A WORLD WITHIN ROOTS

THE ROOTS TRILOGY

BOOK ONE

A WORLD WITHIN ROOTS

ANNE ELIZABETH

*I would never have put the final touches on this manuscript if not for the patience
and support of my loving husband.
Thank you for everything.*

CHAPTER ONE

Vivid greens and reds clashed in an intricate dance with one another as the hazy morning light filtered through the ancient trees. The musty scents of dry dirt and rotting leaves filled my nostrils as branches swayed high above my head, the wind a whistle that hinted at the beginnings of a breezy song.

I glanced over my shoulder, but the parking lot had already disappeared as the leafy giants enveloped us in their still embrace. My pace quickened as my feet carried me closer to freedom.

"Juliet!"

My heart beat faster as reality sunk her teeth into me. I glanced at my companion, her short legs almost jogging to keep up. "What?"

"What do you think your mom will do?" She gasped for air, shooting me a quick smile of thanks as I slowed my stride.

"Cam—"

"No, don't tell me." Camila's fingers played with the end of her black braid. "She probably won't let us go anywhere by ourselves for the rest of the trip."

"*Camila*, we're not children," I protested while failing to push aside the guilt assailing me.

I didn't have their permission. They'll be furious—

Cam laughed, drawing me out of my thoughts. "When does that stop her?" She muttered something else under her breath.

"What?"

Cam raised her hands in the air. "I just said that it won't stop her from freaking out."

Mom's nerves... She didn't use to be so protective. It hadn't always been like this. But when was the last time she hadn't fretted over me if I was out of sight?

"Don't you remember what happened the day before vacation?"

Cam's question pulled the memory to the surface of my mind.

I just needed some last-minute things, so I grabbed the keys and left without telling her. When I got home, she was in tears and pulled me into a hug so tight I worried she'd never let me go. She asked me where I'd been, why I hadn't answered my phone—but I'd forgotten my phone. It lay on my desk. My explanation wasn't good enough. It never was. But it used to be.

Her face filled my mind—warm, kind, with tears streaking her cheeks and fear written in the lines about her eyes and lips—and the pang of guilt inside my chest became a wave threatening to crash over me.

Cam touched me on the arm, her dark eyes serious. "I'm sorry, maybe I shouldn't have brought that up."

"It's okay." I drew in a deep, shuddering breath and forced a smile on my face. "You know, it wasn't always like this. We were happy once, before Eddie—"

"And you still are." She held up a small hand, palm out. "No buts. You all love each other, and you will get through this."

I readjusted the pack on my shoulders and tugged at the straps dangling at my sides. "I hope so, but it's been so long. I'm pretty sure it's gotten worse as I've grown older."

Cam snorted. "You think? It *has*. When is she going to learn to let you go?"

I shoved the guilt deeper down. "You know why—"

"Yes, I do know, but that was a long time ago."

"It doesn't take away the hurt."

"I never said it did," Cam protested. "And I'm not saying it should. But this" —she gestured with her arms— "this isn't healthy. I think it'll be better for you if you start setting some boundaries. It'll hurt her at first, but you need to do it."

I sighed. "It's not as easy as you make it sound. My brother's death made boundaries impossible!"

"Juliet," Cam exclaimed. "You're twenty-two, an adult, and boundaries are part of being an adult. When are you going to realize that?"

Whirling to face Cam, I snorted as tendrils of hair tickled my nose. "Hey, that's not fair," I retorted as I brushed the hair back up into my loose bun. "And you're one to talk."

"Why?" Cam's eyes glinted as her lips pursed. "Because I followed you out here on another one of your whims? Because we left your parents back at the vacation cabin, took their car while they were napping, and decided to go on a lark?"

The pang of guilt grew.

"Why didn't you stop me, then?" I snapped.

Cam groaned. "When has that ever worked?" The corner of her lips tilted upward to lighten the sting of her words. "You know, Juliet, you get so defensive when it comes to your parents, especially your mom, and how they treat you as a child in so many ways, and yet you get so fed up at other times. And it's been almost eleven years since—"

"Let's not have that conversation again," I bit out. Resuming my quick stride along the path, I heard the rustle under her feet as she followed me.

"Wait, all I was going to say is since you stopped being a child in many ways."

"Cam, please, let's just enjoy the hike."

There was no answer from her. But above our heads, birds trilled, high-pitched and rapid, heralding our passing in the trees above our heads.

"Juliet?"

My gaze followed the quick motions of a small brown bird alighted on a branch, standing tall on its thin legs. It swayed with the movements of the wood as the breeze rustled through the treetop.

Cam hurried her step, the leaves under her feet rustling. "What did you say in the note you left?"

"I told her not to worry and that we'd be back soon."

"She'll try calling you, you know," Cam remarked. "Have you checked?"

I shook my head.

"Maybe you should. There is still a week of vacation left. Maybe it'd be best not to have her too upset with us."

"Fine." I slipped my pack off my shoulder and rifled through it. Palming my cell, I glanced at the screen and groaned. "Five missed calls—" My voice trailed off and Mom's face flashed across the screen.

"She's calling again?" Cam guessed, flipping her thick braid over her shoulder.

I nodded and walked away deeper into the forest.

"What are you doing?"

"If I don't have service, the calls won't go through."

"Juliet, are you sure that's the best way to go about this?"

"You told me to create boundaries."

Cam tugged on my arm, her narrow eyes wide.

"Oh, look—" I held up my phone. "No service."

Cam sighed and placed her hands on her wide hips. "How are your parents doing? Your mom seems as clutch-fisted about you as always."

"She is."

"And your dad?"

"He lets her have his way," I added, shrugging. "I don't really want to talk about it."

"But—"

"Cam, please."

She rolled her eyes. "So, when are you supposed to be back at work?"

I shot her a quick smile of thanks. "Next week. Day after we get back."

"Ouch. So soon? What, the coffee shop can't do without you a little longer?"

"Guess not."

She huffed and glanced around. "Speaking of coffee...I need to go to the bathroom."

I stopped short. "We just left the house."

"So?"

"So why didn't you go then?"

"Because I didn't have to then. I'll just find somewhere to go. Be back." Her eyes twinkled and her braid whipped through the air as she strode away, her small figure disappearing into the towering layers of giants. The soft thuds of her hiking boots receded in the air as the ferns blanketing the ground rustled with her passing.

Redwoods.

"You could have just gone behind a tree," I called out after her.

Crouching to pick up a large leaf, I watched as the light from the sun dappled the ground in a myriad of shifting shadows. With a grimace, I peeled my limp and sticky hair off my neck and pressed them back up into the bun.

The wind had gone, leaving the air fetid and stale. I leaned back, looking up overhead. The brilliant blue sky lay far above, a beautiful backdrop for the green treetops. The sun struggled to beat down through the thick canopy, and the heavy branches lay still and silent.

What happened to the wind?

Warm air entered my lungs as I took a deep breath, leaving my throat as dry as a corn husk. Unable to stand still in the heat, I walked forward with slow steps. The air grew stuffier with the passing of time. I tilted my face upward, wishing for a relieving breeze to sweep through, but it didn't come.

"Julieeet!" Cam yelled from somewhere behind me. "Julieeet! Where the heck are you?"

I hesitated, surveying the trees, all of which mirrored one another with their reddish-brown bark, their green leaves changing into reds and yellows, and the pale green moss growing up the trunks. Behind me, the path wound through it all, but there was no sign of Cam.

"Just keep following the path a little ways," I called, looking over my shoulder as I continued walking. "I didn't go far!"

"This isn't your playground, Juliet! Next time don't waltz off on your own! Blasted trees...they all look the same..." Cam's disgruntled voice filtered through the forest.

A grin crossed my face as I faced the sound of her voice and walked backward, ignoring her distant grumbling. "It's not my fault you managed to get yourself lost," I muttered into the dry air, scuffing my boot against the ground. With a sigh, I spun around and jerked back with a sharp gasp—a long, curling stick jutted out mere inches from my face.

Wait.

My eyes widened. My jaw dropped.

"Are those roots?" I whispered. "What in the world?"

Before me, a mass of spindly brown tendrils rose high into the air from beneath the dirt. The smallest roots teased at the air before my face, fewer in number, but the farther back they stretched, the larger and more numerous they were, twisted in a maddening web of interlocking spirals. And there, a short ways farther on, a path led forward, curving into the maze looming over me.

In a haze, I advanced and rested my hand on one of them. The wood was hard, rough, and healthy—not just healthy, but thriving.

How is this possible?

"Juliet!"

I jumped as Cam's voice rang out, closer now.

"Juliet Barrows! Where are you?"

"Cam!" I exclaimed without turning. "Hurry! You have to see this!"

"*Why* did you have to keep walking?" Cam shouted, annoyance lacing her tone. "Can't you—"

The rest of her words faded as the gap in front of me beckoned, the thinner trailing roots on either side pulsing in an effort to pull me forward. My breath caught as I stepped into the shadowed opening. A light cascade of dirt drifted down through the air onto my clothing as my movement disturbed the roots.

The bark was hard beneath my fingers as I slipped through the narrow pathway. Below my feet, the wood was firm but soft, an almost mildewy scent rising into my nostrils with every step.

Snaking my way along the maze-like path became harder as the roots grew larger and denser. Sucking in a breath, I squeezed past a root at least four times as large as my waist, the jagged branches snagging on my shirt and ripping some threads free.

I entered a small, circular area, just wide enough for me to stand tall.

The center.

All noise faded. Silence reigned in this mysterious place. I reached forward and trailed my fingers along a large root, thick with knots and curvatures that time had hewn into the wood.

A soft sound, as of a footfall, came from behind.

Cam.

As I turned, my foot caught on something, and I pressed down on the root for balance—

Then the wood opened up beneath my feet, and I plummeted downwards.

My heart leaped into my chest, and I screamed as blackness enveloped me. The sound was torn away in the passing stream of air, which whipped around me.

I couldn't see. I couldn't breathe; I couldn't do anything. Terror gripped my heart in its iron clasp, and a numbness spread over my soul.

Hair lashed against my face, each strand moving with a life of its own. Time itself seemed to have stilled as I fell. My arms and legs flailed with instinctive action, almost as if I could get them to do the impossible. I couldn't see the opening I'd fallen through. Everything was dark and musty, and I coughed as flecks of dirt fell into my mouth. Gasping for air, my heart racing, I managed to flip myself over so that I was facing down.

A speck of white far below suddenly caught my eye. A pinprick, a strange iota, of white light, growing larger and brighter with each passing second.

The end.

Somehow I knew it to be true. I couldn't close my eyes against the growing brightness. It was a sign of the end, of the bottom of this continual tunnel through which I fell. Tears leaked from my eyes and slid up into my hair from the passing stream of wind. It ripped the air from my lungs, leaving me suffocated within the swelling pressure. As the white light grew brighter, softening the darkness, I could see the rough outlines of walls surrounding me: a tunnel growing up from the glaring whiteness of the light to encircle me.

My sight began to blur. Straining, I reached and touched the tip of one finger to the soft brown wall, feeling damp sponginess slide against my skin.

Blackness surged in at the edges of my vision, and the roaring of the air rushing past dulled. The brilliant white light disappeared under the creeping shroud of black.

And I no longer knew anything.

Chapter Two

Puffy white clouds rolled across the blue sky as I gazed up at the heavens. I basked in the soothing warmth of the sun, time slipping by without end.

With a soft sigh, I clasped my hands over my stomach and smiled. I closed my eyes, letting the grass enfold me in its lush embrace. The quiet chattering of birds in the distance lulled me into a drowsy wakefulness.

Something sharp poked into my forehead as I shifted. With a groan, I leaned my head back and stared cross-eyed at the point of a stick. I lurched into a sitting position and peered around.

The grass grew vibrant and long in the small clearing, interspersed with shrubs and fringed by trees that were pale yellow as if summer turned to fall.

Grass...

I stood up, turning in a slow circle on my heels as my heart rate quickened.

This isn't right.

A bush...a tree...no, neither—

My temples throbbed as I turned around. The stick that had been jutted into my forehead was no stick. It continued onwards, twisting back and away from me along with dozens of others like it.

Roots.

They spiraled up from the ground, reminding me of something akin to Medusa's hair.

Wait.

Camila. She'd been there. She'd called my name, and then—

My eyes widened. The world tilted around me, and the pressure in my temples worsened.

I'm not dead.

"Cam!" I screamed, listening for any sound of her. "Camila!"

The birds went silent as though the world listened for an answer. They resumed their song when none came.

I'm dreaming. This isn't real.

I pinched myself hard on my arm, and a sharp burning spread from the crease in my elbow up and down my arm before fading away.

Dreams don't hurt, not like this.

Fresh air flooded into my lungs as I tried to calm down. After a few breaths, my mind began to clear as the frenzied thoughts bouncing around slowed and quieted. Straightening, I strode towards the roots overshadowing the ground.

Home. Somehow the roots will take me home. Over and over, the thought ran through my mind.

Where is Cam?

My boots made no noise on the soft earth, though rustling filled the air as I sauntered through the overgrown grass and weeds. The roots grew thicker and larger as I wound my way closer, my eyes searching for a way through the seemingly impenetrable mass.

An opening...a way through...it must be here.

Memories returned, memories of the winding path I had followed before, a path that had led me to the center, where the floor disappeared, and I fell.

Pausing, I looked around, searching in the dim darkness. The late-afternoon sun strove in vain to shine through the overreaching roots, but there—in the dim light, I just made out the dark yawn of an opening a couple of feet above my head. Framed by twisting tendrils, it beckoned in an eerie, dark sort of way.

I must get back.

Mom's face flitted across my mind's eye.

Holding my breath, I jumped and grabbed hold of a branch just above my head. Kicking my legs forward and back, I used the momentum to swing up and into the tree, my heartbeat loud in the stillness surrounding me.

The birdsong faded as I entered what almost seemed like another world: darker, quieter, hidden from view by the tangle ensnaring me in their grasp. The roots seemed determined to keep me back—to keep me out—as I pressed on. They clutched my clothing, their tips brushing against me as I walked. I didn't remember the path to the center being so difficult to navigate before. It was almost as though the roots were trying to keep me back.

Once in the middle of the maze, I let my fingers brush over every inch of root I could reach. Fear filled my heart as the memory of falling through the dark tunnel pervaded my mind. Something here must release the floor.

It has to.

Loose dirt fell off the wood in soft cascades, and I coughed, licking my lips as I held back my growing frustration.

Laughter broke the eerie silence. It was me, I realized faintly—the choking sound bubbling out from deep inside.

This isn't real. But I knew better. I tried to push the truth—that this was really happening—deeper inside myself, but it was futile.

I don't know how long I pushed and prodded, my hands brushing over every root I could find in the center of the maze. Sweat beaded my skin, and my throat ached from lack of water. Exhaustion deadened my limbs and numbed my mind.

Looking around one last time, I turned away and snaked my way back through until I stood free of the clinging tendrils again.

I peered up at the brightening sky as the sun continued her trek westward over the horizon. Tears stung my eyes, and a surge of emptiness created a pit in the base of my stomach. Yet the sunlight was warm, and it washed over me with a welcome tingle, keeping the fringe of fear at bay and helping the world to seem right.

I slumped to the ground, crossing my arms over my drawn-up knees. The glade was dotted with trees, smaller and more delicate than the massive redwoods. They grew at differing angles from the ground, slanting up with narrow, pale brown trunks. Their leaves had changed to an orange yellow. Their branches were a little sparse at the tops where the wind must have bit into them.

I closed my eyes, reveling in the cool, damp breeze blowing in gentle gusts.

"Hello," a voice murmured.

A small woman, her skin smooth and flawless, her features dainty in a perfect sort of way, stood scrutinizing me with brown eyes that seemed to see everything. I sprang to my feet.

"Are you able to speak?" Her voice came out in soft tones, dainty even, yet a hardness—almost of a deep, inner strength—underlined the words.

The smell...scents of cinnamon and warm bread filled the air. She drew me in, and my feet felt pulled against their will. I took a deep breath, clenching my fists at my side, fighting against the sudden relaxation filling me and the sense that everything would be alright.

"No. I mean, yes."

She cocked her head.

"Where am I?"

The petite woman blinked. "Not many do not know of where they are. It is a rare occurrence. You are a few miles away from Umi no Machi."

"Umi no Machi?" I inquired. "I've never heard of it."

"Yes. It means 'sea town', and it lies south." She gestured behind herself without looking. "It is small, a peaceful town with few who reside there." She stood, head regal and shoulders back, but her delicate and beautiful features remained as blank as a slate.

Tension grew in the air as we both regarded one another without speaking.

"Your dress is pretty," I blurted out. "I haven't seen anyone wear something quite like that before. It almost looks Japanese."

"Japanese?" the woman inquired, glancing down at her pale green gown with its billowy sleeves. A wide sash tied below the corset-like top made the skirt widen as it fell away. "We are Ryujin."

Ryujin?

"What is that?"

She swept an arm out. "The people of this land. Ryujin. Times have changed much, but we were once the people of the sea." The corners of her mouth tilted up in the hint of a smile.

My lips moved, but nothing came out as I stood mesmerized by her almond-shaped eyes, their depths swirling with hues of brown and black.

"Would you like to come with me?" She shifted a basket on her arm. "I am headed there now."

I hesitated, glancing over my shoulder at the roots behind me.

Home. Mom. Dad. Cam.

The way back home was behind me. Somehow, those roots could send me back. I knew it deep down—

"Umi no Machi is a town worth visiting. You might be surprised by what you find there." Her voice was persuasive, her tone filled with a promise of things unknown.

"I—"

But home. Mom and Dad would be waiting. They'd be worried—freaking out. And Cam— *I should go back.*

"No," I began. "I should—"

The stumbling words on my lips came to a halt. I stared at the woman with her unusual dress and her eyes so full of mystery and intrigue.

She took a step forward, coming closer. "Why do you hesitate?"

"My family. My home. I should go back. They'll be missing me."

"Then why not go?"

Why do I hesitate?

Cam's words flitted through my mind.

"When is she going to learn to let you go? ... You're twenty-two, an adult, so when are you going to start acting like one? ... They treat you as a child in so many ways..."

"What's holding you back?"

I blinked, the words flowing before I could stop them. "My mom—she'll kill me. She was already angry, but" —I glanced up at the sun in the sky— "it's been hours. I've never pushed her this far. She—"

What will she do?

The woman watched me without speaking.

Dad has never been strong enough to stand up to her when she's set on something.

A soft voice asked, "What are you afraid of?"

That my cage will become more of a reality. That the bars will grow thicker, closer together, and I'll never escape.

"I'll go with you." My voice grew stronger and more certain as I spoke. "I can go back later."

A small weight lifted off my chest even as my heart constricted with guilt.

The woman's full lips quirked up in a smile. "Very well. It is a good choice."

"You don't know anything about me!"

"Coming with me will save you much heartache later on."

"What do you mean?"

She shrugged and turned, calling back over her shoulder, "You will know in time. We all know in time, though sometimes we wish we hadn't. But this is the path you are on, and you shall know the consequences soon enough."

"What do you mean?"

"There are always consequences to everything we do." She paused, her dark brown eyes searching my own.

Juliet.

My name hung heavy in the air between us, though I'd never said it.

She cleared her throat. "There are those who will stand by your side, who will earn your trust, but beware the pretender." Her figure glided over the ground as she moved away.

Beware. Beware the pretender.

Her words hung in the air, her voice compelling, urging me to listen, to not forget the warning.

A shiver crossed my skin as I stood rooted in place. Foreboding crept in, but still my footsteps moved to follow. Too many questions ran through my mind.

"Wait, what do you mean?" I called, hurrying forward.

For such a small person, she seemed to float across the ground, the tall grasses surrounding us doing little to hamper her passing.

"What do you think I mean?"

"I have no idea!" I blurted out. "Who are you talking about?"

"You'll find out in time." Her voice was soft, confident, and sure, and the questions that had been building in my mind faded away. "We should hurry."

I hesitated and peered back over my shoulder, a shiver traveling over my body.

And my steps carried me toward the receding figure.

The trees grew sparser and the ground a little rockier as we continued. Raising my eyes, I gaped. There was nothing but blue sky beyond, and the woman was gone.

Hurrying forward, my heart racing, I stopped short.

The ground hadn't disappeared. It fell away to a small, open valley.

Below, my companion picked her way with dainty footsteps around the wind-stripped brush as she descended the slope. The long slits in her gown provided freedom of movement and revealed the tight leggings underneath.

I tilted my head back, licking my lips and tasting the sticky saltiness of the air. The scent was tangy, sharp, and acrid.

Seaweed.

Goosebumps broke out under my shirt as the breeze picked up. The blue sky above accentuated the soft whiteness of the clouds, and gliding across was the sun. I watched as it made its way farther toward the horizon to the west. Afternoon was quickly becoming evening.

"Are you coming?" the woman called, her voice faint but clear as it carried with the wind. She raised a hand over her eyes as she looked up.

I nodded and took the first step down the slippery crag. The brush caught at my hiking pants and pulled at my boots as I descended. Spiders ran before me, stirred by the movement of the sliding rocks. *Gross.* I shivered at the sight of their spindly legs and beady black eyes. The slope was infested with them. *Just don't think of them.* I swallowed and continued on.

I smiled as I reached the bottom, relieved, and stopped beside the woman.

"What is in the basket?"

"Some herbs and such. We should keep going. I would like to be back before sunset."

"How much longer?"

"Long enough. Here." She handed me a waterskin that she pulled out of the covered basket. "Drink this."

Lifting it to my mouth, I felt the life-giving water flow down my dry throat.

A hand tugged on the skin. "That's enough."

"But—" I began, fighting against the irritation building inside me.

"You don't want to make yourself sick."

My eyes widened and I handed the skin back to her. "Thanks."

She inclined her head and continued walking. "Why do you stare?"

"I've never met anyone like you before," I remarked, unable to bite back the words. Heat rose to my cheeks.

She laughed, a twinkling sound which quieted the birdsong as though they, too, stood entranced. "It's quiet out here, isn't it?"

"Yes, almost too quiet, though," I murmured, glancing around at the barren landscape. The grass had gone, and the trees were fewer, their lower limbs thinner and bare from the coastal wind.

A soft smile hovered on her lips. She laughed again. "Sometimes quiet is good for the soul. I like it out here. Do you smell it? The ocean breeze, salty and yet alluring? It fills the air." She closed her eyes, dark lashes in contrast to the ivory of her skin.

What a strange woman.

I ran to come abreast of her. "What's your name?"

"We have not known one another long enough for that."

"What?" I blinked. "What's wrong with sharing names?"

She stopped and turned to face me. "Names are important. You and I have just met. Why should I tell you my name?"

"I—I don't know."

She resumed walking.

A pang of frustration shot through me. "Wait! My name is Juliet."

"There it is," she whispered, giving no sign that she'd heard me.

Out in the far distance appeared the bright sparkle of an ocean, a wide, gray-blue expanse stretching forth till it seemed to drop off the edge of the earth. I could hear the faint, rhythmic pounding of the surf carried on the breeze. White-capped waves shone against the blue of the water, foaming with each thunderous roll. Wheeling overhead, dark birds circled with pride, the natural predators of the skies. Every now and then, one plunged down before streaking back up, water falling in a glittering cascade from their long, dusky wings.

A bird called, shrieking its greeting across the sky, or had it just been an echo of such? Maybe it was but a whisper on the air of a bygone memory—my first memory of the ocean, a time long since passed, but there on the edges of my thoughts.

A different ocean, a different place, and a different time.

Sandcastles built with pails and spades loomed tall as we crouched before them. The sand sparkled in the bright sunlight, and the ocean drummed against the ground with each crashing wave.

Laughter on the breeze. Children laughing... Eddie talking...

"Juliet! A memory has you within its grasp. What do you think of?"

The memory faded, and a tear slid down my cheek. "It was a long time ago."

"How long?" Her voice was soft and placating.

"Years. Almost eleven ago."

"It eats away at you still."

"Yes," I murmured, tearing my gaze away from those deadly waters.

"You fear it. Why did you come?" She regarded me with dark, open eyes devoid of any emotion.

"Because I didn't think about how I would feel when I saw it! I didn't think I'd see the beach!"

"But I told you Umi no Machi is a coastal town. You knew what to expect. You knew you would see the ocean."

I blinked against the tears stinging my eyes and balled my hands into fists. "I didn't think about it like that! Leave me alone!"

Strings of electricity zinged through the air, invisible to the naked eye.

The woman lifted a small hand and pointed, a soft smile tilting her lips upward. "There is Umi no Machi."

Taking deep breaths to calm my racing heart, I followed her gaze to a small town away from the sea and built on higher ground. "I'm sorry."

Understanding shone in the depths of her intense eyes. "Be careful. The rocky crags will confuse you."

"What?" A startled cry escaped my lips.

"Trust your instincts, and at other times, do not trust them. Be wary, yet be not wary. Sometimes you will know, and other times you will not." She gestured, and I looked below to the maze of rocks that lay between me and the town.

"But—" I glanced back. The quick jerk of motion tangled my legs, and I screamed as I lost my footing and slid down the slope. After a few yards, I caught onto a dry shrub and slid to a halt. I struggled to my feet, wincing from the scrapes along my arms. Bright red blood blossomed on my forefinger where something had pricked me. Looking up, I saw no sign of the woman.

She's gone!

Chapter Three

Small, low buildings with thatched roofs and simplistic lines lay before me. The narrow dirt road stretched down through the middle of the town, damp from the ocean breeze.

It was quiet. Without the thrum of cars or electricity, an eerie silence hovered in the air.

The slight breeze rustled the loose tendrils brushing against my neck.

A sharp squeak split the air, raising the hair on my arms. My eyes darted to the right, where an old, petite lady stepped through her front entrance and closed the door with another squeak. She froze and stared at me. Her almond-shaped eyes softened, and she inclined her upper body and head in a slight bow.

"Hi," I murmured, not sure what else to do.

The wood creaked as she settled her small frame on a rickety rocking chair. "Come closer, will you?" She gestured a hand toward me. "My hearing is not so good."

I glanced from side to side before taking a step forward.

The woman laughed, a high and reedy sound. "I'm not going to harm you." Her thin lips pursed, and she tapped an index finger on her chin. The wooden rocker protested with each rock as though about to give way beneath her weight. She smoothed down the skirt of her dress. The material was a soft green, and the high slits on either side revealed thin, olive-green material encasing her legs. "You do not dress like anyone I have seen before."

I looked down at my clothes: the dark gray pants tucked into hiking boots and a short-sleeved blue shirt underneath a light-weight, navy windbreaker.

"I have lived here a long time, long enough to know you are not familiar with our country at all."

"How did you know?"

She smirked and steepled her fingers together. "You did not bow when I bowed. But I am not offended." She cackled, a bright gleam in her brown eyes. "However, it does make me wonder why you are here and where you are from." She looked past me. "The sunset is beautiful, is it not?"

I glanced over my shoulder at the cloudless sky filled with the pale pinks and oranges of a setting sun. The sky had looked similar many a time back home. Mom and I often watched the sunsets together, sitting in silence on our back porch. The few times there was no tension filling the air. *Home.* Guilt assailed me. I grimaced, burying the thoughts and feelings associated down deep inside and returned my gaze to the old woman.

"I come out here every night to see what the sky looks like," the old woman mused, her yellowed teeth flashing at me as she smiled. "It should be a good day tomorrow. Nothing mars the heavens tonight."

I raised an eyebrow and opened my mouth, but she interrupted with another laugh.

"You want to know how I know?" She tapped a small finger on the side of her head. "The clouds and colors of the sky tell us many things. Pay attention and perhaps you shall learn this too."

I blinked. "Okay. Well—"

"If you wish to stay here, go to the inn. You will find lodging there." The woman raised her eyes back to the sunset behind me.

"Where is that?"

She pointed with a short index finger. "It is the only building here that has more than one floor."

She was right. The building loomed over the others lining the dirt road. They all shared a similar square shape with sharp arches coming to a point. The red of the inn's trim was faded and peeling, and a few windows eyed me from the brown wood. The inn was square and narrow, with wood sconces holding lanterns at the corners.

Lanterns.

I realized then that as the light from the sun faded, there were no streetlights breaking through the setting darkness. Nor had I seen a single car.

Nothing modern. This isn't home.

"Go on now," the woman muttered, wrapping a cloak closer around her thin body. "It will be dark before you know it. You should find lodging." She waved a hand and shuffled back inside.

A soft footstep of a man passing made me turn around to face the street. The small man continued walking, the long sleeves on his tunic flowing as he swung his arms. His eyes met my own, and he inclined his head.

I nodded back, swallowing against the dryness coating my throat. Another man stepped out of a building next to the inn, also wearing a mid-thigh tunic belted around his waist and pants tucked into light-weight boots. He hesitated a moment before turning away from me as he strode down the street.

I crept along, studying the few inhabitants who went about their business. Two women passed by me, dressed like the old woman on the rocker. They wore the long and simple-cut dresses in shades of greens and reds over tight leggings. Frowns crossed their faces as they caught me staring, and their eyes traveled up and down my own clothing before the older of the two grabbed the younger's arm and hurried on.

Eyes followed my progress. I could see them, feel them on me even when I passed and left someone behind. They bowed, a slight movement, so I nodded my head, unsure of what else to do.

No one spoke.

Each individual repeated the same bow over and over again.

People back home didn't acknowledge one another like this. *I could pass dozens of people on a walk without a single nod or word of greeting. No, don't compare. Don't think that way.* I placed the tips of my fingers along my temple, fighting to keep my focus on the present, away from the thoughts of home.

When I brought my hands back to my side, continuing toward the inn, goosebumps ran over my arms from the attention. I was the stranger here. My blonde hair stood out in stark contrast to the dark brown and black of those around me, and my pale skin, barely tan from the summer sun, stood out from the deeper, ivory tones of the villagers.

My footsteps quickened as I neared the inn, the tall building throwing shadows across the street.

With an exhale, I felt a surge of relief wash over me as I realized I stood under the awning. Chills spread across my skin as the shadows blocked the warmth from the sun. The front door stood before me, its wood worn with imperfections that time had ingrained in its lines. It was dark and imposing, as old as the peeling paint on the trim above. The faint smell of mildew and rot sifted through the air.

I stepped forward and raised my hand to the door. My index finger just fit into the notch cut in the wood. It was soft, almost mushy in parts where it had decayed in the ocean air's dampness. Pushing, I grunted, but it didn't budge. I took a deep breath and tried again, biting my lip as I ran my fingers over the notch. Suddenly they slid into place. This time, the heavy door glided open.

A dark foyer greeted me, closed off from the rest of the inn by another door waiting to be opened. Something gave beneath my feet, and I suppressed a scream, leaping back. I gaped at the ground. Adrenaline surged through me, but I let out a sigh of relief—they were only slippers on the floor, lined up in neat rows.

"Hello."

The shriek that I had managed to swallow down before erupted from my throat. I whirled around to face the silhouette of a man as tall as me standing in the doorway.

His bushy eyebrows rose. "Are you going to go in?" He stepped into the foyer, and I stared. He was tall, his thick, chaotic hair adding a couple inches to his height.

My mouth opened and closed, but no sound came out. I nodded, turned back to the door, and pushed it open. When I raised one foot to step down into the room, an audible gasp froze me in place.

"There are slippers for your convenience," came a quick explanation from over my shoulder.

"Oh, sorry, thanks." I took off my shoes and placed them on the low shelf before sliding my feet into the firm, flat slippers.

Sliding open the door, I stepped through into a dark, low-ceilinged room. A little light filtered in through a couple of large windows facing the street, but lamps provided a warm glow in the space otherwise.

Except for a large desk, a few armchairs, and a table, the room was empty. I made my way toward the desk and tripped over a bamboo board that had loosened. Biting back a gasp, I regained my footing and looked up to see a man standing at the before-empty desk. I jumped, startled.

The man from the foyer.

My eyes widened. He waited for me, the same thick black hair now sticking up in tufts from his head as he ran a hand through it.

"How did you slip past me?"

He frowned, his dark eyes narrowing under black eyebrows. "Excuse me?" He inclined his head, and I had the annoying urge to awkwardly bob my own, but I refrained from doing so.

My cheeks flushed with heat.

"Do you want a room?" he inquired, cocking his head to the side.

"I—I do."

"Wonderful!" He smiled, his posture relaxing. "For how many nights?"

"Wait," I exclaimed, holding up a hand. "I didn't intend—I mean—I don't have any money."

The smile disappeared. "What?"

"I hadn't intended on staying here, but I don't have anywhere else to go, and I don't have any money or belongings."

The man regarded me, his face devoid of any expression.

My stomach growled. *Without money, what could I offer?* My mind whirred, and my heart beat faster. "Is there any way I could work for lodging? And food?"

"I am not in need of help right now." He hesitated, regarding me as I shifted on my feet. "Where are you from?"

"Far away from here."

"That is not much of an answer. Perhaps you come from the west?"

I stared, my mind blank as to what to say. The words jumbled inside my brain, and I licked my lips.

"The west..." the man continued, and I relaxed when I realized he hadn't waited for an answer. His words were soft like the trickle of water over stone. "Not many come from the west. And even fewer come without horse or pack."

"It was not planned."

"I suppose it is none of my business why you find yourself here without money or belongings. The fair-haired folk do not come here anymore. Not in many years. But if you don't mean any harm, you are welcome."

Fair-haired folk? I fingered the tendril of blonde hair slipping past my ears. My throat tightened. "I mean no harm to anyone here."

"We shall see."

The west...people like me.

The man tapped a slender finger on the desk. "Do you mean to go or stay?"

"You'll let me stay?"

He leaned forward, a puzzled look in his eyes. "Should I not?"

"But why?" I burst out, feeling the edge of the desk press against my abdomen. I hadn't realized I'd moved forward.

"Don't you want to stay?"

I nodded.

"Then why question me?"

Before I could say a word, the man continued, "We will try it out. You may help in the kitchen. In exchange, I will give you food and lodging."

"Are you the owner?"

He closed the ledger in front of him. "I am the innkeeper." He turned from me, and I jumped as he barked, "Saya!"

A petite, young female appeared out of nowhere. No, not as young as I'd first thought, possibly twenty-two, my own age, a woman in a girl's body. She looked up at me, her eyes clear of emotion.

"Saya," the innkeeper instructed. "Please show this young lady to a windowless room on the top floor, then bring her to the kitchen. She will be staying with us for a few days."

The girl blinked. "Kitchen?"

"She'll earn her keep while here."

Saya nodded and marched away without a word.

"Thank you."

The innkeeper inclined his head to me. I turned and hurried to catch up to Saya, whose short legs carried her quickly to the stairwell in the corner of the room.

By the third flight of stairs, my legs began to tighten and burn. On the top floor, Saya led me down a narrow hallway into a square room lined with doors. She strode across and folded her arms.

The gesture reminded me of Cam. She would cross her arms the exact same way. I stared at Saya, her petite stature now reminding me of Cam's, her dark hair a similar color, but finer and silkier...but her eyes, her brown eyes, weren't as bright as Cam's, nor as cheerful.

"This one is yours."

Saya's voice snapped me back to the present. I looked to where she pointed. Inside an open sliding door lay a tiny foyer similar to the one at the entrance to the inn. On a single, low shelf, lay a couple pairs of slippers.

"Put your slippers here," Saya murmured, taking her own off before leading the way through yet another sliding door.

No locks on the doors, I noticed as we stepped down onto a thin bamboo flooring in a small room, which was bare except for a plush mattress and quilt lying folded in one corner.

"Are you ready?"

I looked up at her. "For what?"

She crossed her arms over her chest again. "To earn your keep?"

"Not that I'm not already doing that," I muttered under my breath.

Saya looked at me over her shoulder. "What was that?"

"Nothing." With one last survey of the room, I followed Saya out.

"You're strange," she remarked as I slid the outer door closed behind us.

"So are you," I countered with a frown.

She blinked, her long lashes brushing the skin below her eyes.

"Why are there no locks on the doors?"

"They aren't necessary," she retorted, leading the way to the stairs.

"At all? Do none of the doors have locks?"

"No, we have no need for them." Her breath blew out in a long, drawn-out sigh.

"What about keeping people out?"

Saya gestured with her left hand. "Why would we do that? We are an inn."

I stopped short. "But thieves..."

"There are no thieves here. Nothing is ever taken; thus, we have no need for locks. Any other questions, Juliet?"

"No."

"Good. This way, then."

My jaw clenched and I inhaled the musky air. "Actually, I do have another question."

Saya groaned. "What?"

I couldn't hide the smile of satisfaction crossing my lips. "How did you know my name? I didn't introduce myself."

She shrugged her narrow shoulders. "You must've said it at some point."

Frowning, I hesitated before running forward a couple of steps. "I really don't think I did."

Saya whirled. "Just leave it, will you? How else would I have known it?"

Before I could say a word, she resumed walking across the main floor of the lobby.

"You have a pretty name," I murmured back to her.

"It's a name. Yours is different," Saya murmured, her eyes narrowing as she examined me.

"So is yours," I retorted.

Saya grimaced, her delicate face puckering harshly. "You ask a lot of questions. We're here now. Eat, and then you will work."

My stomach growled, and I grinned as we entered a long, narrow room. Silence filled the room as the mutter of conversation died. A dozen or so faces looked at me, their dark eyes staring. I swallowed as mouth-watering aromas assailed my senses. A long, low table overflowed with dishes and pitchers filled with green and pale white liquids. Flat, square pillows lay stacked in each corner of the room.

Saya held out one of the pillows and gestured to an empty place at the table. I held the cushion to my chest, hesitating as I realized the conversation around the table had halted with our appearance. Saya set down her pillow and sat with her feet curled under her, her bottom resting on her heels.

I set my pillow down next to her and struggled to balance in the same position. Already a burning pain grew in my legs, and my feet began cramping.

Saya nudged the small bowl of rice in front of me and pointed to the chopsticks next to my plate. "You *do* know how to use the wooden implements there, don't you?"

I picked them up and nodded. Saya pursed her lips with a disbelieving air and picked up a thin slice of meat with her chopsticks from one of the plates in front of us. I watched, chopsticks poised in my right hand, as she brought her bowl of rice close to her lips and shoveled some of the rice into her mouth. After chewing and swallowing, she then took some veggies from another plate and ate those.

They share food from the platters.

"I can hear your stomach. Eat," Saya ordered before turning back to her own food.

My stomach growled, and I leaned forward to take some meat. The food was delicious and savory, and juices from the meats and vegetables filled my mouth in spicy bursts. Focusing on eating, I kept my gaze down, away from the stares, the whispers, and the blatant awareness that I was unlike anyone else here.

A constant barrage of sound fell upon my ears: the incessant clink of bowls being set on the hardwood table, the clank of platters being shifted, the hushed requests for a specific pitcher or dish, the clatter of wooden chopsticks against china, the gulping of water, the slurp of sauce, the chewing of food—and then the sudden silence as swallowing commenced.

My bowl of rice was empty when Saya stood. With a groan, I managed to stand and follow her. She led the way down a dark hallway and into a spacious kitchen filled with towering piles of dirty dishes, which lay on the floor next to a large barrel.

She pointed. "The kettles are already heating by the fire."

"For what?"

"For the washing water," she replied with a slight frown.

"There's no sink?"

"What is a sink?"

"Never mind." Rotating on my heels, I surveyed the room. No fridge, freezer, oven—nothing that reminded me of the world I'd left behind.

But not for good. I'll go home. I stripped off my light jacket and rolled up my sleeves to combat the sticky heat inside the large, low room.

I had my chance. The thought crossing my mind jerked me to a halt as I reached for the first dirty plate. *The portal didn't work. It didn't let me go home.* I scrubbed at the plate with furious motions, angry at the argument raging inside of me. The washing water, hot at first, cooled quickly, and I worked hard to scrub the grains of rice and bits of meat and veggies off the plates. I found a thin wooden shelving system, which I supposed could be a drying rack, and placed the clean dishes there by the fire to dry. Two hours flew by before I was done with all the washing and drying.

"Nope, never again," I muttered. "I don't ever want to travel back in time to any era without running water. Or air conditioning."

"Are you talking to yourself?"

I jumped, whirling to find Saya standing behind me, her eyebrows raised and her petite frame somehow hostile with her squared-off stance.

She surveyed my work with a critical air as I examined my poor, wrinkled hands and arms. "You did all right," she admitted. "Someone will put them away. Now you may rest."

She disappeared again before I could say a single word, leaving me to find my own way back up the four flights of stairs and into the room given to me. I collapsed on the mat, not even bothering to pull a blanket over me, and fell asleep, unmindful of how my legs were almost too long for the bed.

⁂

"Wake up."

The voice filtered through my subconsciousness as a foot prodded my side.

"Leave off," I muttered, rolling over.

"Come on, Juliet Barrows, get up."

I blinked and saw Saya's face looming over me, her left hand holding a candle. Its dim glow flickered. Groaning, I sat up. "It's you."

"That is impolite," she murmured, her thick eyebrows furrowing. "It is time to get up. You're needed in the kitchens."

"What time is it?"

"Almost mid-morning. You slept through breakfast."

I rubbed my eyes, brushing away the last vestiges of sleep. "Why do you not like me?"

Saya waited while I stood and threw on my shirt and pants under her averted gaze. "What is there to like?"

I chuckled. "Now *that* is impolite."

"Why do you not like me?" she countered.

"Because you haven't made yourself very likable from the get-go."

She whirled around to face me in the small anteroom, her face mere inches from my chest as she peered up at me. "You don't belong here!"

"I know I'm not from around here," I began.

"No, it's more than that. You shouldn't be here. You don't belong. You're not one of us."

"Woah, I know! Saya, I'm not here to stay. I want to go home."

"Then go." She folded her arms and waited, her black eyes smoldering. "Go back to where you came from."

Jaw open, I gaped at her as she fled the room. Darkness descended as the light from Saya's candle went with her. Blind from the sudden change, I leaned down and felt with my hand over the floor. There, the matchbox I'd seen the night before. A spark flew, and my own candle emitted a small glow. With a sigh, I pulled on my boots and went downstairs. Saya was long gone.

What did she mean? What does she know? I wondered.

"Ah, good," the innkeeper exclaimed, startling me out of my wayward thoughts. "You are finally awake...and still here." He frowned and shrugged. "You slept the whole evening and night away, as well as this morning, so you missed breakfast. Go to the kitchens. There you may eat and then begin cleaning up from breakfast." His thin figure receded down a short hallway and disappeared through a doorway at the end of it. Movement caught my eye, and I turned to see Saya scrutinizing me.

"Come on," she ordered, as though nothing had happened between us.

I followed her down the same long corridor to the kitchen where the cooks prepared lunch. They handed me a plate of leftover breakfast, and I grimaced at the sight before me: fried eggs, but runnier, as if they'd barely touched the pan before landing on my plate. Some vegetables, dried seaweed, and what looked like prosciutto lay arranged on the plate, as well.

Poking my chopsticks under one oozing egg, I grimaced as it slid back onto my plate. Sensing someone watching me, I looked up and saw one of the chefs standing still, a frozen, wide-eyed look on his face. My cheeks warmed, and I took a bite, averting my gaze. It oozed around my mouth before sliding down my throat with a gooey adieu.

"Didn't your parents ever tell you to eat what's provided?"

I jumped and glanced up at Saya. "I—uhh—"

"Never mind. Just eat up. There's work to be done." Her harshness quelled my response.

❧ ❧

The morning pile of dishes had disappeared. Lunch had come and gone, and those dishes also were put away. I rolled my neck, feeling the small creaks and pops that followed as my vertebrae shifted and my muscles loosened.

I made my way out of the empty kitchen and through the corridor to the main room. It was also empty, but a noise filtered in from somewhere outside. I took a step closer to the front door and realized it wasn't closed. Anger and confusion laced the muffled voices coming through.

Slipping out the door, I raised a hand as bright sunlight blinded me. The street thronged with people. Muffled voices cascaded around me, too many to make out what they said. It seemed the whole town had come out for whatever was happening.

I pushed myself into the outer ring. "Hey, what's going on?"

A woman stared at me with a blank expression before turning away without a word. The man next to her tucked her arm in his and shook his head.

There—a glimpse of Saya and the innkeeper, just visible through the roiling midst of people before me.

"Excuse me, sorry, excuse me," I murmured as I pushed my way through the thick crowd. "Sorry," I exclaimed as I stepped on someone's foot.

"Watch yourself!" the man snapped as he shifted away from me.

Turning sideways, I shuffled past a few more individuals, beginning to sweat from the afternoon heat mingling with that of warm bodies pressed close together. I lifted my head, releasing a pent-up exhale as I realized I'd reached a small circular area fringed with people. Saya and the innkeeper stood in the middle, surrounded by pointing fingers and angry glances, though it was quieter here than on the outskirts.

Saya turned a bitter face toward me but gave a slight nod. She folded her arms, her stare piercing the air above the heads of the crowd.

"Hey, what's going on?"

The innkeeper turned to look at me and frowned. "What are you doing here? Rather interfering of you to involve yourself in something that does not concern you."

"Who says I am involving myself? I merely asked what's going on."

"Isn't that involving yourself?" Saya accused, crossing her arms over her chest.

I closed my eyes and took a deep breath. "Saya," I began, "what's going on?"

"Saya"—the innkeeper hesitated, glancing at her—"she thinks—"

"I don't think. I know!" she blurted. "Something is going to happen tonight."

The force of her voice took me by surprise. "What do you mean? What's the something?"

"I don't know!" She glared at me. "Who do you think I am? One of the all-seeing, all-knowing gods? All I know is that it will happen between dusk and dawn, and here in town."

"But that doesn't make sense."

"Join the crowd," she muttered. She looked at the ground, her black hair falling forward to hide her face.

The voices around us grew angrier as hands balled into fists. Tension radiated from the crowd as they became surlier and drew closer to the three of us. Confusion and fear were written across their faces and in their raised fists and hunched shoulders. Even the children seemed caught up in their parents' actions, clinging close to their legs, tears shining in their eyes.

A hooded figure stood off to one side, away from the crowd yet close enough to listen. His face was shadowed by a dark green—almost brown—cowl pulled up over his head, hiding the top half of his face. His posture was confident, his cloak doing little to hide the leanness of his tall body.

I shifted on my feet. "What did you say to them?"

"A warning." Saya flipped her hair over her shoulders and straightened.

"A warning about what?"

"It does not concern you!" she exclaimed, her lips pursing. "You don't belong here. Go back home, Juliet Barrows."

"What do you mean by that?"

Saya threw up her hands. "I am done here!" she yelled, startling me. "You all either listen to my warning or go about your business. Heed my words. If you do not, you will regret it." She strode forward, and the crowd parted before her, none daring to touch her but all observing in silence as she passed.

The innkeeper followed after her, his thin form weaving around the crowd, who mingled together after Saya passed. Beyond them, the doorway to the inn stood empty; the hooded man had gone. I scanned the crowd, but there was no sign of him.

"Wait!" I called after the innkeeper, hurrying to catch up to him.

"What is it?" he inquired as I came level with him before the inn.

"What was all that about? What was Saya warning of?"

"She warned us of impending doom, so to speak. We shall see if anyone listens."

"What doom?"

The innkeeper looked at me and raised his eyebrows. "Pardon me?"

"What is supposed to happen?"

"She does not know." He glared at me as a snort escaped my lips. "She cannot know all," he continued. "Like she has said, she is not sure what will happen or when, but you may depend on it: it will come to pass."

"There is nothing more? How does she know?"

The innkeeper returned his gaze to the crowd. "She cannot tell us how she knows."

"Why do I get the feeling she knows more about me than I think?"

"Perhaps because she does."

I jerked. I hadn't realized I'd spoken my question out loud. *What does he mean?* "How?"

"That's not for me to say."

"Well, that's helpful." Another snort escaped me.

"Do not take this lightly. Do not make the same mistake the townspeople of Umi no Machi are. Ryujin help us all." The innkeeper raised his face to the sky before entering the inn, the door opening with a soft click.

I bit my lip, my eyebrows furrowing in confusion.

Ryujin.

Why did that sound so familiar?

Chapter Four

The scent of jasmine wafted through the air as I stood in front of a wooden door. Now that I was here, I hesitated, unsure whether to knock or just walk away and leave that simple door behind. But the innkeeper hadn't been willing to give me an explanation for what happened with Saya and her warning, so here I was. He'd at least told me where her room was.

I should just leave. I shouldn't be here. I stepped back, turning away, and the door slid open behind me.

Saya stood there, her arms crossed. "What do you want?"

I rotated back on my heels and squared my shoulders. "I need to talk to you."

"About what?"

"Earlier."

She leaned against the doorframe and frowned. "I don't want to talk about it."

"But—"

"No." Saya held up a hand. "It's none of your concern."

"None of my concern? You kind of made whatever that was back there *everyone's* concern. So what did you expect?"

Saya's almond-shaped eyes narrowed. "Why do you really want to know?"

"Because you are an enigma, not just you, but this whole town." I spread my arms out wide. "And because it finally dawned on me that you seem to know a lot more about me than you should."

"I can't help you." She turned to go back into her room.

"Yeah, well, too bad," I muttered, striding past her into the small annex.

"Hey, you can't be in here." Saya followed me and grabbed hold of my arm. "This is my room."

"I'm not leaving until you explain."

She laughed and let go of my arm. "Explain what? The warning I gave the town? Why do you care?"

"Not that. What do you know?"

Saya's shoulders relaxed a little. "Oh, that. What do you think I know?"

"Hang on, that's not what I asked."

"You asked an impolite question."

"You people and your politeness," I muttered under my breath.

"That *was* rude, and you know it."

"Yeah, I do, but when someone is making cryptic comments about me and refuses to answer, it kind of gets under my skin. So what do you know?"

Saya knelt on a cushion on the floor, her eyes watching mine over the seven lit candles in front of her. "You're stubborn; I'll give you that."

"So you'll tell me?"

"No." A soft smile tilted her lips upward, softening her face into something refined and beautiful.

I took a cushion and knelt on it in front of her, the candles between us. "Why not?"

"Because it is my secret, not yours."

"But it has to do with me," I pressed.

"It does not *have* to do with you. It is about me, and you're just a small part of the whole picture." She waved her hands in the air to emphasize. "Just let it be, Juliet."

I sat back on my heels. "You know where I'm from, don't you?"

Saya blinked, hesitating. "No."

"Are you sure?"

"Yes. I don't know where you come from. Now, I think I would like you to go."

Standing up, I walked to the door and placed my hand on the notch. "I'm sorry, Saya. I shouldn't have barged into your room the way I did nor disrespected you." With that, I opened the door and slid through. There was no answer, no voice to call me back.

Deep down, I kept hoping she would come after me and explain all the cryptic comments. Her, the strange woman who had found me, the hooded man outside... There were so many secrets revolving around this town...around *me.*

⁂

My eyes flew open as my limbs jerked from sleep.

Falling.

Without a light, the room was black as pitch.

What woke me?

Sleep tugged at me, pulling me back into its rosy clutches. A thump filtered through the closed door.

Stretching a hand out, I felt the soft pallet, the floor, pallet—there, the matchbox. A spark flew, and a flickering light sprang into life. As the wick on the candle caught, the room flooded with a dim, yellow glow.

I stared at the door, my gaze flickering between it and the cozy, plush quilt covering my body. The urge to go the bathroom grew. With a sigh, I stood, letting the blankets fall to the floor.

My fingers shook as I took the blanket and wrapped it around myself before opening the bedroom door.

The darkened square room beyond was empty, but distant noises floated up the stairwell. I hesitated at the door to the bathroom and jumped as a crash reverberated from somewhere down on the main floor. All thoughts of relieving myself disappeared.

My footfalls were soft on the bamboo floor as I crept towards the stairs. With one foot on the second step, I hesitated. A new, unsettling aura of silence had settled over everything.

Another loud bang set my heart pounding. I blew out the candle and set it down before continuing.

Pausing at the bottom of the stairwell, I peered around the corner into the darkened lobby. The air itself felt eerie, yet my heart beat in even waves, my limbs calm and controlled, my senses heightened.

With a deep breath, I slipped across the room. The door creaked, and I dove behind a chair as heavy footsteps thudded against the floor.

"Dirk," a rough voice ground out.

Frozen in place, I waited, my knees drawn up to my chest.

"Is anyone else 'ere?"

"No."

I peered around the chair, my heart pounding. A large man stood outlined by the dim light coming in through the open doorway.

He gestured. "T'en why are ye still 'ere? Git outside and 'elp. T'e sun will be up soon."

The other man, shorter, burlier than the first, threw up his hands. "They have ale in the kitchen—"

The large man laughed. "We 'ave enough ale! Come on." He turned, his heavy tread receding as he left the inn. The burly man's booted footsteps followed.

I waited, frozen as screams filtered into the room from the street.

Move.

But I didn't go back upstairs. Instead my feet carried me toward the front door.

A dark shadow appeared, and I dropped behind another chair. The figure's chest heaved as it paused at the entrance. *A woman*, I realized. She waited a moment before streaking forward, her skirts swishing and her eyes glinting white in the darkness.

A man entered the room behind her and, with long strides, caught up the fleeing woman and grabbed a fistful of her blouse and hair. She screamed, and I suppressed a shriek of my own as he flung her against the wall with a sickening thud.

Sweat dampened my clothing as I watched the woman's chest rise and fall with rapid breathing. Her terrible screams rang through the room as she pummeled the large man, the air sharp with the sound of her cries.

He laughed.

A heavy fist rose into the air and fell. I stifled a scream, but not soon enough as a small hiccup escaped. Clamping a hand over my mouth, I stopped breathing, unable to tear my gaze away from the man as he held the limp figure of the woman. His head swung around as he looked about.

I couldn't breathe, couldn't take in air, even though my lungs burned and my throat ached. The woman moaned, drawing the man's attention back to his burden. It wasn't until they left that I could draw in deep gulps of life-giving air into my lungs.

With shaking feet, I rose and paused in the doorway. Torches blazed up and down the street, illuminating the large figures of men running back and forth, loading a line of carts and horses with goods they carried out of the surrounding homes and shops. Cries of pain and anger, the screams of women, and the sobs of children rent the air.

"Hurry up!" one of the men called out. "We've almost outstayed our welcome!"

Echoes of laughter rebounded up and down the street. Tears stung my eyes before running down my cheeks.

A small child stood strapped to the back of a cart nearest me. His eyes rolled, and his mouth stood open in a silent wail.

Eddie. He looks like him—

I'd hesitated before, long ago, in a different time and a different place.

Never again.

Sounds dulled as I ran across the street toward the little boy. A shard of glass lay on the ground, and I scooped it up. Arriving at the boy's side, I sawed at the rope with the glass. The shard glinted in the surrounding torchlight as I worked. The child stared at me with eyes wide and terrified.

"Come on!" I exclaimed as the last of the rope strands gave way. I clutched the boy's hand and pulled him along behind me towards the inn.

"You there!" a voice called out behind us.

Throwing a quick glance over my shoulder, I saw the dark form of a cloaked figure striding toward us, something glittering in his hand—then we were through the doorway.

An echo of heavy breathing and the stomp of boots followed us as we climbed. Higher and higher we ran, until we reached the fourth story. I dragged the boy across the room to a door adjacent to my bedroom. I closed the door behind us with a soft click and looked about.

There.

I pulled the boy behind me down a passage to the second to last door. Inside, a small bathing chamber with a shallow pool greeted us. I groaned and shook my head.

Nowhere to hide! The thought raced through my mind. I was about to whirl around when I spied a large cabinet.

"Come on," I whispered, leading the way. The door came open with a sharp squeak, and I winced before shoving the boy inside and following in after him.

He whimpered as I half-lifted, half-dragged him onto my lap. He buried his head in my shoulder, his little body shaking. The door clicked as I pulled it closed.

"Shh," I whispered. "Stay quiet now."

I may have sat hours or mere minutes, but time continued on with no chime to herald its passing. Pain throbbed across my right palm and fingers. I looked down at my palm, unable to see more than the silhouette in the dark. I frowned.

The memory of using the glass to cut at the boy's bonds flitted through my mind. *I must have cut myself.* Adjusting my stiff and numb legs, I tried ignoring the aches in my hand. The boy's body leaned against me in the peaceful relaxation of sleep. His eyes were closed, his mouth slightly open as he breathed. I brushed back his dark brown hair and shifted him off my lap.

Opening the door a crack, I looked through, but the room was dark and there was no movement. I slipped out of our hiding place and laid the boy carefully back into the cabinet. Sneaking to the doorway, I paused again. The hallway was also empty, as was the room beyond. The faint light of early morning sifted through the cracks around the curtains. Muddy footprints marked the bamboo matting.

I edged to the stairwell and listened to the faint hush of voices drifting up. *What could they be saying?* My feet made little noise as I inched down the stairs. The voices grew stronger, and I strained my ears, taking another step—and slipping on the last stair to the second-floor landing. I cringed as I regained my footing, waiting. The voices grew quiet before resuming. I let out the breath of air I'd been holding.

A form burst around the corner of the stairs onto the landing. I shrieked, turning to run, but a hand grasped my wrist and pulled me back.

"Juliet?"

I froze, looking up into the shadowed face of a tall man, his cowl drawn up over his head.

The man standing at the edge of the crowd. The one who watched, his face hidden, before disappearing.

He let go of my hand. "I won't hurt you."

"I saw you outside yesterday!" I exclaimed. "How do you know my name?"

"The innkeeper is downstairs, and Saya, as well."

Another figure appeared around the corner, her breathing fast.

"Saya!" I almost cried with relief. "There is a boy upstairs, fourth-floor bathing chamber. He's in the cabinet."

She nodded. "I'll fetch him." Her footsteps thumped against the bamboo flooring as she bounded up the stairs.

When I turned, the hooded man had disappeared. I recoiled. *Where did he go?* Peering around the landing to the next set of stairs, I found it empty, and no sound of receding footfalls echoed up the stairwell.

On tired feet, I trudged down the rest of the steps and entered the lobby, where a dozen or so people sat on cushions in a circle. I slipped onto an empty one near the innkeeper.

He nodded to me, his eyes lined with weariness. "A meeting will be held soon," he whispered. "A count of the missing and of the dead is being taken."

Saya and her warning. She was right. The realization hit me in full force. My mouth moved, but no words came out. *Her warning. She tried to tell us, but no one had listened.*

I turned to look at the innkeeper. "Saya was right, wasn't she? This was what she spoke of yesterday."

Sullen looks were thrown my way.

"She was right, but how did she know?" a woman asked, her voice high and reedy. "Maybe she was in league with them."

"Quiet!" the innkeeper barked. "There will be no accusations here, not now."

"But who were they?" The thin woman sent a resentful look the innkeeper's way.

"I think they were from up north."

"Northern raiders?" she gasped, leaning back on her heels.

"Yes, Ai," the innkeeper replied with a heavy sigh.

"But how? They've never come down this far before."

The innkeeper shook his head and shrugged his bulky shoulders. "I don't know. But they had all the markings of the northern raiders."

"What markings?"

As soon as the words left my lips, everyone stared at me. The antagonism from before had not disappeared from their eyes. I turned to the side to see the innkeeper regarding me with a puzzled look in his eyes.

"What do you know of the north?"

"I—nothing," I admitted, crossing my feet at the ankles.

The innkeeper grunted. "We are connected to a large country by a thin strip of land. Some of the people up there, whom we refer to as the northern raiders, they deal in the slave trade."

A sudden intake of breath from those around the circle interrupted the innkeeper.

He looked about with weary eyes before settling his gaze back on me. "The men last night, they were large men and spoke with the accent of the northerners—"

"Maybe they weren't," a man broke in. "We don't know for sure."

"They didn't take any goods or try to steal our possessions. They took people. Men, women, and children, all in good health. The elderly were left. Why do you think that is?"

My eyes shot back and forth between the two men. The face of the man who had spoken paled, and he cast his eyes downwards to the floor in dejection.

"Ask Saya," the same woman grated out. "She knew they were coming; she should know who they are."

A footstep behind us silenced her, and we all turned to look as one. Saya walked in from the stairwell, the boy's hand clasped in hers. He pulled away from her as he caught sight of me and ran over. Heaving him up onto my lap, I winced as I examined my right hand for the first time. The skin was brownish red from dried blood, and lacerations spread over my palm and across my fingers from where the shard of glass had cut into me. Blood matted the boy's hair, and bloody handprints stained his shirt.

"Does anyone know who his parents are?" I inquired, looking around at the weary faces around me.

"His parents were taken," the innkeeper replied in a low tone. "How did you find him?"

"He was tied to the back of one of the wagons."

The innkeeper's eyes widened. "You rescued him?"

"I did."

"Your hand?"

"Glass," I answered.

"You could have been taken," he remarked. "That was stupid."

"And rather brave," someone added. The new voice was deep and curt.

I looked up at the speaker. It was the man from the stairwell, his cowl still drawn and his eyes hidden in shadow. Short, bristled hair stubbled his chin and jaw. He dipped his head towards me. Heat rose into my cheeks, and I looked away.

"Yes, I suppose so," the innkeeper agreed. "But you put yourself and your life at risk."

"Better than doing nothing," I responded.

Ai leaned forward, her hand tapping her knee. "Is he hurt?"

"No."

"Where did all the blood come from, then?"

My fists tightened as I remembered the glass glinting in the light from the torches and the boy's face, pale and frightened before me. I forced myself to relax, looking down at my palms and the dark red streaks of clotted blood and the brighter red of fresh blood. They stung, the pain throbbing through my skin and deep inside my tendons and nerves. When I looked up, I was surprised to find everyone watching me. The woman's face hadn't changed as she continued to eye me, suspicion pouring out of her narrowed eyes and thinned lips. Material rustled, and I glanced at the innkeeper. He looked at me also and blinked before giving me a slow nod. But the stranger, the unknown man—his was the most unnerving of all. He had removed his hood, and his gaze penetrated my soul. His eyes, dark green with flecks of gold, were blank, showing nothing of his emotions.

I turned away, trying to gather my scrambled thoughts back together. A single drumbeat drifted through the inn's walls. I looked up, my head tilted as I listened to the sound.

The people around me stood without a word, and the hooded man had disappeared yet again.

How does he do that?

I leaned closer to the innkeeper. "What's going on?"

"It's time." The innkeeper rose and led the way outside.

Chapter Five

A few dozen men, women, and children thronged in the street before the inn, but most of them were the elderly, the young, or those with infirmities. They shuffled their feet on the dry dirt and avoided one another as though betrayal ran amongst them.

The innkeeper cleared his throat, and complete silence fell. "How many were taken?"

A middle-aged man stepped forward. "Just over three dozen."

The innkeeper swore under his breath. "By the gods, so many?"

"How could this happen?"

I craned my neck, looking to see who the speaker was.

The innkeeper began, "Akio—"

"We've had peace for years until now." The man, Akio, strode forward to face the innkeeper. "We can't allow this to pass."

The innkeeper's posture went rigid. "Yet it did." He surveyed the townspeople. "We all had family and friends taken. But I don't know if there is anything we can do."

Silence met his words, heavy and stifling.

Akio took a step, turning to face those gathered. "The king has men; he can help us."

The innkeeper laid a hand on Akio's burly arm. "Have you not heard the rumors?"

"I have!" he spat. "But they are just those: rumors."

"And yet my inn has lain empty these many months. Few ask for lodging."

"Wait," I blurted out. "But you have tenants. I don't understand."

The innkeeper frowned as he turned to face me. "They live here in town. My inn is also somewhat of a boarding house."

"None of that matters," Akio interrupted. "My mother was taken. We must do something. We're not fighters or trackers, but we can plead to the king."

"Stop fidgeting," Saya snapped, glaring at me.

"I'm just trying to listen," I whispered.

"Then do it quietly."

I rolled my eyes and leaned forward as Akio continued, "A rider will be sent. The king cannot ignore his duty to protect his people. Even though we live on the edge of the kingdom and are small in number, it does not mean we deserve less protection than the people from the capital."

"The king won't help you." The words rang out from a tall man in a long cloak.

It's him. I watched with interest as he strode forward, the crowd parting before him. *The man who appears and then disappears without anyone noticing.*

The hooded man stopped mere feet from me. "It would be a fool's errand."

Akio frowned. "What do you mean?"

"The king doesn't care for the well-being of his subjects. The country has changed much in the past years, and it is not the peaceful little hamlet of Umi no Machi."

"We've heard the rumors," Akio remarked.

The hooded man's fists clenched at his sides. "They aren't rumors. I come and go. I see things and hear things—"

"We all know you travel, unlike the rest of us," the innkeeper broke in.

"We could still try the king," Akio declared, his voice soft. "Perhaps you exaggerate."

"You could petition, but I would be surprised if you're even admitted before the king. He has too many enemies. If you want to rescue your loved ones, you must do it on your own. There won't be a king nor his soldiers to help."

The innkeeper raised his hand as he gestured. "How do you know? You are gone so often, but where?"

"I know. I don't need to explain how."

"Why wouldn't you have warned us before of how dangerous it has grown inland?"

"Would you have listened?"

Silence met his words. The crowd seemed to strain forward on tiptoes as though waiting for someone to step up and answer.

Edging my way to the innkeeper's side, I whispered, "Who is he?"

"He's lived here for a long time. We call him Shizukana. He is the quiet one." *The Unknown.*

"He doesn't interact much with anyone. I doubt there is a single person he cares about in this town. He is a loner, a man who has shut himself off from the world around him, but he minds his own business, and he pays well."

"Pays well?"

The innkeeper leaned closer. "He rents a small shack from me."

"Saya!" a woman yelled, shoving her way past me.

I rubbed my ear with the back of my blood-stained hand as her voice vibrated.

"How did she know this was going to happen?" The woman's deep voice belayed her short form. "She warned us all that something would happen during the night hours, and it did! What does she have to say?"

"Druselle!" Akio called, a warning in his voice.

"No, Akio, I will have my say." Druselle took a few steps forward, joining him and Shizukana—or "the Unknown", as I now thought of him—before the assembled people. "How do we know Saya wasn't working with the bandits?"

"Why would she have warned us?" the Unknown asked.

"Maybe she got cold feet at the last minute."

"I agree with him." Akio jerked a finger towards the Unknown. "Why else would she have warned us?"

"Maybe she feared a reckoning from the bandits if she gave them away completely. Or maybe she feared the gods' retaliation against her!"

"Druselle, enough!" Akio up a hand. "This is getting out of control."

The crowd's murmuring grew louder, accusations pouring in from every quarter. Saya stood without flinching, but my gaze flickered toward the inn. The boy I saved grabbed my hand and squeezed, and I winced as pain flared across my lacerated palm. Leaning over, I loosened his grip and transferred his hand to my left instead.

Saya stared out over the crowd, her gaze glassy and unseeing.

"Look at her!" Druselle yelled, her long dress rustling as she strode back and forth. "She doesn't care! Orphan! She has no one!"

"Enough!" the Unknown barked, his voice cutting through the air. The crowd fell silent. "No more. Saya is not with them. Cease this talk. Go back to your homes, plan a rescue, whatever you'd like, but no more about Saya."

"Who are you to say what we do?" a man called out, stepping forward. "You are not one of us. You never have been."

The Unknown turned to face the shorter man, who shrank back.

"What about the new girl?"

Wait! That voice! I whipped around. The woman who had found me at the roots stood there, almost lost amongst those pressing in around her: small but standing straight, her features calm.

"Yes!" Another woman took up the call. "What about her? Could you have anything to do with last night?" Fear laced her words, blatant in the brisk morning air.

In my distraction, the woman who had found me had disappeared. I frowned. She'd been there.

"Juliet, right?" someone shouted. Everyone's gaze turned toward me now, more suspicion filling their faces as they looked for another to blame.

I took a step back.

"Why is she still here, then?" the Unknown bit out. "Now disperse—be about your business." He brushed past me, the innkeeper right on his heels. Saya and I exchanged a glance and hurried after them.

Before I could usher the boy into the inn, a woman came forward, and the boy clasped his hands around her waist.

"I'm his aunt," she explained with a soft, sad smile. "Thank you for caring for him."

I nodded, watching them walk away with a pang in my heart. *He survived, unlike Eddie. Even though I froze the first time, this time I didn't. And now he's safe.* My heart constricted within my chest. A single tear slid down my cheek, but I dashed it away.

"Come on. He'll be fine." Saya proceeded into the main room of the inn, where we joined the Unknown and the innkeeper in the circle of chairs. Akio also sat there. The innkeeper stood and left the room, leaving silence in his wake.

It stretched on until he returned with a tray of drinks. I wrapped my hands around the cool glass and bit back a groan. Forcing myself to relax, I let the cool moisture soak into my aching palm.

I glanced up to see the Unknown staring at me.

"Saya," Akio began, "I don't believe you are in league with the men who attacked us last night." His brow furrowed. "But how did you know something would happen? Yesterday you warned us all, yet none of us believed you, and now I am sorry for that."

Saya peered at him with her usual unemotional face. The innkeeper fidgeted a bit in his chair but didn't say a word.

"Saya?" Akio repeated.

"I don't know," she admitted. "It's not the first time."

The Unknown's gaze again slid over to me, catching my own before moving back to Saya.

An unbelieving noise issued from Akio's throat. "There are no seers left in this world. They've all died or been killed. It is not possible."

My lips opened as I sat up straight in my chair, but then I caught the Unknown looking at me.

He raised an eyebrow. "You have something you wish to say?"

"No, I—no."

"Ask what you wish."

"I don't understand. Seers? People who see glimpses of the future?"

He crossed his arms. "Yes."

"They exist?"

"Yes—"

"No!" Akio exclaimed at the same time.

The two men looked at one another.

Akio leaned forward. "They don't exist. Not since the king went on a rampage. They've either died or left the country."

"They *do* exist," the Unknown reaffirmed.

Akio waved a hand. "It does not matter. Juliet, where do you come from?"

"Earth."

Akio snorted. "Yes, we're all from Earth, but where on this wide planet?"

"West."

"That's where the king's family is from." Akio's gaze grew distant. "Where exactly?"

"It's a long way from here. The woman in the crowd, who is she?"

"Woman?" Akio repeated. His foot beat a slow rhythm against the floor. "What woman?"

"The one who cast blame on me."

"I didn't see her." Akio frowned. "Why do you ask?"

"Just wondering. I've seen her before."

"That hand of yours needs bandaging."

I glanced down, having forgotten about the wound, but now I felt that stinging pain again as if hundreds of needles had punctured my skin.

The Unknown waited, his arms folded, a daunting figure in his long cloak. He turned and strode away, so I followed, catching Saya's inscrutable gaze as I went.

He led us to the kitchen, and I flinched as he laid both of his hands on my waist and hoisted me onto the table. Heat flushed my cheeks, and I looked down at my hands in my lap.

I watched as he began cleaning away the blood on my palm. "What do you know about me?"

"You appeared in this town two days ago, have been working in this inn to earn food and lodging, and in that short time have embroiled yourself in affairs that don't concern you."

My jaw dropped open. "I haven't chosen to do so!"

"No? Well, you ought to be more careful."

"You seem to know more about me and where I came from than anyone else."

"Do I? Interesting."

I leaned forward. "Do you?"

"Do I what?"

"Do you know more about me than you're telling?"

"Should I?" He raised his head. I blinked, unable to glance away from his green eyes, fringed with lashes, long and dark.

Pain lanced across my palm, and I gasped, looking down to see clear liquid falling over the torn skin.

"I don't know where you come from, Juliet, but I know it isn't here." He took a thin strip of fine linen to wrap around my palm. His touch was firm but gentle.

"What do you mean by that?"

"I don't know you, and I don't trust you. For now, you will have to take it as you will. Perhaps in time we may both be straightforward with one another. On the other hand, this might be the last time we ever speak. Sometimes things are meant to stay a mystery." He lifted me off the counter and onto the floor. "Be careful, Juliet Barrows." He stood there a moment, staring down at me, before leaving, his long strides carrying him out of the kitchen.

I waited, mulling over his warning before following him out. He wasn't in the room when I returned; however, Akio and the innkeeper still sat, talking in hushed voices. A footstep—there, Saya had just disappeared up the stairs. I hurried over to the stairwell and ran up, taking them two at a time.

I passed an open window on the second floor, the warm afternoon air rustling my hair as I peered out at the bright blue sky. She was fast. There was no sign of her. I continued on, hesitating before the familiar door, so like every other one in the inn.

With a deep inhale, I rapped my left hand on the door. Somewhere inside, the wood floor creaked, and the door slid open.

Saya raised her eyebrows. "Yes?"

"Can we talk?"

She stepped back so I could enter and took a seat on the floor. I knelt on an empty cushion, twisting the hem of my shirt between my fingertips. The closet door was open a couple of inches, and even with the low lighting, I could make out the straps of a pack and garment sleeve trailing across the floor.

Saya snapped her fingers, drawing my attention back to herself. "What do you want?"

"You're going after them."

Her eyes narrowed. "Yes."

"On your own?"

"I can find them."

"But it's too dangerous," I blurted. "What are you going to do by yourself against all those men?"

"What chance do you think a group of noisy townsfolk not used to going outside the boundaries of their own town have?" Her lips curved downward. "We both know the answer. And the longer we wait, the less chance of freeing them we have."

"And what chance do you have?"

"The best chance they have. With the gods' help, I can find them." Saya stood up and placed her hands on her hips. "Juliet, I don't understand. Why don't you go home? What's keeping you here? Do you not want to go?"

"Seriously?" I stood as well. "You hate personal questions, so why ask them?"

Saya laughed. "I *hate* them? More like it is against our custom, our culture, something you obviously do not understand. Go home."

"I can't."

She cocked her head. "Why not? Go home. You don't care about us or what happens to us."

"You know nothing of my life, Saya," I snapped. "You have no right to judge me."'

"As you're judging me?"

I reeled back. "Fine. You know what? I may not have known anyone taken last

night, but I still know the pain of having someone taken from me."

Saya's hands fell by her sides. "Who does the boy remind you of?"

I took a deep, shuddering breath. "My brother...it was a long time ago."

"Your brother?" Her voice was a soft whisper.

My eyes closed against the onslaught of memories. "Yes. I both love and hate the ocean. We used to go every summer, not just once, but multiple times, any weekend we could. My brother was several years younger than me, but we were so close. Neither of us had many friends, and it was often just us two as playmates." I licked my lips as Saya nodded for me to go on. "One summer, eleven years ago, we were at the beach. We built sandcastles, buried one another in the sand, and played in the waves. We knew not to go too far into the ocean, but we dared each other—and the tide was coming in." The images danced before my eyes, as clear as the day itself.

"What happened?" Saya whispered, her eyes soft and damp.

"Mom and Dad called out to me, waving their arms as they ran forward. But I couldn't hear them. They were too far away. When I looked around, he wasn't there. I couldn't see him anywhere. Just water." Tears filled my eyes. "Then he came up, but another wave came, and he went under again. I froze. I couldn't do anything. I don't know how long it was before I ran forward, but it was so hard in the water. I was too slow. As the wave receded, I found him, I pulled him to me, but his body was limp. He wasn't responding." My shoulders shook. "I never heard his voice again. It's because of me he's dead." A sob wrenched out of my body, and I buried my face in my hands.

"That's why you saved him," Saya whispered. "You wanted to do what you couldn't before."

Taking deep, calming breaths, I raised my head to look at her. "Let me come with you." The words were out before I could stop them.

Saya blinked. "What? Why would you do that?"

"I don't know."

"You're strange."

I sighed. "Maybe I am, but even if I wanted to, I'm not able to go back home."

"Why can't you go home?"

"I've tried. I'm not sure how to." I shrugged as I dried my face on my sleeve. "So I might as well go with you."

Saya laughed and held up her hands. "You really are strange. Why wouldn't you just stay here until you can return?"

I blinked. "Because you shouldn't go alone."

She snorted. "You're not experienced enough. No, I'm not trying to offend you, but I'll do better on my own."

"Maybe, and maybe not. Two will be better than one. I'm fit. I'll keep up."

Saya's dark eyes regarded me, her dark pupils dilated in the dimness of the room.

"Do you ever feel," I began, "an urge to do something that may be so stupid, and you can't explain the reasoning, but you know if you don't go through with it, you would regret it? Miss out on something just beyond your reach, but you don't even know what it is?"

"No."

"Let me go with you," I pressed.

"Alright, but I won't be blamed for your choice, bad as it is."

I smiled. "The choice is mine, so the fault is mine as well, whatever happens."

"I hope you know what you're doing."

"Me too," I whispered.

"Here," Saya said, handing me a black rucksack. "I'm leaving tonight. Bring what you need in this."

"I don't have any belongings."

"Nothing?" Saya frowned. "You have nothing with you?"

"No."

"How—" She bit her lip and stood up. "We're about the same size. Take these. You'll probably want to change out of the clothes you're currently wearing. They smell."

"Thanks."

"No, really. They do. Go to the bathing chambers before we leave."

I nodded, turning to leave.

"How do you know him?"

"Know who?"

"Shizukana."

The hooded man.

I shook my head. "I don't know him."

"Yet he stood up for you against the crowd, then he bandaged your hands."

"Is that his real name?"

Saya's eyebrows drew together. "No, but no one knows what it is. Go, I'll see you when night has come and everyone is abed."

⁂

Darkness had fallen as day descended into night. Shifting my position, I waited in the lobby for Saya to appear. A stair creaked, but no one appeared. I glanced down at the pack at my feet. Inside lay my clothes, still a little damp from washing them, as well as the other shirt that Saya had given me.

A soft rustle alerted me.

"Follow me," Saya whispered as I reeled back. Her dark form moved past.

In the kitchen, she lit a small lantern and set it down on the table before bustling around, gathering supplies.

I set my pack on the table. "Did you leave a note?"

"No, the innkeeper would come after me."

"Who is he to you?"

"He's the innkeeper."

"Nothing more?"

"It's none of your business," she hissed, whirling on me. "My life is none of your concern."

I held up my hands. "That's fair. I'm sorry."

Saya handed me my pack. "Done. You sure you want to come?" Her shadow stretched out behind her, long and thin.

I nodded and swung the pack over my shoulders.

"Alright then." She carried the lamp before us as we walked down the silent hallway and left the inn. The street was still and quiet, the night cold. Nothing about it whispered of the terror of the night before, of the screams and wails of men, women, and children.

"Wait here," Saya murmured, disappearing into the fog.

I shifted my weight from foot to foot, eyes darting toward every tiny sound and shadow that moved. Everyone was asleep, yet I could still hear echoes of shouts and harsh laughter from last night. They hung in the air, begging to be heard, to be understood—

Someone stepped up behind me. I jumped, a shriek rising in my throat, but Saya's small hand clamped over my mouth.

"Shh, it's me. Do you want to raise the whole town?" Over her arm draped a similar cloak to the one she wore. "Here. You'll need it to keep you warm."

I swung it over my shoulders. It fell almost to the ground, its thick material already beginning to warm my body. "Where did you get it?"

Saya blew out the lantern and strapped it to her pack. "Never you mind." She strode off, the mist enveloping her in its wispy hold.

With one last glance at the inn, I took a deep breath and followed her into the dark haze. A sliver of moon lit our way. The nighttime noises created a cacophony, which burst upon us from every direction. Up in the sky, millions of stars glittered, decorating the dark, velvet expanse. My breath caught in my throat at the calming beauty. Resuming my gaze upon the ground ahead of me, I quickened my stride. Saya had pulled ahead in those brief seconds.

Brushing fallen strands of hair behind my ears, I burrowed my hands under my cloak. My legs tingled with the warmth from the walk and the brisk chill of the night air, and as I exhaled, my breath blew a cloud into the mist.

"Saya?" I asked, breaking the peaceful silence.

"Yes?"

"How do you know which way they went?"

"They left a trail."

Chapter Six

S aya veered off the narrow path and stopped underneath a thick copse. Bright orange hues streaked the sky as the sun rose above the horizon.

"Eat something and take a few minutes to rest," Saya muttered as she set her pack on a fallen log.

I sat down with a deep groan, my back against the rough bark of a tree trunk. My eyes closed.

"Don't sleep."

Opening one eye, I peeked at Saya, who regarded me as she ate.

"We won't be here long enough," she added. "Once the sun is higher and it's warmer out, we can stop and sleep."

I glared in the direction of the birds chirping in the trees, unseen in their perches. Their bubbly songs seemed to be aimed at Saya as though to push back her serious demeanor.

"I love the trees this time of year." Saya gazed up into the tree above me. "The soft reds and brilliant yellows against the fading green—soothing colors, at least to me." A tinge of pink entered her cheeks, and she glanced down at me.

"Me too," I replied, looking around. The trees here were shorter, their trunks and branches more delicate and swaying, and their colors both brighter and softer at the same time. "The scenery is changing."

"We've left the coast behind. The deciduous trees are numerous here. They'll grow a little sparser and intermix with conifers as we leave the coastal forests behind. Then we will truly be in a forest."

I wiped my mouth after drinking some water. "What do you mean?"

"Those forests are harder to traverse. They stay green all year around and are tall and wild."

"You've traveled through them before?"

"Not for a very long time."

"And you haven't left Umi no Machi since?" I guessed.

She nodded and crouched down to rifle through her pack.

"That was impressive, how you knew about the trail. I wouldn't have thought to check to see if the ruts from the wagon wheels were fresh or not, or even to know which way the raiders had left town."

Saya nodded and rolled up her sleeves. "There aren't many trails they could've taken anyway. Most people come and go by the harbor, not over land."

My blue eyes widened, and I sat up. "Why do you think they came by land then? Why did they risk coming all the way from the north on foot?"

"I don't know," Saya admitted. "It doesn't make much sense. Even if the king is ignoring what's going on in his kingdom, it seems like it would have been better for them to go by boat. Maybe they didn't know much about our town."

I grunted. "Maybe."

But something still doesn't seem right. I watched as Saya shouldered her pack.

"Alright, I'm coming," I muttered with a groan. Heaving myself to my feet, I felt a deep ache settle into my legs.

"Now you know why I didn't sit," Saya remarked, hoisting her pack over her shoulders.

"You don't say." I jogged forward a couple of steps and fell in next to her. What's your plan?"

Saya frowned. "I don't know. We have plenty of time to figure it out between now and then."

I glanced at the ruts in the road. "They have wagons—we're on foot. And we don't have weapons."

"Your point?"

"Come on," I replied, gritting my teeth. "You can't be that naïve."

Saya's gaze didn't leave the path. "Maybe you should go back if you're not sure about this." Tension radiated from her raised shoulders and compressed lips.

"Do you want me to?"

"No."

Stumbling, I missed a step at her quick answer.

"What, you thought I didn't want you to come?"

"Pretty much," I muttered. "Hold on one moment."

Saya stopped and watched as I slipped my cloak off and stuffed it into the top of my bag. "It's kind of nice having a little company," she confided. "And as annoying as you are, you speak your mind, which I like."

I stepped over a large branch laying across the narrow road. "How come you didn't ask anyone else to go?"

"How do you know I didn't?"

"Because I know you well enough already that I'd very much doubt you did."

Saya flicked her gaze up at the sky and sighed. "Who would want to go with me? None of them trust me."

"Akio seems to trust you."

"As much as he's able, yes. But it would've taken too long to try and convince him to go." Saya shifted the pack on her shoulders. "He's set on pleading to the king." She stared into my eyes and tilted her face as she scrutinized me.

I raised my hand to my hair. "What? Do I have something—"

"You have blue eyes," Saya interrupted, leaning forward to peer closer.

"You're just now noticing?"

Saya frowned and took a step back. "No, but I'm mentioning it now."

"Why now?"

"Why not?"

I bit back the retort hovering on my lips and sighed.

Saya shrugged and continued walking.

I ran a couple steps to catch up. "Why did you comment on my eye color?"

"I've never seen anyone else with blue eyes before."

I blinked. "I'm not from around here."

Saya stopped. "So you've said." Then she continued along the trail, her small frame belying how quick she was.

I stared at her back, watching as she was forced to take two steps for each one of mine. *The west, the king's family...me.* Akio, the Unknown, and the innkeeper—they had all mentioned the king and his family. *But why do I feel there is some connection? What am I missing?* I cleared my throat. "Saya? I've heard the king's family mentioned a few times now."

Saya glanced over her shoulder and slowed a little.

"The innkeeper seemed suspicious when I first came to the inn, too. Why?"

Saya's eyes narrowed. "You're from the west, same as them. They are fair-haired, light of skin, blue eyes—like you."

"Why do they not look like you?" As Saya frowned again, I added, "I mean, everyone else I've met is the opposite—ivory skin tones, dark hair, dark eyes, small of stature..."

Her face lightened a little. "It's been that way for centuries as far as I know. It was a very, very long time ago when people from the west came and defeated my people. The conquerors have ruled us since. It's always been that way."

"So your people don't actually rule this country?"

"Ryujin? No, they do not."

"Does the king's family still look like me? Haven't they intermarried?"

Saya smiled and her eyes returned to the path. "No, they bring spouses from the west when it's time. It's how they've always done it."

"This is a strange place."

Other than the birdsong trilling in the trees around us, I heard only the soft tread of our boots on the dusty ground. I turned to Saya, who was watching me out of the corner of her eye.

Her gaze shot forward, away from me. "And you're a strange woman."

My lips split in a smile, and I laughed. "That's fair."

∗ ∗ ∗

The late afternoon sun glared down on me, warm and soothing. Saya still lay on top of her cloak near me, her snores gentle and peaceful.

Sitting up, I shaded my eyes and peered at the horizon. A wide yawn popped my jaw, and I grimaced at how tight everything felt. Pulling my knees up to my chest, I rested my chin on them—and froze.

A hooded figure sat on a log at the edge of our makeshift campsite. His fingers played with the tip of an unstrung bow.

I shrieked, springing to my feet as I yelled, "Saya!"

Saya's eyes flew open, and she sat up. My eyes flicked back to the tall figure, and my hand clenched into a fist as the person brushed back his hood. "Oh! It's you."

The Unknown. The fear that held me in its feverish grip relaxed.

Saya took a step forward. "What are you doing here? You followed us."

He stood and folded his arms. "Yes."

"Why?"

"I was there the night you left Juliet standing outside the inn so you could *borrow* a cloak." He stepped closer to Saya, ignoring me.

I frowned. "You've been within sight of us this entire time?"

He gave the briefest hint of a nod.

My right eyebrow rose. "And you could hear us?"

He nodded again.

A shiver ran over my body. "That's—"

Saya cleared her throat and narrowed her eyes. "Why didn't you show yourself before this?"

"Why would I?"

"Because it's more polite than spying."

The Unknown raised an eyebrow, and I could've sworn a small smile crinkled the corner of his lips.

I stepped forward. "You know why we're here?"

He inclined his head.

"Why show yourself now?" Saya demanded.

"It was time," he murmured.

"Are you going to join us?" I pressed. Saya stiffened from where she stood next to me.

"Why would I do that?" he queried, his voice low.

Though I couldn't meet his gaze, I put my hands on my hips. "Why else are you here?"

He turned to look down at me but said nothing.

Saya and I exchanged glances, and she cleared her throat. "Are you here to make us turn back?"

"Why do you think I care that much about your welfare?"

I blinked. "Then why are you here?"

"Neither of you knows what you're getting into nor the full extent of the danger you face."

"So you do care?"

"No."

"Then why?"

"I know these lands." He hesitated, his eyes darkening. With a sigh, he continued, "You could use my help."

"So you *are* here to help."

Saya threw her shoulders back, letting a soft huff escape her lips.

A gleam lightened the Unknown's dark green eyes. "You both need to be more alert. I've followed you for hours, and you had no idea. Neither of you knows what lies out there...nor who." He gestured and shrugged his cloak back, revealing a long, curved sword at his side. "Now, how about we get moving?"

"Wait!" I blurted, my mouth dry. "If you don't care about our welfare, why help?"

"I suppose you'll just have to trust me."

I pulled Saya away from the Unknown and leaned my head close to hers. "We could use him," I whispered.

Saya's eyes flitted from my face to his as he watched us.

"He defended you yesterday."

"I don't trust him," she replied.

"What's the saying? Keep your friends close and your enemies closer?"

She lowered her eyes in resignation. "Fine. But I still don't trust him."

"I don't either, but I would rather know he's within sight than wandering around out there watching us. Hasn't he lived in your town for years?"

"He's been around as long as I can remember," Saya muttered.

"Yet you don't know him?"

Saya glanced at me. "He isn't around much and keeps to himself when he is. I know nothing about him beyond he's as slippery as an eel. He's hard to pin down about anything."

"That's pretty much what the innkeeper told me when I asked him."

Saya raised her eyebrows.

"Well, too late now," I muttered. "If he didn't harm us before, why would he now?"

Saya blinked and shrugged. "Alright then." She turned to the Unknown and raised her voice. "Shizukana, you may come with us."

He nodded. "Let's go then." He turned and walked off, and we were left to follow in his wake. We had to hurry to keep up with him, as his long legs ate up the ground beneath them.

"Hey," I whispered, nudging Saya with my shoulder.

"What?" she snapped, her brown eyes sparking.

"Why are you so angry?"

Her gaze shot toward the Unknown before lowering to the path we tread.

"It's him?" I guessed.

She shrugged and sped up.

"Saya!" I called, but there was no answer as she caught up and fell in behind our new companion.

The trees hid the falling sun from view, but the sky above shone blue and bright, a cheering sight. I sighed. *Or, at least, it should be cheering. What is Cam doing right now? What day is it?* My eyebrows drew together as I considered. *September seventeenth, that's when I arrived here.* I looked down at my boots as I walked. *How long...?* I grinned and glanced up. *Three days. Only three days since I came. It was Wednesday. So today is Saturday.*

The smile disappeared.

Are they looking for me? What did Cam tell them? Do they think I'm dead?

My heart wrenched deep within my chest.

Cam would've assumed the worst. She always does. I took a deep breath and glanced over my shoulder. *It's too late. You can't turn back now.*

"I'll come back," I whispered, but there was no one to hear me. Cam couldn't hear me. My parents couldn't hear me. Even Saya and the Unknown couldn't catch a word as they strode ahead, the distance between us widening.

I swallowed the lump in my throat and took in deep, even breaths. Saya's head turned as she peered over her shoulder at me. My pace quickened.

She didn't look back at me again. As I drew near, she hoisted the pack up her back a little. Taking a couple of running steps, I caught up. Saya stared forward, her gaze unswerving.

"Saya?" I prompted, eying her.

She didn't make a sign that she'd heard me. The birds twittering in the trees above our heads accompanied the soft thuds of our boots on loose earth, and the rustle of fallen leaves began to dry in the warm sun.

The Unknown's tall figure led the way, his steps sure and even. His cloak swirled around his legs, and his hair was hidden under his cowl. As we walked, the sun continued to lower below the skyline, mirroring my own depleting energy.

Not a word passed between Saya and I. Whenever I glanced at her, she would not look at me, and her shoulders remained raised and tense.

The Unknown glanced back at us over his shoulder. "It'll be dark in an hour or so. We'll stop soon."

Saya's shoulders straightened, but otherwise she gave no sign she'd heard.

My feet dragged with exhaustion, hurting so much I wasn't sure I would be able to limp, much less hobble, after the day ended.

"Juliet," the Unknown murmured, stopping as he let Saya pass him. He stooped to the ground and brushed the tips of his fingers across the ground. "Why do you believe this is the right way?"

"I suppose," I began, glancing at Saya, but she continued walking as if she hadn't heard, "because the shrubs are beaten down. You can see the faint markings of wagon wheels in the dirt, and there is horse dung everywhere." I wrinkled my nose against the potent smell radiating through the warm, dry air. "And Saya saw them heading in this direction when they left."

"Anything else?"

I shook my head.

"This could have been made by a different group."

The Unknown shifted and I froze as I saw a flash of a slender knife hidden in his left boot. *Why so many weapons?*

"The track led out of town in the direction the bandits left," Saya observed.

I jumped, glancing up to see Saya had walked back to join us.

"Couldn't it have been the traders?" he pressed.

"No, they only come once a year or so," she replied. "The track we followed was new and joined this more-used one."

The Unknown smiled.

My jaw tightened as the realization hit me. *He's been testing us.*

He pointed at a faint smudge on the ground. "What is this?"

Why? Why are you doing this? The thoughts circled around my mind before I followed his gaze to the smudge on the ground. Looking back up, I found the

Unknown waiting, his arms crossed over his chest. I shrugged and forced myself to speak without a hint of the annoyance building within me. "No idea."

He raised an eyebrow. "They have scouts. This was made by a person."

I crouched down at his feet to peer at the marks. "Couldn't it have been an animal?"

"No, it's smudged a bit too deep for one animal. Plus, look on the thorns here: a thread. There's similar evidence on the other side of the path from scouts walking near the main group. Know your enemy beforehand. Learn to read tracks, and it will help."

Saya snorted.

I stood up, my lips parting, but before I could say a word, she glared at me and strode away. "Saya," I called out, but she didn't turn. I glanced at the Unknown, whose eyes followed Saya, his expression blank and unreadable.

I jogged a few steps to catch up to her. "What's going on?"

"You don't need to treat him as though he's all-knowing."

"I wasn't! I just..." Hesitating, I felt a gaze on me. When I looked over my shoulder, I saw the Unknown watching me. I fell silent. A shiver ran up my spine. *Who are you?*

❧ ❧

The ringing cadence of crickets and the clicking of other insects had sung me to sleep the night before, and now the herald of morning birds woke me. My body ached. Groaning, I moved first one leg and then the other.

Every. Single. Part. Of. My. Body.

Hurt.

I sat up. *Breathe in, breathe out.* One by one, I stretched each limb until I gasped from the fiery pain shooting through them.

The Unknown stood with his back to me, his pack lying ready at his feet. Saya stepped forward, her eyes narrowed and her lips curving down at the corners. She nodded in greeting.

The Unknown turned around. "You snore."

I stiffened. "I do not."

"Yes, you do."

"No—"

"You could hear yourself while you were sleeping?"

My mouth opened and closed.

"I thought not," he noted.

"It didn't help that I don't have a pillow."

He turned around and looked at me, his eyes piercing, something indiscernible in their depths. "A 'pillow'?" he repeated, the word sounding odd when he said it. "Should I know what that is?"

"Never mind."

Something in the harsh stance of his body told me he'd expected me to give up. My lips parted, but Saya nudged me.

"Don't mind him," she bit out. "You hardly snore at all."

I swallowed, forcing down my anger. "It doesn't matter," I replied, pulling a small bag out of my pack. Under the layers of cloth, I pulled out a thick strip of dried meat and chewed on the tough substance. It was like the jerky I was used to, but thicker and harder. I eyed the long piece I held. Saltier, too. Stowing the cloth bag back in my pack, I froze as Saya approached.

She took my hand in hers.

"What are you doing?" I mumbled around the mouthful of dried meat.

She unwrapped the linen strips. "I brought some salve for your palm."

"Thanks."

"Why does it bother you?" she blurted.

"What?"

"Him—why did it bother you that he said you snore?"

I blinked and peered over her shoulder. The Unknown's head tilted back as he drank some water.

"Juliet?" Saya prodded.

Why did it bother me?

"I—I don't know."

Saya finished wrapping my palm back up and let my hand go. "You don't know?" Her warm brown eyes stared back at me, confused.

I shook my head. *No, I don't know.* My gaze wandered over to where the Unknown pulled his pack over his shoulders, his brown and green cloak rippling.

"You'll fall behind," the Unknown called, striding off into the forest. "Let's go."

Saya glared at his back as she finished tying a new strip of linen off. "Here." She handed me my pack and shouldered her own. "We'd better get going."

"Or should we?"

Saya eyed me. "What do you mean?"

"What would he do if we don't follow?"

The corner of her lips tilted upward. "Wish we had that luxury."

I stood and swung my pack onto my back. The first few steps were agony. My feet ached even worse than the night before.

Saya trudged on next to me, her eyes fixated on the back of the man we followed.

A weariness settled over me as we walked, aware of nothing except the unignorable pain in my legs.

"Juliet—" Saya motioned with her head. "He's gone."

My eyes snapped forward. There was no sign of the Unknown. He'd vanished. Saya picked up her pace and in the rush of adrenaline, I forgot the aches in my legs as I kept pace with her.

"You didn't see what happened?"

"No," she responded, her tone grim.

My eyes flicked from side to side. *Where did he go?*

Like a wraith, the Unknown materialized from behind a tree, his hand on the grip of his sword.

I gasped, stopping short. "Where—"

"Where did you go?" Saya demanded, placing her hands on her hips.

The Unknown's eyebrow rose, and a gleam entered his eyes. "Scouting."

Saya's shoulders relaxed, and her arms fell by her sides. "Why didn't you tell us you were going to leave?"

"Because last I checked, I don't answer to you."

Steeling myself, I stepped in between them and held up my hands. "What did you find?"

"There's a steep slope just ahead. Looks like they took the long way around on the trail. We can cut some time by going straight down."

"Lead on, then," Saya muttered.

"It's steep," he warned.

"We can handle it," she affirmed with a steely look in her eyes.

The Unknown looked to me, and I nodded back in confirmation. "Very well," he acknowledged. "Let's go."

Not another word was spoken as we crossed the short distance through the last of the trees. The ground sloped away, sparse with wind-bitten trees and long, trailing gray-brown plants. My jaw dropped. The earth looked as though it would shift and carry me away with it if disturbed.

"Be careful. Follow in my footsteps as much as possible," the Unknown said, raising a foot to begin the descent, but Saya pushed past him.

"I'll go first."

"Be my guest," he replied, sweeping his arm out. We watched as she began the slow descent. With each step, she slid a little and used the shrubs and trees when she could for stabilization.

The Unknown looked at me. "I'll go first. Pay attention to where I'm stepping."

I inhaled the crisp fall air and grinned. "I can go next."

He paused at the edge and glanced back at me. "It'll be safer if I go first."

"I've got this…" I began but hesitated as the corner of his lips curved.

Was that a smile?

Before I could decide, he turned and stepped off onto the slope. He hadn't listened to me. A flare of annoyance washed over me as I watched each step he made and how he angled his body, but even then, he began to draw ahead of me, surer of his balance and of the terrain than I was.

Something skittered to my right. My eyes snapped in that direction, my concentration broken. The dirt gave way beneath my foot, and I screamed. Dust swirled through the air as my body slid forward. I grasped for anything to stop my fall, my other leg caught beneath me and to the side, as momentum carried me forward. A hand caught my right arm, and another wrapped around my midsection, halting my slide. Gasping for breath, my heart pounding, I looked up to see the Unknown crouching beside me, one leg braced against the slope, the other under my own legs. His arm left my waist, and he helped me into a sitting position before releasing his grip on my arm.

"Are you all right?" Saya called up from below.

I nodded, licking the dust from my lips. My heart pounded from the adrenaline rush.

"Do you need a minute?" the Unknown asked, his green eyes piercing mine.

A sharp pain lanced through my left leg from being pinned in an awkward position under my body during the fall, and my palms burned from scraping against the ground and grabbing onto the rough branches of shrubs. "No, I'm all right."

"The palm you injured rescuing that boy," he began, taking my hand in his larger one. "You're favoring it."

I tried pulling away, but he wouldn't let go. Heat rose to my cheeks. "It hurts, but it'll be fine."

"Let me look at it."

"I can make it to the bottom."

The Unknown looked up at me then and nodded, his hair falling forward to frame his face. "I know you can."

My eyes widened. He was so sure, so confident. I pulled my hand out of his grasp. *But why? What has his life been like to give him such confidence?*

He stood, digging his right foot into the earth to brace himself, and held out a hand for me.

I stared at it a moment, hesitating.

"You can accept the gesture," he remarked in a mild tone. "It doesn't mean I think you're weak."

My jaw clenched. *He's right. Accepting help doesn't mean I'm weak.* I took his hand. His skin was rough, calloused but strong. He pulled me up and helped me balance before letting go.

"Thanks," I murmured.

He nodded and continued his descent. This time, I couldn't fail to notice how close he shadowed me. Often, he paused as though to study the terrain, but I caught his eyes shifting toward me more than once, keeping an eye on me.

Saya waited, arms crossed, at the bottom. When I reached it, without further mishap, I grinned. I'd never felt so glad to be on level earth before. Saya raised her eyebrows in a silent question.

"I'm okay, just glad to be off the slope."

"Come on," the Unknown interrupted. "Let's get a move on. The morning hours are dwindling."

Saya frowned and I waited back with her as she watched the Unknown take the lead.

I sighed. *What is it this time?* Tapping my index finger on Saya's shoulder, I asked, "What's wrong?"

She placed her waterskin back in her pack. "You heard him saying we would pass a village sometime around midday?"

I hesitated. "Yes..."

"How does he know?"

I blinked. "He said he's been there before."

"And he seems to spend an absorbent amount of time teaching you how to track. Too much time. Why you? And why would he wish to teach you in the first place?"

"I don't know, but I also don't see you jumping to learn. Why would he teach you if you don't want to be taught?"

Saya frowned and her eyes grew icy. "I think he knows far too much about too many things." She pulled on her pack and took a step in the Unknown's direction, but I tugged on her arm.

"Wait, Saya—"

She wrenched herself out of my grip. I sighed and followed after her.

As mile after slow mile passed, the monotony was broken up by the Unknown continuing to instruct me. Every paw print, every imprint in the ground, every broken twig meant something.

Sounds filtered in more vividly under the Unknown's tutelage. I became more mindful of my surroundings, listening and breaking down the differences in tone, cadence, and pitch, differing them to the types of animals, birds, and insects that surrounded us.

Branches lay broken, marring the almost perfect illusion of a lived-in forest. I stopped, peering at the ground.

The Unknown appeared next to me and stooped down. "What did you find?"

I shrugged. "I don't know, but it leads away from the main path for a bit."

He stood up and brushed his hands off. "Someone tried to escape."

"But they didn't?"

"No."

Saya cleared her throat. "How do you know?"

"There was a struggle, but the escapee was brought back to the main group."

Her shoulders drooped. I laid a hand on her back, but she shrugged it off.

"Did either of you have anyone close taken?"

Saya shook her head, but the Unknown just stared at me with his dark green eyes.

"What about friends?"

"No," Saya grunted.

"How come you're doing this?"

The Unknown set the tip of his bow on the ground and looked over the top of it at me. "We could ask you the same question, Juliet. You haven't even been in town for a whole week."

He's right. Why am I here? I toed the ground with my right boot. *My brother is dead. All adventure died with him.*

I looked up at the Unknown. "I suppose—I want a bit of adventure, but—" I hesitated. *I've never had this freedom before.* Taking a deep breath and closing my eyes, I focused on pushing the guilt deep inside. *Freedom. I want the choice, the choice to make my own decisions...to choose to stay or choose to go.* I opened my eyes. This time my voice was stronger and surer. "I want to help. I know I'm not used to this." I gestured toward our surroundings. "But the least I can do is try."

He folded his arms. "Why don't you go home?"

"I can't."

"Why?"

Warmth flushed through my body, and I clenched my left hand into a fist. "Because I can't!" Tears stung my eyes and I looked away, biting my lip.

Saya took a step forward. "Leave her alone."

He regarded both of us. "Juliet, what kind of tracks are these?"

I peered up through my lashes but didn't raise my head. He pointed at something by his feet.

My knees brushed the dirt as I knelt, thankful for the change of subject. "A rabbit?"

"No, think."

"A fox?"

A rare smile crossed his lips. "Do you realize why you were wrong about the rabbit tracks?"

I shook my head.

"I'll keep an eye out for the tracks of a rabbit. For now, remember that the width between the four toes of a fox is farther apart and more circular, and a rabbit's is more oval and narrower. The pad is also of a different shape, with foxes shaped more like a"—he grimaced—"a tooth, such as a shark tooth."

"Why do you care to teach her this?"

I jumped, thinking I'd spoken my own thoughts out loud before realizing it had been Saya. When the Unknown didn't answer, Saya grabbed me by the arm, dragging me along with her down the path before letting go.

"Don't let him in," she snapped.

"I'm not."

She stopped and whirled around, her face mere inches from my own. "Well, you sure are acting like it. Do you trust him more than you trust me?"

"I haven't seen anything not to trust—"

She snorted.

"But I'll admit he's mysterious, and he hasn't told us everything. Saya—" I grabbed onto her sleeve. "Just because I don't trust him fully doesn't mean I should ignore him. There's something about him; I don't know, there are times I could completely put my life in his hands—and I know that's weird, believe me—and there are other times I'm not sure what to think."

"You're crazy." She strode forward. "Or brainwashed."

"Saya, have you looked into his eyes?"

"Juliet?"

I blinked. "What?"

"Was there something else you were going to say? Or were you lost in his eyes?"

"What, no! My point is that there is no emotion in his eyes. I've only seen him smile once. Once, Saya."

"You love his eyes."

I peered at her, my eyes wide. Shock rippled through me. "What are you talking about?"

"You don't understand him, though."

"What is that supposed to mean?"

"Nothing," she muttered as she walked away. I watched her a moment, listening as the Unknown's footsteps came up behind me.

She was right; I didn't understand him. One moment he would be the silent, brooding type, and another he would give me the feeling he'd known me for a long time, as if he knew more than he let on.

The Unknown halted next to me. "The village is but a mile or two from here. I think we should stop there."

"Saya!" I called. "He said we're not far from the village and that we should go there. What do you think?"

Saya turned and stared at the Unknown with narrowed eyes. "Considering you have taken charge of this little company," she spat, "it is your choice."

"That doesn't mean I don't listen to others. Or at least give the semblance."

A chuckle escaped my lips, but I hushed up when I saw Saya's eyes shoot daggers at me.

Saya stared the Unknown down. "Why are you here?"

"Why do *you* think I am here?"

"That's not what I asked. You ask us to trust you, yet we know almost nothing about you."

"I never asked either of you to trust me." He sighed. "What do you want to know?"

I cleared my throat. "What's your name?"

"I am known by what I am known. To those at Umi no Machi, I am Shizukana." He paused. "But as for why I am here, I do not have anything better to do, and the two of you intrigue me. I do not know that you will succeed in your mission, but I will see it to the end."

"How can we trust you?" Saya hissed.

"Trust? Because you have no choice."

Laying a hand on Saya's arm, I shook my head. *It's no use.* Raising my eyes from the fury racing across hers, I gazed up at the birds flying high above us; the white tips on their wings caught the light as they soared through the air.

"I could use a bed," I murmured, still looking up.

"As could I," Saya admitted.

"We can't stop."

I looked back at the Unknown. "I know. I was just wishing."

He followed my gaze up to the birds wheeling overhead. "They're starlings. Not common to these parts."

"Sometimes I wish I could be one," I whispered. Catching the confusion in his drawn eyebrows, I sighed, realizing I'd spoken out loud. "To just fly wherever I wished, see everything from way up there—a quick escape…"

"They have their own dangers up there," he said, his eyes boring into mine. "It doesn't matter who you talk to or see; no human can escape from everything. There is more freedom in your mind and soul than you will ever have in your body." He glanced up, and I followed his gaze to see small black and white birds flying in and out of the branches of the tree above us.

Starlings.

The Unknown whistled to them and waited as they echoed his song. My breath caught in my throat as I listened to the haunting melody. *They have freedom. They fly where they wish, eat what they wish, do what they wish.* A starling plunged from the tree toward the ground before its wings caught a draft of wind. It soared up and away in an arc. *The townspeople won't find freedom.* I bit my lip. *They've lost it, just as I've found it.*

With each step forward, my pace quickened, and an exciting sense of elation grew within me. The Unknown's words ran over and over through my mind against the backdrop of the birds singing.

"There is more freedom in your mind and soul than you will ever have in your body."

Chapter Seven

The scenery had been slowly changing, just as Saya had said it would. The colorful, deciduous trees grew fewer and were replaced with the dark green of tall, slender conifers. Hills slowed our progress as the elevation ebbed and flowed. Patches of trees with red and yellow leaves appeared here and there to break up the ongoing sea of green.

Saya gazed about with lips parted and eyes wide.

"It really is beautiful," I murmured, brushing wisps of hair back behind my ears.

A soft sigh escaped her parted lips. "I hadn't remembered. It's been so long. Umi no Machi is all I've really known."

"Why did you come to Umi no Machi?"

Saya glanced up at me, and her dainty shoulders rose.

"None of my business?" I guessed.

She shook her head, her dark hair threatening to come loose from the bun coiled atop her head.

"I'd like to know."

She blinked and lifted a hand as though to ward me off, but it fell. Eyes trained forward, she did not speak. A muscle in her jaw pulsed.

"Saya?" I prompted. "Maybe I haven't earned your trust yet, and rightfully so, but I care about who you are and would like to know your story."

She looked at me then, her thin eyebrows drawing down in a 'V'. Her arms swung at her sides, and her pace slowed. "Why?"

"I guess I care about who you are—hold on," I muttered, bending down to retie the laces on my right boot, which had come undone.

Saya's snort sounded above my head. "You guess?"

"Yes...no—I mean, I *do* care. We've been traveling together for a few days now, and I've entrusted you with some of my biggest secrets. Sometimes we must take a leap." I paused and inhaled before standing up, readjusting my pack. "But you don't have to share with me if you don't want to. I'll be here either way."

Saya's arms stilled as she tensed.

"And I know that I've been irritating you lately," I continued. "And that it has to do with the Unknown..." I trailed off, noticing the way Saya's shoulders had relaxed back down and her hands had unclenched. "I'm sorry for that. I'm not trying to create a wedge between us, but I *am* trying to make the best of what we have—and to learn. And I think you should, too." My breath caught in my throat as the words faded into the silence that fell.

The Unknown continued ahead, his cloak rippling in the air as he strode along. His figure was smaller in the distance, and I realized we'd begun to fall behind.

"My parents died."

I blinked and tilted my head to look down at Saya.

"It was a long time ago," she added, her voice soft and distant.

I touched her on the arm. "I'm sorry. What happened?"

The silence stretched between us, a layer of thickness that became almost suffocating.

A small sigh escaped Saya's lips, and she halted in the middle of the path. "Fever. It took perhaps two dozen people, mostly children and elders, but my parents were among the dead. It was quick but painful. Many fell sick—most survived. It was a hard time for all. Even those who hadn't lost someone faced the fear that they might. It took me a long time to be okay with what the gods allowed to happen. They had a reason, but I don't know what it was." Her dainty shoulders rose in a shrug.

"Saya...that's—that's awful."

A hint of moisture shone in her dark eyes before she blinked, and it was gone. "Everyone has their stories. Now you know mine."

"And the innkeeper?"

"He's my uncle, not by blood, but he might as well be. He left the capital long before I was born, but he and my father kept in touch; they were best friends.

When my parents died, he took me in. If he hadn't, no one would've. I was seven."

"I can't imagine how hard that must've been. You were taken away from everything you knew, all that was familiar."

Saya nodded, her eyes dry and expressionless, but a muscle twitched in her jaw.

"Did you make any friends after you came out?"

"No. There was no one my age."

My heart wrenched inside of me.

She stopped walking and turned to face me. "And what about you, Juliet Barrows?"

"What about me?"

"What is your story?"

I hesitated, toeing small circles in the damp earth with my boot. "Everything was great until Eddie—until he died. It was a happy childhood. After Eddie, though, things changed. Mom and Dad changed...I suppose we all did."

"Is that why you're here instead of trying to go home?"

I glanced up at the Unknown, who walked far ahead, his bow strapped across his back. *No arrows,* I realized. *He has no arrows.*

"Juliet?"

I shook my head. "Oh, sorry, I did try...it wasn't that I didn't. Saya, this is my first time feeling free! Feeling like I can do what I would like without my parents' permission, or checking in with them, or without them worrying about where I am when I'm late in coming home."

Saya frowned. "It was that bad?"

I sighed. "Yes. No—"

"It was," she declared, nudging me with her shoulder. "Did you ever talk to them about it?"

"No, not really. Sometimes I tried, but it never went well, and I know it's because of my brother. They weren't like this before. And I have so much—so much, I don't know..."

"Guilt?" Saya supplied.

"Yes."

"It's not your fault."

"It's easy for you to say." I watched the ground as it passed under my feet. "You weren't there."

"No, no, I wasn't. But I know how much guilt can eat one alive. I've been there. I still am in some ways." She stared straight ahead, her eyes unwavering.

The Unknown had pulled ahead a little, his strides longer and quicker than our own flagging ones.

Saya nudged me with her shoulder. "You know, you're going to have to set boundaries at some point."

Cam.

"That's what Cam also told me," I whispered.

"Who?"

"Cam. My best friend. She told me that the day I—the day I came here."

Saya blinked and glanced at me. "Is that why you came?"

"No, I had no intention of coming here."

Saya took a deep breath and returned her gaze to the narrow dirt road. "I know you appeared here...somehow. You didn't just travel normally into Umi no Machi, did you?"

I shook my head. "No."

Saya nodded.

"I came here through a portal."

Saya stopped short and stared at me. "What? You did what?"

"I came through a portal. I know it's hard to believe, but I was on vacation with my parents and Cam just a few days ago. Cam and I left to go hiking and—"

"Just jump to the last part. What happened?" Saya took a step closer to me.

"I found an upside-down tree and fell through the bottom of it and ended up here."

Saya snorted. "That's—that's—"

"I know."

"But you're serious." Saya resumed walking. "It's almost unbelievable."

"You don't think I'm crazy?"

"A little." She grinned. "But I do believe you."

My lips parted, but the words were forestalled as the Unknown's voice called down from where he stood, watching us.

"Are you two ladies going to get a move on? We're almost to the village."

Saya and I exchanged glances.

"Talk later?" she asked.

"Definitely." I called up to the Unknown, "What are we hoping to find there?"

"Information. The raiders would have gone within a couple miles of the village, so someone may have seen something. We might as well eat a hot meal while there," he added as we approached.

"A hot meal?" Saya repeated. "We don't have time for that."

"We do when spending money and taking our time may help us get the information we need." He shifted his pack, checking to make sure his bow was secure.

No arrows. I took a couple steps to catch up with him. "Why do you have a bow and no arrows?"

"Because I don't have any arrows."

I rolled my eyes. "Yes, I see that, but why keep the bow?"

"It's mine," he replied. "Now quiet."

"Don't tell me to be quiet." I kept my voice even, but I couldn't keep out the edge. "You don't have the right—"

"Hush, we're here."

My mouth closed and I craned to look around him. The first house came into view, then another, and another. The run-down homes with sagging roofs and patched-up walls dotted the landscape along a wide dirt road.

As we walked down it, I shifted closer to the Unknown and Saya, unnerved by all the empty stares of those we passed. Few villagers were about, but their eyes were narrowed, and their lips thinned. Their clothing was worn, patched in places with varying shades of material.

With every step we took, the silence grew. A child stared at us, clinging to a woman, his face smudged with dirt. The woman looked up as we passed, her eyes wide and empty. No emotion shone there. It was as if—

I hit something solid and broad and gasped. The Unknown glanced over at his shoulder at me.

My cheeks began to burn. "Sorry." I drew back and waited for him to keep moving.

"Stay close," he uttered in a low tone. "Just not that close."

"Don't have to tell me," I muttered. Saya shadowed us as we entered a low-hanging building, ducking our heads to avoid the frame. The darkened interior felt even more oppressive and lifeless than the village. I wrinkled my nose at the pungent air that filled the room.

Saya coughed, lifting a hand up to her mouth from the smoke swirling through the murky air. Two men with dirty clothes and ragged hair stared at us over long pipes. Another man tilted his chair back with a chilling scrape, his wide-brimmed hat hiding his face from view.

The Unknown gestured to a table by the wall. "Sit down."

Saya and I sat, watching as the Unknown strode to the bar. My chair clanked against the wall as I leaned back. A yawn split my jaw open, and my eyes closed.

A grunt brought me leaning forward, my chair dropping to the floor with a sharp clack. Steam rose from the plates in swirling curls as the Unknown set the dishes down on the table. Tantalizing smells of spices teased me, driving away some of the sharp odors swirling about the room.

When the last bite of rice and meat sautéed with veggies was gone, the Unknown leaned back in his chair, his eyes on the ceiling. Saya gazed off into the distance, her expression unreadable.

The Unknown grunted and stood. "Let's go."

I yawned. "Did you find out what you needed to?"

He glanced about the room. "Not here."

Saya shifted on her feet as an unkempt man with a tangled beard lifted his mug in a salute to her. "I don't like this place."

"Me neither," I agreed. "There's no life, no laughter."

The Unknown glanced at us. "Keep your voices down. We'll talk later."

Saya and I fell into step behind him. Birds chirped in the distance, and somewhere a dog barked, but a silence continued to lie heavily over the village.

I glanced over my shoulder as we left the town behind. No one but the little boy still clinging to his mother's skirts watched us go. "What did you find out?"

The Unknown glanced at Saya with a raised eyebrow. "Is she usually this impatient?"

I rolled my eyes, glad Saya didn't give him an answer.

"Apparently this is not the first band that has passed near the village. The increase in activity has the villagers scared."

Saya straightened her shoulders as she took a step forward. "So they did see the raiders?"

"Yes."

I glanced around but were alone. "What do you think they're doing with the townspeople?"

"They deal in slavery," Saya blurted. "They're northern raiders." She shrugged as though that was to explain it all.

"I know that," I rejoined with an eyeroll, "but do they use them as slaves themselves, or...?"

"They'll do as they've always done," the Unknown broke in. "They'll take them to some land where slavery is allowed and sell them to the highest bidder. They do use slaves in their tribes, so it's possible they'll just take them home to be sold."

Saya quickened her step. "We should pick up our pace."

I moved to follow her, but seeing that the Unknown did not speed up, I remained by his side.

He cleared his throat. "Is there something you wish to ask?"

"Why would anyone condone slavery?"

"Many do. It's the world we live in, Juliet. Slavery is not uncommon." He laid a hand on the hilt of his sword to keep it from swinging as he walked. "Perhaps more so than in the past, but there are still many countries that utilize slaves, especially in the north. There aren't any recognizable kingdoms up there like down here. Dozens of tribes war and fight one another without respite, most of whom will even sell their own countrymen for a payday."

"But that's horrible. They'd sell their own countrymen?"

"They don't see it that way. And they're one of a few."

I raised my eyebrows and almost tripped over a root. "How do you know all of this? Umi no Machi seems such a peaceful town."

"I didn't always live there."

"But how—"

"What I am curious about is...where you come from," he interrupted.

I hesitated, my lips moving but no words coming out. Clearing my throat, I began, "I—it's too far away, you wouldn't know it."

"Try me."

With a quick inhale, I returned my gaze to the road. "How come Umi no Machi has stayed out of trouble?"

"They've had rumors of towns ransacked, but they were always just that—rumors. Most of their visitors come from close by, in the outlying villages and farms, or from other towns along the coast that are farther away from the king's stronghold, away from the northern borders and the threat therein."

"What are you doing?" Saya snapped, facing us with arms crossed. "We shouldn't have stopped at the village. We're never going to stop them at this rate, and here you two are chatting away as though we have plenty of time to kill."

I flinched at the anger lacing her words and took a step forward, but she crossed her arms over her chest and glared at me.

"We don't have a chance, do we?" she inquired, looking past me to the Unknown.

"I could move faster, but you two—"

Even with the distance, it was clear Saya glared at him.

The Unknown continued, "This means we need a faster mode of transport."

"Horses?" Saya called back, her features coming into focus as we neared her. "Where are we going to find horses?"

"We'll need to find a town."

I held up a hand. "Wait, I don't understand. How come we couldn't get horses at the village we *just* left?"

The Unknown resumed his stride. "Did they look like they'd have any?"

I frowned, thinking back to the haggard look of the villagers and the lack of any visible horses. "They have to have some—"

"For farming, but not for riding."

"I still don't understand. What horses aren't for riding?"

"Not plodders like they'd have."

I looked back and forth between the Unknown and Saya. "Then why didn't we bring horses with us?"

Saya huffed. "Umi no Machi doesn't *have* horses. You didn't see any stables, did you?"

"I have a horse," the Unknown acknowledged.

Saya slapped her forehead. "You do! Why didn't you bring him?"

"Because I had no intention of chasing after the raiders."

I raised my shoulders, feeling the strain from the pack straps as I did so. "He has a point, Saya."

"None of this matters," she exclaimed, raising her hands. "How far out of our path would we have to go to get some?"

"Quiet," the Unknown ordered. "Let me think. We might have to go out of our way, but we'll gain back the lost time easily. It'll be worth it in the end."

"Let's get a move on then." Saya fell into step next to the Unknown. "The villagers were more suspicious of us than I realized they'd be," she murmured.

"Times are worse than they used to be and more so than you could imagine." His eyes drilled into the distance ahead. "That village back there has probably seen better than most, being so far in the woods. I don't think many know of its existence, and it was clear they want to keep it that way."

"How did you know of it?" I asked.

"I've passed through before." He picked up his pace, leaving Saya and me behind in a matter of seconds.

Saya kicked at a rock lying across her path. "You must not have a very good view of my country so far."

I brushed my sleeve across my face and looked down at the dust now coating it. "Doesn't seem like a nice place to live." I motioned to the Unknown's receding figure. "And some of the company is questionable."

She sighed. "It used to be. It was different."

"How do you remember the good ones when you were so young?"

"I don't, but I have stories. So I know things can change."

"*If* someone changes them," I replied. "But if no one lifts a finger, they'll get worse."

Saya stared straight ahead, her eyes unseeing, her mind lost in thought. "Do you ever wish you were in a different time? Or a different world?"

I almost stopped short but forced my legs to keep moving. "Is that a joke?"

Her eyes widened, and she grinned. "You do think this is a different world, don't you?"

"I—I suppose I do. It's the only thing that makes sense even when it doesn't make sense."

She nodded and winked. "Yes, that makes a *lot* of sense."

I grinned, but it faded as I watched the Unknown's receding figure. "He asked me where I'm from."

Saya followed my gaze. "Oh? What did you say?"

"I changed the subject."

Saya sighed. "That's one way to do it."

"What, do I sense a note of rebuke?"

"No."

"You sure?"

"I just think you can't run away forever."

I stopped walking. "And you can?"

"You're right."

My jaw dropped. "You're agreeing with me?"

"I'm a seer."

I stared at her. *A seer.* The crowd in Umi no Machi flashed before me. *Akio...all this time.* "Akio was wrong then, and the Unknown was right. There *are* seers left."

A wry smile curved her lips. "I'm sorry I didn't tell you sooner. But it's true. It's how I knew you weren't from around here. It's how I knew something was going to happen the night the raiders came."

"Why didn't you tell me sooner?"

"Because I've hidden this for so many years. The king would kill me if he found out. I was scared."

"Akio mentioned the king went on a rampage," I remembered. "He said they'd all been killed or were driven out. What happened?"

"I don't know. The innkeeper thinks the king was jealous because he's not one himself. Who knows. But I've grown up with the stories, told in hushed voices late at night."

"He does sound a little crazy." Catching the look Saya shot at me, I added, "Okay, more than a little. But why are you telling me now?"

Saya resumed walking. "Because I trust you. I may not understand you, but I trust you, and I like you."

I laid a hand on her arm. "Thanks for telling me."

We continued on in silence, the tall pines looming over us and the ground beneath my feet firm and a little spongy from a recent rain.

"Juliet—"

I jerked back, startled.

Saya regarded me. "What's wrong?"

I raised my eyebrows and shrugged.

"Then why do you look troubled?"

"I'm not."

She frowned. "There's something. Talk to me."

The ache deep in my chest grew, creeping in around my heart.

What is Cam doing? What are my parents doing? Do they miss me? Are they still searching?

The thoughts swirled around my brain like fog in a fortune teller's ball.

"You're doing it again," Saya pointed out.

My lips parted, but no words came out. *What could I say? What did I want to say?*

"It's nothing," I replied, looking down into the valley where the tall trees gave way to maples full of red and yellow leaves, their blossoms gone as the trees heralded the end of summer. "I'm just tired." A cool breeze blew through the trees, forming goosebumps on my bare skin. Burying my hands beneath my cloak, I sniffed the air, breathing in the rotting wood, musty earth, and the clean scent of pines wafting through the trees.

"There's no going back anyway," I muttered, following Saya as she picked her way down the hillside.

"Juliet?"

My heartbeat quickened. *Had she heard me?*

"He's gone."

I glanced up, scanning the trees. There was no sign of the Unknown. "Where did he go?"

"I don't know." Saya looked like a coiled snake ready to strike.

"Relax, Saya. I'm sure he'll be back. We probably just lost him amongst the trees and undergrowth. He'll double back if he gets too far ahead."

"I'm not worried."

I raised my eyebrows.

"I'm not," she protested. "I just don't trust him, and you shouldn't either."

My step faltered, and I raised my eyes toward the sky above, a narrow, snake-like path formed by the foliage banking it. The feeling that this wouldn't be the last time the Unknown vanished crept over me, and a chill settled over me even though the afternoon sun warmed the fall air.

CHAPTER EIGHT

The sun dropped over the tree line. Shadows stretched their clinging fingers across trunks and over shrubs.

"He's back."

I started at the sound of Saya's voice and scanned the direction in which she looked, but I saw nothing. "Where?"

"Just watch."

He appeared in the distance, winding his way between the trees in the steadily darkening forest.

She foresaw it. She knew before I'd even noticed.

I watched as the Unknown drew ever nearer.

"I saw him appearing as he just now did, through the trees there, when the sun was just over the horizon and our shadows became long and narrow."

"Do you have any control over this?"

She shook her head. "No, I don't even know if it's possible to." She went silent as the Unknown came within hearing distance.

My eyebrows furrowed.

"Why the look?"

My eyes flew to his as he spoke. "Your cloak is gone."

"Yes." He stopped short in front of me. From his hand dangled two limp forms, their fur stained with dirt. "Let's stop here for the night. I need to clean these up."

Saya crinkled her nose. "Where have you been?"

"Can you get a fire going?" he asked her, ignoring her question. "I'm going to skin these."

Saya cleared her throat. "Not until you answer me."

He grunted. "I thought it was obvious. Hunting." He held the rabbits out. "We need to eat."

Saya crossed her arms, her jaw clenched. "I'd appreciate if you'd let us know when you leave."

"Why?"

Saya blinked at the challenge, her small frame almost shrinking back into itself.

"Why should I answer to you?" He pushed, stepping forward and towering over Saya.

"Hey," I interrupted, forcing my way in between them. "There's no need to intimidate her like that."

A muscle in the Unknown's neck pulsed, but he pulled away. "What have I done that makes you feel I need to inform you of my every move?"

We both looked at Saya.

Her eyes flew from one to the other of us, and her cheeks reddened. "I don't trust easily—"

"You don't say," the Unknown muttered. I shot him a glare.

Saya flinched but continued, "I didn't even know my parents were unwell before the end. They didn't tell me. The innkeeper kept things from me as well to protect me, or so he said. I should've known something was wrong. That they were dying." She paused, watching as she toed a circle over the ground. "I don't like not knowing. It makes me feel..."

"Helpless?" I supplied.

"Vulnerable," the Unknown interjected. His eyes softened around the edges. "I'm not trying to protect you. I just don't think to tell you."

"Good." Saya turned away, throwing a quick glance back over her shoulder. "Let's keep it that way."

She dropped her pack on the ground and headed off to gather wood. I set my own pack down, and the Unknown headed off a ways and squatted over the carcasses. Lost in thought, I stared, watching as he pulled out the knife I'd noticed in his left boot and began skinning the rabbits. I jumped as a stick cracked. Saya watched me from where she built a fire. She grunted, and after a few deft movements, a small flame flickered in the middle of the bare patch of soil. Warmth bloomed, small at first but growing hotter as the wood caught fire. Sparks flew up into the air, and thin curls of white smoke wafted upwards.

I leaned closer, my gaze lost in the numbing brightness of the light as I relaxed, exhaustion spreading across my mind and body.

Saya knelt next to me. "Let me check your palm."

I held out my hand, watching the Unknown return with the skinned carcasses. Kneeling, he sorted through the pile of wood and drew out two long sticks.

"It looks good," Saya noted, drawing my attention back to her. "Healing nicely."

I nodded and continued watching as the Unknown wormed the meat onto the sticks. The sinew and muscles shone a dark reddish-purple, almost translucent in the firelight, detailing the forms of thin bones beneath.

"What are those?" I asked, gesturing toward whatever he'd taken out of the packet he held.

"Spices," he answered as he rubbed the contents into the meat, ignoring the heat beneath his hands.

The longer they slow-roasted, the more I forgot what they used to look like, all furry and soft. Now they looked more like skinned rats being seared over the hot flames.

My mouth watered as tantalizing smells wafted up into the air, and my stomach groaned. A small grin curled Saya's lips upwards.

"Good timing," the Unknown said as he took the spits off the fire.

Under the cover of darkness, I took my first bite of the burning hot meat, and juices exploded across my palette. "It's delicious," I sputtered with a quick inhale.

Saya nodded as she wolfed down her share. She licked the juices off her fingers and gave a contented sigh.

The fire crackled and spat, the flames licking at the air. I folded my arms over my belly. My eyes began to close as the minutes slid by and a drowsiness washed over me.

"Alright, up, you two," the Unknown ordered as he rose.

Saya yawned. "Why?"

"You both need some training."

"Training?" I echoed.

The Unknown considered both of us. "You two might be fitter than most people, but you haven't been trained in defense—or offense, for that matter. There isn't much time for it, but something is better than nothing.

"Is that important?" Saya asked. "We should keep moving."

I stood up with a grunt. "Saya's right. Shouldn't we save our energy for finding the slavers? Besides, we don't even have any weapons."

"No, but we'll make do."

Saya shuffled to my side and whispered, "I don't think he's as weaponless as he seems to claim, and I'm not talking about his sword."

"He's not weaponless," I offered. "Haven't you noticed the bow and the sword?"

"Thank you, yes, I have."

I blinked. "I wasn't—" I sighed. "He also has a knife in his left boot."

Saya's eyes gleamed in the light reflected by the fire. "That's what I mean. He's hiding things."

"Ready?" The Unknown regarded us as neither of us made a move to stand. "Have either of you had any self-defense training?"

I shook my head.

"Weapons?"

My lips parted in a wide smile. "Not unless you count word quips." The smile faded as my gaze met the Unknown's icy glare. "Alright, I'm up, I'm up." With a sigh, I stood and heard Saya do the same.

We stood side by side facing the Unknown.

His arms hung by his sides. "One of you come at me."

Saya stared askance at him. "How?"

His shoulders rose in a small sigh. "Pretend I'm a threat, and you can't run, so you're going to need to take me down."

I gestured. "Go right ahead."

Saya rolled her eyes. "Fine." Narrowing her eyes, she ran at the Unknown and dove for his legs. He sidestepped, giving her a light shove as he did so. Saya sprawled on the ground, her lips downturned. Her brown eyes shot sparks at him as she rose to her feet.

"Try again," he instructed. Before he'd finished speaking, her fist came flying toward his side in an upper cross. He deflected her with ease, his movements light and quick. "Better. Juliet, your turn. You're already tense," he noted with a gleam in his eyes. "Breathe."

I gritted my teeth. "Easier said than done."

"Practice." His lips creased at the corners.

Over and over again, we went through the motions until my hair grew slick with sweat and my clothes became damp.

The Unknown held up a hand. "Alright, that's good for now. If you feel like you're beginning to forget the three defensive moves I taught you tonight, then practice them. Remember them."

We staggered into the clearing after him, our clothes plastered to our bodies, limbs already beginning to stiffen.

"He enjoyed that," Saya muttered with a quick look at me as she dropped onto her bedroll.

"I know. It was obvious."

She grinned and gulped down water. She wiped her mouth and collapsed back against the bedroll. "I. Am. Exhausted."

"Me too." I wrinkled my nose from the potent body odor washing over my senses from Saya and me. "And I feel disgusting."

The Unknown stood above us, hands on hips. "You two don't smell much worse than you did earlier."

"Thanks," I muttered. "Though not sure we could say the same about you."

The Unknown turned away without acknowledging if he had heard me or not.

"Why are your cheeks red?" Saya whispered, leaning closer.

"Are they?"

She frowned. "Yes."

"It's nothing," I hissed in a low voice.

She shrugged. "Shizukana—"

He turned to look at her.

"I noticed you didn't sleep last night. I can take a turn tonight."

My lips parted but froze as I realized the seriousness and yet a hint of surprise shining in Unknown's eyes and in the set of his raised shoulders.

He nodded a grave, slow nod. "Alright."

Saya inclined her head back a little deeper than necessary.

Oh, I realized. *Whatever is going on, she's trying to make peace.* When it became obvious there would be nothing more forthcoming, I cleared my throat. "Take a turn at what?"

"Saya," the Unknown began, not taking his eyes off her, "take the first watch."

Oh...so we haven't all been sleeping without a thought for who else might be out there.

"I can help, too," I said.

"Good," the Unknown replied. "Saya, wake Juliet when you can't keep your eyes open any longer. Juliet, the same goes for you. Don't stare into the fire on your watch. Your eyesight will be impaired, and you won't be able to see well if you aren't accustomed to the darkness. Stay further back, out of the light from the fire, and pick a place that's easy for you to see but harder for others to see you." He stirred the fire up before lying down and wrapping himself in his long cloak.

I yawned and watched as Saya rose and strode out of our little circle of light, disappearing into the inky blackness of the night.

"Get some sleep while you can," the Unknown instructed from his bedroll.

⚜ ⚜

My eyes snapped open, and I struggled underneath the trappings of the cloak. Saya removed her hand.

"It's just me," she whispered. As she shifted, the embers from the dying fire revealed the outlines of her face, and her grip on my shoulder loosened.

I stood, flapping my arms and wrapping the cloak closer around me as I stamped my way toward the edge of the campsite. Shivering from the sharp, cold breeze, I settled down and glanced towards the small fire. Dim as it was, it beckoned to me with warm, dancing fingers.

Up above, the stars twinkled, thousands of little glittering dots speckling the velvet-black expanse. My breath caught as the noises around me began to register, pounding in on my eardrums. A cacophony of sounds echoed: hoots, chirps, buzzing, sticks cracking, bushes rustling, the air whistling across the forest floor, and the falling of leaves as animals skittered about in the trees above.

I blinked, trying to block out the endless number of bugs that could be around me. There was nowhere I could go where I wouldn't feel numerous tiny legs crawling over my body.

"Stupid imagination," I muttered, tensing as yet another scuffle happened in the bushes nearby. "Small animals, they're just small animals," I whispered.

"They can hear you better than you can hear them."

I jumped, biting back a scream as I clasped my mouth.

"Be quieter," the Unknown grumbled, shifting on his back and pulling his cloak tighter around him. I glared at him, almost disappointed he couldn't see my eyes boring into his shadowed form by the fire's embers.

A howl shattered the air, joined by others within seconds. They were distinct yet overlapped one another, rising and falling. I stiffened. They were coming closer.

"They are far away." The Unknown's voice sounded resigned from where he lay by the fire.

"How do you know?" I hissed back. Ears perked, I waited, but he never answered. Drawing my knees up, I peered through the darkness but couldn't see anything. Chills ran through my body. Those weren't coyotes; I had heard them before. *The preserve is—was—Eddie's favorite place to go.* I clenched my jaw, my teeth grinding. *The howls, long, mournful, yet defiant and freeing...*

Wolves.

The call snaked its way through the forest. A chilling sound that rocked me to my core.

These were wolves.

After a time, the howls faded into the distance. They had done their job in keeping me awake, at least. I sighed and wrapped my arms around my chest as I shivered. The potent smell of sweat wafted into my nostrils from my clothing, and I gasped, leaning my head back against the tree trunk.

What am I doing here?

Burrowing my hands under my armpits, I shifted into a more comfortable position, my teeth chattering from the cold.

Does time work the same way back home?

My parents would be in bed, and mine—mine would be empty.

Mom's distant voice filtered through the walls enclosing my room. She laughed. I perked up, ears straining to hear that long-awaited sound again. My lips moved in a silent plea, but her voice had already died away.

"Mom," I whispered.

My body jolted as my head fell forward. The room was dark—no, *forest,* the forest was dark. I scanned the undergrowth and the trees, tall and slender, surrounding me. *It was a dream. Mom can't answer.*

I leaned back and peered up at the sky. It was as black as ever. I couldn't have slept long. My limbs refused to move, numb and cold as they were.

The slightest rustling sounded next to me, and a dark form leaned down. I jumped, a low groan escaping my lips as my back slammed against the bark of the tree. Blinking back tears, it took me a moment to see the Unknown standing before me.

"I'll watch now." He wrapped his cloak closer around him to ward off the night chill.

I yawned as I stood. An owl hooted a call somewhere in the blackness of the night. The moonlight shone down through the branches, leaving shadows crossing over the Unknown.

His eyes glittered bright without the cowl drawn over his face. "Get some sleep."

I hesitated. "What are you thinking?"

An eyebrow rose as the Unknown looked down at me.

"You were thinking something. You had a look in your eye, distant, but almost troubling somehow."

"That this is only the beginning," he answered, his voice low and even. "You and Saya have chosen a journey that will be filled with difficult choices, but you've already made the most important one."

I tilted my head, raising an eyebrow in a silent question.

"You've chosen to go," he replied, making to turn away.

"And what about you?"

He froze. With a quick movement, he whirled about to face me. "I have chosen to accompany you."

"Why do I feel like I didn't have much of a choice in all this?" I whispered.

The moonlight shone down on his face as he looked upward for a few brief seconds. "You'll have to wrestle with that yourself." His shoulders rose. "Each of us has our own demons we fight."

"What are yours?" The moment the words were out, I almost wished I had given some more thought before speaking...but at the same time, I waited for an answer.

His voice low and deep, he answered, "Too many to name. Get some sleep," he reiterated, stepping away.

The owl that had hooted from time to time fell silent, as though listening to my thoughts. *No one told me to come. I made this choice.* My limbs creaked as I limped toward the fire, or what was left of it. A shiver ran its course over my body in anticipation of lying next to the glowing embers. It was useless to wish for roaring flames and the heat that would go with them. *My dream—Mom. Was deciding to go on this journey worth it?* I stopped, staring down at the ground.

The fire.

He'd built it back up. It didn't matter if it had been for him or for me. The flames, low and controlled, licked at the air. I couldn't help grinning as I sank to the ground, letting the warmth blossom over me.

Chapter Nine

There was no need for an alarm clock; the sunlight woke me. Rolling over with a slight groan, I rubbed the small of my back where a rock had made its bed.

"I didn't realize you were that weak."

I blinked, squinting up at the Unknown's tall silhouette. It was too bright to see him clearly, but I could sense an abnormal smile crossing his face.

Sitting up with a grunt, I muttered, "You haven't been the one lying on a rock most of the morning." A grin split my face as I felt the culprit and pulled it out—a small pebble. I scrambled to hide it behind my back, but it was too late.

"Yes, that is one big rock. Your pain must be beyond bearing."

I glared at him. "Do you want to switch places?"

"Why would I do that?"

With a shake of my head, I stood and dusted myself off, studying the Unknown as he turned away.

Saya watched from where she stood a few feet away, chewing on something.

"How far behind them are we?" I had to bite back a groan as I rose.

"Maybe two days or so," the Unknown stated, his tone grim.

A weight settled over my shoulders. "Two days?"

"Yes," he answered.

"There's no way we'll catch up," Saya murmured, her petite frame drooping.

I looked back and forth between my two companions. "We can't stop now, though, right?"

He held my gaze. "We'll go as far as it takes. Nothing was ever accomplished by giving up without seeing it through. Don't accept defeat yet. There's a chance we may still catch them."

Saya folded her arms over her chest. "We haven't found horses yet, and with each hour they draw farther away."

The Unknown loped forward a few steps, calling back over his shoulder, "It shall be made known when it is made known."

A chuckle escaped my lips.

Saya raised an eyebrow. "You shouldn't encourage him."

I struggled to force the smile from my face as she glared at me. "I'm not. Maybe you just need to relax—"

Saya's eyes narrowed, and her lips thinned.

"Saya, I can't explain it, but I trust him, and he's done nothing to make me doubt his word. He's had numerous opportunities to hurt us, kill us, whatever he could want, yet he hasn't. Instead, he has protected and respected us. I know you're scared—"

She stiffened. A flash of red appeared in the center of her cheeks.

"I am too." My eyes flashed up ahead to where the Unknown strode, his broad back to us. I hoped he was too far away to overhear, yet I wasn't sure.... "Just don't let that fear rule your emotions. Keep your mind clear. It's hard, believe me, I know—"

Saya picked up her step, and I watched as her short legs carried her further away without a single acknowledgment of my words.

Is my judgment impaired? What if she's right? I sighed and wiped away a sudden tear. *Whoever may be listening, please, please give me strength.*

I let the distance grow between Saya and me. *First Eddie, and now the Unknown.* My teeth ached as I clenched my jaw. I winced. *But what if I'm not wrong? Even with all the layers of mystery, I think we can trust him.*

The Unknown's head swung to the side.

He can't hear my thoughts. The snap of leaves reminded me of the passing days. The Unknown had done nothing to harm us or hinder us. *I was right in that.* He had done nothing to cause mistrust. *He has done nothing.*

The Unknown halted and swung around. "I'll be back."

Saya increased her pace as she called, "Where are you going?"

But he was gone.

As the hours passed, we became jumpier as we walked along, still following the faint indentions of wagon wheels in the ground. Exhausted and thirsty, we stopped to eat and rest a little.

"It's not really the Unknown that has you so pent up today, is it?"

Saya adverted her gaze.

"Saya?" I pressed, tugging the flap of my pack open.

A heavy sigh escaped her lips. "No, it's not."

"Then what is it?"

"I don't want us to fail. I had another vision last night."

When she didn't go on, I waited, trying to be patient even though every nerve was surging with anticipation. I followed her gaze up to the still branches of the trees around us. The ground lay littered with more fallen leaves than when we'd left Umi no Machi. Fall was now in full swing, red and yellow leaves marking the passage of time.

"I saw the wagons, the raiders, and the townsfolk." She closed her eyes. "There wasn't any hope in their eyes."

"Did you hear anything?"

"No, it was more like snapshots, just glimpses that flew across my mind's eye."

"Could you tell where they were?"

She shook her head.

"Was there anything else?"

"I saw us returning to Umi no Machi. We crested a rise, and there it was in the distance."

I stood up from where I'd been kneeling by my pack. "So we did it?"

A tear slid down Saya's cheek, and her voice was hoarser this time. "No. We were alone. It was just the three of us. We failed."

"But..." My mind grasped at something—anything—to say. "It doesn't mean that's what happens, right? We can still rescue them. Just because it's what you saw doesn't mean it'll come true."

"I see glimpses of the future," Saya acknowledged. "But I've never tried to change what is seen."

"So it's possible then?"

"I guess."

I ignored the dubious look she gave me. "Chin up, Saya. We haven't failed yet. Pray to the gods that you speak of so often."

Saya frowned. "Do not take the gods lightly."

I held up my hands, palms out. "I wasn't."

"Alright, I will. You're right. I shouldn't lose hope yet." Saya's eyes searched up and down the path we stood beside. "He's been gone a long time now."

"Maybe we should keep walking?"

Saya shrugged, but neither of us made a move.

A soft drumming filtered through the trees. I held up a hand. "Do you hear that?"

Saya cocked her head, listening. "Hoofbeats," she murmured. The faint sound echoed through the woods, growing louder with each passing second. Saya's fingers twitched, and I rolled my weight onto the balls of my feet. "Quick, hide!"

Dead branches cracked and shifted under our feet as we darted into deeper cover. The birds around us chirped their protest before falling silent. In the hushed stillness, we waited, our breathing loud in the abnormal silence enveloping us. My heart pounded as vibrations from the horses' hooves beat through the dusty ground and up into my body. Leaves prickled against my face, but I didn't dare move.

Minutes seemed to tick by, though it couldn't have been longer than seconds before a figure on horseback appeared through the trees. Two riderless mounts followed after—but there was something familiar about the shape of the figure—*the cloak*—

My eyes widened, and I stood up.

"Juliet!" Saya's dainty hand gripped my sleeve with a sharp tug.

"It's him." With a grin, I pulled away and jogged back toward the path. Raising a hand as I came into view, I called out, "Where did you get them?"

He pulled the horses up, their hooves stamping and puffs of air shooting out from around the bits in their mouths. "I found someone who needed the money more than he needed the horses."

I stepped back as one of them pranced closer to me and watched as Saya encircled them with wary footsteps. The tall horses dwarfed her small frame, making her seem shorter and the beasts taller than either truly were.

"These must have fetched a pretty price," she pointed out. "They aren't cheap. These are some of the best I've seen." She approached the nearest one, a pale chestnut, the smallest of the three, and let it nuzzle her palm. "I'll take this one."

I eyed the last one; he, or maybe she, was a dark brown, almost black on the legs.

"He's yours," the Unknown affirmed. "Here."

I caught the smooth, leather reins the Unknown tossed me. Taking a deep breath, I lifted my foot into the stirrup, grimacing as my thigh tightened. Settling into the saddle, I rocked a little on my tailbone as I adjusted. *This is different*, I thought. *Interesting.*

"What is it?"

My gaze flickered over Saya before settling back on the reins in my hands and the saddle beneath me. "I've never sat in a saddle like this before. There's not much between me and the horse."

"Juliet," the Unknown broke in, and I froze. "When was the last time you rode?"

I ignored the skeptical look on his face. "It's been a while, and I've never ridden in a saddle like this," I repeated, unsure if he had missed what I'd told Saya.

"I caught that," he replied, coming alongside me. "It's light, durable, good for fast travel. But it won't provide much cushion."

Saya groaned, planting her face in her right palm. "Don't remind me," she muttered. "I haven't ridden in a long time either, but I remember."

The Unknown's lips tilted upward in the corners. He clicked his tongue and led the way. I watched as Saya followed without any trouble.

"Come on, boy," I whispered, nudging the horse's ribs with my heels. A grin spread over my face as the horse began to move underneath me, but then he stopped. Warmth flooded my cheeks as I struggled to get the horse to move to no avail.

I was aware the moment the Unknown's head swiveled as he glanced over his shoulder and circled back to me, the faint clip-clops of hooves on the ground providing a gentle staccato beat in the background of my ears. Not a sign of emotion showed on his face, yet he met my gaze straight on, his eyes boring into mine. So many layers were encompassed within that I couldn't begin to delve into them, nor even to crack the surface.

"What is it?" he asked, flicking his hood off his head so that it lay behind his shoulder blades.

"He won't move," I murmured, shrugging. Using my heels, I nudged the horse. I sat back in the saddle with a sigh. "Nothing."

"Utilize the reins, as well as gentle motions. He's a smart horse, so for one thing, he's testing you and two, he responds better to verbal cues and body movement than with your heels. Have more confidence, look where you want him to go, and he'll feel it. Try it."

Taking deep breaths and forcing myself to relax, I felt the horse beneath me begin to move. The Unknown turned his own mount and followed.

"Good, just keep him nice and steady. We'll increase our speed as you become more comfortable."

⁂

I stretched out on the ground, unmindful of the dirt clinging to my already-dirty clothes. My thighs and backside screamed in rage at me.

"It'll get worse before it gets better," the Unknown grunted, stretching out his legs before the fire. The material stretched tight over his muscular—

I shook my head. "Thanks," I muttered, watching the fire smolder, the light dying as the wood turned into charred black lumps.

"Speaking of which," the Unknown murmured, closing his eyes. "Time for some practice."

"But it's so late!" I protested, my body already groaning in anticipation.

"There is enough light from the fire."

Saya removed her cloak before rising to her feet. I followed her a short ways from the fire, where the light still reached, but we couldn't feel the heat.

"Same moves as last night," the Unknown called from where he still lay by the fire, his cloak serving as a pillow underneath his head.

Saya shot a glare at him and muttered under her breath, "By the gods, you drive me crazy."

"I can hear you," the Unknown acknowledged. "Probably better than the gods can."

"Be careful what you say," Saya spluttered, glancing around, fear written all over her face in her raised eyebrows and wide eyes. "Any one of them could be listening!" She muttered what sounded like a quick prayer.

I took a step toward the Unknown. "Do you not believe in the gods?"

He shrugged.

"How could you—" Saya began.

"I've not seen anything to prove the existence of Ryujin or any of the other gods."

"It does not mean they aren't real!" Saya exclaimed, her face pale.

"True."

"So then—"

"It just doesn't seem right to me."

Saya opened her mouth, but he held up a hand.

"Time to practice."

Her mouth snapped closed at his words, and I raised my hands as I slipped my left foot forward into a defensive stance.

"Please don't take it out on me."

She nodded, tight-lipped. "This isn't over," she called over her shoulder without looking at the Unknown. "Ready?"

I nodded, but she was already charging at me.

Over and over again we practiced the same moves. This evening, though, it wasn't long before the Unknown called us to a halt.

"I'm going to sleep. Juliet, take the first watch, then Saya."

I gritted my teeth, knowing that soon the wave of adrenaline would fade, and the exhaustion would set in.

Lying down, the Unknown drew his cloak closer and pulled his hood down. Saya shot me a quick smile before also rolling up in her cloak. Heaving to my feet, I passed out of the ring of light, watching as my shadow stretched out long and thin on the ground in front of me. Settling myself against the back of a slender pine, I let my eyes grow accustomed to the darkness. The stars glittered in the heavens, visible through the large gaps in the sparse trees above me.

It'll be okay. I stared at a lonely star shining brighter in contrast to those further away. *It may feel like I'm alone right now, but I'm not.* My two companions, still and sleeping, lay by the fire. I bit my lip. *I don't need to be afraid.*

As the time passed, it grew harder to keep my eyes open and my mind alert. The fire had died down; it was but a faint glow in the near distance.

A sharp crack reverberated through the trees.

I startled, my heartbeat quickening as one of the horses snorted and stamped his hoof. My eyes jumped from shadow to shadow as I scanned the undergrowth, but I saw nothing. My ears strained to the point I felt a pain forming in my temples. A low whinny came from the dark chestnut just before something large rustled in the direction I'd heard the stick crack. A shiver ran its cool fingers over my skin, spreading faster than a wildfire.

Maybe it's just coyotes.

I rubbed a small rock between my thumb and index finger, letting the same thought ring in my head. *It's just coyotes,* I repeated. *Or rabbits, owls, raccoons...*

I froze as shuffling came from the forest, like that of a large animal. With tense shoulders, I spotted the Unknown's dark shape lying by the embers of the dying fire and threw the small rock I'd been holding.

His tall form rose, and with deft movements, he scooped up some dirt and threw it on the embers. What faint light they'd emitted disappeared. Footsteps echoed out of the surrounding darkness, and a dim form appeared amongst the shadows. The figure slowed and stopped as though listening for something. The silhouette of broad shoulders and a hefty build met my eye. He was so close I could almost see the clouds of breath swirling in front of his face.

My heart raced, and I made a small movement—

Wait, I told myself, hesitating. *He can't see us from there.*

My eyes flicked to where the Unknown stood next to the horses, a vague dark shape blending in with the surrounding shadows. I focused on my breathing. *In for four, hold for eight, out for three.*

Another stick cracked. The man moved away, his footsteps dying away. As the last sound faded, I took a deep breath of fresh air, my lungs hungry. I watched, numb, my limbs frozen as Saya stood and made her way toward me. The Unknown remained by the horses, keeping them quiet.

Saya's soft footsteps approached, and she whispered, "Are you alright?"

I shook my head. Tension had strained my muscles to the point where I could hardly move.

The Unknown walked back to the fire, his figure a shifting shadow that glided across the ground.

"Come on," Saya urged. Inhaling, I followed in her footsteps.

He watched us approach but remained silent until we stood next to him. "Well?" He folded his arms over his broad chest, dark eyes gleaming as he toed the ashes from our fire.

Saya glanced at the dark trees surrounding us. "Who do you think they were?"

"I don't know, but no one should be moving around at this time of night. No more fire tonight. I'll keep watch. Saya, get some sleep before I wake you." He turned without waiting for an answer.

Saya looked at me. "You should try to sleep too." She dropped down and rolled herself back into her cloak.

The Unknown pointed to the ground, and I laid down without protest, asleep before my body had even stilled.

⁓⟫⟫⟩⟩ ⟨⟨⟨⟨⟪

I raised my hand into the air, watching the shifting of shadows dance across the palm of my hand, the branches above swaying with a gentle breeze. Dawn had chased away night and light streaked across the sky in varying hues of orange.

Standing up, I glanced around, stretching my arms. The clearing was empty. There was no sign of the Unknown and Saya, and the horses stood silent nearby, still picketed where we had left them. Raising each knee in succession to stretch my hamstrings, I noticed the leaves littering the ground. Fall touched the landscape. The tall pines had thinned the further west we traveled, and the deciduous trees became more numerous.

"Juliet!"

I spun around at the sound of Saya's voice. They wove their way toward me across the plain, its tall brown grass brushing against Saya's waist and the Unknown's thighs as they walked. Fronds waved in the slight breeze.

"Where were you?"

Saya skipped a little in her excitement. "Scouting the area where those men traveled last night."

The Unknown strode straight to the horses and began saddling them.

I walked forward to help. "What did you find?"

"Not much, nothing of importance. They were clumsy; quite a bit of brush was trampled down along their path. I would say a group of about five men, but they don't appear to be heading in the same direction as us."

"Why were they out there in the first place?"

"Don't know," he admitted, "but they're up to no good. Honest men sleep during the night; they don't crash around a forest in the dark."

"They seemed to be looking for something or someone." Saya hesitated, her eyes lifting to where the Unknown saddled his horse.

"Someone?" I questioned, forgetting about the saddle in my hands. "Saya?"

"It's just what *he* said." She inclined her head toward the Unknown, avoiding looking at me.

"Raiders?"

The Unknown shook his head. "No, these men are traveling too carefully to be raiders."

"So, who do you think they are?"

The Unknown dropped the reins he'd been holding on the ground. "I don't know."

I lifted the saddle onto the horse's back with a soft grunt. "What is she talking about?"

He stepped away and picked up his pack to secure behind the saddle. "Based off the tracks, they were searching."

"For what?"

"I don't know. But it's time to go."

It wasn't until he said my name that I realized he was waiting for me to mount. Beyond him, Saya finished cinching her own saddle.

I patted the horse's sleek neck, crooning in a soft voice as I placed my foot in the stirrup. Gritting my teeth, I pushed down and gasped as my thighs protested. Fire soared through my veins.

The Unknown strode over to me.

"I'm fine," I groaned. "Just give me a minute."

Without a word, he reached out and gripped my waist. In one swift movement, he lifted me up into the air, and I swung my leg over the saddle. "We don't have a minute," he murmured, his green eyes expressionless.

I nodded and exhaled, every part of me tense as I watched him wheel around and mount his own horse. As he swung his mount around and forward, I realized I was still staring and averted my gaze—yet even then I seemed aware of his every move. I jerked in surprise as Saya drew abreast of me.

She frowned. "You look serious."

"Just thinking."

Saya's eyebrows rose, and she cocked her head to the side.

"Do you think I made a bad mistake in coming with you? It's been a week since I came here."

"Do *you* think you made a mistake?"

I considered her question, the hooves beneath the horse drumming in a soft cadence. White clouds slid across the blue sky as the wind high above drove them forward. "No, I don't think I have."

"There you have it, then." Her words didn't ease the heartache within me. "It's alright to still feel regret."

"It's not regret I feel. It's guilt."

"We all feel guilt at times...even when we don't need to."

My shoulders dropped as the tension eased away. "Thanks, Saya." I dipped my head, and a smile lit Saya's face.

"You learn quickly, though the deeper the bow, the more respect you show."

I grimaced. "Ouch." Taking a deep breath, I asked, "Did you foresee this conversation in order to know what to say?"

A smile lit her face. "No."

"Saya, I've heard you and other mentions the gods several times now. When you use that term, what do you mean?"

Saya's eyes widened, and she blinked in surprise. "You don't have the same gods back home?"

"I don't know." I chuckled.

"Well, usually we refer to seven gods. There are more of course—the seven are the ones most prayed to and revered. They're the gods of fortune, of luck." She raised a hand in the air. "You really haven't heard of them?"

I shook my head. Raising a hand, I peeled off the hairs clinging to the back of my neck. It was hot. A black bird with beady eyes regarded me from a branch overhanging the trail. The muffled clip-clop of hooves striking soft earth reverberated through the ground as we fell in behind the Unknown.

I wiped my face with a sleeve. "Can we go any faster?"

He ran an assessing gaze over me. "Of course, but are you ready for that?"

"Yes."

"Then go on ahead and scout. We'll catch up."

"Me?" I squeaked, leaning back in the saddle as though I had an avenue of escape.

"Yes. It'll be good practice for you. Enable you to practice the tracking I've been teaching you."

How do you know so much? Again, the question flitted through my mind. *Tracking, fighting, hunting, so many skills.*

"What?" the Unknown quizzed.

I gulped. "I was just wondering..." I trailed off. *He wouldn't have gone after them. He came after us.*

"Juliet?" Saya prodded.

My eyes didn't leave the dark green ones staring back at me. "You wouldn't have gone after them."

The Unknown regarded me, still and silent save for the slight shifting of the horse beneath him.

"You said you didn't expect us to come so far, and you didn't bring your horse."

"You're right. I didn't plan on it. But you knew that already." He raised a hand to shield his eyes to better look at me. A shadow fell across his face, making the stubble there even darker. "I think I made that clear, so what are you really asking?"

"Why?"

He blinked.

"I know you didn't have any loved ones taken. You didn't have any personal reason..." I paused. "But nor did Saya. And yet she is here, trying to save peo-ple—because who else was going to do it? You came to bring us back, or you came out of curiosity, which I'm not sure...but you ended up joining us instead. Why?"

Several moments of silence passed before he parted his lips to speak. "You surprised me."

"You joined us on a whim?"

He shrugged. "I suppose you could call it that. Be glad I did, for you would never catch up to them without me, nor can you free them without my help." He nudged his horse forward, and Saya followed with a quizzical tilt to her face.

He's right. We wouldn't.

We have a chance because of him. *But how does he know so much?* He'd had training...experience—he knows how to track. But how?

His words replayed in my head as I moved past my companions to take the lead. They were almost arrogant, too confident, too sure...yet he'd said them so matter-of-factly. As though how could Saya and I ever doubt him?

The trail below the horse's feet was faint. *Who used this other than the raiders?*

What is the Unknown hiding? *What is his real name?* I chewed on my lower lip. *It's not the Unknown and it's not Shizukana...* I sat up straighter and shifted with a small groan. My limbs were stiffening, and my butt ached from sitting on the thin saddle.

⚘ ⚘

The road continued ever on, winding through another valley and up a shallow slope. Plains filled with brown grass stretched out before me, broken here and there with copses of trees.

My horse brushed his soft, velvety nose against my skin. "Sorry," I crooned under my breath. "I wish I had an apple or carrot to give you, but I don't."

The wind rustled across the long grass and whistled through the green, scarecrow-like trees.

I sighed and dropped the reins as I walked around the small glade. The undergrowth was trampled, heading off to the west as far as I could see. Broken branches and foot imprints lay scattered across the ground. Picking up my pace, I jogged down it, following the remnants of the trail.

It continued with a gradual change to the north but west, nonetheless. I stopped around a bend in the trail. It stretched on as far as I could tell, lost in the unending plains. With a deep breath, I turned to head back. My breath came in short gasps by the time I reached the clearing. I nodded to the Unknown and Saya, who stood waiting.

Saya put something she held back in her pack. "Where were you?"

"The trail, there—" I pointed. "It leads to the west but with a slight curve to the north. I followed it for a little while, and it didn't change. A small group must have split off, but the others seemed to have continued on their way."

The Unknown didn't move from where he leaned against the narrow trunk of a maple. "You're right."

Saya's mare whinnied, and she rubbed its nose. "Where does the trail we've been following go?"

"Through a small village in the north before becoming a fork, one of which goes to a coastal town and the other further inland."

"And the path Juliet found?"

He shrugged. "Seems like that is veering toward the coast."

Saya handed me the reins while looking at the Unknown. "What do you think?"

"The coast makes sense. I should've thought of it sooner, but this trail gives an idea of where they're headed. They'll have a ship waiting. I don't know why a few branched off to keep going further inland. Maybe they plan on hitting another village before they rendezvous." He stroked his chin.

Something isn't right. I blinked. *Wait.* Umi no Machi—*it's a sea town.* "If they have a ship, why didn't they just sail to Umi no Machi?"

Saya's thick, dark eyebrows rose high, and her eyes looked extra wide in her delicate face.

The Unknown shot an appreciative nod toward me. "That's what I was wondering. Maybe it wasn't planned. Maybe they didn't realize how far south they'd come." He rotated his shoulders and rolled his neck before mounting. "Who knows. It would've been smarter."

I heaved myself up into the saddle. "So the coast then?"

"Yes. Saya?"

I followed his gaze to where Saya stood by her horse, silent, her eyes unfocused and staring. "Saya? Saya?" I made to get off my horse when she blinked and looked up at us.

"They will be there." She pulled herself up and swung her leg over the chestnut's back. "I know it. Is there a stretch along the coast that has a small cove that would be perfect for hiding them? Maybe a sparse stretch of coastline?"

My breath caught. *She's had a vision.* I tried to get her attention, but she ignored the question in my eyes.

The Unknown raised an eyebrow. "Yes, there is. I think I know where they'll go."

The horse under me danced as it felt my growing anticipation.

"I don't understand how the king can allow any of this on his land." Saya voiced the thoughts that had been flitting at the edge of my own mind.

"Because he only wants what benefits himself, and right now, that's behind-the-scenes condoning the raiders taking his people for trade."

I pushed the strands of hair that had fallen back from my face. "How do you know he isn't openly condoning it?"

He blinked. "What?"

"The king, you said he wouldn't condone it, at least not openly."

He shrugged.

"How come he wants to hide it? Is he afraid of how his subjects will see him?"

"Wouldn't you?"

"Yes," I acknowledged, "but is he afraid they'll do something to stop him?"

"Like depose him?" the Unknown challenged.

My ponytail bounced as I bobbed my head.

"There's been rumors of some trying to do just that, but they're rumors. I doubt those involved will succeed."

"Why?"

"Because I know." The tone of his voice took on a new edge.

"How do you know all this? Have you met the king?"

"No more questions."

"Have you been to his palace?"

"Juliet—" he growled.

"What?" I raised my hands in the air. "Don't tell me you have a soft spot for this so-called king?"

He whirled his horse around and drew it alongside mine. He leaned down, his several inches on me feeling even greater as he snapped, "There's much you don't know."

"Shizukana," Saya interrupted. "That was uncalled for."

The Unknown's long, dark lashes lowered over his eyes as though biting back the words springing to his lips.

"How long will it take us to reach the coast?" Saya asked, her tone making it clear the previous conversation was over.

"A day, maybe less."

"Then we should go." Saya nudged her horse into a walk.

The Unknown dropped in line and followed, muttering, "Hopefully we're on the right trail."

"The gods help us if we're not," Saya muttered, casting her eyes up to the heavens.

The Unknown snorted. "They won't—"

"Alright," I cut in as I saw storm clouds gather over Saya's face. "Let's just save our energy for what's to come, gods or no gods."

Chapter Ten

The green plains stretched out around us, the trees growing in sparse patches. Dust clogged the air from the breeze blowing across the open ground.

My gaze flicked toward the Unknown, his face hidden beneath the shadow thrown by his cowl. It was a warm day, and yet he had not removed his cloak.

Licking my lips, I grimaced as I shifted in the saddle, my thighs flaring with pain from the strain. I looked down. My legs were thinner than they used to be and more toned beneath the pants I'd borrowed from Saya. The hem was too short, but at least they weren't as tight as they used to be. Raising the waterskin, I swished a mouthful around before spitting it out on the ground.

The Unknown glanced sideways. "Are you all right?"

"Yes. The water is just a little gritty."

He nodded, his gaze clear and focused. "Try to relax. You've been tense all day."

I took a deep breath, the air hot and heavy as it entered my lungs. "How did you know?"

"Your horse. He feels your tenseness. It's really starting to grate on my nerves."

My mount danced to the side, and I pulled on the reins.

"Why are you tense?"

"My body hurts."

The Unknown adjust the reins in his hand. "Where?"

"Everywhere."

His lips curved upward a little, almost imperceptible. He seemed to hesitate. I nodded in encouragement. "What is it?"

"Where is your family?"

Oh, maybe I shouldn't have asked. I swallowed down, trying to push back the guilt that had already begun growing within. "Far away from here," I replied, my voice not as steady as I'd have wished.

"Why aren't you with them?"

"Unexpected circumstances," I responded. "What about your family?"

"Far away from here."

I shot a look at him. If that repeat of my answer was a sarcastic rejoinder, I couldn't tell. I laid the reins across my lap and reached up to pull my single ponytail holder out, sweeping my thick hair up into a loose bun. "Do you see them often?"

"No, not for many years." He pushed back his cowl, letting it drop off his broad shoulders, and flicked a glance at me, watching with a raised eyebrow as I finished with my hair.

"What kind of king would really let all this happen?" I waved my hand through the air as though the townspeople and slavers stood before us.

"A man who lives only for himself. One who doesn't care for people and uses them for his own gain. He is corrupt."

"You said there were rumors of some fighting against him?"

"Most don't have the willpower to do anything, or they live in ignorance, much like those at Umi no Machi. And those who have enough power to do something, well, the king keeps their pockets lined so that they don't do anything."

I tilted my head to the side as I studied him. "You sound like you know him."

"I know what he's capable of," he spat. "There are many just like him in this world."

He's hiding something. I ignored the shadow darkening in the Unknown's eyes and the way his jaw clenched. "What do you know about this king? What haven't you told us?"

"He goes wherever a favorable wind takes him—"

"What does that mean?" Saya broke in, leaning forward in her saddle as though to better hear the conversation.

The Unknown slowed his mount a little as he considered. "In this case, I think the raiders are paying the king off, which I think I've already told you.

The king has many who work for him…" He trailed off and took a deep breath before continuing. "The slave trade is not all that goes on in this kingdom. It is rotten at the core, and it has been so for a couple of decades now."

A sharp hiss rent the air as Saya spewed her anger. "I did not realize it was so bad." She pushed the sleeves of her tunic up towards her elbows. "The gods curse him and remove him from his throne."

The Unknown raised an eyebrow, and even I was a little taken aback at her outburst.

"What?" Saya raised her hands in the air, letting the reins drop onto her mount's neck. "He shouldn't be king. No man should be king who has not a care for the people under him or the land. He abuses the power and privilege he has."

"He does," the Unknown agreed. "But are you to remove him from his throne? Am I? Is Juliet?" He spurred his horse forward without waiting for an answer. Dust billowed up in small clouds behind him. Birds chirped their cheerful heralds to our passing, but now that the Unknown was up ahead, the silence that lay around me did nothing to relieve the tension crackling the air.

Saya gestured toward the receding figure of the Unknown and his horse. "What was that all about?"

"I was asking him about his family."

She smirked. "Oh. That explains it then."

"What do you mean?"

"You really think he"—she jabbed a finger towards the Unknown—"is going to tell you? Do you know what Shizukana means? Silent. Quiet. Why do you think we call him the silent one? Because he doesn't speak. No one knows anything about him."

"Doesn't mean I can't ask."

Saya huffed and rolled her eyes. "Haven't you learned anything about our culture? If he is even more reserved and secretive than most, and yet none open up lightly to a stranger, why do you think *he'll* do so?"

"I'm not a stranger!"

"No?" Saya eyed me and leaned down to scratch a spot on her calf. "Perhaps not a complete stranger, but what does he know about you?" She spurred her mount forward in pursuit of the Unknown and called back over her shoulder,

"Besides, he has secrets for a reason, Juliet. Are you sure you want to know what they are?"

It was early evening when we found the stream. Saya and I didn't have to do more than send beseeching looks the Unknown's way before he relented and told us we could stop for the evening.

"As long as you train first."

I groaned.

"Fine!" Saya exclaimed, dismounting with a low moan. She removed the saddlebags and dropped them on the ground. "I'm too tired," she explained when she caught the look on my face.

"You two done yet?" The Unknown stood by his horse. "No? Then hurry up."

I gritted my teeth and set the saddlebags on the ground. "He's really starting to drive me crazy."

"Starting to?" Saya repeated. "Try since day one."

"Fair enough." I stooped down and picketed the dark chestnut loosely beside the Unknown's mount.

"Saya?" the Unknown inquired as I came to stand next to him.

"Ready," she affirmed, coming to join us.

"I'll show you the third move to add into the rotation that you've been practicing." He looked back and forth between us for acknowledgment before continuing. "After you knee the groin, I want you to hook your right leg around their right leg and push. With the correct momentum and shock factor, they will fall to the ground."

I placed my hands on my hips as I considered. "What do we do after they're on the ground?"

"Oh, and don't forget to tuck your chin to your chest as you fall, and don't break your fall with your hands, not unless you want them sprained or broken. You'll learn that later. Now, get started." He wrinkled his nose and strode away, calling over his shoulder. "When you're done, rinse off in the stream. You could both use a bath."

"So could you," I muttered to his back.

Saya curled her dark hair behind her ears and watched as a bird alighted on the ground a few feet away.

"You seem to be getting along with him a little better—" I began, watching the bird as well, but the words were cut off as my body fell to the ground with a heavy thump. Air whooshed out of my lungs, and I groaned.

Saya held a hand out, her eyes wide. "Did I hurt you?"

"I'll be fine," I huffed, allowing her to pull me to my feet. "I just wasn't expecting it. Forgot what we were doing for a moment."

She squared up in front of me. "Ready this time?"

I nodded and stepped forward—tripping over a long, thick stick. Pain lanced through my leg. Hopping up and down on one foot, I clutched the injured leg as I glanced down at the offending piece of wood. Reaching down, I picked it up. The wood was rough and grainy but light and strong.

Eddie. Dad used to carve pieces of wood like this down for him—we'd have mock sword fights. I blinked, the soft echo of wood-on-wood fading as reality resurfaced. *Staffs!* My lips tilted up in a smile.

"Saya!" I called out. "Do you have a knife?"

"Yes, why?"

"We could make some staffs," I suggested, flexing the wood between whitened fingers. "They'd be better than nothing."

Saya knelt beside me and tested the weight and flexibility of the wood. She grunted in satisfaction. "Good idea. How about you find another one? I'll start trimming this one."

"As long as I don't find one by banging my foot on it," I muttered.

"You'd be fine if it was the other foot." She grinned and winked. "Even you out a bit."

"I see you found some sticks," the Unknown noted, setting down a large armful of wood.

Saya held one out. "We're going to make some staffs."

He nodded. "Might want to bathe first while there is still light."

We dropped the staffs next to our packs before grabbing a set of fresh clothes. *Clean clothes.* Just thinking of washing made my skin itch in anticipation.

By the time we finished bathing, night had fallen. He was right. Saya finished before me and headed back with a wave while I continued wringing my wet clothes out.

The air was still and quiet, the nighttime animals and insects not having yet fully awoken. Grabbing my dirty clothes, I squeezed more water out of my hair with one hand as I walked back. The low drone of voices drifted around a grove of bushes as I neared our makeshift camp.

The Unknown's deep voice asked, "What do you know about her?"

I froze.

"Nothing," Saya blurted, a note of irritation lacing the single word.

"I think you do know something. What has she told you?"

"Why don't you ask her yourself?"

I crept forward, each nerve taut as I took one slow step at a time. A stick cracked under my foot. With a deep breath, I walked around the bushes and came face to face with two figures. Saya stood with her arms crossed over her chest, several inches shorter than the tall, broader shape of the Unknown standing mere inches away from her.

"Well? What do you want to ask me?"

He regarded me with his dark eyes and grizzled face. "I think it's high time you tell me the truth."

I blinked once, twice. "About what?"

He crossed his muscular arms over his chest. "You know." His green eyes narrowed, and a tendon pulsed in his neck.

My story, I realized. *But why should I tell him?*

"I don't owe you that."

He took a step forward, and I shrank back unconsciously. He stopped short. "You're right. You don't. But I would like you to."

As the echo of his words faded, the silence emanating from him and Saya weighed on me like a ton of bricks. I licked my lips.

Saya shrugged and returned her gaze to the Unknown. Her arms dangled at her sides, and her gaze remained clear and expressionless.

What harm could come of it? I mused as I studied the Unknown's almond-shaped eyes. *Opening might give him incentive to do so as well. Maybe Saya's right. Maybe I need to be first for him to be willing to tell us more.*

I sighed. *It's time.*

"Very well." I kept walking, the fronds from the surrounding bushes brushing against my legs and leaving the air full of rustling. The soft tread of my companions echoed as they followed. I entered the small clearing, trying to ignore the aches in my body as I sat against my saddlebag. With a sigh of satisfaction, Saya dropped onto the ground. She grunted as she nudged the saddle down a little lower and leaned back against it.

"Whenever you're ready," the Unknown murmured. He stood over me, his towering form daunting.

"Do you want to sit first?"

He dropped onto the ground and crossed his arms behind his head.

"I come from Gig Harbor."

"I'm not familiar with it. Which kingdom?"

"Gig Harbor is a city—town—in the United States. It was, I suppose, a couple of weeks ago now, when I was in a forest…" I summarized the events that had happened in the forest that day, leading up to finding myself in a different environment. "I was found by a woman who lives in your town, and I ended up at the inn. You know the rest of the story." I swallowed some water to ease my dry throat. Once I'd begun, the words had flowed out without effort. A burden had been lifted off my shoulders, a burden I hadn't realized I'd been carrying up to now. I felt free and light; it was euphoric.

The Unknown stroked his jaw with long, slender fingers. "Who was the woman who found you?"

"I don't know. She didn't give her name and disappeared before I could ask. I've tried to find her, hoping to find a way back home, but obviously that didn't work. I saw her once, but even then, I couldn't get to her fast enough."

"Sounds like a ghost."

"I wouldn't put it past her," I muttered.

"This is one of the most fantastic tales I've heard, but it seems to be true." The Unknown stood up and began pacing. "And it explains a few things I've wondered." He caught my gaze as he finished, a flicker of emotion showing for a millisecond.

He recognizes something…there's a familiarity— I blinked, and the flicker was gone.

Saya set her waterskin down. "I think this should just be kept between the three of us."

The Unknown's boots continued to tread the ground as he walked back and forth. "Others would not be willing to believe your tale. The people here are full of superstition and suspicion. It would not go well for you if unwelcome ears heard."

"How come you both have taken it so well, then?"

Saya poked the fire with a long stick. "I don't think I would have if I hadn't already known there was something different about you and that you didn't seem to be from anywhere on this world from what I—" She broke off whatever she was about to say.

"So you *did* see that with your abilities." I bit my lip. *Too late.* The words were out.

Saya's gaze shot to the Unknown. "What are you talking about?"

"I—I mean," I faltered.

"I already know you're a seer," the Unknown stated, gesturing to Saya. "You don't need to hide it."

"How did you know?"

"You've let enough things slip in the past that I guessed long ago."

Saya's face reddened and her lips moved, but she didn't speak.

"I won't tell anyone," the Unknown assured her. "If I'd wanted to, I already would have. Your secret is safe with me. I hold nothing against seers."

The fire crackled, the low flames warm upon my face. I stifled a yawn, sinking a little further back onto my saddlebag.

The Unknown tilted his head to one shoulder and then the other in a stretch. "I'll take first watch. Tomorrow will be a long day."

Chapter Eleven

My boots dragged across the ground, stirring up little pebbles along the rocky trail. With dulled senses, I plodded along behind the Unknown and Saya, stifling the yawns threatening to split my jaw. Invisible weights drew my limbs downwards, creating an even more invisible slough that bogged me down. I blinked, my eyelashes fluttering as I tried to focus my wavering vision on the trail in front of me.

In the last hour or so, we'd found a bay: small, secret, and perfect for docking. The Unknown figured the raiders would spend the night on the cliff before heading down the treacherous, rocky trail to the beach. We entered a wide glade, the last grassy area free from the rocks covering the cliff.

"They'll camp here," the Unknown observed. He shaded his eyes, peering at the position of the sun to the west. "Wait here. I'll be back soon." He gathered up his reins and left with the three horses following.

"And there he goes again," Saya muttered, her eyes boring into his back as he left. The slight breeze ruffled her thick, dark hair.

She still doesn't trust him. I dropped my pack on the ground and rubbed my wrists to ease some of the tension. Taking my waterskin, I licked my lips before asking, "Saya, don't you think he's earned at least a modicum of trust by now?" As the silence stretched out with no answer, I forced my eyes open and propped myself up with one arm. "Saya?"

"I don't trust him, but nor do I *not* trust him."

I cocked an eyebrow. "You didn't trust me, but now you do. What's different with him?"

"It was only recently I realized I do trust you. Before that, it was just that I trusted you more than I trusted him." She waved a hand in front of her face. "It's really warm out today."

"Saya," I began. "Every time he disappears, you tense up until I feel tense and annoyed myself. You can't keep it contained. I don't understand. Is there something you're not telling me about him?"

"No, there's nothing. But that's just it," she murmured, lacing her hands behind

her neck. "I know nothing about him."

"You trusted me after you believed I had told you the truth, after you knew where I stood—"

"Well," Saya interrupted, "to a certain extent. I still don't know you very well. But I now understand why you're here and why you couldn't go back home."

"Why don't you ask him what you want to know?"

Saya looked out toward where the Unknown had disappeared. "Why don't you?" She turned and walked away to the edge of the clearing without waiting for an answer. I watched her in silence, pondering her words.

Why don't I? Why don't I ask him what secrets he hides? How does he know so much about tracking? About fighting?

My feet tread the hard ground as I paced. *Where does he go so often when he leaves town?* I didn't have to look to know Saya watched me from where she stood. Her eyes bore into my back with every step I took.

"You're right," I muttered as my feet led me in a wide circle back toward Saya. She blinked, and her thin eyebrows rose.

"It is hot." A soft rustle filled the air as I rolled my sleeves up close to my elbows.

Saya rolled her eyes, but I ignored her. She wanted to know why I wouldn't ask the Unknown what I wanted to know, but I wasn't ready to answer that. Not to myself or her.

"The coast here is rockier than around Umi no Machi," I observed, sitting down. "There aren't any sandy beaches."

Saya squatted onto her ankles. "It's wilder."

"Does it make you miss the town?"

"A little. The ocean reminds me of home."

The Unknown strode up to us. "There are almost two dozen men."

Saya stiffened, and I leaned forward.

Two dozen?

"Do you have a plan?" Saya inquired.

"Not really," he admitted. "I think the best option will be to free them under the cover of darkness."

I rolled my eyes.

"What about sentries?" Saya stepped forward, gripping her staff in a possessive manner.

"They shouldn't prove much of a problem."

I stood up and brushed the back of my pants off. "Why wouldn't they be?"

He motioned to the staffs.

"Oh, right. Just knocking someone out, easy." I raised my eyebrows when I found both Saya and the Unknown staring at me. "Did I say that out loud?"

Saya nodded.

Great. "How will we free them, especially the children, without alerting the whole camp?"

"It will be hard, but it's our one chance. There are too many of them," he replied.

"What about—" Saya broke off as soon as she started. "Well, you mentioned them falling asleep. What if we were able to put them to sleep?"

I started and blinked. "What?"

"That just might work." the Unknown hesitated, stroking his chin as he thought. "There are herbs that have that property. I just can't remember them."

"I know of one," Saya whispered, and I had to strain my ears to hear her. "Valerian. It's often used as a sedative. My mother would use it from time to time. She was a healer. It can come in handy."

"We don't have much time to find it—if it does grow around here."

"It does," she said with a heavy note of confidence. "The roots and rhizomes are what I need. And the plant is distinctive. Give me an hour or so. I'll find it."

The Unknown nodded and sat down. "We'll wait here."

I watched as Saya strode off into the forest with a determined set to her posture.

"Get some rest," the Unknown murmured, lying down and closing his eyes. "You'll need it."

I chewed my bottom lip as I sat down. Anticipation thrummed within my body as the minutes ticked by. My foot tapped a soft rhythm on the ground. Sleep wouldn't come. I glanced over at the Unknown. He hadn't moved a muscle.

Saya entered the clearing, a slender plant gripped in her small hand.

Energy coursed through my veins as I bolted upright. "You found it."

She nodded, a grim smile decorating her face. "I'll have a brew whipped up in no time."

"Do you need help?"

She shook her head, her dark hair falling over her shoulder as it came loose from the thin leather securing it. Saya set the plant down and swept her hair back before sitting down next to her pack.

I sat with my back to a tree, half-watching as she rummaged through her pack.

The temperature began to drop with the sun, but it was a welcome and cooling relief from the heat. Shadows set in, still and long, cast by the overhanging trees and shrubs lining the top of the cliff leading toward the bay.

Saya looked up at us. "Ready," she exclaimed.

The Unknown opened his eyes and stood up. "Good. It's almost time."

I grunted as I heaved myself to my feet. Saya's gaze flickered over me. *She's worried. Her vision.* My eyes widened.

I reached forward and placed a hand on Saya's arm, giving it a soft squeeze. "Don't think about it. We can change things."

"About what?" the Unknown inquired, sheathing the sword he had been examining.

"Saya had a vision."

"We didn't rescue the townspeople," Saya broke in, her voice bitter. "We failed."

"Juliet is right. Just because you saw something doesn't mean that's what will happen."

"But—"

The Unknown took a step forward, his hand clenched over the hilt of his sword. "Do you want to give up?"

Saya shook her head.

"Good, then chin up. Let's go."

I followed him as he hid Saya. He was good. I wouldn't have known where she was if I hadn't seen the Unknown place her there. Next, we found my spot. He sat me there, and after reminding me not to do anything rash or stupid, his lithe form disappeared into the trees with the slightest of rustles.

I smirked. *Something rash or stupid... I probably would, even if I thought whatever I was doing was a smart move.* The ground moved a little as I settled into a more comfortable position.

It was a long time before I heard voices and sounds of movement.

They're here. My throat felt dry as parchment.

The sound of boots came first, trampling the ground underneath bulky bodies. Harsh shouts rang through the warm air. Already a cask of alcohol had been cracked open and wooden mugs filled with the cloudy, white liquid. Thick foliage was all that separated me from the men. They laughed, joked, swore, and—as the camp fell into a somewhat organized manner—slurred their words and cast ribald jokes. Most of them were about the women tied up at the far end of the camp.

A pair of shuffling boots alerted me to another man passing within feet of my position. Heavy breathing filled my ears as I sat, waiting with bated breath for him to move on. As his footsteps finally receded, my shoulders relaxed, and a little relief entered the cramping tightness of my muscles.

The light grew dimmer as night fell, and a thick blanket of darkness fell over the grove. The two large fires near the middle of the encampment roared high and bright. Their flames sent shadows flickering over the trees and ground.

Though I knew where Saya hid, I couldn't see a sign of her. Nothing stirred; not even a breeze seemed to distill the air. Anticipation grew, heightening my senses until I ached for something—anything—to happen. The Unknown had disappeared into the trees after he'd hid me, a wraith of the night, yet I wished I knew where he was.

They had almost finished erecting low tents in half circles around the fires. The townspeople sat at the far end of the campsite, on the very edge and furthest from the warmth of the fires. My jaw locked. Weariness weighed down their bodies. It was obvious in the way their shoulders slumped, and some even slept stretched out on the ground.

One of the tall men released two of the townspeople, both women, and beckoned them to follow. As he turned, a third form—slight and thin—appeared out of the growing shadows to join them.

Saya.

Gnawing on my lip, I waited for the man to notice her, but he paid the women no mind as he led them to a large fire and beckoned to the cart nearby. He drank from a large mug in his hand, watching the goings on in the rest of the camp more than the three women. Saya leaned over the large, open pot at the fire, stirring the contents before walking with unhurried and short steps over to the other fire. The tall flames silhouetted her petite, thin form as she bowed her head over the pot.

A heavy-set man, his footsteps clumsy in his drunken stupor, blocked my view of Saya for a moment as he passed. The tension in my shoulders eased as I watched her step back. After a quick look around, she darted into the surrounding shadows. Camp activity proceeded as normal. No one had noticed.

One by one, the men crawled into their tents and the camp began to grow quiet. I didn't dare shift my position for fear of the pain I knew would come as soon as the blood circulated in my stiff limbs again. The savory smells from the cooking fires wafted across the camp. My stomach growled and my breath caught, but no one seemed to have heard.

The guard at the other end of the camp rolled his neck and yawned. The surrounding shadows merged with his form, causing him to blend in.

A soft rustle sounded behind me. I jumped as a strong hand clamped over my mouth, stifling a rising scream. My heart thudded as warm breath blew against my ear.

"It's me," the Unknown whispered, his head brushing my own. His hair tickled the back of my neck as he released his hold over my mouth. "It's time."

I crept out of my hiding spot after him, every swish, every snap of the smallest twig beneath my feet sending my heart thudding. I gripped the staff with clammy hands, my breath catching as I realized we should've passed the first sentry, but there was no sign of him. The Unknown moved in front of me, his movements phantom-like, his cloak a darker shadow in the night.

My eyes slid past him as we reached the edge of the encampment closest to the townsfolk. They made no sound, not even the children. Saya must have seen us, because she reappeared and walked through the townspeople, urging all those sitting or lying down onto their feet. One by one, they passed by me, following the Unknown.

The last person, a man, strode by me, the grass rustling under his feet with his passing. Saya nodded at me and followed him. I turned to join them, but a movement in the shadows caught my eye, and the faintest sound, as of a moan, flitted on the air. *Did we miss someone?* Creeping forward, I squinted through the darkness.

The faint form of a large man rolled over in front of me. Holding my breath, I took a careful step backward. With a grunt, he sat up. I froze, sweat trickling down my cheek. He mumbled something about water and my breath caught.

That voice! I froze. *Their leader—the man from the inn that night—it's him.* I stared down as he cocked his head, his face scrunched as he tried to concentrate through the brain fog.

Hit him.

I swung the staff at his head as soon as the thought came. A soft thud preceded him falling onto his back. I whirled on my feet, and my heart thudded deep within my chest.

What did I do?

A grunt pierced the air behind me. My legs wouldn't move fast enough. The staff tangled between my feet—large hands engulfed my shoulders and pulled me around. I gasped.

His deep voice soared into my eardrums. "What do ye think ye're doin'?"

Rough hands yanked my hair back as a man peered down at my face. A surge of energy tore through me. Again, I swung at the hulk looming over me, but he blocked it with one forearm and tore the staff out of my grasp. My palms burned from the friction. His arms crushed me against him, and I tasted the saltiness of warm blood on my tongue. Tears sprang to my eyes, and I shuddered.

"Wha's goin' on?" a voice muttered from a short distance away.

"Nothin', go back to sleep." The man let go of my arms and gripped my hair, yanking my head back as he peered down at me, his face inches from mine. "Now then, what 'ave we here? How'd ye get loose?" His breath was pungent with the scent of stale, spicy alcohol.

Some distance separated us now that he had leaned down. I paused.

Don't hesitate. Do. The Unknown's voice spoke in my mind, yet I wasn't sure he had ever even said them. With a quick intake of air and my arms pinioned, I kicked upward, aiming for between the man's legs, but I missed. He grunted as my foot met his knee, but his thick fingers only tightened around my arms. He jerked the side of his arm hard against my face, throwing my head back.

I swallowed the scream back, spitting out the blood and mucus coating my mouth.

Don't cry out. Don't!

Licking my lips, I tried to wrench my body out of his grasp, but he was too strong, his grip like iron as he shackled me against him.

"Now there," he murmured, his voice a grating rasp above my head. "Let's go this way." He pulled me into the trees, away from the sleeping men. "I may not be able to see yer face in this infernal black, but it don't matter."

Shivers ran across my skin, and pain beat a dull rhythm in my temples. A memory of my training filtered through my mind. *Relax.* Inhaling, I forced myself to go slack in his arms. His grip loosened.

With a sharp twist to the side and away, I felt his hold break.

"What the—"

I danced back a step or two, trying to regain my balance. His form teetered for a moment before taking a thudding step forward into a sliver of moonlight. It revealed the scowl twisting his features.

"Come back 'ere," he growled, running forward.

Saya, not him. Saya—I've done this before. I brought my arms up and gripped my neck, elbows out in front as I stepped forward and rammed him. He grunted as the air left his lungs, and I grabbed his shoulder as my knee came up into his groin. The deep groan leaving his lips was cut short as I swept his leg out and shoved him backward to the ground.

I whirled and crashed through the bushes, fading into the shadows as heavy footsteps followed me. My breaths came in ragged gasps as branches whipped against my face. Everything looked the same in the dark forest, and all the bushes seemed to hide potential enemies. With every step I took, it seemed my pursuer gained on me. A half-sob tore itself from my throat, and I slowed and whirled behind a tree, hugging its trunk as I waited. The seconds ticked by as the enemy's footsteps faded and the distance widened.

I hurried in the opposite direction, no longer sure which way to go. The hair on the back of my neck tingled, and I glanced over my shoulder, but I couldn't see anything through the darkness. I swung my head forward—

Wham!

Tears stung my eyes, and I gripped my nose, my other hand reaching out to touch the rough, spiny bark of the tree I'd hit. I blinked, my vision shifting in and out.

In the silence of the forest, I turned to face the surrounding, looming trees. I was lost, with no idea if I was heading in the right direction. Helplessness clawed its way over me, dulling my senses and leaving me without clarity. My tears mingled with the anxiety I now couldn't shake. I'd been left behind. They probably hadn't even noticed I was missing. Pain constricted in my chest as anxiety wormed its way through my mind.

How am I going to get back? Reaching up, I brushed the hair out of my face. It came away wet with hot sweat. *Which way?* My heart hammered in my chest, my breathing too loud in the quiet stillness around me. I was alone. *This isn't the first time. I've been alone before.* A quick glimpse of the day I'd arrived ran through my mind's eye.

Here, not even a bird called; no chirp of an insect nor rustle of a small animal marred the disturbing silence. Pain filled my lungs as I gasped for air, blackness surging in at the corners of my vision as thoughts flew across my mind—wild and incoherent.

A soft rustle as of a footfall sounded behind me, and a sound escaped my lips. A small hand grabbed my arm, and I struggled out of its grasp as a voice—lighter, sweeter, and softer than that of the slaver—drifted over the short distance separating us.

"Juliet, it's me."

Relief washed over my body as hope flooded back in.

Saya.

"Come on." Her small, familiar shape moved away from me with quick strides. "We must hurry."

Chapter Twelve

Grass bent with a soft whisper from the many feet trampling it down as the townspeople passed. Saya and I glanced at one another and hurried our pace until we reached the stragglers. A stitch grew in my side, and I clasped a hand to it as I straightened and took in short breaths. My upper arms burned where the slaver had gripped as he'd hauled me further into the forest.

The trees grew more numerous, the foliage thickening above as we entered a small swatch. Almost no light from the full moon shone on us.

Every now and then Saya and I had to encourage people to keep going, keep walking; we had to put as much distance between us and the slavers as possible. The stronger carried the children, who had long since grown tired.

For the past mile or so, I had carried a little girl, her weight growing heavier on me and her hair a soft tickle against my cheek. Her breath issued in small, warm puffs of air. The slow thrum of her heart beat gently into my back, her head bumping against my neck as she dozed.

I peered over my shoulder, turning a little as I did so, but it was too dark to make out the trail we left behind.

How long before they come for us?

"I don't think they can make it much farther," Saya murmured, coming alongside me.

"Me neither. My legs feel a little numb."

Saya looked up at the sky. "It looks like it might be lightening a bit."

I followed her gaze. "How can you tell? The trees are blocking most of the sky."

She shrugged. "Just looks like it."

Within an hour, sure enough, a clear dawn approached. The first streaks of light filtered through the trees, driving away the horrors of the night. Feet laden with exhaustion tread the earth. Heads bowed, backs bent, shoulders drooping, we trudged on. With each step of the people in front of me, little bursts of dirt swirled up into the dull gray light that followed the heralding of day. I shifted the little girl up higher on my back, grunting as her weight settled back down. My thighs burned and my calves ached. The struggle to keep moving grew as my energy depleted. I peered forward. The light was too dim for my eyes to see through the shadowed forest to where the Unknown led the group.

Footsteps slowed, and people began splitting off from the path as they mingled amongst one another. As the trees thinned, I saw why. A steadily flowing stream divided the landscape before us, halting our progress. The water glittered in the morning brightness, but the beauty was marred as dissatisfied voices rose into the air.

"Now he's making us ford a stream," a short man muttered a few feet away from me.

An older woman sniffed. "We'll be dead before we get home."

"If he would just allow us to rest!" the man added, his dainty features coming down in a sharp 'V' as he scowled.

The voices ground into me, and my shoulder rose as I took in a deep breath. "Stop your complaints and muttering!" I exclaimed. "Think about what you're saying and how ungrateful you're being. You've been rescued from a life of slavery and are on your way back home, where you can reunite with your family. Isn't that what you want? We didn't have to come after you. We could've left you to the life you were about to begin." Seeing the shock radiating on the faces of the man and woman who had first spoken, and noticing their averted eyes, I lowered my voice. "I know you're tired, hurt, hungry, and want to rest. I do too, but we must make our way as far as possible before the slavers notice you're all gone. It will be a long journey back, but we can make it. I know it seems difficult, impossible even, but if you set your mind to it, I know you'll be fine. The Un—Shizukana—knows what is best. I trust him."

Saya nudged me, and my eyes widened as I realized every one of the rescued villagers now stood around me. She motioned over her shoulder with her eyes, and I turned to see the Unknown standing behind me.

"Let's move," he ordered without a hint of emotion, brushing past me to pause at the edge of the river.

I set the little girl down and pulled off my boots and socks before picking the girl back up. The water rippled as I dipped one foot in and pulled it back out with a grunt.

Freezing cold.

Gritting my teeth, I set my foot back in the water, followed by the other one. The slight current swirled about my bare ankles. I kept all my attention focused on the rocky riverbed, feeling for each treacherous step. Coated with a slimy substance, the rocks sometimes shifted beneath my weight, threatening each time to throw me off balance and send both of us into the cold water.

Little yelps alerted me every time I reached a critical point of unbalance. The girl's arms gripped my neck with strength I didn't know she possessed.

With relief, I stepped up onto the bank on the other side. I set the girl down, where she drew up her bony knees and rested her small chin on them. "Your mother will be here soon," I murmured, watching as the young woman crossed, her attention focused on the rocks beneath her.

My teeth chattered, and I leaned down to massage some feeling back into my numb feet as the girl's mother crossed and climbed up to join me.

"Thank you," she murmured, taking her daughter. My lips curved upward, and I nodded. I rolled my shoulders, listening to the small pops as the tension began leaving them. *She was heavy.* Not holding her anymore felt like the greatest burden had been lifted from me. I returned my gaze to the river where the rest of the townspeople struggled over. A woman slipped and fell, and I winced as her shriek rent the air. The Unknown traveled back and forth, helping the younger ones across or providing support to those too weary to balance themselves on the slimy rocks.

Wading into the shallows, I pulled my left sleeve high up on my bicep and laid an index finger on the bruises darkening into a deep blueish purple. Leaning over, I splashed water over the area and gasped. The cold acted as a natural numbing agent against the painful flaring of my sore muscles. I cupped my palm, letting the water slide over my skin, and brought the cool liquid up to my swollen bottom lip.

"Juliet—"

Yanking my sleeve down, I turned and stepped out of the water.

"Everyone is across," Saya observed, gesturing over her shoulder at the townspeople, most of whom sat down in small groups.

"They shouldn't sit." I grimaced. "I learned that the hard way with you."

A soft smile curved Saya's lips. She took a step closer and looked back the way we'd come. "Are you hurt?"

"Nothing that won't heal."

"He doesn't know what happened."

I watched a bird swoop across the surface of the water before flying up and into the trees on the far side. "He doesn't need to know. It was my mistake."

"How so?"

"I walked toward that man. I don't even know why I did it; I can't explain. In one brief second, I saw movement and turned toward it even as you disappeared into the foliage. I could've followed you none the wiser, instead—" I sighed and played with the hem of my tunic lying across my lap. "I remembered him, Saya. His voice. It was the same as the one that night during the raid. He was the one barking orders. I've never felt such terror before."

Saya squeezed my left arm, and I moaned.

She winced. "Sorry. Can I see?" At my nod, she rolled up the sleeve to reveal the bruises. Her eyes widened. "That looks painful."

"You don't say." Shrugging the sleeve back down, I smiled at her. "This was all worth it."

She grinned. "It was."

The Unknown stooped down next to us and handed my boots to me. "We should leave."

Saya stood up with an obvious burst of energy. "I'll go check on the others."

"They can't go on much longer," I murmured, sitting to lace up my boots with shaking fingers.

"I know," he replied, lifting a hand to stroke his jaw as I stood. "We must go a bit further, away from the river." He took a step closer to me and peered at my face.

I froze, watching as his tall frame leaned closer.

His fingers rose, hovering just in front of my lips before his hand dropped back to his side. "What happened?"

"One of the men—the leader—woke up..." I hesitated, shuddering. "It was my fault."

"Are you all right?" His hand rose again, and I couldn't help shrinking back, unsure of what he was going to do this time. My breath caught as his stare held my own.

His finger rested on my cheekbone, just below my eye. "That wasn't there before."

"Is it bruising?"

"A little."

His eyes hardened, and a muscle twitched in his neck. The green in his eyes blackened into such darkness and pain that I recoiled.

A light voice cleared her throat from behind us, and just like that he resumed his normal, controlled composure and turned around.

A woman stood there facing us. "I am grateful for everything you've done," she began. "But we cannot go on much farther."

"A little longer. We need to put as much distance as possible between us and them. Tell the others."

She nodded and turned away.

"You inspired them, you know."

My eyes widened. "Who?"

The Unknown turned back around to face me. "Your little speech. It rallied them."

"It was nothing."

"It helped them." He licked his lips and averted his eyes. "Thank you." He strode away.

He just thanked me. I watched him encourage the exhausted townspeople to their feet. *Maybe there is hope for us all after all.*

⁂

The sun had risen high in the sky when we stopped for rest. With no food, and the Unknown not wanting to risk a fire, everyone huddled together for warmth. Most slept fitfully.

Saya had woken me from my own restless slumber to take watch. I'd been torn from a dream, flashes of which still assailed me as I picked my way around sleeping bodies.

My family had been there; Cam had been there—a peaceful, comforting, happy time. But the memories faded, and the aches and pains filling my body reminded me that I had a different life, a life I may never see again.

Out of sight of everyone back at camp, I stopped, looking down the obvious trail we had left. With a series of pops, I stretched, the tension in my muscles releasing and sending relief into my exhausted body. The cool morning air smelled damp, and dark gray clouds collided high above. A breeze, stronger than it had been earlier, blew against my skin, bringing with it the fresh scents of dirt, leaves, and a faint smell of water, like fresh rainfall.

The bird calls sounded distant to my ears, my mind fuzzy as an hour passed and then another.

Brushwood rustled, and I glanced over my shoulder to see Saya appear through the trees.

"I brought you some food," she called. "We thought you'd be hungry."

My stomach growled. "Where did it come from?"

"Shizukana set some traps before going to sleep, and most of them were full when he checked a while ago." She shrugged. "I have to get back, though. We should be leaving soon; I'll send someone for you when it's time. You haven't seen or heard any pursuit, have you?"

I shook my head, my mouth full of meat, and watched Saya stride off toward the main encampment. Licking the juices off my fingers, I grimaced as my stomach growled. The few mouthfuls of meat had done nothing more than whet my appetite. With one arm behind me, I rotated my shoulder blade back.

The sharp crack of a stick reverberated through the forest.

I stopped, straining my ears, but nothing sounded again. The trees had grown silent. There was no birdsong, no noise of any kind. It was as if the forest was watching and waiting, but for what?

A muscle in my neck pulsed as I tensed. Thick, mottled shadows lay over everything. I took a step backward. The ground beneath my feet rolled, the leaves rustling as they bore the brunt of my weight. My other foot followed, and my heel sent a rock flying with a thump. I froze as the sound seemed to echo in the stillness.

Something was there, something that didn't belong.

I swallowed, my mouth sticky and dry. I turned, ready to make a dash back towards the others—but a dark, hooded form stood in front me, its cloak a familiar blend of browns and greens. The cry on my lips was bitten off as a sharp pain ricocheted through my temples and everything went black.

Chapter Thirteen

Excruciating pain rang through my head. I blinked, but everything was fuzzy. My heels bumped across the hard ground, and hard fingers dug into my armpits.

They must be warned.

I couldn't move. My limbs wouldn't respond to the signals I was sending. The figures around me focused in and out through a dream-like state; misty, the silhouettes blurred, never becoming clear but also never fading away.

Warned about what?

My eyelids closed and opened again.

The pounding in my head worsened, but my vision began to clear, the muddied images coming into greater focus. *So dark. Why...why...* I struggled to form coherent thoughts.

It was dark—no, the light of the moon was illuminating my surroundings to a certain extent. The blurred silhouette of a man's leg lay outlined in front of me.

"She's awake," a voice rumbled.

"You know what to do," another answered, harsh and commanding.

A gloved fist entered my peripheral, and searing pain shot through my head. Black filled my vision again.

⁂

Light filtered in bit by bit.

Water dripped down my face. I shivered in my drenched clothing and recoiled from the potent stench.

Warm, musty, leather—horse.

A soft nicker, trilling and short, came from the animal as though it had heard my thoughts. I opened my eyes, blinking as a splitting pain pierced my skull. It was as though a dozen icy spikes drove themselves through my head. Rain beat down over my body in heavy sheets. Something rough and hard pressed against my lips. I raised my unbound hands and pulled my head back. The pain broke a hundred-fold from the whiplash and tears streamed down my cheeks, mingling with the rain.

"Drink," a man ordered, his form fuzzy and swaying as he stood in front of me. He shoved a bottle against my lips. Gripping my hair, he wrenched my head up and away as he tipped the bottle. I choked, spluttering as the water ran down my throat, overflowing down my cheek and into my hair.

"Make sure she drinks enough. We don't want her dying."

"Not yet, anyway." The man holding the water grinned at me, his yellowed teeth glinting in the hazy darkness. He took the skin away and slid it into a saddlebag.

What happened?

The thoughts inside my mind were sluggish and incoherent. I craned my head, blinking back against the bright light. I was alone. *Where is everyone? I can't remember. A forest?* I blinked. *What was I just thinking?* I tried to catch onto my thought, but it disappeared. *It doesn't matter.* I shook my head, closing my eyes against the hammering inside my skull. *Why does everything hurt?*

"I got her good," the short man laughed. He leaned down in front of me and prodded my shoulder. His face went in and out of focus. I blinked.

"Put her back on the horse," the other voice answered, its owner out of sight. "Don't rough her up too much. We need her alive."

I know that voice. It's so familiar.

I struggled to hold onto the thought, but it slipped away.

⁂

When I came to, the pain had receded somewhat. From under half-closed eyes, I saw the shapes of two men standing a short distance away. The sun had risen high in the sky, its heat beating down on me.

It's not raining.

I peered down at my hands. There was something about them, something I knew I should realize. A creak of leather caused me to lift my gaze. Two figures, one tall and cloaked, the other short and squat, took care of a packhorse and stallion a short distance away.

Two men. I looked down at my hands again. My fingers moved, but the action was slow and difficult. I flexed one leg, then the other. They were heavy under my damp clothing, and my brain was dull. Thoughts drifted in and out like the *drip, drip* of ice melting.

I was taken. The realization hit me like a ton of bricks. My eyes widened and my heartbeat quickened. *Something hit me. I blacked out.* The two men continued in their work of rubbing down the horses, unmindful of me sitting a few yards away. The packhorse nickered, a familiar trilling sound. I'd heard it before.

How could this have happened? Mom warned me to always be aware of my surroundings, told me stories of women taken—how is it me? My hands trembled. *This isn't real.*

Leaves lay around me, their fall colors dulled by dirt from the heavy soaking they'd received. *I must get away.* I laid a hand on the tree behind me and pushed off it, staggering to my feet, my head pounding with the slow movement.

My hands, I realized. *They're not* bound. *They were...at some point.* Leaning against the tree, I steadied myself and glanced once again at the two men. They still busied themselves with the horses, unaware.

With halting footsteps, I stumbled away from them, the sound of every step ringing in my eardrums. My breaths grew short and ragged, my chest tight. I leaned against a tree, gasping for air as I pressed a hand to my side. It was like when I was a child. Eddie and I would play tag until I would collapse against the tree in our backyard, gasping for breath. But this wasn't tag with my little brother.

Something is wrong with me.

A heavy hand dropped onto my shoulder. I shrieked as he swung me around. "Didn't get far, now," he chuckled. His thick lips parted as he leered at me.

Why am I so slow? "What did you do to me?" I gasped.

"The water," the man responded with a grin.

"What about the water?"

"The water we gave you did this." Over his shoulder, I caught a glimpse of his hooded companion turning back.

Drugged.

"Yeah, right," I disagreed, staring at the ground swaying beneath me. "Water rejuvenates; it revives."

"Think you're smart? Come on." He pulled me forward so that I almost lost my balance and forced me to walk before him, propelling me along.

It took all my concentration to keep from falling. *I'm so weak.* "Who are you?"

He shoved me faster, forcing me to pick up my pace. If it wasn't for his hands on my shoulder and arm, I would've fallen.

"I'm impressed." His grasp tightened. "Most are knocked out from the dose we gave you. And ye're a small slip of a girl."

Seeing the hooded man standing next to the horses, I motioned toward him. "Who is he?"

"None of your business." He pushed me to the ground and handed me the skin of water. "Drink."

"What's his name?" I tried again, looking at the tall figure facing away from us.

"Bagu!" the hooded man exclaimed. "Hurry up."

Bagu.

Bagu slapped me on the side of the head. "Hurry up."

A strange name. I lifted the waterskin, angling away from Bagu as I did so. Tilting my head back, I let the water run over my cheek and down my shoulder and back before handing the empty skin back to him. He turned away, and I sighed with relief.

⁂

The smell hit me first. I didn't remember blacking out, but here I was, slumped over the back of Bagu's horse. I felt damp from the body heat seeping into me from the horse. The sun lowered toward the horizon, and the light no longer hurt my eyes. Although my mind felt clearer, the fog still hovered at the edge of my consciousness.

A familiar pressure filled my abdomen. I craned my neck and peered up at Bagu. "I need to pee."

His broad shoulders slumped, his silhouette sharper than it used to be. "Wait."

"No, I really have to go."

Not drinking the water is working. The drug is wearing off.

Bagu pulled the small, sturdy horse to a halt and grabbed me by the waist, swinging me to the ground. "Come on."

With a small gasp, I swayed and fell against the horse. Bagu planted me back on my feet with an annoyed grunt and gestured to the forest.

I looked down. *They tied my ankles together.* "My feet are bound," I noted, for my benefit as much as his.

Bagu peered at me, his beady eyes becoming even smaller. "What?"

"How do you expect me to walk?"

He grunted and leaned over to untie the rope around my ankles.

"Come on," he repeated, leading me a short ways into the forest. "Hurry up." Spittle followed his words, and a drop hit my face.

Raising a sleeve, I wiped it off, disgusted. "Can you undo my bonds?"

"No, you can make do. Now hurry up."

"Not until you turn around."

He huffed but did turn, crossing his arms. Using a tree as half a cover, I kept my eyes on him and hurried.

"You're pretty, you know."

My eyes snapped up, but he still faced away from me. *At any moment he could turn around.* I rushed, praying silently for him to remain facing the other direction. *Please.*

"But you don't have to worry," Bagu explained.

"Why?"

"We're under orders."

What? My ears perked. "Whose orders?" I pulled the tunic's hem back down over my pants.

"Wouldn't you like to know." Bagu laughed.

Who? Who wants me? I took a step closer. "Are you taking me to whoever gave the orders?"

"Yes."

I licked my dry lips. "Then there should be no reason I can't know."

"Bagu!" the stranger shouted, the word snapping through the trees.

Bagu turned around, and I cursed under my breath. His meaty hand grabbed my upper arm, and he dragged me toward the horse. My feet wouldn't cooperate with the speed at which he walked.

The stranger sat on his black stallion, his hood pulled low over his face. "There isn't much time," he snapped. "Get her on the horse."

Time for what?

I stared at him. *Where are they taking me?*

The stranger spurred his horse forward. "Hurry up, Bagu."

Bagu grabbed my shoulders and whirled me around before slinging me over the horse. Placing a foot in a stirrup, he mounted with a loud grunt. I moaned, shifting so that the rim of the saddle wasn't jabbing into my ribcage.

"Quiet." Bagu jabbed his booted heel into my side. I closed my eyes against the pain throbbing in my side.

He urged his mount forward, and my head slammed against the horse's flank.

Bagu reined in when we caught up to the hooded man. "How long before we stop?"

"Why?" The hooded man's voice was smooth and silky.

There is something so familiar about him.

"I'm hungry," Bagu muttered, tapping my thigh with his foot.

The other man snapped, "Will you stop talking if we eat?"

Bagu grunted.

"Very well."

I took in a deep breath as the horse stopped and Bagu swung his legs over and slid off. He pulled me down like a sack of potatoes. My knees buckled as my feet hit the ground, and I fell onto the damp ground, the impact aching in my side.

"I'm not undoing your bonds, so stay there if you can't stand," Bagu snapped. He took out a pouch and grabbed some dried meat out of it. With a quick gesture and a smirk, he asked, "Want some?"

I shook my head, but my stomach growled.

He grinned and tossed a hunk of bread over. I leaned over and picked it up from the ground, dusting the flecks of dirt and leaves off. The bread was crumbling and dry, almost disintegrating. Stuffing a piece into my mouth, I felt it soak up what moisture was left in my mouth and choked it down. I licked my dry lips.

"Eat." Bagu watched me, his brows furrowed.

"I'm not hungry."

"Eat," he growled, walking over to me.

"Why are we heading east? Away from the coast?"

His eyes narrowed in puzzlement. "You'll find out."

"You aren't with the raiders, are you?"

He grinned, his yellowed teeth flashing at me. "No."

"Who is giving you orders? What do you want with me?"

"Bagu," the stranger bit out, "she doesn't need to know anything."

Bagu glared at me. "Stop talking and eat." He forced the bread into my hands. "Chew."

I chewed and choked, crumbs flying out of my mouth.

"Give her water," the stranger ordered. "She needs more."

"Who are you?" I called out, peering around Bagu at the hooded man. I couldn't see his eyes, but somewhere under that shadowed hood I knew he was watching me. "You seem familiar."

"Do I?" He crossed his arms over his chest. "Perhaps we have met before."

"What's your name?"

The man strode to the horses, his long legs eating up the ground.

"Wait!" I yelled, but Bagu shoved the skin into my hands.

"Drink," he ordered. "Enough talking."

I hesitated. *Could I?* My mouth clenched at the thought of cool water sliding down my throat. *But it's drugged. I need to make it seem like I'm drinking it.* Raising the skin, I tilted my head to the side and held up a hand as though I had to scratch my nose. With the skin hidden behind my hand, I pretended to drink. The water dripped down my cheek and onto the ground. My heart continued to pound as the seconds ticked on by.

"Oh!" Bagu grunted. He slapped my head to the side and the waterskin flew out of my hand. I gasped, looking up to see him doubling before my eyes.

"She hasn't been drinking the water," the stranger snapped, his voice distant. "Fool!"

"I didn't see!" Bagu protested, cringing.

"She's been talking more, hasn't she?"

Bagu shrank back.

"Has she been questioning you?"

Bagu's silence was answer enough.

"I'll deal with you later." The stranger's voice was icy. "Be more careful."

Bagu grabbed my jaw, his fingers gripping like iron.

No, no! My vision blurred with pain, and I opened my mouth. He tipped the water down my throat, but I couldn't swallow fast enough. It spilled over my cheeks as I sputtered. His eyes hardened, and a gleam entered them. He stood up, glanced at the stranger, and kicked me hard in the ribs. I gasped, tears flowing down my cheeks, mingling with the water as he strode away. Curling into a ball, I watched through slitted eyes as the tears hit the dry earth, soaking into the ground with barely a trace.

"What did you do?" a voice asked, cold and hard as steel.

"Nothin'," Bagu muttered. "She's just angry, is all."

Nothing prepared me for this. Mom and Dad have no idea where I am, what's happening to me...please, someone, help me. I felt the familiar, dense darkness penetrate my mind. *Not again.* The tears renewed in a silent frenzy. I tasted salt on my lips. The drug pulled me from reality until all I could see were muted glimpses.

A horse. The ground passing beneath my feet. A tree.

Then no more.

⚘ ⚘

My eyes fluttered. I swallowed, my throat raw and swollen. My tongue flicked out over my lips, heavy and thick. *The effects of the drug*—the dull thought swam across my mind.

A wooden gate—a pair of legs—more legs swam through my blurry vision. Through the haze of my drug-induced stupor, I heard mutters filtering through the air as we passed. One man came just close enough for me to see the whites of his eyes as he looked down upon me.

Help me.

I moaned, but the man hurried on, avoiding my gaze. He wasn't the only one. Bagu and the stranger walked the horses by others, but they also turned away as though I was not there.

I tried to speak but couldn't get words past the gumminess in my mouth.

Something sharp and heavy drove into my side and I gasped, losing my breath as tears sprang to my eyes.

Bagu leaned down. "Not a word from you."

The horse stopped moving, and another kick from Bagu's boots caught me in the ribs. Everything hurt. Shifting my head to the side, I tried working the dry gag out of my mouth. My breaths came in hard and fast. A small grunt escaped my lips.

"Keep her quiet," the hooded one bit out.

"You heard him. Not a peep." Bagu gripped my chin in his hands, wrenching my head to the side with a jerk, before following the stranger into a dilapidated building, leaving me slung over the horse. Dizzy from the blood pooling in my head, I craned my neck to look around. Those standing there were few, their clothes dirty and torn, their faces devoid of emotion. They didn't lift a hand or say anything—just watched and waited. My eyes pleaded with them, but there was no response.

I sucked the last bit of moisture from my mouth. "Please," I whimpered.

The people turned away, leaving me alone.

The small horse nickered, and its tail whipped across my legs as it flicked back and forth. A few strands of my hair fell across my eyes, brushing the tip of my nose. I snorted, but they didn't move, no matter how much I wrinkled my nose and growled in frustration.

Someone...anyone... But it was a silent plea that no one would answer. *I have to get away.*

Tugging my wrists back and forth, I rubbed them against the coarse grain of the ropes, my eyes smarting as the skin was rubbed raw. A trickle of blood ran down my left hand, dripping onto the ground below my head. Tears slid down my cheeks, and my head fell back against the horse. I slid my face back and forth against the horse, gagging at the smell. The gag loosened, and I spat the thick material out of my mouth. Using my teeth, I gnawed at the rope binding my wrists.

A pair of feet came into my line of sight, and I froze, glancing up to see the hooded one standing before me.

Gripping my hair and heaving my head and upper body up, he spoke, his voice like silver, smooth and cold to the touch. His form wavered like liquid.

Why won't he hold still?

"Have I not given you enough warning?" His fist slammed into my ribcage.

A half-sob escaped my lips.

"Do. Not. Try. That. Again." He accentuated each word with another punch. My world was ending. The warm saltiness of blood filled my mouth, and my vision wavered. Waves of pain spread across my ribcage, pulsating and unending.

He slipped the gag back into my mouth, tightening it till I groaned from the pain. Gripping my wrists, his fingers pressed into the raw flesh. Fresh blood squeezed out, trickling down my arms. "Serves you right," he hissed, his voice distant as though I was listening underwater. "Don't cross me again." He let me fall back against the horse. "Bagu!" he roared. "Time to go."

Bagu ran out of the house, his knife unsheathed.

"We're leaving," the man interrupted. "Watch the girl. You fail again, and you won't survive."

I blinked, my head slack against the rough coat of the horse. *What was he going to say?* Even through my bleary state, I saw Bagu approach, a twisted scowl twisting his lips. He grabbed a fistful of my hair and stared into my eyes. He held up a knife and slid the tip of it across my cheek.

"You give me more trouble, and I'll make sure you regret it, darling," he snarled. He mounted, and I gasped as a searing pain pierced my side, crossing over my stomach and onto my back. I screamed.

A boot slammed into my temple, and oblivion welcomed me into her arms.

Chapter Fourteen

Time passed without a conscious thought. The drug-induced stupor holding me within its grasp so encompassed me that I did not care when water was forced down my throat. The time of day did not matter, nor even what day it was. I no longer felt the gnawing pains of hunger nor knew how long it had been since they had given me something to eat.

Numb. I tried to shift my feet. *Move.* Nothing happened. They wouldn't respond.

Footsteps approached and receded as I flickered in and out of consciousness, a gleam of light, a fire, then darkness.

My eyes fluttered open again, the fire a blurry haze in the night. The cold air cut against my skin as my head lolled to the side. I blinked heavy eyelids and saw two dark forms lying close to the fire. There, just in front of me, lay my own cloak.

My cloak.

I'd forgotten I'd even had a cloak.

Saya had given it to me.

A shiver wracked my body, and my head lulled to the side.

Crickets chirped and other bugs clicked, their cacophony of sounds keeping me company. I sniffed, closing my eyes against the pain throbbing in my head. The wind died down a little, easing the biting chill that had been wracking my body. Taking in a deep breath, I bit my lip, gasping as a sharp pain rent my side.

Lifting my fingers, I probed my right side, closing my eyes as I struggled to keep from crying out. The tunic was dry and caked with something, and I noticed a tear in the cloth. Tears streaming down my cheeks, I slid my finger through the opening in the material and closed my eyes against the searing pain.

Bagu's knife.

A vague memory of the sharp piercing pain that had burned through my side as we'd left the village...

It was him. He cut me.

Something touched my hand and I flicked my wrist, coming back to the present. A small, furry animal scampered over my elbow.

A rat. The thought flitted through my brain, my reaction too slow.

Another shape loomed behind me, throwing a shadow over the ground as dawn broke over the skyline. My jaw dropped as the shadow moved, and a gloved hand clamped over my mouth.

"Shh." The voice was a warm whisper in my ear.

I swallowed.

That voice.

A knife appeared, glinting as it cut through my ropes. The hand moved away from my face and slid down to my feet as the figure moved into view.

The Unknown.

Relief filled me, and the aches and pains faded.

With a feathery touch, his fingers grazed my hand, and he motioned upward. He took my cloak off the ground and secured it around me with a soft rustle. Taking his hands, I let him heave me to my feet. My head spun, and I felt myself falling to the side. The ground loomed before me at an alarming rate, but my fall stopped as strong arms caught me.

I clutched at him, staring around his arm at the two cloaked forms beyond. They lay still, unaware of what was happening. I blinked. The Unknown pulled me upright and let go. I swayed, struggling to stay balanced.

"Can you walk?" the Unknown whispered in my ear. I shook my head, my throat dry, and my limbs numb. He swung me into his arms and strode away from the campsite, the forest swallowing us whole. His muscles strained beneath his cloak and tunic.

I'm safe. I blinked and slipped my arm around his neck, my head lolling against his shoulder. His arms were like a cloud of comfort surrounding me with its strong embrace. *I'm safe.* The words replayed over and over. I closed my eyes, listening to the beat of his heart—a perfect, slow rhythm. *He came. He came for me.*

A new, soft voice issued from the darkness. "Juliet?"

"Saya!" I exclaimed, my voice hoarse.

She moved forward and peered at me. "Are you all right?"

"I will be." My lips curved up at the corners in a weak smile.

"Let's go," the Unknown whispered, leading the way to the two horses. One was large, black as night, and the other was small and round.

I recoiled, my breath hitching, my right-hand grabbing at the Unknown's tunic. "That's—"

"Shh, it's okay. I took their horses while they slept."

My hands shook as memories flooded through my mind. The shape of the horses there were so familiar. Bagu's packhorse—short and bulky—stamped its feet. *How many days did I lie slumped over that horse?* The smell hit me. *Bagu.* Sweat, potent body odor, the tang of blood in the air—my blood. The stallion had a familiar bow strapped to its saddle.

I leaned back. "Where are our horses?"

"We left them with the townspeople to use. They needed them."

"I can't—"

"Juliet," the Unknown murmured, his breath a warm puff of air against my ear. "You can do this. You're strong."

I shook my head, the words frozen on my lips, but he swung me up into the saddle before I could resist. Clutching the pommel, I gritted my teeth, my head buzzing.

"Relax," he whispered, looking up at me.

Relax, relax, relax, I chanted in my mind. The drug still pulled at me, and tears threatened to spill forth.

"Saya, take the other horse." He swung up behind me, reaching his arms around my torso to take the reins.

"We'll ride for a few hours. Dawn is here, and they'll wake up soon."

Exhaustion overrode the adrenaline, and the drug hampered my system and numbed me. Slumping back, I felt my head rest against the Unknown's shoulders even as his arms tightened around me, holding me upright. I didn't fall asleep, but neither was I awake. Instead, I swam in and out of a dreamy state.

We rode until the sun had risen and shone down upon us with a warm light. A stream wound through the trees to our left, the water clear and gentle. I sighed.

It looked so inviting. My eyes followed a bright red leaf as it swirled in the slow current.

Almost as if the Unknown had heard my thoughts, he pulled the horse to a halt at the water's edge. He dismounted and let the reins fall to the ground. Lifting a leg, I swung it over and dropped to the ground. I sank onto the long grass, the sunshine unable to warm my shivering body. Something hot and sticky trickled down my stomach and side. I placed a hand there. *I'm bleeding.* The dark blue fabric of the tunic hid the darker patch of blood pooling. I kept my hand there as though something itched my side.

"Go wash in the stream," the Unknown observed, looking down at me. "You'll feel better for it."

Saya knelt in front of me, her face soft, concern creasing her eyes at the corners.

"Come on," she whispered. "I'll help."

It wasn't until then I noticed the pack slung over her shoulder.

My pack. Fresh clothes.

She hoisted me to my feet, and I swayed, the landscape before me blurring.

"Come on, lean on me." Her voice was distant.

"I'm fine. Just tired." I swayed as I took one step and then another, supported by Saya's small form on my left, her arm wrapped around my upper back. My limbs trembled harder with each step, but we made it to the river.

"Do you want me to help you?" Saya asked, her eyes flickering at my clothes.

"No," I murmured. "Just give me time."

Saya's slight form swam before my eyes, sometimes melding into two or three of her. "Here," she muttered, taking hold of one of my feet. "I'll get these off you at least."

With a sharp pull, I was tugged back to earth as she removed one boot.

"There you go. Here are fresh clothes." She handed me the extra set from my pack.

I took the clothes, hesitating as I watched Saya sit down. She laid back, lacing her hands behind her head, and stared up at the sky. Sucking in a deep breath, I scooted down to the water and dipped my feet in, gasping from the piercing cold of the water swirling around my skin.

"Argh," I exclaimed. "It's freaking cold."

Saya didn't move. "Snowmelt. We *are* in the mountains."

"What?"

"The men who took you. They headed straight east, into the mountains."

The mountains? I stepped back onto the bank and pulled my shirt off and over my head, teeth clenching as my side seared with agony. *How much time passed?* I slipped my pants off and shuffled back into the stream. As the numbness spread over my feet, driving away the aches, I sighed. The farther I went, the colder it became. Rocks lined the riverbed, covered in moss and as slippery as an eel. More than once I sucked in a breath as I lost my balance, and my feet sought a footing on the rocks.

I reached the middle of the stream. It came no higher than my shoulders. Teeth chattering, I watched as a slight red hue swirled off my skin and flowed down the stream.

Numb from the biting cold and free from pain, I leaned back and finger-combed my hair, working out the knots and massaging all the dirt, sweat, and oils from my scalp.

When the cold became unbearable, I left the gentle stream. With shaking fingers, I washed the shirt I'd been wearing and tore it up. Using the strips, I wrapped them roughly around my side. I couldn't help gasps from escaping my lips or the tears from stinging my eyes. The pain burned. I looked to see if Saya had noticed, but she still lay farther up the riverbank, basking in the sun.

I eyed my boots lying next to me. I flexed my hands. Even if I could muster up the will to try and pick them up, I knew the boots wouldn't even make it off the ground.

"What is it?"

I jumped at Saya's voice.

"You've been staring at those boots." She stood over me, her hands on her hips.

"I'm—" I hesitated. "I'm bruised and am not sure I can bend over."

Her lips thinned as she clenched her jaw. She crouched down and maneuvered my foot into one of the boots. Black spots danced before my eyes as my torso jerked with the movement. Biting my lip, I fell back against the ground, staring up at the cloudless blue sky above as I fought the waves of pain and nausea sweeping over me.

"Alright," she grumbled. "Come on."

"Just leave me here for a bit."

"Come on," Saya pressed. "There's a fire going. Can't you smell it?"

Blinking, I sniffed, surprised to smell smoke and something gamey wafting through the air.

When had I last eaten?

Saya shifted beside me. "Juliet, come on, I'll help you."

"Saya," I muttered. "I truly cannot walk. My head is spinning."

She stood up. "What happened to you?"

I closed my eyes. *Everything. I was drugged, starved, beaten—*

"Juliet?"

"Not now, Saya. I'm so tired."

A faint patter of footsteps made me open my eyes. Saya disappeared up the bank and into the trees. I sighed and felt my eyelids flutter shut again, blocking out the bright sunlight that warmed my cold body as I lay in the soft grass bordering the stream. The warmth soon stopped the tremors wracking my body.

Before long, vibrations through the earth alerted me that someone was coming.

"Saya," I murmured, fighting against the drowsiness, "I really can't—"

I yelped, my eyes flying open as someone's arms slid underneath my legs and upper back. The Unknown loomed over me, tightening his hold as he lifted me off the ground.

"Let me down," I protested, lifting my head with effort. "I can walk."

He strode up the bank. "That's not what Saya says."

"I can—"

"Quiet," he ordered, but there was no malice.

He hasn't told me to be quiet in a long time. I stared at him unabashed, knowing his eyes were still trained straight ahead.

"You can barely lift your head. You're covered in bruises." His voice took on a softer tone. "Remember, it's not weakness to accept help from time to time."

"Do you ever tell that to yourself?"

He blinked and glanced down at me. His lips parted as though to speak, but Saya's voice interrupted further conversation.

"Set her down here." She stood next to my saddlebag.

A slight stab of pain lanced through me when he set me down on the ground. Relaxing back against the rough leather, I sighed, enjoying the peaceful calmness surrounding me. It was quiet. *Safe.* I closed my eyes, my mind drifting. The sound of the slow river provided a calming background as I listened to the sizzling of fat dripping into the fire. The soft sound of boots against the earth made me look up. Broad, green leaves in the trees above swaying in the slight breeze, acting as the perfect lullaby.

"Here." The Unknown handed me a bowl of the stew, and I sniffed as savory smells arose with the steam. I reached out, placing my hands around the bowl, but he didn't let go, his eyes staring at my shaking hands. A glimpse of red, raw skin peeked out from under my sleeve. He let go, and I nursed the bowl, sliding the sleeves back down to cover my chaffed wrists.

After a few bites, I set my bowl to the side.

"What's wrong with the food?" Saya mumbled around a mouthful of meat.

"Nothing," I protested, feeling my stomach gurgle. "It's delicious. I'm just full."

Saya raised an eyebrow before shrugging and continuing to eat.

The Unknown set his own bowl to the side, regarding me. He stroked his jaw, fingering the beard that had grown even more since last I saw him.

I forced myself to sit up straighter, to hide the pain I feared shone in my eyes. "What?"

"If he won't say it," Saya blurted, "I will. You look awful."

"I'm fine."

They exchanged glances.

"I'll be fine," I persisted. "How did you find me?"

Saya stretched her slender legs out in front of her. "You know how good he is. Found your trail quickly."

"So you left the villagers?" I leaned forward, biting my lip against the onslaught of throbbing over my whole body. "What if something happens to them?"

"They'll be fine. Seems the slavers were more interested in you than them."

"They're the priority," I mumbled.

"So are you. Your captors didn't try hiding their trail, so tracking you was easy. Whether it was arrogance or stupidity, it doesn't matter."

"Do you know who they are?" Saya asked. "I thought at first they may have been scouts, but that doesn't make sense. They didn't take you back to the coast."

The Unknown's eyebrows creased. "Did they say anything to you? Or did you overhear anything?"

"I—no, not really. All I heard was that they were short on time. One of the men's names was Bagu."

"How did you receive the wounds?"

I shivered at the icy anger lacing his tone. "I didn't listen, so I had to learn my lesson."

The Unknown squatted down next to me. "May I see them?"

I nodded, watching as he rolled up my sleeves to examine them with a gentle but firm grip.

Darkness swirled through his green eyes. "What else did they do to you?"

I blinked.

"Juliet—" He leaned forward. "Did those men assault you?"

"What? No! No, they didn't. What wounds I do have will heal. Someone wanted me unharmed...for the most part. They kept me drugged, so I don't remember a whole lot."

Saya's eyebrows rose, and her eyes widened. I twirled the hair lying over my shoulder with my fingers, feeling the intensity of the Unknown's gaze on me. Heat filled my cheeks, and I knew they were reddening. *I don't need their pity.* I survived. *I am none the worse for wear.*

"Did you hear any other names besides Bagu?"

I looked up at the Unknown, relief filling me as he and Saya turned their attention to who my captors were.

"No, none. The hooded one never gave his name. Bagu feared him, and I did too," I added after a moment. "He never showed his face, either. For that matter, they weren't part of the slave traders."

Saya stirred the coals of the fire before adding more wood onto it. "How do you know?"

"Because I asked."

Saya sat back down. "So who were they?"

"I don't know. They wouldn't tell me."

"I don't understand," she exclaimed. "Why you? What is so special about you?"

"Nothing," I protested.

"Except that you came through a portal from a different world," the Unknown pointed out.

"But no one knows that except the three of us."

The Unknown rose and went back to his bedroll. "Not anymore. They came purposefully for you, and the only thing that makes sense is they know where you come from. Someone must have come to know of it. I don't know how, but I doubt they'll give up on finding you either."

His brow furrowed, and his eyes grazed over my head. He was mere feet away, yet I felt he was much, much farther. Flames danced faintly across his distant, green stare. *Where is he right now?*

I cleared my throat and yawned. "I know. There's not much I can do about it, though."

"I won't let anything happen to you."

"There might not be anything you can do. Don't blame yourself for my own decisions."

He frowned and stood up. "Get some rest. We should leave soon."

I watched as he disappeared into the tall pines filling the forest. "What did I say?"

She shrugged. "Don't mind him. Try to get some sleep."

I nodded, tearing my gaze away from where he'd disappeared and closing my eyes. But no matter how many times I shifted, I couldn't find a comfortable position. Saya dozed by the fire, and the Unknown still hadn't returned. My thoughts were consumed with the nightmares of the past few days.

With a deep breath and a hand on my side, I got to my feet. I dropped my cloak on my bedroll and swayed, waiting for the dizziness to pass. Saya's still form lay by the fire, wrapped up in her own cloak. Step by shaking step, my boots crunched against the dry leaves and debris littering the forest floor.

He hadn't gone as far as I thought he would've, but I was still drenched in sweat when I fell with a sharp gasp beside him.

"Sat down too hard," I explained.

"You're sweating," he commented, peering at me.

My mind raced for an explanation. *The fire.* "I was too close to the fire. It was too hot."

It sounded weak, even to my own ears, but he returned his gaze to the valley stretching out below us. The forest lay in shadows, a void, oppressive and dark beneath the thick canopy. *Maybe this was all a mistake.* My throat tightened. *What if I never return home now? All because I wanted some freedom, some adventure—*

"What's on your mind?"

I glanced at the Unknown, his silhouette still. His chest rose a little as he breathed in and out. "Why do you think something is on my mind?"

"You've become quieter than normal. And you play with the hem of your shirt when you're concentrating."

I gaped at him. "I do not do that."

His head swiveled to look at me. "Yes, you do." He returned his gaze to the valley. "You can talk to me. I know how to keep secrets."

Yes, you do.

I took a deep breath. "I'm starting to think I should never have come. I suppose there was no way of avoiding it, but I shouldn't have left the town. I've endangered everyone."

"It's not your fault."

"But twice now I've put you and Saya in danger."

"We could never have known the alternative if you had stayed. The future is uncertain. None of us have the ability to see that far and thus make our decisions. We cannot know the results of our actions until they come to pass."

"Yes, but—"

"No, don't blame yourself. Juliet?"

I looked at him.

"Don't hold your emotions or feelings back."

Don't you?

I wanted to say it, but the words would not come. I watched the trees swaying in the distance as I murmured, "Part of me wishes I'd never come; another part is glad—"

"Am I interrupting?" Saya asked from behind us.

The Unknown swung his head forward.

"No, of course not," I reassured. Yet a pang of disappointment washed over me. The Unknown didn't move, his eyes focused on something far out below us. But all I saw was the dark green blanket of treetops covering the valley floor and sides.

The Unknown cleared his throat. "I think it's time you return home."

Home. A bug, its many legs splayed as it crept along the ground, drew my attention. *Say goodbye to my freedom?*

The Unknown's voice broke into my reverie.

"As long as you're here, they'll come after you. You would have to constantly watch your back and be on the run if you stayed. Besides, you have a family waiting for your return."

Mom and Dad...how long has it been now? I shut my eyes. A pang pierced my heart. *I miss them.*

"No excitement?" Saya probed. "What's wrong?"

My lips opened and closed.

"You're at war with something," the Unknown observed. "You're not ready to go."

I shrugged.

"You'll be able to see your parents again," Saya jumped in. "And your friend, Cam. This isn't your home, Juliet."

I rubbed my temples, which had begun to ache.

"Especially not now," the Unknown added, his voice deep and low. "It's too dangerous for you here. After what you experienced..."

A sharp pain pierced my side as memories of my captivity assailed my mind. I sucked in air.

A rough, calloused finger tapped my hand, which trembled. "You see now?" the Unknown whispered.

I hadn't forgotten, I wanted to say. *The pain and fear filling me, especially at night, don't allow me to forget.*

"Juliet?" Saya questioned.

The Unknown nudged me.

I looked at Saya, the concern written across her face. *I endanger them by staying.* "You're right. You both are. It's time I go home." The pit in my gut didn't disappear. It remained. *And when I return? What then?*

I bit my lip, watching as Saya rose.

"I'm going to get some sleep," she muttered, stalking off.

"She'll be fine," the Unknown reassured. "Just give her some time. She doesn't want you to leave even though she knows it's best." He inhaled, sitting up a little straighter, "What are you thinking now?"

"How things might be when I get back...how much has changed, and—" I hesitated.

"You won't know how it will be till you return," the Unknown interrupted. "Don't worry about that yet. Come on." He stood up. "We have a long day tomorrow."

"What's the plan?"

"We should catch up with the townsfolk and accompany them the rest of the way back. When we arrive at Umi no Machi, we'll try to find the portal, and if not that, then the woman who found you."

A small wave of dizziness washed over me. I leaned back against the sun-warmed moss. I cleared my throat, trying to concentrate on the Unknown's tall figure. "How long will that take?"

He brushed off the leaves that clung to his trousers as he answered, "It will take time to catch up with them. The men who took you traveled in the complete opposite direction of the town, toward the heart of this country."

He speaks of Ryujin as though he doesn't belong to it.

"We'll rest today and tonight, then leave." As he spoke, a heaviness descended over me.

I yawned. "Is that wise?"

"We'll have a better start well-rested," he answered. "The horses could use some rest as well..."

But the rest of his words were lost on me as my eyes closed and I drifted into a deep sleep.

Chapter Fifteen

I t was the shivering that woke me.

Dusk.

The sun had dropped below the tree line, and the trees dappled the ground with shadows cast by their branches. Staring upward with drowsy eyes, I shifted and hissed through my teeth from the pain. Tears sprang to my eyes as I rolled to my side and lifted myself away from the ground into a sitting position. I didn't have to look to know I was bleeding again.

A dark shape stood up and stepped out of a patch of shadow. "I didn't realize you were awake."

"Saya? What are you doing here?"

"Keeping watch. You fell asleep within minutes of the three of us talking about staying longer before continuing our journey. We didn't want to wake you, so we've been taking turns keeping watch while you slept."

"You should have woken me."

Her shoulders rose in a shrug. "Are you hungry?"

I nodded, taking her hands as she helped hoist me to my feet.

"Come on, then." She led the way back across the dry ground, the ferns pulling at our legs. A flicker of light from a fire beckoned to us with its pale gleam.

The Unknown stood as we approached and handed me a platter with food. As soon as I sat down, I angled my body away from Saya and the Unknown and examined my side. The blood had soaked through the shirt I'd been using as a bandage and now was seeping through my tunic.

Wiping the grimace from my face, I turned back towards my two companions. "You two get some sleep. I'll keep watch."

"Wake me for my turn," Saya mumbled, already stretching out next to the fire.

With a sharp intake of breath, I rose to my feet and ambled off out of the ring of firelight. It wasn't difficult to find the stream in the darkness. Once there, I rinsed out my tunic and the bandages on my side before replacing them. I shivered from the wet clothes, but they were all I had.

My silent companions lay by the fire, seemingly unaware of my excursion. I sat with my back against a nearby tree, tired but with a mind too active for me to give in to the fatigue filling my body. I knew I couldn't sleep through the pain and the dreams. They danced on the edge of my memory, out of focus and surreal. A hooded man—tall and cloaked—a low voice, hoarse and guttural. The slight bitterness of laced water lingered on my tongue.

I cringed, touching the bruises on my swollen side. The pain was almost unbearable, and it had taken most of my strength to hide it from Saya and the Unknown, but now I lay back against a tree, crying without a sign.

⟫⟫⟫ ⟪⟪⟪

Exhausted as I was, I felt no urge to sleep and was still awake when the Unknown stirred and walked over to join me.

"You've been awake a long time. You should go get some rest."

"Have I?" The dark horizon showed no sign of lightning. "Will dawn ever come?"

He didn't answer.

"I don't feel sleepy."

"You should try to sleep anyway. Tomorrow will be a long day."

"Perhaps."

"You can't ignore the nightmares. They'll only get worse if you don't sleep."

My eyes shot toward his face. "I—"

"We're heading to town after we meet up with the townsfolk, which should take two days at the most."

"Can I ask you something?"

"What is it?"

"Your name?" A hesitant smile curved my lips. "I don't know your name. I probably should've figured it out by now—or at least asked—but for some reason, 'the Unknown' just stuck. And I know I've called you 'the Unknown' a few times already."

A sound issued out of the darkness next to me.

It was laughter: a deep, throaty laugh. I stiffened in shock, a smile crossing my own face as I listened.

"Go rest. I'll keep watch." He touched me on the shoulder.

"Your name?"

"You don't give up, do you?" He helped me to my feet. "The villagers call me Shizukana."

"I know, but that's not your real name."

He looked down at me, a muscle in the side of his neck pulsing.

"Fine," I whispered, tearing my gaze away from his face. "But you can't keep expecting everyone else to open up to you when you never give anything in return. This works two ways, *Shizukana*."

His hand shot out and gripped my arm, pulling me back towards him. "Adnan. My name is Adnan." A note of defeat filled his voice. He turned away, but not before I saw pain filling his eyes.

Adnan. A tingle of warmth spread through me. I studied the outline of his face. The dark stubble that had used to line his jaw and cheeks had grown and was now more of a full beard, unkempt as it was. *Adnan,* I mused. *Maybe if he was less rugged and not so mysterious.*

He shifted back to face me. The pain was gone from his eyes, but the way his eyebrows drew forward was somehow plaintive.

"Hm, I think I like 'the Unknown' better."

He laughed, a rare sound. A smile crossed my own face. His laugh was catching.

"Thank you for telling me."

His laugh faded and he nodded. He pulled his cloak over his sword and wrapped it around himself. "Keep it between you and me."

"What about Saya?"

He sighed. "Shizukana is fine for her to use. Goodnight, Juliet."

"Juliet, you need to stretch," Saya remarked. "You're walking around as though you've turned into clay that's been baked in the oven."

"Maybe later."

"You'll feel better for it," she pressed.

"Later."

"Come on, follow my lead."

With a sigh, I leaned over toward my toes. Black clouded my vision, and I gasped from the sharp ache piercing my side. Eyes closed, I straightened and pressed my hand against my side. A warm dampness oozed through the material onto my skin.

"Juliet—"

I shook my head, focusing on staying upright even as the world swayed around me.

"What's wrong?"

I glanced up at the Unknown—I shook my head. *Adnan. His name is Adnan.* He stood before me, next to Saya, his hand stretched out as though to steady me.

"I'm fine," I whispered through pursed lips at his raised eyebrow. "It's just warm out, and I'm still weak from the lack of food and water."

"Sit down," he ordered. The soft moss cushioned my body, and I angled myself to the left to relieve some of the pressure in my right side. Sliding my hand through my hair, I looked up at the sky, trying to block out the numbing pain.

Adnan crossed his arms. "What haven't you told us?"

"It's just bruised," I murmured around clenched teeth, sitting up.

"Ribcage?"

I nodded, forcing myself to sit upright, despite the pain.

"It could be broken."

"Maybe," I admitted. "But it would just have to heal either way, right?"

Saya nodded. "Yes, but could I look at it? My mother was a healer and taught me some."

The pain seemed to increase tenfold the more I thought about whether to let Saya examine the wound I hid. *It's always there, even when I sleep.* My fingers curled. *And the bleeding hasn't completely stopped. I'm so tired. I don't have the energy to hide anymore.*

I nodded to Saya. "Sure, but you'll have to help me remove the cloak first." *She can help me.*

She knelt next to me and undid the clasp at my throat. Adnan stood, watching without a word as she removed my cloak.

"Juliet!" she gasped, revealing a dark stain covering my upper right side. "What is this?"

Before I could say a word, she pulled up my tunic to reveal the blood-soaked bandage I'd created from my old shirt.

"Juliet!" she snapped again, her voice ringing through the air. "How could you not have told us?" Her hands had already begun loosening the knot I'd tied in the cloth.

"I don't know. I suppose I just thought it would heal on its own."

The bandage fell away, and Saya's eyes widened. I followed her gaze to see the gash was even worse than before. The flesh was raw and inflamed, and mottled bruising covered both sides of my ribs.

"Here," Saya murmured, biting her lip. Her face had paled. "Let me help you lie down."

"That's a knife wound," Adnan observed, his tone icy. "Who?"

"Bagu," I replied as I watched Saya hurry away to her saddlebag. "He was angry with the hooded one and took it out on me. I hadn't realized until later that he'd even stabbed me because he knocked me out right after it happened. And I think the drug impaired my ability to think through things."

Adnan's lips thinned as his jaw locked. His eyes were stormy.

"Shizukana," Saya blurted out, kneeling back next to me. "Do you have anything to put on this?"

He nodded and handed her a small leather flask.

"This is going to hurt," she explained.

"What is—"

My side burned as though on fire.

I cried out and clenched my teeth so hard my jaw ached. Tears streaked down my cheeks as I stared up at the sky, my hands curled into fists at my sides.

Saya tore one of her shirts into strips and glared at me. "You stupid girl. Hopefully this isn't infected. And look at you. You're pale, weak as a kitten, and now that we know, you aren't even trying to hide it from us. You don't even realize that, do you?"

My lips parted, but she cut off anything I was about to say.

"I don't think it is infected, but it could've been. I can't believe you didn't tell us. I thought maybe there was bruising because of how you've been favoring your side, but this?"

Guilt lanced through me. I avoided Saya's penetrating gaze.

Wait—

She turned her face down, her hair falling forward, but I'd seen the wetness in her eyes.

"I'm sorry, Saya."

"You should be," she murmured, her voice raw. "Why didn't you tell me?"

"I think it was some stupid way of trying to prove myself."

"It *was* stupid," Adnan confirmed and muttered something under his breath.

I blinked, recoiling from the anger radiating from his tense posture and his green eyes.

Saya pressed her fingers over my sides. "I think you have at least one broken rib on your left side, but the bruising around the gash is probably just from the injury itself. Riding is going to be hell for you."

"It already has been," I whispered.

Saya stood and looked at Adnan. "She can't ride any more today. I'll go take care of the horses."

He nodded, still watching me with intent eyes as Saya walked away. I shifted under the intensity of his gaze. Guilt grew in the pit of my stomach. *He's right. I should've told them.* I tugged the hem of the tunic down over my thighs so that it lay straight across them. The disappointment spewing from Adnan was almost too much. Even when he'd just been the Unknown, he had never looked at me that way. *Cool indifference, maybe, but never with deep disappointment.*

"I'm sorry," I whispered, wishing I could replace the consternation in his face with one of respect. *Even his previous indifference would be better than this.*

He placed another large piece of wood on the fire. "For?"

I lowered my gaze, shrugging. "I should have told you both."

"You already apologized."

I blinked. "Yes, but I'm trying to help you understand. They drugged me, and I don't know, I didn't feel myself. I—"

"Partially that, and partially your damnable pride."

"What?"

"Your pride. You could have killed yourself if that had become infected." He gestured at my side, his anger boiling under the surface, fury filling his words.

"Why do you care so much?"

His eyes darkened in the shadows thrown across his face. "I don't."

My eyes narrowed as I tried to make out what I saw in the dim firelight on his face. Something had flickered across his brow, something gentle below the disappointment and rage. "You do care," I reiterated. "Why? I want to know."

He whirled around on his feet and strode off, calling over his shoulder, "Get some rest." He disappeared into the forest, his back ramrod straight, and didn't look back.

The moment I think he begins to open up, his shell snaps shut again, letting no one in.

⚜ ⚜

For three days we'd ridden at a slow pace, and even that was painful.

The Unknown sat behind me, his strong arms wrapped around me to hold the reins. "I don't like to see you hurting."

I opened my eyes but didn't turn to look at him. "I don't like it either. The Unknown—" Heat crept into my cheeks. "I mean—"

"Either is fine."

"I'm still getting used to it."

He glanced over his shoulder to where Saya rode behind us. "The Unknown is fine when she's around."

Adnan is still so foreign. I looked down at his hands holding the reins, so strong and yet gentle at times. *There's still so much I don't know about him. The Unknown just fits him still.*

"Listen," he murmured. "The townsfolk are just ahead."

I cocked my head to the side. Faint sounds of rustling of bodies and feet treading earth filtered through with the soft breeze.

"They haven't made great progress," he noted. "Hopefully we'll be able to speed them up a little."

"After all they've been through," I began, "you'd think they'd want to return to Umi no Machi as soon as possible."

The Unknown grunted in agreement.

"I can hear them!" Saya exclaimed, spurring her horse forward from where she'd been riding along behind us.

I cocked my head to the side, listening.

"Wait," the Unknown called to her.

Saya reined in her mount. "Why?"

"Shouldn't we warn them or something?" I inquired. "Won't you startle them if you just charge right in?"

Adnan nodded. "She's right."

"Fine, I'll just keep walking the horse, slow and steady."

"And we'll follow along right behind you," I replied with a cheerful smile.

"Come on," Adnan began. "Enough jabbering."

"But I thought you were the jay," Saya rejoined. A couple birds broke out into song as the last words left her mouth, and I struggled to hold down my laughter.

After one pained looked toward Saya, he called out, his voice loud above my head, "Jirou! Jirou!"

"Who?" I asked.

At the same time, a very deep voice replied, "Who calls?"

"Shizukana." Adnan adjusted his arms around me, the reins loose in his grasp, and murmured, "Jirou is one of the men from the town, and his voice is very distinctive."

A short man, his tunic sleeves rolled up to his elbows, stepped out into view. "Welcome back," he called as he walked down a small path that cut through the dense grove.

The Unknown swung off his horse, careful not to jostle me, and he followed Jirou in a short bow.

Jirou swept a quick glance over me. "You found her."

Adnan nodded and looked up at me. "I'm going to help you down," he murmured in a low voice as Jirou greeted Saya. I swung my leg over and grasped his shoulders as he placed his hands on my waist and swung me down off the horse.

Jirou inclined his head to me. "We are glad you are safe, Juliet Barrows." He glanced around at the people who'd flocked to us and drew the three of us away, ignoring the annoyed looks from the circle of curious bystanders. "Come on, we need to talk."

Trepidation filled me at the serious tone his voice had taken on. Following in the Unknown's shadow, we walked back a little way until we were out of earshot of the rest of the townspeople.

"Two men found us several hours ago," Jirou began. "They were asking some odd questions, which I suspect were about Juliet."

Bagu and the hooded stranger.

My hands shook. "They're looking for me, aren't they? I didn't realize I was so famous." I grinned despite the tension stiffening my body.

Three faces swung to look at me, two with a reprimanding seriousness and the other with puzzlement.

Heat flushed my cheeks. "Sorry, carry on."

Jirou cleared his throat. "Something was off about them. They claimed to be looking for someone in the king's name, a young woman, matching your description"—he nodded at me—"but they weren't dressed like the king's men. And one of them, he gave me the chills, he did, and never showed his face. He—" Jirou hesitated.

"What?" Adnan asked.

"He reminded me of you," Jirou exclaimed. "I thought he was you when they first rode up."

My jaw dropped as I gazed at Adnan.

He's right. I knew there had been something familiar about the hooded man. *The voice, the clothing, the long legs, the cowl pulled low over the face...*

A shiver wracked my body. *Why does he look different? He stands out from everyone else. Where is he from?*

"What do you mean?" Adnan's voice broke the silence.

"Well," Jirou hesitated. "He looked like you."

"That's it?"

Jirou blinked and cowered back a little. "His voice reminded me of yours a little. It took me a bit to realize it wasn't you. I may have called him Shizukana, and—and he responded to it as if it was his own name."

"Did you tell them about Juliet?"

An icy finger traced a line down my heart. I gasped as though I had become submerged in frigid water.

What if...

I took a step back from Adnan, struggling to take in air as I remembered the hooded stranger.

Adnan shot a quick glance at me.

Jirou continued on without noticing anything amiss. "I told them I didn't recognize the girl's description. I don't know that they believed me. I wouldn't put it past them to still be close by. You should take care."

"What did the other one look like?"

"He was gruff, small, burly, and thuggish-looking."

I perked up. "Was his name Bagu?"

Jirou turned to me with a grimace. "I don't know. Like I said, they gave no names. The other, the hooded one, there was something about him...something that didn't feel right. He carried himself with a certain air, had more command than the other. Gave me the shivers, he did."

"It's them," I murmured.

The Unknown held up a hand. "When exactly did you see them, and how long were they here for?"

"Early this morning, soon after sunrise. They stayed long enough to question and search us before leaving."

"Where did they go? Did you hear anything that could be of use?"

Jirou shook his head. "No, I am sorry to say. They didn't say a word other than attempting to extract information. I think at one moment, the rough man had been about to voice a thought out loud, but before he could say more than two words, the cloaked one cut him off. It was odd. They left in an easterly direction."

"Thank you, Jirou."

Jirou's eyes darkened as he took me in, and his jaw clenched. "What is it about her? What has she done?" He returned his gaze to the Unknown, but not before a flicker of fear contorted his features.

"Nothing. Whatever they want with her, she has done nothing to deserve it."

"Are they the ones that took her?"

"I think so. From your description, it sounds like them," Adnan replied.

Jirou stood close to the Unknown and lowered his voice. "I don't want her around my family and friends, not when she is being sought. No more trouble."

I knew he'd tried to hide his words, but I'd heard them all the same. My chest tightened. The air seemed to grow heavier, harder to take in, as I struggled against the pain filling me.

The Unknown glanced at me, sending a silent message to not say a word. "I will leave with Juliet and travel separately from you."

No.

"Maybe I should just travel by myself."

All three looked at me. Saya gaped, but Adnan didn't look surprised at my quiet outburst.

"No, I'm going with you," Adnan remarked, turning back to Jirou. "We'll leave now."

"I'm coming with you," Saya broke in, addressing Adnan.

He protested, "The townsfolk need someone to guide them, watch after them—"

"They'll be fine. Jirou is a good man. He'll be able to take care of them. Besides, they are a couple days' journey from home. Juliet is my friend. I'm not leaving."

I laid a hand on Saya's arm. "Thank you, Saya, but—"

"I'm coming," she affirmed. "Besides, things are never dull with you around."

"But—" I began.

"Very well," Adnan acknowledged. "Jirou, until we meet again."

Jirou bowed to the three of us. "Goodbye, and may the gods be with you all."

Chapter Sixteen

Two days later, we crested the rise and saw our first glimpse of the ocean in the far distance. Gray clouds lay overhead, and the air smelled of rain.

"There it is," Adnan murmured over my head.

Faint lights gleamed through the thin fog shrouding the coastline.

Umi no Machi. I straightened in my saddle. *Saya's vision—this is it.*

"Saya!"

The Unknown jerked as if startled behind me.

"Saya, it's just like your vision. You thought it meant we had failed in rescuing the townspeople, but we didn't!"

Saya's eyes widened in dawning comprehension. "By the gods..." She nudged her horse forward, her brows furrowed in concentration.

Adnan's breath tickled my ear. "You're tense. What is it?"

"Nothing." *Though your warm breath on my ear is distracting.* I leaned forward a little, furthering the gap between his body and mine.

"Does it have anything to do with the vision you and Saya are talking about?"

"No." I sighed. "It's just the pain, and I've been plagued by a headache most of the day."

"What else?"

I stared up at the blue sky. "Is it really time to go home?"

"It's time," he said, his voice gentle.

"You know I've been here for about a month now."

"Yes, it's been twenty-five days."

I shifted in the saddle, glad for the warmth Adnan provided against the slight chill in the air. "That's pretty exact." When he didn't answer, I continued, "So it must be approaching the middle of October then."

"Something's wrong," Saya muttered, sitting up straight. "We can't go into town."

"What do you mean?"

Saya blinked, her lashes brushing her cheek in a slow movement. "Someone is there who is looking for you. We can't go down there—at least, you can't."

"Very well," Adnan said, taking it all in stride as he had with every other thing that had happened to us. "Let's go straight to the portal. Juliet, tell me everything you remember about where it is."

"Wait a moment!" I exclaimed. "Saya, how do you know?"

"I can see glimpses. Two figures, searching for someone—that's about it."

I twisted my neck as I looked at Adnan over my shoulder. "Maybe we should go down there. We can find out who is really behind it all."

"It's not so simple," Saya snapped. "Have you already forgotten what happened to you? You don't know what could happen or what can change. That's not a good enough reason for you to stay. I think Shizukana is right. It's time for you to go home."

"But this might be the chance to find out what's going on."

Adnan shifted in the saddle behind me. "It's time."

"But what about you?" I asked, my heartbeat quickening.

"I think the threat to us will dissipate once you're gone," Adnan pointed out.

They're in danger because of me. My jaw clenched as I looked upon the distant town. *Because of me.* Exhaling, I blinked, my hands clenching into fists. *I couldn't save Eddie, I couldn't save myself, and now I keep putting them in danger.*

Adnan leaned down, his head brushing against my own. "Juliet."

I closed my eyes as I felt his warm breath blow against my ear. *It's because of me. Saya and Adnan have been here for me over and over again—I owe my life to them.*

"Stop," he commanded, yet still a low whisper. "It's our decision to be here. Don't try to control what is not yours to control. Where is the portal?"

I nodded, swallowing away my guilt and fear, and pointed. "I think it's a few miles that way, to the east. There were sparse trees and grass, long and wild growing everywhere, and there was an upside-down tree with its root system in the air. The trunk looked like it was underground."

Saya snorted. "What? That's ridiculous."

"But it's true," I insisted.

"I've never seen a tree like that," she muttered. "Trees don't grow—and can't survive—with their roots above ground. It's impossible, right?"

"I know, but that one can, and so can the one back home. I think I somehow fell through the roots and the trunk and ended up here. The two trees must be portals of some kind."

Saya looked askance. "I can't think of where you could have arrived…" she trailed off, looking for confirmation from the Unknown.

"Neither can I. It could be one of several places, but never have I seen a tree like the one you describe."

"There is one who could lead me there." I remembered the woman. Someone had led me to Umi no Machi. "Why not find the woman who first found me?"

"You don't even know her name," Saya stated.

I shook my head.

Adnan turned the horse to the left, toward where I had pointed. "Can you describe her?"

I nodded. "She was probably in her late twenties. She looked timeless, though, somehow, and she was beautiful. She had dark hair and large, brown, almond-shaped eyes with thick eyelashes."

"She doesn't sound like anyone from the town," Saya remarked.

"She looked regal, somehow," I added. "I think you would know if you'd seen her."

It struck me. Adnan—he didn't look like anyone else either. *Why him?* I glanced over my shoulder, taking in his dark hair that was several shades lighter than everyone else in this country, his deep bronze skin, which was far darker than the fairer skin tones of—

"Quiet," Saya ordered, pulling her horse to a halt. We all cocked our heads, listening. All I heard were the birds singing in the trees. I opened my mouth, but Saya held a finger up to her lips.

A branch snapped somewhere to our right.

Something flickered in the corner of my eye. Another flicker, and I saw them. Two men, treading with stealthy and careful movements, unaware of our presence. One did look our way, but they passed on without locating us—if it was us they looked for.

Saya's shoulders relaxed. "Did you see anyone?"

"A glimpse," Adnan responded. "Juliet?"

"They both wore the same clothing, with similar haircuts, actually." I concentrated. "Pants, jerkin, boots and tunics, all black. Looked like leather. They seemed to be looking for someone or something."

Adnan's body stiffened. "Sounds like the private guard."

"Who?"

"The king's men, his private guard."

"If the private guard are here, then they must be looking for Juliet," Saya exclaimed. "The king's men never come here; no one of importance does."

"What if those two men who took me work for the king, too?"

Adnan stroked his chin. "Jirou did say they asked in the king's name."

"But why me?"

Saya glanced at me and shrugged.

Adnan shifted in the saddle, his arms tensing around me. "Someone must have found out about you coming from another world."

"But how?"

"It just had to take the right person at the right time to overhear you telling either Saya or myself. Getting to the portal will be more difficult now with the king's men combing this area." He swore under his breath. "We'll wait for the cover of darkness. If they've confined their search to daylight, we can make our way safely southwest around the town." Adnan swung to the ground and waited while he held the reins.

I swung my leg over and gasped as pain stabbed through my ribcage. Placing a light hand over the stab wound, I grimaced. *You can do this.* I stared at the ground. It seemed so far away. The Unknown reached up to help me down.

"I think I can do it," I began, but he placed his hands on my waist anyway.

"You need to take it easy." He lowered me down and set me on my feet. "Let's get some sleep. We'll continue on at nightfall."

Sleep eluded me, and the pain in my sides did not abate long enough for me to relax and drift off. My nose crinkled as something wet splashed on my face. Opening my eyes, I reached up and felt more raindrops land on my palm.

Adnan sat with his back to a tree, his eyes distant.

I stood and walked over to sit next to him. "I can't sleep. Why don't you go and get some rest?"

"I won't be able to sleep either."

Silence settled between us. I shivered as the storm thickened.

"Pull your cloak closer around you and draw up your hood. It will help keep you warmer."

"Thank you," I murmured, feeling his shoulders and arm touch my own as I settled back against the same tree trunk. "Sometimes I feel like this is all a wild dream. It's almost unreal."

"But it is real. Everything you see and hear, everything that has happened to you, is real. Never forget that, hard as it may be at times."

I glanced up at him. "After this, I'll go home and never be able to tell anyone where I went or what I went through. If I did, I'd probably be sent to a mental asylum."

"Bitter much?"

"What? No, I mean—" I sighed. "All of this, how could I ever keep it all a secret? What excuse could I give them for what I've been doing?" Looking down with a dry chuckle, I asked, "What about me? How can I explain this?" I gestured to my side.

"Perhaps it doesn't work that way."

"And perhaps it does," I countered. "If I arrived here with everything I'd left with, why wouldn't I return in the same manner I am now?"

"That is something you can deal with when the time comes," Adnan murmured. "Do you miss your home?"

"Yes and no. Of course, I miss my family—and Cam. But everything we've been through...going through something like that changes a person. I'll miss both of you. And, this might sound terrible, but I'm not ready to leave," I admitted. "I feel like there is much more to experience and see, as though by leaving, I'll miss out on something I'll never know about unless I stay. It's something I'll wonder about for the rest of my life…but I miss my family at the same time. I miss home."

"You seem to be handling all this much better than most would."

I laughed. "Do I? There's only so much you can do to try to convince yourself you're in a dream or that everything is okay. I suppose once I realized there was nothing I could do, I just had to deal with it and take everything in stride. I'm not making much sense, am I?" I grinned.

"Not really."

I raised my eyebrows.

Adnan took a deep breath. "I'd imagine you'd be sick of this world—" He hesitated. "After what you've been through."

"I suppose if you'd told me what would happen and asked me before I came here, I would too. I don't think I would've come, given the choice. I would've laughed, thinking it all one big joke, no matter how much I may have daydreamed in the past."

It's not just me in this world. It's not just my pain. There are so many others besides me, so much hardship, and each has his own burden to bear. I squared my shoulders.

"I don't regret it." I grimaced, my eyebrows furrowing as I considered my words. *Striving after a goal with others, day after day, to save lives, even when hope seems lost…* I looked up at the Unknown, who watched me with his dark green eyes. "I did something that mattered. I can be very naïve—"

He lifted an eyebrow as though to say, *Really? I would never have guessed.*

I looked away at my hands lying folded in my lap. *But those two men…I want to forget them. Forget what happened at their hands.*

"Learn from the past. Don't bury it."

At the sound of his voice, I glanced up.

"You're not the same girl who slunk into town that first day."

"I'm not, am I?" It was phrased as a question, but I knew the answer. *I'd never be that girl again. She's gone.* I laid a hand on my side over the stab wound. It never stopped pulsing; even, now when I sat unmoving, it still throbbed.

"I've made that mistake over and over again. I can tell you better than anyone. Don't bury it all so often that you get to the point where you don't even know how to dig your way out." He leaned closer to me. "You're in more pain after the last three days of riding. Have you asked Saya to take a look?"

I shook my head. "No."

"You should." He nodded and returned his gaze to the water-drenched forest surrounding us, the rain drumming on the leaves and ground with a dull, soothing thrum.

I am hurting. I wrapped my cloak tighter around me. My lips parted, but the words wouldn't come. Warmth blossomed in my chest as I continued sitting next to him.

Why do I want to tell him all my complaints? All my aches and pains, hopes and fears?

Chapter Seventeen

"We should get moving." Adnan's voice jolted me awake.

"What?" I mumbled through the wide yawn threatening to crack my face in half. "I don't remember falling asleep."

"It didn't take you long."

My clothes were damp from where I'd lain against the earth, but everywhere else was dry. I struggled under the heavy folds lying on top of me and pushed them off. *Two cloaks.* "You gave me your cloak."

Adnan nodded. "You were shivering."

Saya strode up to join us, forestalling any more conversation as she demanded, "Why did you both let me sleep? I didn't take my turn." She placed her hands on her hips.

I handed Adnan back his cloak and flung mine over my shoulders. "Don't ask me."

"Both of you should eat," Adnan suggested as he stood. "We have a long night ahead of us. Besides, we can't have your stomach alerting everyone to our presence."

His eyes are puffy. Dark circles surrounded his eyes from the lack of sleep. "You've barely slept," I realized out loud.

"I didn't need to," he said with a sardonic twist to his voice. He poured some of the clear liquid from his waterskin onto his hands and splashed it against his face. Small droplets clung to his beard, glistening in the late afternoon light.

"I'm drenched," Saya complained. "Why are you in such a good mood?"

I eyed him. "And how are you still going?"

"Contrary to your beliefs," Adnan replied, "I am able to stay up for two days and a night and continue on the night after."

"I don't doubt," I murmured, adverting my eyes from his own piercing ones.

Saya cleared her throat. "We should get moving. It'll be dark soon."

She was right; the sun had dropped below the tree line, and deep shadows lay across the ground. I waited, watching Adnan and Saya prepare the horses.

When we left, there was no sign we had been there. The gentle staccato sound of the horses' hooves drumming against the earth reverberated through the air. Tension began filling my limbs, my body tightening with the anticipation of being found. *Any sound could be them.* My fingers curled and uncurled in my lap, and my eyes darted from shadow to shadow.

"Relax," the Unknown whispered into my ear.

I took a deep breath of the crisp night air. With each inhale, a little tightness left my body.

The way the Unknown had chosen led us in a varying direction around the town, sometimes nearing it, other times drawing back into the forests again. We were at the liberty of the rough terrain. Sometimes we were close enough to see the lantern lights brightening the darkness, gleaming from where they were placed throughout town. A hushed quietness stole over us, and I felt some more of the tension ease as I looked upon those little lights, so inviting and peaceful—

"Juliet," the Unknown said softly. "Explain again what you noticed between where you arrived and the town."

I cleared my throat, striving to bring my thoughts back into a semblance of order. "I think we walked in a pretty straight line from there towards the ocean. When we arrived at the edge of the forest, the dunes spread out before us, and the town lay ahead. I didn't notice any landmarks."

The Unknown mumbled something under his breath, brow furrowed in concentration.

"I grew up here, but I can't think of the spot she's talking about. I didn't go out much and explore when I was a child," Saya said from where she rode behind us.

"I might have an idea," Adnan mused. "Let's go."

Hours passed, and dawn had just begun to stretch pale orange fingers over the sky.

Adnan walked just ahead, holding the reins of the horse I rode on. "Hush, Juliet," he soothed. "It's just an animal."

I glared at him, watching as he stroked the horse's nose. "Are you calling the horse Juliet now?"

Adnan frowned. "No, I was talking to you. He can sense your nervousness."

Resisting the urge to snort my annoyance at him, I studied where we were, having paid scarce attention beforehand. Trees, their branches sparse and their trunks ill-formed, lay scattered here and there around us, with long, weed-infested grass thriving in abundance. Yet there, in a patch of moonlight, before the small circle of grass, lay the upside-down tree. Its roots stood up in the air, larger and wilder than I remembered.

I trembled, all signs of fatigue gone. *I'll be home soon.* I glanced at my companions, neither of whom seemed to have noticed the tree yet. *Will it work this time? Will the portal let me through?* I was so close to finding out. *Are they still looking for me? Have the police found any leads? Mom and Dad wouldn't have given up on me...they wouldn't.* I shook my head, trying to push aside the doubts rising within me. Soon, I'd be leaving this world behind.

I studied the back of Adnan's head, his hair grazing the top of his shoulders. My gaze traveled up and past him. *There.*

"There it is," I whispered.

Adnan stopped walking and peered around. "What?"

"It's even more amazing than I remember."

Saya also halted, standing on her tiptoes as she searched. "I just see trees. What are you looking at?"

"It's not just a tree!" I exclaimed, pointing. "It's upside-down. The trunk is down in the ground, and the entire root system is in the air, thriving. It's impossible, I know. The roots are healthy, enormous, growing—twisting up and around. This is what I found back in the redwoods and how I came to be here."

Saya glanced back at me. "I only see a normal tree, though a bit on the scrawny side."

Adnan froze and looked back at me, his eyes widening. "Only you can see it."

Saya's heels hit the ground. "How is that possible?"

"How is any of this possible?" I replied. The saddle creaked as I shifted.

"She has a point," Adnan stated.

Saya glared at him. "It doesn't explain why you can see the tree how it really looks, but we can't."

"Saya, what does it matter right now?" My chest tightened and my breathing grew harder. I swept my hair back over my shoulder and out of my face. *It's a portal, a portal that brought me here against my will. What does any of it matter other than going home?* My eyesight blurred. *Do I want to go home? Why is this so hard?* Drawing in air, I forced the shakiness away from my tone. "I'm supposed to go home, and none of us ever see each other again, and we're arguing over who can see the tree?"

Saya nodded. "You're right. I'm sorry. What do we do now?"

Adnan resumed walking. "Juliet, tell us where to go."

"Keep walking straight ahead," I instructed. "We're nearly there." My heart rate rose as we neared the tree and the memories resurfaced. "Stop. We're here."

Adnan swung me down. "I just see a normal tree in front of us. A weirdly shaped tree, but still a tree."

I walked around the base of the tree and saw an opening in the roots.

There it is.

Turning, I gestured over my shoulder. "The opening is behind me. I don't know if this will work, but I'll try everything I can to open the portal."

Adnan stepped forward. "I'll come with you."

My heart pounded. "If you'd like."

He doesn't need my approval. And it wasn't a question.

"It's time to say goodbye," I murmured, looking at Saya.

Her brown eyes widened, and she frowned. "I'll miss you, Juliet Barrows. I needed a friend, and you have been the best I could ever ask for." She hugged me, her head turned away against my upper arm.

Why is this harder than I thought it would be? I sniffed. "I'll miss you too. I wish—"

"Shh." She stepped back and smiled. "Don't. Safe travels, Juliet."

"You too." I turned around, staring at the darkness before me, unable to see anything but the shadowed silhouettes of curled and twisted roots.

One foot in front of the other.

The awning did not beckon as it had a month ago, when I'd stood among the redwoods and stared in awe at the phenomenon. The same faint light drove back the darkness in the skies above, but this time it did nothing to drive back the darkness before me.

A shiver ran over my skin as I stepped forward. In the opening, I hesitated, glancing over my shoulder back at Saya.

She smiled past the tears in her eyes and bowed. When she came back up, she held up a hand. "The gods be with you, Juliet. Maybe one day we'll see one another again."

I nodded and looked at the Unknown.

"It's time," he murmured.

"You two! Halt!" The voice rang out across the glade, harsh and commanding.

"Hell's teeth!" the Unknown bit out. "Go!"

I took one more step into the mass of roots and froze, watching as a small group of men advanced on my companions. There was no time. The horses lay a few yards away. We'd left them when we'd navigated through the reaching tendrils of the roots.

Saya and the Unknown walked forward, away from me, as the men approached.

"Juliet, hurry," Adnan called over his shoulder in a soft hiss. "We'll fare better without you here; they haven't seen you yet."

I couldn't move; my limbs wouldn't respond.

"Where is she?"

A cricket chirped in the background, high and reedy.

"Answer the question. Where is she?" the man demanded.

My heart thudded in my chest, too loud in my dark hiding place. *He told me to hurry.*

"I am not sure who you're talking about. I've not seen another soul tonight," Adnan answered.

My stomach dropped, my gaze flying to the man interrogating him. *Leave.*

"You know of whom I speak. We want the Otherworlder."

Adnan's hand didn't leave the hilt of his sword. "Who?"

"Enough pretending. We need her, and you know where she is." With each word, the man's voice grew more impatient.

I blinked. Sweat beaded on my face. *But what can I do?* The sole sound of leaves whispered in the wind, rustling through the air as I waited with bated breath.

"Fine, we'll soon find out. Take them." The man snapped his fingers, and his men surged forward, surrounding Saya and Adnan. "We'll get what we want."

No, no, no! I watched, my mouth open in a silent protest as the men forced Saya and Adnan to their knees and tied their wrists behind their backs.

The man stood over them, saying nothing as two of his men held their knives to my companions' throats. "Last chance."

Neither of my companions said anything.

"Let's move." The leader nodded to his men, who gagged Adnan and Saya.

Eleven years ago I did nothing, and someone died—my brother died. I can't do nothing again. I stood. *They want me, not them.* "No!" I cried. "I'm here!"

"What was that?" someone shouted. "A ghost!"

"She's here," their leader, a slender man of average height, announced, a note of satisfaction in his voice. His hand reached down, slipping an object out from his belt—something that gleamed. He walked toward Saya.

I stepped out from the tree and tripped, falling hard on one knee. My head spun. Pulling myself to my feet, ignoring the dampness seeping into my shirt. "Stop! Let them go. I'm the one you want."

The man who had given an alarmed shout took a step back. "She's right there," he babbled. "How did she do that? There's nowhere to hide. She just appeared. Is she a witch?"

The rest of the group began muttering under their breath.

"Markai, enough!" the leader barked.

"We should leave, leave this place, and leave her alone. We'll die, we'll all die—she'll kill us with her magic," Markai continued.

"Markai!"

The man shut his mouth but still looked uncertain.

"I am not a witch," I reassured, holding up my hands. "Please let them go, and I'll go with you."

The leader laughed. "No, we have orders to bring you in, but we'll bring your friends along, as well. What's a few more?"

"Let them go first, and I'll come with you, no trouble."

"I don't think you're in a position to make a demand like that." He looked at his men. "Markai," he snapped and waved a hand toward me.

The one who had called me a witch started forward with hesitant strides. I backed up near the Unknown and Saya, who both watched but were unable to say anything through the gags in their mouths. But I could see it in their eyes.

Run.

The tree was just behind me. I could still make it. It was so close. I looked back at Adnan and Saya. The darkness and distance hid their eyes from me but not their postures as they leaned forward as though to help me. '*Neither of you knows what lies out there…or who.*' Adnan's words replayed in my head. '*You'll just have to trust me.*' I steeled myself and faced the men approaching me. *It's his turn to trust me. It's my decision—*

Heavy hands pulled my arms behind my back. A searing pain shot through my side. I moaned. It felt as though my wound had torn back open. A man laced my wrists together, jerking me almost off balance. The leather bit into my still-healing skin. Another man, his long black hair falling over his shoulder, laid a hand on my forearm and pulled me toward Saya and Adnan.

"Down!" he ordered and shoved me. My knees jarred as I hit the ground.

"Search them," their leader ordered. The man with long hair crouched down in front of me, his eyes focused. He reached forward. *I have nothing to hide.* I stared past him as he searched first me, and then Saya. He hesitated before reaching for the Unknown.

My eyes widened. *His weapons. Maybe they won't find them all.* My heart beat faster as I watched.

With a sharp hiss, the man pulled the knife out of the scabbard Adnan kept at his low back. Then the knife in his left boot. His hands slid over Adnan's bound arms. My eyes widened as he pulled out a small, curved knife attached to the inside of Adnan's wrist. The man stood and laid the knife on the ground next to the others.

"Check his tunic, under his belt," their leader barked.

Something glinted in the moonlight.

"There are three *shuriken*." He held up three small circular objects.

My eyes narrowed as I peered at the tiny metal object glinting in the moonlight. *Throwing stars.* I strained against my bonds as I watched. *What else does he have?*

"Put them with the sword and bow."

"That makes seven weapons, seven!" Markai blurted out, eyes wide. "Daimyo—"

"Quiet. Get them to their feet. We're moving out."

Markai shrank back, as though wanting distance between him and Adnan. *He said seven weapons...that's a lot, but why the reaction? The seven weapons mean something—*

Markai's rough hands hauled me to my feet.

"What about our horses?"

The leader glanced from the animals to me. "They will be taken to one of our hideouts. We're traveling on foot."

Adnan stiffened.

His weapons. I looked back and forth between the horse and Adnan. Licking my lips, I blurted out, "And the weapons?"

Ko stroked his beardless jaw as he considered. "You and you—" He pointed to two men. "Take the weapons. We'll bring them with us." He strode off, leading the way. A small knot of men fell in around us. As we walked, I realized there were other men in the shadows of the trees. Glimmers of a silhouette, rustles as they moved, glimpses of those who walked in the darkness.

Adnan jostled me, and I looked up at him. Muffled sounds filtered through the gag around his mouth.

I shook my head. "I can't understand you," I whispered. He shrugged, unable to say anything through the gag.

Saya mumbled through her gag, but the words were unintelligible. She shook her head in annoyance.

❦

My side continued to seep wet blood as we journeyed; the cut had reopened from my fall. The hairs on my arms stood on end, and my heartbeat quickened.

Do these men work for the same person that my first captors do? Why do they want me? My imagination grew wilder as mile after slow mile passed beneath my feet. *What do they know about me? I'm not valuable. I'm not even from here.* I walked but did not see where I was going. Everything in the real world became blocked. I couldn't hear; I couldn't process anything in my surroundings. *I should never have come.* My parents' faces filled my vision, beautiful and caring. A knot of homesickness grew in the pit of my stomach. This was all my fault. *Maybe I should never have told anyone who I was.*

Something brushed against my side, and I snapped out of the prison my mind had placed me in. The Unknown walked close beside me, looking down, eyes glinting with reassurance. I smiled, blinking back the tears and focusing on breathing as I ignored the ache in my throat.

Be strong.

His eyes told me what I already knew. *Don't lose hope. This is not the end.*

"Daimyo Ko," Markai began, shooting a quick glance at me over his shoulder. He lowered his voice so I couldn't hear the rest.

Daimyo...is that some sort of rank? My eyes widened. *Are they with the king?*

"Back to your position, Markai," Ko barked.

He must be the leader. He's been the one giving the orders.

"Daimyo Ko," I called out, my voice quivering. I cleared my throat and repeated, "Daimyo Ko!"

The man didn't turn or acknowledge me.

"Where are we headed?"

"You'll find out when you get there."

I forged ahead, ignoring the warning glance Adnan sent my way. "Who are you taking us to?"

"You'll find out when you get there."

"The king?"

Markai spat on the ground.

"You'll find out when you get there."

I didn't miss the warning glare Ko shot Markai.

"Why do you want me?"

"You'll find out when you get there."

"Seriously!" I grunted with annoyance. "May we not know anything?"

Silence.

"Are you taking us to the king?"

Markai, who walked next to me, gave a start, his eyes darting to Daimyo Ko.

I followed his gaze. "I'll assume that is a yes. Firstly, I'm wondering why in the world three small-town locals, who have never seen or done anything spectacular, would come to the interest of the king."

Ko grunted, his disbelief evident. "Otherworlder, you have come to be of interest to more than one person."

I blinked in surprise. *They called me that before.* I widened my eyes. "Otherworlder? What are you talking about? You think someone has come over here from another world? But"—I pretended to be incredulous—"that's impossible."

"Not anymore. You know that very well."

"Even if someone did, why do you think it's me?"

"I've had enough of this banter. We know you're from another world; nothing you can say will change that. Suffice it to say, I will not tell you how I nor my leader knows, but know that we do. You would be wise to stop trying my patience."

"I—ouch." I grunted as Adnan butted me with his elbow. I hissed, "I probably have a bruise now with how many times you've done that."

Be careful, his eyes responded.

He's right. I'm being a fool. My lips compressed together, and I grunted as I tripped over a sharp object in the pale morning light, falling flat on my face. Pain streaked across my torso, and I gasped as large hands wrapped themselves around my arms and hauled me back up. I stared straight into the eyes of Ko, his angry face mere inches away.

"If—you—say—one," he paused, seeming to collect himself, "more word, I swear you will not like it. Do you want to walk, gagged, like your companions?"

"No."

"Speak up."

"No," I stated.

"I thought so."

"Why—" I clenched my jaw shut, eyes wide.

One more word.

He hesitated.

Was that admiration?

He blinked and the glint in his eyes disappeared. A long sigh escaped his lips. "What were you going to ask?"

I searched his face and licked my lips.

He nodded for me to go on with an air of resignation.

"Why did you gag them but not me?"

His eyes flashed, but he turned away without a word. The Unknown brushed against me again.

"I wasn't going to say anything else," I hissed, but he just raised an eyebrow.

⚜

Another day and night passed by with another rising and falling of the sun. We continued walking northeast. Forests upon endless forests passed us by with varying shades of green—sometimes we traversed flat ground, other times with more slopes than I wanted to count. I was tired of the trees. My feet ached, my ribs ached...even the soft grass under my boots felt hard. The weather was growing colder and damper, and even my cloak didn't keep out a pervading chill that continued to worsen.

Ko had elected another man to guard me in place of Markai, as he would not stop muttering and complaining about being so close to a witch. Now he just did it from afar. Otherwise, our guards were our silent companions and hardly spoke.

"I think they'll be stopping soon," I murmured to my companions, not waiting for a response. While I continued to remain without a gag, theirs were only taken off for food and water. And there was little food to be had. Dried meat, dried seaweed, dried fruit... I sighed, and my stomach growled as I swallowed the last bite.

It was another hour before the Daimyo called for a halt. My feet dragged, and my breathing was shallow. I lay down on the ground, unmindful of the damp leaves and dirt entangling themselves in my cloak and my hair. I closed my eyes, listening to the footsteps of someone approaching.

Ko removed the bindings on our wrists and handed us each some more of the same food, but this time with a small, hard rice ball and a waterskin. "Hurry up and eat. We won't be here long."

I watched as Saya wolfed hers down. "Saya?"

She raised an eyebrow as she finished off the rice ball.

"Have you seen anything that might help us?"

The small lines around her eyes deepened. She shook her head. "No, I haven't."

"Have you tried?"

"No, not really." She laid back and closed her eyes. I looked down, fighting waves of exhaustion and pain. My stomach turned at the sight of the small pile of food lying on my lap.

"Here," I murmured, handing my food to Adnan, but he made no move to take it. "Eat," I urged, fighting back a yawn. I swallowed against the nausea.

"No, you need it."

"I'm too tired. I'd rather just close my eyes for a few minutes."

"You should eat, Juliet." When I didn't respond, I felt him take the food from my hand. I smiled and rested my arms at my sides.

"I'm not sure where we're headed," Adnan noted. "At first, we journeyed east toward the palace, but we've been traveling along a different course all day. I'm stumped as to the destination."

"Some fortress of the king's?" Saya suggested, opening her eyes.

"I don't know." Adnan stroked his chin. "But I have a feeling we'll find out soon."

"We'd better be close," I murmured. "I'm honestly not sure how much longer I can keep going."

"I know." Adnan shifted before brushing the palms of his hands over his pants.

"Is it that obvious? Actually, don't answer that." I grinned. "I'm trying, and—and I'm afraid of what's ahead, but at the same time I want it over with."

"I know what you mean," Saya agreed, frowning.

I turned my head to look at her. "What is it?"

"You know," she declared, "I think curiosity might someday be your downfall."

I laughed. "Perhaps, but it can also be a good thing."

"Wariness is, too," Adnan interrupted.

With a shrug, I brushed him off. "What's on your mind?"

"I'm not sure," Saya began. "I've been thinking about it on and off, but it might not be important. Never mind."

"Saya, we're in this together. Don't be afraid to say what's on your mind," I repeated.

She scooted a little closer and glanced around before opening her lips. "You're being treated differently from us, as though at great lengths to pamper you. And they're not treating you the same as the two men who took you before. I don't think they work for the same person. There is something strange about—"

I snorted and shifted my head over into a more comfortable position. "That's obvious."

"Juliet," Adnan warned.

I lowered my eyes. "I'm sorry. I don't mean to pass off what you're saying, but what is normal about any of this?"

"Something is different. It feels odd. We've not been badly treated—"

"So, what?" I replied. "Are we supposed to be? No, don't listen to me—I see your point. There must be orders not to harm us."

"There's nothing we can do right now," Adnan murmured as he stroked his bearded jaw. "Be patient, watch, and wait. Stay strong. Don't let them break you down." He went silent as Ko walked up to us.

He leaned down and, one by one, retied our wrists. "Get some sleep. We have one day left."

One more day.

"Good, because I don't think I could move," I mumbled around a yawn.

"Both of you, get some rest," Adnan ordered.

I closed my eyes and focused on breathing to calm my body down. *In for four, hold for eight, out for three.*

As my mind and body grew drowsy, I felt someone tuck my cloak close around me.

Chapter Eighteen

C old, musty air seeped through the heavy cloak trapping my limbs. A single candle burned on a circular table, emitting a small glow of light.

I sat up, and Ko loomed over me.

"Where am I?"

"Calm down," he reassured, laying a hand on my shoulder.

The room was empty but for us.

Wait, a forest. We were in a forest...

I struggled to get out of the blankets entrapping me. "Where am I? Where are the Unknown and Saya? What have you done with them?"

"Calm down, girl. I haven't done anything with them."

Free at last from the cloak, I sprang up, fighting the onslaught of panic. Clutching my head, I reeled, leaning against the wall for support. What seemed to be memories in the form of dreams flitted through my head—a forest—my captors—Adnan, Saya. The motion of being carried, and now here.

A small room, dark except for the light from the candle. The earthy smell of dirt pervaded my senses. Ko watched me, his face cryptic, his arms crossed over his chest.

A door was just there, mere feet in front of me. *Go! It's so close!* I lunged forward, but before I could even land, Ko slammed me back on the bed. The mattress slid, and my head hit the wooden slats of the cot before bouncing back up, sending shockwaves down my neck and spine. Vision blurring, I began slipping under, listening to Ko's voice from down a distant tunnel.

"Why won't you listen? You have no patience!"

My head lolled, and my eyes closed.

"Oh, no you don't."

I gasped as something wet and icy was thrown in my face.

"That's better. Now come, there is someone waiting whom you must meet."

"First answer my question," I sputtered, struggling to recall my fleeting thoughts.

Ko folded his arms. "You're in no position to make demands."

"Quite right. But I can make your life a living hell trying to get me wherever you want me to go."

He sighed and waved a hand.

"Where are the Unknown and Saya?"

"They're on their way as I speak. We brought you on ahead. Now come." He hauled me to my feet, and my head spun.

I blinked, and the walls stopped spinning and came into focus a little. "Why—?"

"No more questions. You said *one*." He led me outside of the room into what seemed like a narrow corridor. As we walked, shadows flickered on the rough walls from the candle Ko held. The light from the candle lit but a foot or so on either side of us, and the rest lay in darkness. I stumbled on the uneven floor. *Pay attention.* Rock protrusions stuck up from the floor, which rose and fell without rhythm. And it was cold. The brisk air I breathed in was stale. Our footsteps made soft thuds upon the floor, and an eerie silence seemed to follow us.

Where are we? I ran my fingers along the wall and the rough irregularities, wondering at the dry cold that seeped through my skin. *Somewhere underground.* I shivered at the cold draft running through the corridor. *Deep underground.* I focused on my footing as the ground grew more treacherous as it sloped down.

Ko doesn't act like the two men who took me. He couldn't be with them. The truth of the thought seeped into my heart. *Nor could it be the king. He wouldn't live here.*

Ko gripped my arm harder as my toe caught an indent in the rock. "Careful."

"Where are we?" I asked aloud, the echoes of the question thrown back at me.

"You'll find out."

Pain grew in my temples, and I struggled to keep my head clear. My foot caught on the floor, throwing me against the wall. I flung out a hand to break my fall and bit back a gasp as something sharp pierced my skin. I glanced down. A small rivulet of sticky, wet blood ran down my palm and onto my fingers.

Ko prodded me forward. "Hurry."

As I followed, I ripped off a piece of material from the bottom of my tunic and tied it around my hand, wincing at the sting of the dirty fabric touching the open wound.

Ko stopped in front of me. "Here."

A large door stood before us, hewn into the wall. I swayed as Ko walked forward and rapped on the door with a strange sequence of taps. After a moment, the door opened with a grating rasp.

The man just inside eyed me with suspicion. "Is this her?"

Ko ignored the question. "Is he here?"

"Yes," the guard responded.

"And the others?"

"They'll be here soon."

"Very well, we'll wait." Ko laid a hand on my shoulder and led me into the brighter antechamber beyond. The bolt slid shut behind us as the guard secured the door.

I sank into the closest chair, one of several arranged about the room. My head buzzed and I blinked several times, squinting against the blurriness at the edges of my vision. Ko and the guard muttered to each other, their voices a low drone in the background.

A set of double doors in the far wall heralded another room. Made of dark wood, the doors hid in the shadows, dominating in a foreboding way.

The shadows dance. A dull thrum filled my temples. *Do shadows dance? I suppose...sometimes. Why do I even care?*

The buzzing in my head grew worse.

I swallowed, my mouth dry, and stood up, another wave of exhaustion sweeping over me.

"She doesn't look well."

The words drifted through my mind in a dreamy haze.

"She'll be fine."

"Maybe we should give her some water."

"I'm fine," I said.

Did I just speak?

"Here." Ko handed me a glass, and I took it with a shaking hand, lifting the glass to my lips. Ko grunted. "You're pale."

The water slid down my throat. "I'm fine."

"What happened back there when you passed out? You were out for several hours."

I heard words coming from his lips, but they didn't make sense. "I'm fine," I repeated and motioned to the blurred door. "What's through there?"

Ko shrugged and walked back to the other guard. "You'll find out soon enough."

Why wait? I leaned forward, ignoring the blurriness at the edges of my vision. My eyebrows furrowed as I peered at the closed door. *Whoever wants me so badly is behind there. So close.*

I stood. My headache worsened.

The door grew more formidable as I approached, and the quiet conversation of the guards behind me continued, both unaware of my movements.

So close.

"Stop!"

My hands on the handles, I looked over my shoulder. Ko started toward me, his mouth open and eyes wide. The other guard was frozen in place, his eyes moving as his gaze flicked between Ko and me.

"Stay away from there," Ko ordered.

I flung open both doors. The momentum jerked me forward, but my eyes widened as I took in the dozens of lanterns brightening the room in various hues. Tapestries covered the walls, ancient with faded colors and frayed threads. Beneath my feet, a plush red carpet stretched away down the hall towards a raised dais. A large chair rested upon it, and a man sat atop.

He was surrounded by five others who stood. As one, their heads swung towards me, and the two guards who stood to either side of the door started forward.

A hand clenched my arm and squeezed it with a vice-like grip. "What do you think you're doing?" In the same breath, Ko yanked me off balance, back toward the outer chamber. Eyes wide with fury, Ko tightened his hold as I struggled to escape. Another pair of hands grabbed me, and Ko's face swam over my head.

"Enough," commanded a voice. "Daimyo Ko, release her."

At once, all three men let go. I fell to the floor, the coldness of the hard, dank stone seeping into my skin. I gasped as the forceful shock rippled through my ribs. My left arm felt immobile, the nerves around my ribcage pulsing with pain. A numbness grew, spreading from the shoulder downward to the tips of my fingers.

A hand appeared in front of my face.

"Let me help you up." The voice was gentle and somehow reassuring.

I placed my hand in his and hesitated. The contrast—mine, small, dirty as a street waif's, engulfed in his large, soft, clean one. With a sturdy pull, he hauled me to my feet and steadied me. My jaw dropped.

The king.

My heart pounded, and I yanked my hand out his grasp.

The king is here.

I took in a deep breath, struggling to keep the fear from exploding outwards.

Before me stood a man as fair as the Unknown was dark: a picture of health, youth, and strength. His tunic hung loose but did nothing to hide his athletic form. His blue-green eyes stared back at me, mirth visible deep within their depths.

He's not what I expected. My heartbeat slowed.

"Are you done looking?"

My cheeks flushed red, and I let my hands fall at my sides as I stifled the urge to reach up and touch my messy hair.

He smiled, his teeth flashing white. "Where are my manners?"

"Who are you?"

"First, let me apologize. I kept you waiting in the anteroom for your companions to arrive as I would prefer to explain the whole at one time. I see I should have been a more gracious host." His gaze shifted for a mere second. "Ko, she does not look well. What happened?"

Ko flicked his long hair over his shoulder as he took a step back. "My lord..."

"I'm fine," I said as I fought to control the fiery streaks running through my side, the tingling numbness spreading down my arm and into my fingers, and the wooziness making my head spin. "Where are they? Why am I here in your underground…" I paused, my brain struggling to connect words together.

"Palace, fortress, hideaway, prison?" He supplied the words contritely.

"Are you speaking from my view or yours?"

"Both?"

I eyed him and folded my arms with a wince.

He grinned. "Are we done with the word games?"

"Possibly."

"No offense, but you seem as high-spirited as I have been led to believe."

"None taken. But the report seems to have been given by those whom I believe you sent to kidnap me. 'Oh please, take me where you will. I love being kidnapped.'" I clasped my hands in front of me. "Do you expect me to have acted docile?"

"Yes and no?" he queried.

I blinked.

"Yes, quite a few people would be vulnerable in some way toward those who hold them in their power, possibly to escape attention or maybe to throw their captors off their guard. I cannot tell whether you are extremely smart or foolish to act the way you have done. From what I have seen, I doubt you show submission easily. But I understand it; I would not, either."

"Easy for you to say," I spluttered, my hands curling into fists as I looked up at him. "Do you even know the meaning of submission? You're the king."

"He's—" Ko began, but the blue-eyed man held up a hand.

"Interesting." He tapped a finger on his chiseled jaw. "That's a *very* interesting observation."

The soft thud of footsteps caused him to turn. Ko stepped closer to me as I also looked through the open doors in the anteroom. A couple of men appeared with Saya and Adnan.

"Juliet!" Saya called. Adnan's green eyes met mine.

"How about we all sit down?" suggested the young, blond man. "We have a lot to discuss." He led the way toward the dais.

Adnan fell in beside me. "Are you all right?" The intensity in his gaze seared into me.

My heart beat faster.

"No, but I will be." I smiled, turning tired eyes up to him. "I was so worried about you both. They wouldn't tell me anything. What's going on?"

"I don't know," he admitted. "We just arrived."

"That's just it, though! Arrived where? And how long have we been apart? I can't remember."

"We'll talk later. You're sure you're all right?"

I took a deep breath.

"No." His eyes hardened. "You're not telling the truth. You're white as death and you're clenching your jaw, not to mention you've stumbled twice now."

"I'm fine. How long have we been separated?"

"You don't know?" Saya asked.

"No, I don't even remember parting. I have vague memories, but I can't tell if they are dreams or reality."

"You collapsed a few hours after dawn this morning," Adnan murmured, his eyes boring into me. "A couple of men went on with you, taking turns carrying you. We tried to stop them, to keep us all together."

"It's alright. I'm fine. We're all here now, for better or worse." I stumbled on the first step leading up to the dais. Adnan took hold of my arm under the elbow as we neared the steps and lent a supporting weight as we walked up. He let go as soon as we reached the top stair.

The green-eyed man looked at those sitting around the table. "Leave us. Please sit." He motioned for me to sit on a cushion to the right of the one man who had not gotten up and left: a man dressed in a robin's egg blue tunic, the only bright thing in the entire room. I started, realizing my companions had already taken seats. I lowered myself onto a cushion. The blond-haired man sat down on my right, his shoulders brushing against my own.

Shivering, I edged away and caught Adnan's gaze. His eyes remained emotionless, stony, cold.

"Now that we are all here, I hardly know where to begin."

"A good start would be your name," Adnan suggested, folding his arms across his chest. He looked like a snake coiled to strike.

The man's eyes narrowed. "Yes, of course. I am Tristan Geoffrey Bernaeon"—he paused—"Gorvenal."

Adnan leaped to his feet. "You can't be."

A slow smile spread across Tristan's face. His eyes gleamed. "I can be. I am here in the flesh."

I looked from one man to the other. "Would someone care to enlighten me?"

"You're supposed to be dead," Adnan murmured, his words devoid of emotion.

"Supposed to be, yes; in reality, no."

"The king's not the last—" Adnan broke off, his eyebrows drawn together.

This was the first time I'd seen him so out of his element. It disconcerted me. Shock and uncertainty radiated off him in waves.

"No, he is not. Not many know the truth." Tristan paused. "Now, the two of you." He gestured to Saya and Adnan. "Who are you? There is a rumor...circling of one called Shizukana. Is that you? It is a name I have heard before...amongst others."

"I am known by that to some," Adnan gritted, his jaw locked.

Tristan inclined his head, not bothering to hide a sparkle in his eyes. "Well, I am glad to have made your acquaintance at last. You are a hard man to find. And you?" He turned towards Saya.

"Saya."

"Saya, and is there anything special about you?"

She shook her head, her long dark hair flicking through the air. "No."

He can't know about her. "What do you want? And who exactly are you?" I demanded, drawing the attention away from Saya.

"I apologize. Momentary forgetfulness." He inclined his head in a shallow bow. "Juliet, Saya, I am of the house of Gorvenal, one of the last of that house. Perhaps I should start at the beginning." He tapped his head with a forefinger before going on. "Just over two decades ago, the house of Gorvenal ruled this land. We were strong and numerous. Peace reigned, and the people flourished. My mother, daughter to the king, was the first and only direct heir to the throne. The king, my grandfather, had no male children of his own. Though he had but one child of his own, his siblings had many. Our house grew tenfold." He paused and leaned back in his chair. "One nephew of his, my cousin, Creulon, longed for the throne. Being the oldest male child and succeeding heir if I had not been born, he was devastated when I came along. With his hopes dashed, his greed for the throne and power grew even more. Yet my grandfather was overjoyed when

I was born, and, wanting to pass the throne down directly through the line, he named me as his heir. Being so young, all of this was unknown to me, of course."

My head began to swim again as I strained to keep track of all this information.

Tristan's eyes held my own, a dark emotion shining deep within their depths. "Creulon continued to grow in power after I was born and gained many followers. One night, exactly a week after my younger sister was born, hired assassins killed everyone in my family—any person of the bloodline of Gorvenal. It was a bloodbath.

"And now, my cousin, the heir apparent, sits on the throne. But he is the one who orchestrated the mass murder of his own family. *My* family," Tristan spat, running a hand through his hair. "That night, my entire family lay dead, assassinated in their beds, homes, wherever they happened to be. Some by those whom they trusted who worked secretly for my cousin, others by trained assassins." Tristan's voice grew bitter. "I survived because of my mother and my nurse. I do not know how nor by whom my mother was warned, but she knew we weren't safe. She had just enough time to send my nurse and myself away from the palace. And we hid. My nurse raised me and is with me even now. As the years passed, I grew older and stronger, slowly gathering around me those loyal, biding my time." He hung his head.

That's awful. His family is gone. I wished for water to ease the tightness in my throat and mouth. *I was right. He is the king...or should be.* I watched as Tristan closed his eyes, hiding the sheen of emotion there. *But there's something else—* I rubbed my temples, but the throbbing didn't ease. My thoughts were becoming harder to form through the aching in my head and side. *He's fighting for justice.*

A low rumble came from deep within my stomach. *I'm so hungry.*

Tristan sat up straight, but his eyes stared, unseeing, at the wall.

His mother died. But why? Why couldn't she get away too? He was so young. I cleared my throat. "Why was your mother unable to get away?"

Tristan turned pain-filled eyes on me, their twinkle gone. "My mother had given birth barely a week before. It had been a hard birth, I am told, and my mother was weak."

I barely remember Eddie's birth. He was so small. So vulnerable.

"She knew she would put me in danger if she came," Tristan continued, "and my sister would not have survived the cold of winter, so she stayed."

I twisted the hem of my shirt in my lap as I listened.

A muscle pulsed in Tristan's neck. "She stayed to die, knowing her newborn daughter, my sister, would die as well."

I'm alone here as well. But at least my parents are alive. Tears slid down my cheeks. *I have them. He had no one but his nurse.* "That's awful." My voice quavered. "Where is your nurse now?"

Tristan swallowed. "She is in a small village, living comfortably, away from all of this." He waved a hand in the air. "I keep an eye on her," he admitted.

Part of me wanted to reach forward and lay a comforting hand on his arm, but then I remembered why we were here in the first place. I cleared my throat. "So, Creulon is the present king, your cousin, and the one who killed your family?"

"Yes."

"Does he know of your being alive?"

Tristan shrugged. "It is possible he suspects, but I have made sure not to let any rumors circulate the land, which is why I asked you all to keep my secret." Tristan gestured at the silent man next to me. "Shogun Haniel, my right hand, is the only person who knows, besides my nursemaid, and they both would take it to the grave if needed."

But how does Adnan know so much? He must have sensed my eyes on him as he shifted to face me. I waved a hand towards Tristan, my voice hushed. "How did you hear about this, about him?"

He glanced at me, his eyes unreadable. "I've traveled quite a bit."

That's not the full story. There is far more you won't tell me.

"Yes." Tristan's smile returned to his face as he leaned back in his chair. "Shizukana, is it? I had wondered who you were, when I received word that a man and woman traveled with Juliet. But I thought you had a different name you would prefer to be called. How about Benkei? Or *Oniwaka*?"

Saya jolted upright in her chair, her face pale.

Why the reaction? I leaned forward. Saya stared at Adnan, unblinking. Adnan's jaw clenched, but he said nothing.

"No preference?" Tristan steepled the tips of his fingers together. "Then I shall use Benkei, unless you tell me otherwise. What a surprise to find you here, in my underground fortress. I must admit that I am surprised."

Benkei? Oniwaka? I watched Adnan. His jaw was clenched, his eyes dark, and his hands lay curled in fists in his lap.

He has so many names. With every layer I uncover, I find more.

"Now," Tristan continued. "My cousin's treachery was three decades ago, but his overthrow was well executed. It passed into legend and was soon forgotten."

I shook my head. "How could anyone forget something like that? The entire royal family dying?"

Tristan shook his head. "Most fear for their lives and so do not speak of it. You would be surprised how many prefer to forget the past rather than live with the memory of it."

Would I? No, I wouldn't be surprised. I know. I have fought this for years. I closed my eyes. *It would be so much easier if the memory of Eddie was gone, if I didn't remember that it was me who couldn't save him.*

"Juliet?"

I looked up to see Tristan staring at me. Adnan and Saya watched me, their brows furrowed in concern.

"Is everything all right?" Tristan looked at the pitcher on the low table in front of him. "Do you need water?"

I nodded. "I'm fine."

Tristan hesitated before settling back on his cushion. "Those who could have had a chance to do something about it were killed or have been scared into hiding." He gestured with his hands. "This has become my sanctuary. It is well hidden and vast."

I can relate. But he's fighting; am I? Or am I just running? I set my hand down on the ground and leaned back a little. "But it wasn't that long ago that this all happened."

"No, not in terms of the countless centuries of history we have. But minds are fickle and memories can erode. We have been here for a few years now, beginning the resistance to the king, what we call, the Uprising."

Haniel spoke up for the first time. "Going on four years now, my Lord."

"Has it been so long?" Tristan mused, seemingly lost in memories.

"We've barely had to work on these tunnels," Haniel interposed. "This used to be a quarry. All these tunnels had been long forgotten. We constructed supports and did a few things here and there, but otherwise they were ready for our use."

"An act of providence," Tristan murmured. "We have grown greatly in numbers. I do not know where we would have hidden if not for this labyrinth."

"Where do we come in?" Adnan leaned forward. "Why hunt us down and take us without saying a word about who you were or why we were wanted?"

"I trust none of you were mistreated," Tristan began.

"That depends on your view of mistreatment."

"That is fair," Tristan acknowledged. "But telling you was too dangerous. What if someone overheard? There are ears everywhere. No, I could not say anything to you before you arrived."

Adnan's eyes were stony. "What's to say we won't turn against you anyway?"

"I hope after you hear me out, you will not."

"And if we do?"

"I will be forced to constrain you. I won't kill you, but you will be under lock and key indefinitely."

Great.

Both men gazed at one another with stubborn, unresisting looks. Neither gave in.

"Why risk all of this?" Adnan gestured around the room, breaking the tense silence.

"Because I have no choice."

I shifted in my seat. "Why us?"

Tristan sighed. "It was more specifically you, but now, it is Benkei as well. I did not know he was with you before. But he would be instrumental to our cause."

I glanced at Adnan, but he was concentrated on Tristan. If he noticed my attention, he gave no sign of it.

"And you, we know who you are." Tristan's white teeth flashed in a smile.

"Who am I?"

"You came through a portal from another place. You're the Otherworlder."

Saya, quiet until now, spoke, "How did you find out?"

"There are ears everywhere. My cousin somehow found out, and my spies in his court alerted me. He is hunting for you, and believe me, he will stop at nothing until he owns you."

"He doesn't scare me," I replied.

"He should." Tristan's face hardened. "Juliet, you could be the answer to all our hopes."

Adnan interrupted. "She is not a weapon nor plaything for you."

"I know. Which is why I will not force her. It is her own decision to make. I will lay out why and what I require, and she will be free to take it or leave it."

"You give her little choice in the matter," Adnan spat.

"But it is still a choice, *Oniwaka,* and the best I can offer. Believe me, I do not wish this, and I mean no harm towards any of you. I would have you be on my side wholeheartedly and leave any grievance you may have against me in the past."

"That's easier said than done," I muttered. "As this conversation progresses, I think instead of having my questions answered, you're leaving me with more questions than ever."

"Please ask me anything, and I will do my best to answer."

"Why do you need me? What do you think I could possibly do? What is your plan?"

"Several questions," Tristan noted. "But good ones, nonetheless. You will be instrumental in the retaking of my kingdom. I doubt we could do it without you and Benkei. As for my plan, it is still in progress..." He hesitated.

"You don't have a plan," Adnan stated.

Tristan grimaced. "We have half a plan. There is not much time. It is now or never. We are as ready as we will ever be, and it will not be much longer before my cousin's spies find us."

Adnan leaned forward, stroking his beard. "There's more to it than you're telling us."

Tristan sighed, his brow furrowing. "Word came weeks ago that my cousin had heard of a rebel group planning to overthrow him. He is not one to pass up any rumor, no matter how small nor insignificant it might seem. His spies go out to the furthest corners of the land, and they draw ever nearer. The kingdom is falling into ruin faster than ever."

"We've noticed," Adnan murmured.

Tristan flicked his gaze to Saya.

"I am sorry about your home."

"Not much escapes your ears, does it?" Saya flicked her brown hair over her shoulder.

"No; my followers have grown greatly, but I swear I did not know anything until it happened."

"And would you have done something to help?" Adnan asked. "Umi no Machi is a small town, more for trading than anything else."

Tristan hesitated, his eyes showing the conflict within. "I would like to give you an unequivocal yes, but I cannot. To be honest, if I did save every city, town, or village, I would spread my men too thin, and even then, I would not be able to be everywhere."

"Why are Shizukana and Juliet instrumental to your plans?" Saya inquired.

Tristan regarded her. "I am not ready to reveal that yet. I do not know the half of it myself."

I cleared my throat. "I don't see what you think I could do. You're about to fight a war—"

"We do need you," he interrupted.

"And I'm not helping anyone who doesn't tell me why or for what they need my help. Why do you think you'd make a better king than your cousin? You could be as bad, if not worse."

Tristan stiffened. "Do—not—ever—compare me to my cousin. I am nothing like him."

I shrank back as he leaned closer, fire shooting from his eyes and his lips thinning.

"Leave her alone, Tristan."

I looked up to see Adnan standing tall, his fists balled at his sides.

Tristan's face cleared, and he relaxed. "I apologize. Juliet, I overreacted. I am nothing like my cousin. He wants chaos in his pursuit for his own pleasures. I want to return to the peaceful kingdom we used to have under my grandfather. I want what we used to have, what we had under the kings of old; I want the people to not have to live under tyranny, afraid for their lives or of consequences for doing something right. My family needs to be avenged. Judgment and sentencing by trial must happen. Justice must happen."

No one said a word.

I licked my lips. "Why do you think you need us?"

"I know I do because I have a seer."

"What?" Saya leaped to her feet.

Tristan leaned back and looked up at her. "I do not know if that was quite the sort of reaction I had in mind. They have not died out, you know."

Adnan opened his mouth. "Saya—"

"I know better than most," she spoke over him.

"You are one yourself," Tristan guessed, his eyes beginning to sparkle. "We thought there was something special about you."

Saya stiffened and coiled back.

"You don't have to be afraid here. Seers are to be respected—possibly feared, in some cases—but always respected and honored." He swept his hand out. "Please, sit down. We will talk more about this later."

Saya sat on the floor, her hands shaking at her sides.

Tristan exchanged a glance with Haniel, who still had not said a word. "I hate to break this up, but I would like your answer before I do."

I frowned. "We don't have a choice, though." The pounding in my head worsened, lancing behind my eyes.

"Yes, you do," Tristan assured with a wry smile. "It's just not the choice I know you want to make. Prison or join me."

Adnan stood up. "We agree to join you, but by the gods, you had better swear to be honest with us. Be open about your plans and what is going on. If you want us fully committed, you will earn our trust; make us part of your inner circle, and you had better pray we find you worthy."

Wow. My jaw dropped. *That was impressive.*

"Very well, I swear on the gods." Tristan sighed. "Thank you. As a sign of my good faith, I will take you to meet the other seer. One who no doubt would like to meet you, Saya."

"What? Me?" Her voice squeaked, and I glanced at her with surprise.

"Yes."

A small shiver ran through me at his smile, leaving me uneasy.

Everything had rushed by too fast. I couldn't hold on to the moment, and understanding flew away under the ache in my temples. My stomach turned, and I swallowed down the nausea.

"My guards will accompany you to the dining room for a meal," Tristan uttered as he stood. "The seer may not be up to meeting you today, but if she is, I will bring you to her. Until then."

Tristan swept us a low bow.

"Wait, one more thing." He looked each of us in the eyes. "No one here knows who I truly am. I ask that you keep my secret."

I stood. "How could they not know? I thought you were the king when I first saw you."

Saya raised an eyebrow. "How?"

"He looks like he's of the king's family. Blond, pale skin…" I shrugged. "How do they not know?"

"They think I am a noble," Tristan explained. "Those are the rumors circulating anyways, and I do not agree or disagree with them, which keeps them guessing. It works for us. There is an air of mystery, being distantly related to the same line, but not a direct heir." He ran his fingers through his hair. "They know me as Lord Tristan; you may address me as such as well. Now, do I have your vow that you will keep my identity secret?"

As one, we all muttered our promises of assurance to the man who stood before us.

Chapter Nineteen

Tapestries hung on the walls of the cavern. Darkness spread its wings into the far corners. The dimness was a stark contrast to the bright brilliance there had been in Tristan's council room. The glow of the sparse candles was dull.

The seer faced us. Her robes, a flowing clash of muted purples and grays, swept the ground. Her hair was pulled back in a loose bun, leaving her bright eyes clear. She held out her hands in a gesture of welcome.

Tristan smiled. "Drielle, it is good to see you, as always." He pointed at each of us. "Juliet, Benkei, and Saya, this is Drielle."

I shifted on my feet. Once the seer had heard my name, her gaze hadn't left mine.

"Juliet Barrows," she murmured. "It is nice to finally meet you."

"Drielle," Tristan interrupted, turning her attention away. "Saya is the seer I spoke of to you."

"Saya," Drielle murmured, smiling at Saya. "When did you first realize your abilities?"

"I've known for as long as I can remember," Saya replied. "But I didn't realize they were more than dreams till I grew older and made the connections. The things I saw happened."

Drielle nodded, fingers pressed together under her chin. "That is young."

Saya shrugged her comment off. "Are you the only one besides myself? I thought I was alone."

"No, you're not. There are others, besides you and I, in hiding. And there are many in various countries who look more sympathetically on our kind." Drielle exchanged another glance with Tristan before continuing, "I would like you to stay with me, so I can train you and help you to hone your abilities."

What?

I looked away from Saya's shining face to Adnan. A gleam shone in the green of his eyes. *He knows more than he's letting on.* His expression was clear, empty. *He's too careful. What is Tristan's plan here? First me, then Adnan, and now Saya.*

"You really mean it?" Saya took a step closer to Drielle.

My shoulders rose as I tensed.

"Yes." Drielle laughed. "What is your answer?"

"I—yes!" Saya swallowed as her voice squeaked, eyes shining.

No. It'll take her away from us. I shifted on my feet.

Drielle's gaze flickered over me before she strode to a circle of cushions within a bright circle of candlelight. "Juliet, may I know your story?"

I followed the others over to her. "My story?"

"Yes, how you arrived here."

"Oh." I looked to Adnan for approval, and he nodded his head once.

My story? The portal that brought me here and the journey that led me to this moment... I tapped a finger against my leg. *I chose the townspeople, Saya, Adnan, over my own family.* I sat down on a plush pillow next to Adnan. "It began during a hike in some woods back home..."

I licked my lips when I finished, my mouth dry. *How far is home now?* I waited, my foot tapping.

Drielle clasped her hands in front of her. "Interesting."

"Who is the woman who found you?" Tristan asked, his tone serious.

"I don't know," I admitted. "She was nowhere to be found. I saw her once more, the day Saya warned us of the attack, but she disappeared into the crowd before I could say anything."

Tristan looked at Adnan. "You do not know who she was?"

Adnan shook his head. "No, I tried to find her, but without success. Juliet is right; no one remembers seeing her. I myself do not remember her."

"Wait, you tried to find her? When?" I exclaimed.

Adnan cleared his throat. "Before we even left Umi no Machi. It was after she'd spoken up against you in the crowd."

"But—"

"Is everything fine here?" Tristan smirked.

Heat flooded my cheeks. "Everything is fine."

"Juliet," Drielle interjected. "What planet do you come from?"

"Earth."

Drielle's eyes flickered toward Tristan, and something I couldn't quite detect flashed across her face. "I see. This is Earth, so you must come from a different time—the past, the future?"

"I—I—"

"We aren't sure exactly what is going on," Adnan interrupted. His leg brushed against mine.

He wasn't adjusting his position.

"I want to hear from Juliet," Tristan interjected, his voice smooth and polite.

Adnan's warning me. "I don't know," I replied after a brief hesitation.

"Alright." Drielle raised a delicate eyebrow. "Your time on Earth, it is ruled by many kingdoms? Many nations?"

"Yes, more than I could possibly count."

"Do you think this is a different world altogether?"

"I—maybe, yes—I don't know. This country reminds me of one back home called Japan, but they aren't ruled by a succession of people from another country. And there are other, small differences as well." *There's no electricity here, no humming of powerlines, nothing from the modern world. It's medieval.*

Adnan stiffened next to me.

Tristan leaned forward, his blue eyes gleaming. "What else?"

"It's not an island, from what I understand, which Japan is." *It's a bygone era…and yet I'm here.*

Drielle steepled her long fingers together. "Could it be the past?"

I couldn't ignore the stiffening of Adnan's leg against mine. "I think I would know if I had traveled to the past." I took a deep breath. "But none of this should be possible or make sense."

"Do not hang yourself up on the possibilities or lack thereof," Tristan interjected. "Do so, and you hold yourself back. Without self-restriction, who knows what you can do or can achieve if you are only willing to take the chance."

"It may be a different world, but please do not ask me to explain why I think so because I can't. I don't understand any of this, nor how I came to be here, nor if I can even go back." I raised my fingers to my temples and rubbed as a pulsing pain spread.

"I see." Drielle smiled. "You all must want to rest now. Saya, would you be willing to stay so we can talk some more?"

"Yes!" Saya blurted and took a deep breath. "Yes, I would like that."

No, we should stick together, I wanted to say. My shoulders rounded as I slouched on my cushion. I tilted my head, trying to get Saya's attention, but she only had eyes for the other seer in the room. *We're supposed to stay together. It's safer that way.*

"Juliet, Benkei, until we meet again." Drielle nodded to each of us as she stood. "I'm sure it will not be long before we do."

I rose, still unable to get Saya's attention. Her face shone with excitement.

Tristan placed his hand on my back. "Juliet, Benkei, I'll have you both shown to rooms where you may rest. Please let me know if you need anything. I'll have someone posted outside of your rooms."

Someone to fetch and carry for us, or someone to keep an eye on us?

⊱⊰

Our two guards, Ko being one, led the way down the dark passageway. I shivered at the dank breeze sweeping through.

Adnan placed a hand under my arm. "Woah, steady there," he murmured. "You stumbled again."

My legs moved slower, more sluggishly, and his words took longer to register. I opened my mouth, but Ko interrupted.

"This is your room, Otherworlder."

The other guard gestured, holding his lantern a little higher. "Benkei, this way."

"Wait, A—" *That was too close.* I bit my lip and glanced at the guards, but by the uninterested looks on their faces, I knew they hadn't noticed my abrupt halt. *I can't slip up, not with a secret that's not mine to tell.* I hesitated and looked up at Adnan. "Would you mind coming in so we can talk?"

Adnan nodded.

"Here." Ko handed me a lantern.

Adnan followed me into the small room, leaving Ko and the other guard standing outside. A thin mat lay on the floor.

I sank onto the mat with a grunt and leaned my back against the wall, watching Adnan as he paced back and forth. "I'm sorry I almost called you Adnan out there."

He let out a sigh of satisfaction as he sat down next to me. But he kept his gaze adverted.

"I'm sorry. I'll be more careful."

His eyes closed, but not before I saw the fear he tried to hide.

"Adnan, I won't give up your secret." I nudged him with my shoulder. "But what do I call you in front of others?"

He tilted his head to look at me. "The Unknown is fine, as you have been doing, or Shizukana."

"And the other names he mentioned? Benkei and Oniwaka?"

Adnan's face darkened. "Not those."

"What do they mean?"

"Nothing." He looked at the far wall.

"But Saya's reaction—"

Adnan interrupted me. "I don't understand Tristan's game. I want to know why it's so important to him to know whether it's another world or time."

He changed the subject. What do those names mean? Why won't he tell me? I gritted my teeth. "If you don't want to tell me yet, that's fine. Earlier, when Tristan was questioning me, you warded me off."

"Yes, but what's done is done." Adnan drew his knee up and laid his hand over it. "His reaction isn't what I expected."

"What do you mean?"

"I suppose," he began, studying the floor in front of him. "I expected him to be more disbelieving of your coming from another world."

"I suppose. But you and Saya took it well. You've probably taken it the best so far. Why?"

Adnan turned his head and looked at me, his stare piercing.

Unable to hold his gaze, I looked down at my lap.

"Juliet. Look at me. I know you're hiding what you feel. Never be afraid of fear. It is alright to be scared, to be uncertain. Better to have fear than none at all."

"What if I never get home?" The words escaped before I could stop them, voicing the empty ache inside of me.

His eyes tightened.

The air felt trapped in my lungs. "What?"

"You will return home. Maybe not for a while, but have faith. I will do everything in my power to make sure that happens. I swear."

"Why do you care if I return home or not?" The hem of my shirt wrinkled under my fingers.

"It's where you belong. You're not supposed to be here."

I let go of the material and folded my hands in my lap. "Yet I am." I shrugged under his searching look. "I'm here, aren't I? Which means it was supposed to happen...because it did. Saya would say it was fate."

He arched an eyebrow. "Is that supposed to be a joke?"

I rolled my eyes. "Yes. At least, the last part was." A small sigh escaped my lips, and I leaned my head back against the wall. "We're in this together, for better or worse," I murmured. A warmth grew in my chest until I relaxed back against the wall, a new strength coursing through me. "I wouldn't be able to go through this without you or Saya."

"Our fates are bound together, for better or for worse."

"Fates, hm?"

Adnan took his cloak off and laid it on the edge of the mat. "I never said I didn't believe in fate."

I reached for my boots and gasped as pain shot across my ribcage. "By the—" Closing my eyes, I gritted my teeth. The mattress shifted a little as I felt Adnan move.

"Here." He tugged on my boot, removing first one and then the other.

Curling my toes, I arched my feet, sighing. "Thanks."

He sat back down. "What do you think of the seer?"

"She's—she's, I don't know. I don't like her, but I'm not sure if it's because of her or because I'm irritated that we're breaking up."

He crossed one ankle over the other knee. "Saya's still here."

"I know!" I snarled. But the anger fizzled out as soon as it had ignited.

Adnan's face remained sincere, unchanged.

"Sorry, I didn't mean to snap. It just feels like everything is out of our control, and I hate it. Plus, she and Tristan aren't telling us everything." *And nor are you.*

"There are things they're keeping from us," he agreed, stroking his beard. "It's enough to make me wary, but at the same time, it could be a point in their favor, that they want to trust us before revealing their secrets about the rebellion. If so, it'll take time for them, as well as us, to earn one another's trust."

"I don't want a part in all of this," I admitted. "But I do think they're telling the truth, or at least what they believe to be the truth. I got the feeling Tristan knew something about Saya already."

"I think he did," Adnan agreed. "My guess is the seer knew something about each of us. Tristan may have just been playing with us for confirmation."

"But I don't understand why they want me, or you for that matter."

Adnan quirked an eyebrow. "Am I that useless?"

I chuckled. "That's not what I meant. But why you?"

A small sigh escaped his lips as he stared straight ahead.

"Adnan?" I asked, placing a hand on his forearm.

"You don't want to know why."

Ignoring the pain throbbing in my side, I leaned forward. "What do you mean?"

"I'm not who you think."

I grinned. "And you know what I'm thinking?"

"Juliet—"

"Wait, Adnan. You're right, I don't know who you are, but I think I trust you." I laughed. "Maybe I'm crazy, but you've been there for both Saya and me. I know I thought one of the men who took me was familiar—I still don't understand what was going on there with you both sharing a name and similar clothing, but I know it wasn't you. I *do* want to know why Tristan knows of you, and more than that"—I hesitated, taking a deep breath—"I want to know why you have so many different names."

"I can't tell you what you want to know."

"Can't or won't?"

His jaw clenched. He looked at me, and what I saw in his eyes halted the harsh words on my lips. He looked down, and his jaw clenched. "What is this?" He unwrapped my hand and turned it over to see the thin, jagged red line crossing my palm.

"I cut myself in the corridor earlier. On the wall. It was stupid."

Adnan stood up and walked to the door.

"What are you doing?"

"Tristan said we could ask for things." He grinned and opened the door, speaking to the men outside. "Could we have some fresh clothes, if possible, and linen strips for bandages?"

A faint repetition of the orders filtered through the doorway before Adnan closed the door and came back to the mat.

"I overheard the guards talking earlier," he began, a frown crossing his face. "Seems there's been more chatter than normal with the king's men. They're worried that something is going on. By the sound of it, more than Tristan told us."

"Did you hear anything more?"

"No, they stopped talking as soon as they realized I was listening."

I groaned. "People have too many secrets. I'm sorry, that wasn't aimed at you..."

He raised an eyebrow.

"Okay, it was a little bit. You're a great tracker, Adnan. You carry a sword, a knife in your left boot, another one in a small scabbard in the small of your back, and—"

Adnan cleared his throat. "How—"

"We've been traveling together for a few weeks now. I've *noticed*. Besides the unstrung bow and sword, I didn't notice the rest until you were searched."

"You're right on those."

"What else do you have hidden away?"

He raised his eyebrows. "Like what?"

My cheeks burned. "Anyway, several weapons, you can obviously use a staff well though you don't carry one, and you're in and out of Umi no Machi. You live there but don't live there. No one seems to know anything about you or even your real name."

"Juliet, enough," he snapped.

"Just answer me one thing—is Adnan your real name?"

He blinked and relaxed back against the wall. "It is. I told you the truth."

Is it? I studied him. His green eyes reflected nothing but honesty. *It is. I believe he's telling the truth.*

"Who else knows?"

"No one. I've never told anyone else my name. No one here knows me by it."

And what about Benkei? I thought. *Or Oniwaka?* Saya had reacted so strongly when Tristan had said that name. *What does she know?* Unease rippled through me. And now she was closeted away with the seer. There had been no chance to question her.

Adnan continued to watch me, unmoving and silent.

He can't hear my thoughts.

"I wish you would tell me the truth."

He jerked as though I'd punched him. "I have."

"About your name, yes, but everything else still lies in mystery."

"Keeping silent doesn't mean I haven't told the truth."

I blinked. *He's right...again. But it's still not enough.* I shied away from him a little and laid down. I drew my legs up, my feet planted on the bed, and groaned from the pressure it put on my ribs and wound.

Adnan scooted down to the edge of the mat so I could stretch my legs out.

He does little things that are thoughtful, but he keeps pushing me away. The silence stretched on, and I closed my eyes. And *right now it's harder to continue as we've been with Saya gone.*

"Juliet?" He crossed his hands behind his head. The familiar muscle in his neck pulsed. His lips didn't open to speak. "I'm just not ready yet."

He's in pain. I stared up at the ceiling. "What happened this morning?"

He released his hands and tilted his head to look at me. "What?"

"What happened this morning? I don't have any memory of it."

"You passed out. They tried to revive you, but you remained unconscious."

"I don't remember any of that."

"With each hour that passed, you were fading, your skin paling. Remember last night?"

I shook my head. "Not really."

"You fell into a fast sleep the moment you finished eating, and you'd mentioned some dizziness. This morning it was hard to get you moving. You were traveling up ahead with Ko when the next thing I knew, you'd fallen. They wouldn't let me near you. Ko and another man carried you away, mentioning some small outpost nearby that had horses."

"I vaguely remember the forest we were walking through, but the next thing I knew I woke up in a small room here. Do you know where we are? Other than being underground?"

"A vague idea...but no. We were blindfolded the last several hours of the journey."

I crossed my ankles. "And you don't know where we are?"

"Meaning?"

"You were only blindfolded for a few hours."

"I know," Adnan admitted, rolling his head as he stretched his neck muscles. "I should tell Tristan he's not guarding his secret underground cave system very well."

"Well?"

A slight smile of satisfaction flitted across his face. "I think I know exactly where we are."

"Does that mean we have a choice about staying, then?"

"No." Adnan glanced at me. "Not yet anyways. We need to bide our time for now."

"You've never met Tristan before?"

"No." Adnan stood and paced the floor before me. "My name is not unknown in this world." He smiled at the askance look on my face. "That was not purposeful."

A rap sounded on the door three times. Adnan opened the door, and Ko handed him a pile of clothes, a small pitcher of water, and bandages.

Adnan set the clothes down on the stool. "Juliet, here. I'll wait outside."

With a weary sigh, I heaved myself up. Dipping a finger into the water, I shivered, but I couldn't help smiling as I washed my face and pressed the soft towel to my skin. The material kissed my face with its delicate softness.

I slid a black tunic from the pile of clothes over my head, watching as it fell almost to mid-thigh. Something thumped on the floor as I picked up the pants: a belt. But there were no loops on the pants. I left it on the floor.

With gentle fingers, I lifted my tunic back up as I pulled on the pants and buttoned them. I touched the cut over my ribs. It curved from under my top right rib to just above my abdomen. The line was red, angry, and swollen. With the blood washed away, I could see it still hadn't closed properly. Biting my lip, I looked down at my other side, where dark green and blue bruising mottled the skin.

Taking the end of the bandage in hand, I began wrapping my ribs, sucking in air and gritting my teeth from the pain as I twisted. My hands shook. A sharp stabbing shot across my ribs and torso until I leaned against the wall with my hand clasped to my mouth. The contents of my stomach threatened to come up, and tears slid down my cheeks. Biting my lip, I reached up and held back a small scream.

The door slammed open, and Adnan crossed the floor. "Juliet? What's wrong?"

I held up the bandage. "I'm having trouble bandaging my ribs," I mumbled, avoiding his gaze.

"Why didn't you ask in the first place?" He took the linen out of my hands. "No, I should've thought better. Come here." He took the material from my hand and slid the door closed.

Heat rushed to my face as I raised the tunic and looked away.

"I think you need stitches," Adnan informed me, examining my ribcage. "It's just not closing up like it should." He turned his gaze to my left side and ran his index finger over the skin.

I flinched.

"Sorry," he apologized.

"It didn't hurt. It was just reflex."

"Saya was right, though I think there might be two ribs broken, not one." He strode to the door and opened it, addressing the guards again: "I also need a needle and thread, and some alcohol."

Needle and thread? I examined the angry red line across my ribcage. *He's going to stitch me up himself.*

"Wait, you're not going to—" I began, losing my voice.

"Yes."

Saya examined it. She never mentioned stitches. "Why didn't Saya—"

"Perhaps because she doesn't know as much as she thinks she does."

I blanched and sat down on the edge of the cot.

⚶⚶⚶ ⚶⚶⚶

When the knock came, my hands shook as I looked up at the door.

"Do you need any help with anything?" Ko asked, glancing at me from over Adnan's shoulder.

"No," Adnan responded, closing the door. He set the items down and threaded the needle with deft fingers. Taking up the small flask, he poured some alcohol on the needle. "Pull up your shirt."

"But—"

"Pull it up, Juliet," he repeated, gentler this time. "It'll hurt, but it'll be better than letting it open up again and again."

I pulled up my shirt to expose my ribcage and laid down on the mattress. My fingers whitened as I clenched the hem of my shirt in my hands, keeping it in place.

"Juliet," he murmured. "You risk infection. I need to do this." He poured some of the alcohol over the wound without a word of warning.

I sucked in air and gritted my teeth as my black blurred my vision.

"Alright," he murmured. "Now I have to stitch it up."

My heartbeat quickened and I turned my head toward the wall, away from that small, silver needle approaching. The needle felt like a bee sting, over and over and over again, as it threaded down my side onto my abdomen. I glanced down, my stomach turning as I watched Adnan pull it out with a small tug before turning it point-down again and piercing my skin. It burned as though on fire.

"There, done."

I sighed with relief even though the pain had dissipated with his finishing.

He placed one hand behind my back and the other under my shoulders and helped me sit up. Taking the strip of linen, he began wrapping it around me with deft fingers. "I've tied the thread. It's neat, but it'll probably scar."

I nodded and released the tunic, letting it fall away and cinching it with the belt. "Thank you."

"Those clothes fit you well," he commented. "The ones Saya lent you were short in the legs and arms."

My lips quirked up in a grin. "True. I'll wait outside while you change." I turned to leave, but something caught my eye. "Is that—"

"A brush?" Adnan supplied, picking it up. He reached out to hand it to me but hesitated. "You won't be able to brush it on your own, will you?"

The thought of working out all the tangles with broken ribs was too painful. I shook my head.

"I'll help."

All the tangles removed from my hair? Yes, please. I turned without a word and stood in silence as he lifted my hair with gentle fingers and began brushing. I hadn't expected the gesture of him brushing my hair to feel so... *Intimate,* I realized. An icy dread trailed through my veins, but I shook the feeling. *Stop worrying. He can't hear your heartbeat. He's so gentle.*

My head jerked back as he encountered a knot.

"Hell's teeth."

"Not easy, huh?" I laughed.

He grunted. The motions became smoother, and soon he set down the brush with a sigh. "Done."

I walked to the door and glanced over my shoulder. "Thank you."

Ko closed the door behind me and regarded me with me thoughtful eyes. "What were the bandages for?"

I reached up and swept my hair into a low bun. "A wound that hasn't been healing properly."

The other guard nodded. "Painful."

"It was."

Ko grunted. "Do you need anything else?"

I shook my head. "Thanks, but no."

The door creaked as it opened to reveal Adnan in clean clothing. "Come on." He led the way back into the room and helped me lie down on the mattress. Pulling the blanket over me, he stood looking down.

I yawned. "It feels so good to be in fresh clothes."

"You should get some rest. I'll leave."

"I'm fine." I blinked, trying to keep my eyes from drifting closed.

"You're pale."

"Thanks."

"I'm serious. Get some rest."

"No, I mean," I hesitated. "Could you stay a little longer?"

He gazed down into my eyes, his own swirling with emotion.

"I'm sorry," I rambled. "I'll be okay. You must want some sleep."

"I can stay," Adnan said, his gentle voice stopping the stream of words on my lips. He sat down and drew a knee up to rest his arm on it.

I bit back another yawn. "Do we just wait and see what happens with all of this?"

"For now, yes. We don't really have a choice," he replied.

"That's"—another yawn, and my eyes closed—"true."

Chapter Twenty

Footsteps pounded down a long, dark hallway, drawing closer. The sound of a door thudding against a hard object echoed. Something shifted next to me, but when I looked, no one was there. My gaze had become blurry and unfocused.

"—out!" an urgent voice filtered in as I woke.

The slight form of Ko stood just inside the doorway, his stance ready. The other guard, weapon in hand, was just outside, scanning the corridor in both directions.

"Let's go." Adnan, standing before me, gripped my arm and hauled me out of bed.

Ko waited in the open doorway, the other guard just visible over his shoulder. "Here, take these." He thrust Adnan's weapons at him.

Eyes wide, I gasped, "What's going on?"

Sweat beaded on the guard's forehead as he fell in behind us. The light from the single lantern Ko carried flickered on the walls as we ran.

A lump formed in my throat. *He's afraid.*

"We're under attack!" the guard blurted out.

"No more talking," Ko grunted. "We have to hurry."

I panted, all my focus on breathing and placing one leg out in front of the other. Exhaustion filled my body, making it feel as though I ran through water. My breathing grew more ragged, and I stumbled to a stop and leaned against the wall.

"We have to keep going," Ko urged. He nodded to the other guard. "Go ahead and make sure the way is clear."

The guard nodded and ran off, his lantern flickering.

"Juliet—"

"I can keep going. Just give me a minute."

Ko eyed us both. "She doesn't look like she can."

"She will. Where are we going?"

Ko rocked on the balls of his feet. "To meet up with Tristan."

"Is he making a stand?"

"No, we've been given orders to evacuate and meet up at another location." Ko's eyes shifted up and down the passageway. Distant shouts echoed up and down the enclosed corridors.

"And Saya?"

"I don't know," Ko admitted. "I have no news of her or the seer."

"We can't leave without her," I said, pushing off the wall.

"There isn't much we can do," Adnan replied. "I won't put both our lives in danger when we don't know where she is. Tristan would not leave a seer behind." He grabbed my arm. "Come on."

"One more moment," I gasped.

The shouts behind us grew louder.

"We must go now!" Ko exclaimed, beginning to run.

I glanced behind us, but there was nothing to see but black outside of the small circle of light we stood in.

"Come on." Adnan grabbed my arm. "I'll carry you."

I gritted my teeth and stumbled forward. "I can run."

The torch above our heads created flickers in the pool of darkness surrounding us. A footfall behind, muffled but quick. I glanced over my shoulder as a man entered the ring of light, his sword raised high over his head.

A hiss whistled past my ear, and the man's eyes widened. His momentum would have carried him right into me if Adnan hadn't grabbed him. Blood darkened the man's clothing from the hilt protruding out of his chest over his heart. Adnan pulled the knife out and dropped the man on the floor.

I watched, frozen, my hearing fuzzy as though I was underwater.

Adnan wiped the blade on the back of the man's uniform. "We should go. He won't be the last."

Ko shook himself. "This way."

My legs wouldn't move. Adnan grabbed my arm, forcing me forward.

He killed someone. I looked back, but the darkness of the tunnel hid the man's body from sight. *The man is dead.* Breathing grew difficult and I gasped for air.

"Juliet?" Adnan stopped and grabbed me by the shoulders. "Are you hurt?"

I shook my head, mute.

"They're coming," Ko exclaimed.

Booted footsteps echoed from behind us.

I shrugged Adnan's hands off, but he didn't seem to notice.

"Run," he ordered, pushing me in front of him.

"We're almost there," Ko exclaimed, shooting a glance over his shoulder.

The gleam of orange light spread over us, casting our shadows down the corridor in front of us. I looked back. Two men, both holding torches, curved swords in hand, caught sight of us. Two more appeared out of the darkness behind them.

"Go!" Adnan barked at Ko. He pulled his own sword out of its scabbard with a sharp hiss.

I watched, unable to move. Men poured down the corridor, dressed in black, their curved swords reflecting torchlight.

Adnan strode forward to meet them. "We can't outrun them. Take her and go!" He looked at me, his expression hidden in shadow. His head dipped in a brief nod before he turned away.

Wait.

Ko grabbed hold of my arm and tugged, but my feet remained glued to the floor. "There are too many of them. He's giving you a chance." He jerked me off my feet and I stumbled, watching as Adnan took down one, two, three men in seconds with the fluidity of a snake, his motions a blur as he carried out a dance that only he knew. Ko shook me. "There's nothing we can do." He pulled me after him, his hand gripping my forearm, but I hardly felt it.

The passageway swept by in a dark, dull blur as we rushed to the exit. My mind was numb as I followed. I moved mechanically.

The corridor brightened against the backdrop of daylight streaming through the opening at the end. Ko pushed back the brush in front of us, and I stepped through, blinking as my eyes accustomed themselves to the bright sun. Tristan stood beside a large bay. Haniel and two other horses stood there, as well.

Ko dropped his hand to his sword and peered back over his shoulder as he called to Tristan, "Benkei is back in the corridor a short way, dealing with the advance guard."

Killing them. He's killing them.

Tristan nodded at him. "Go back and see if you can help. If he's alive, escort him to the rendezvous. Juliet, we need to leave."

I licked my dry lips. "We should wait."

"There is not time."

Haniel grabbed me around the waist and hoisted me onto a horse.

"We can't leave yet," I urged, slipping my leg over the saddle. *He's not here.*

"If Benkei is alive, he'll follow," Tristan ordered, spurring his horse forward. "Don't worry about him."

Haniel placed a hand on my leg and nodded. "Benkei can take care of himself. Go." He slapped my horse on the rump, and it shot forward, following Tristan's lead. I bounced along until I was able to swing my leg back over. I gritted my teeth and shot a quick glance over my shoulder to see Haniel following—

But there was no sign of Adnan.

⚜ ⚜

Dusk fell. After hours of riding, Tristan finally raised his hand, and I pulled my horse to a stop with a groan. My mare frothed at the mouth, a thick sheen of sweat glistening on her hide in the dying light. I dismounted and moved to unsaddle her, but Tristan moved in front of me.

"Haniel will take care of her."

"I can take care of her myself."

"Just sit down. Please."

I wrenched my hand out of his grip and sat where he motioned.

"I'm afraid we do not have much in the way of comfort." He gave me a wry smile. "There will be no fire tonight, as there aren't many trees here to hide the glow."

"It's not like I have had much in the way of comfort lately."

"Perhaps. But it is what you deserve. You have been through so much. I swear that I will do whatever it takes to keep you safe, Juliet."

Adnan did everything he could to protect me. And he's missing. I closed my eyes, forcing the doubts from my mind. *Why does Tristan want to do the same? He doesn't know me.* I watched Haniel as he began stripping the saddle off one of the horses. *Yet he's not the one who killed three men with ease.*

Tristan stood up with a slight groan and walked over to Haniel.

Within a day, the trio is broken. I rubbed the spot below my thumb, feeling the rigid muscles begin to loosen. *Tristan is the opposite of Adnan. One is open, the other hides, one smiles and laughs, the other gives nothing away.*

The two men left the horses and walked back over.

Tristan handed me some fruit and dried meat. "It is all we could grab with such short notice."

A waterskin was passed around to finish off our small repast. Tristan laid back against his saddle and handed me a cloak.

"This is for you."

From out of the corner of my eye, I saw Haniel glare at me. "It's yours," I replied.

Tristan smiled, his eyes crinkling. "Yes, which is why I am giving it to you. It is a gift."

Before I could say another word, he swung it around my shoulders and tucked it around me. Scooting back, he laid down a couple feet away from me and crossed his arms behind his head, gazing upward at the heavens. "Go to sleep, Juliet. You will be safe."

"That's not why I am not asleep," I responded, lying down. "Why didn't you go back for him?"

"Because I know he can take care of himself." Tristan closed his eyes. "Have more confidence in yourself and in him."

"You barely know either of us."

"I barely know you, but you know I'm right."

⁂

"Sorry to wake you," Tristan whispered, nudging me awake. "But we should go. You've slept for a few hours now."

Every part of my body ached with a growing intensity. I sighed and sat up with his help. "I feel so gross and dirty."

Tristan smiled and offered a hand. "You do not look as bad as you think."

I stood and let go of his hand. "Even when I have not had a bath in days and have been traveling for even longer?"

Tristan eyed me. "It shows you to have a certain aptitude—a strength to go along with your delicate femininity."

My delicate femininity? Could I feel further from the truth? I looked down at myself. Dust clouded me from head to toe and I could only imagine what my face looked like. Dirt filled my fingernails. *I look awful.*

Tristan preceded the way to the saddled horses. His skin was clean, and his clothes looked almost immaculate.

I stepped forward. "Do your clothes and skin magically banish the dirt? If so, I would dearly love some such clothing myself."

"No," sighed Tristan, flashing me another smile. "But if I had, I would gladly gift you with such articles."

I chuckled. *How does one go through so much and yet always have a ready smile?*

"It is good to hear you laugh. You have a beautiful smile." He grabbed me around the waist, and I gasped, shrinking back.

Tristan let go, his light blue eyes wide. "What is it?"

I backed away from him, aware of Haniel now watching. "What are you doing?"

A light dawned in his eyes. "I was going to help you into the saddle. I am sorry. I should have asked first."

I swallowed. *Accept the help. You need it.* My shoulders straightened, and I stepped forward. With slower movements this time, Tristan placed his hands on my waist and helped hoist me to the saddle.

My breath caught. *Adnan.*

"Juliet? Are you alright?"

"Yes," I exhaled. The warmth of Tristan's hand left my hip as he walked away. *Adnan's not here. He isn't here to help me.* Flashes of him killing those men ran through my mind, his sword but a gleam in the dim light. I closed my eyes against the memories.

"Are you thinking of your companions left behind?" Tristan brought his mount up alongside me.

The saddle creaked as I shifted in my seat. "Do you know where Saya is?"

"With the seer, Drielle. They'll meet up with us at our destination."

I frowned.

"Don't worry about her. I sent several men to escort them."

I nodded. *I knew we shouldn't have split up. If Saya had stayed with us, she might be with me right now.*

"We will arrive soon," Tristan said. "I am sure they will show up within a couple of days. You will see."

"Where are we going?"

"You shall see." He looked ahead. "It might be a bit of a surprise for you."

"May I ask you a question?"

He nodded and mounted his own horse. "Never fear asking or telling me anything that is on your mind."

"Well, I don't mean any offense, but..." I hesitated. "Shouldn't you be more worried about your men and the country? You seem to act as if nothing happened yesterday. I admit, I am partly to blame, flirt—bantering"—I reddened—"with you. But we left before anyone else. We do not know what happened back there. What if—"

"Juliet, I have confidence in my men and those I left in command. They are well disciplined. Yes, I do worry, but I have to hope for the best. Sometimes a leader must take himself out of danger for the greater good. Do you think that because I act differently, I do not feel worry or anxiety?"

"I'm sorry. I just—I worry about A—the Unknown and Saya. Everything's happening so fast."

"They'll be fine. Your two friends have more to them than you realize."

Before I could ask him what he meant by that, he pointed. "Look."

We'd come out of the forest and before us lay a rocky mountain, its peak hidden in the clouds. My jaw dropped. How had I not noticed it before now? It seemed to have appeared out of nowhere. Snowcapped sides lay beneath the cloud cover, glistening in the afternoon sun. Sparse patches of trees grew, thick and numerous, the tall pines and evergreens reminding me of home.

I tightened my grip on the reins. "It's a beautiful country."

"It is. And one day I hope it'll be more so once the politics are different." Tristan rolled his shoulders and neck. "One day. Creulon cannot be allowed to remain on the throne. This country and its people have suffered enough." A scowl twisted his features.

"I hope so too."

Tristan sighed. "I've missed this. It's been far too long since I was last here."

"When was that?"

He turned his face back to the mountain. "Many years ago. My nurse and I hid here for a time with some bandits who took us in. Her brother was part of their group. They hid us until Creulon killed them. Then we moved on."

"What? What happened?"

"They were stealing from one of his caravans, but Creulon must have found out somehow, because he had men hidden in the wagons. The bandits were completely wiped out. My nurse was afraid they would somehow find out about our hiding place, so we moved on."

"It's here," Haniel pointed out. "The trail."

I craned my neck. "Where?"

"You can't see it very well until you're pretty much on top of it," Tristan admitted, leading the way. Haniel rode his horse around a bare twiggy tree and through several shrubs—or what had seemed like intertwined shrubs. A narrow pathway trailed through them. Tristan rode through, and I followed close behind.

The path was rocky and could hardly be called a path. It snaked along the side of the mountain, climbing higher and higher with every foot. The horses took to the trail like seals to water, their hooves sure on the rough terrain.

Tristan's voice broke into my reverie. "We should be there within a couple of hours."

"Will anyone else have arrived before us?"

"Possibly," he called over his shoulder. "But most will come on foot, so we should see the majority of my people trickling in over the next few days."

As we wound our way, I had a hard time keeping my eyes on the path when, to our left, spread the blue-green valley below, the bottom hidden in mist, and the tree-filled hills in the distance.

Tristan glanced over his shoulder. "We're almost there."

I peered around him and noticed a crop of rock rising over the path. "Tristan—"

"Trust me." He grinned, looking more boyish and innocent than I'd seen him yet.

The crag of rock loomed above us, looking impenetrable. In that brief moment, Tristan had disappeared. There was no trace of him. I yelped, jerking on the reins.

"Come on. It's alright," Tristan called, his voice strong and clear. "Just ride through. It's an illusion."

I took a deep breath and clicked my tongue. The horse moved forward, and I had to urge him forward again as he shied away. It wasn't until we were about to run into the rock that I realized there was a narrow opening, just wide enough for the horse. My jaw dropped as we were through and entered a gloomy darkness, lit by the faint light of a single lantern.

A dark smile curved Tristan's lips and tightened the lines around his eyes.

"My lord, we've been expecting you." A man strode forward, the lantern in his hand swaying. "This way, if you please."

Tristan gestured for me to precede him as we followed the guard down the tunnel, the light throwing dark shadows that danced upon the walls. It opened up into a large cavern; men moved about, scurrying about from one table to the next, or in and out of the corridors that stretched out from the cavern.

Tristan strode forward, and one by one, the men and women filling the cavern stilled, frozen in place. When all had grown silent, Tristan stopped. Heads bowed in a wave, sweeping the room.

A sign of respect.

I followed their example, lowering into a slight bow, but Tristan touched me on the shoulder.

"Please don't, not to me," he whispered, a pained look crossing his face for the barest instant. I straightened, watching as, one by one, the people raised their heads, but not a word passed their lips.

Tristan extended his hand to me and drew me forward so that we stood abreast. "This is Juliet. She is under my protection, which means you are to guard her with your lives as you would me. Honor her. Respect her. Obey her wishes."

I rolled on the balls of my feet as the attention shifted from Tristan to myself. I curled and uncurled my fingers, uncomfortable with the stares. *Why is he doing this? They don't need to know about me.*

Tristan's gaze swept the crowd as though looking for something.

One of the men closest to me bowed his head. "My lady."

I don't want this. I took a step back.

Tristan stepped closer, his shoulder brushing mine.

"What's going on?" I whispered to him as more and more followed suit.

"They're acknowledging you," he murmured, turning to face me. "Haniel, take Juliet to her quarters, please. And fetch one of the women to help her."

My shoulders sagged in relief. I could still feel the stares from those around us on me.

"Go with him," Tristan urged. "They'll bring you food and drink. I have some work to do, so get some rest. We'll talk later. Anything you need, just ask."

"Tristan—"

"My lady, this way," Haniel interrupted, gesturing with his arm.

I nodded and looked at Tristan, but he was already deep in conversation with men whom I recognized from the caves. With a sigh, I followed Haniel into one of the many openings. It led into another, smaller cavern. Curtains hung here and there on the walls, and in the middle a little over a dozen women worked, chatting and filling the air with laughter. They fell silent when they became aware of our presence.

"Mari," Haniel called. "This is Juliet. She is under the protection of Lord Tristan."

A woman stepped forward, eying me from top to bottom, before nodding. "Come this way." Her face was a blank mask, emotionless and distant.

I looked over my shoulder to see Haniel leaving the way we'd come, so I was left once again to follow someone. Mari wound her way in front of me across the room, past each woman, who watched with curious eyes.

"Here we are," Mari muttered, pushing aside a curtain and ushering me into a small alcove. "You will sleep here. I'll fetch you some clothes and food. Make yourself comfortable." She curtseyed and backed out.

As the veil fell back across the entrance, I heard the chatter resume outside. A plush mattress lay rolled up against the back wall.

A bed.

I took a step forward, but the curtain rustled behind me. I turned to see a silhouette in the opening.

She inclined her head and stepped forward. "Here are some fresh clothes. They look to be about your size, but we'll have some new ones made for you as soon as I can have the ones you wear. If you will please follow me, you may have a bath before you change."

The tunnel she led me through sloped downward. The air changed, becoming warmer and thicker. I sniffed as my breathing eased. We entered a small cavern, and my jaw dropped.

A spring bubbled up from the rocks beneath into an oval basin. Steam rose in thin curls above the water, and a soft, gurgling noise floated through the room. Part of the pool-like basin's rim tilted down toward the floor, allowing the water to flow over its sides and onto the rocks below, following a shallow dip until it exited through a crevice near the base of the wall. The path it followed was not man-made. It must have been flowing that way for quite some time to have carved out the floor.

She handed me a towel and a bundle of clothing. "You may bathe here. There is soap over there."

I took the items. "Thanks."

She tucked her dark hair behind an ear. "I'll wait just up the tunnel."

It had been too long since I'd bathed and even longer since I'd used soap. My scalp itched, and I resisted the urge to reach up and scrape my fingers along the skin.

The steaming water scalded my cool skin as I stepped into the basin. I sighed and lowered my body in, being careful not to immerse the wound on my side. Using a towel, I sponged my neck and upper body until red blossomed on my skin. Cleaning my side and back, I grimaced through the pain as I tried washing my hair. My gooseflesh disappeared as my body temperature rose.

Time passed without thought before I stepped out and dressed. Made for a larger woman, the clothes hung on me, but at least they were soft and clean.

Outside the cavern I found the young woman waiting, toeing the ground with the tip of her boot.

She smiled and nodded. "I'll wash these clothes and get your measurements off of them."

"There's really no need—"

"They will be done and delivered to you tomorrow. Now I will lead you back to the cavern."

Chapter Twenty-One

Without any natural lighting or sight of the sun, time streamed by in an irrevocable manner. My body gave in to the exhaustion that had been settling in for days, barely dented by the sleep I'd acquired before the attack. But it was a fitful sleep, and I woke often, my mind plagued by bad dreams in which I relived my capture.

The curtain rustled, and Mari entered.

I yawned and struggled into a sitting position.

She set a bundle of clothing on the bed. "We finished your clothes."

"Already? I thought they wouldn't be ready until tomorrow."

"The women finished them quickly."

"Thank you."

Mari walked over to the side of the bed. "Are you hungry?"

"Yes, very."

"Come on then." She held out a hand and helped me up. "Get dressed, and I'll show you the way when you're done."

I let her heave me to my feet. "What time is it?"

"It's mid-afternoon, or thereabouts."

I sat up. "Mid-afternoon?"

Mari's mask slipped a little as her eyebrows drew together in a frown. "Yes, you slept through the late afternoon, night, and morning again."

"Have you heard if my friends arrived?"

"No, that is none of my business." She turned and left through the curtain.

I looked down at the stack of clothes. On the top were the clothes I'd worn here. They'd been cleaned and pressed. Below were two more sets of clothing, both similar in style. I fingered the material and picked up the smokey-gray pants with a dark, blue-green tunic.

I pulled the pants on one leg at a time, moving slow and steady. The shirt was a little less painful as I didn't have to bend over. My boots had been cleaned and polished, shining in the faint light from my candle.

Mari came in as I struggled to pull on my left boot, my right one on but not laced.

"Are you ready?"

"Not quite—"

She turned to leave.

I need help.

Mari reached forward and laid her hand on the curtain.

Adnan and Saya have helped me before. I was better off for it.

I cleared my throat. "Mari, wait, could you help me? It's too hard wrapping my ribs on my own."

Her gaze flicked down to my covered torso. She snapped her fingers, and a young girl with apple cheeks appeared within moments. "Linen strips. Bring them to the Otherworlder's alcove."

The girl bobbed a small bow and flashed me a mischievous smile before rushing off. Mari stood with her arms crossed, her eyes penetrating me while we waited.

She's not like the others. She's not afraid. According to Tristan, Mari was beneath me, and yet she held eye contact as though she were of a higher rank. *Why?*

The patter of light feet on stone preceded the girl reappearing with the bandages.

"Lift up your tunic," Mari ordered. She didn't flinch when she saw my mottled skin. The blue and green were fading into more of a dark, purple-gray shade. With deft fingers, she began wrapping my ribs, holding one hand onto the strip to keep it in place as she tightened it. Securing it, she stood back and put her hands on her hips.

I let out a deep breath and felt the resistance of the bandages across my ribcage.

Mari pulled the tunic down at the edges until it fell in folds to the top of my thighs. She took my belt and cinched it around my waist. "You're ready; come."

She led the way down the tunnel from the cavern where I'd slept. "That was the women's cavern," she instructed over her shoulder. "Down that fork there is the men's. Off limits. Just as ours is to the men's."

I blinked. *Adnan was in my room in the underground caves.... Different place, different rules,* I supposed. "What about families?"

"They sleep elsewhere. Just know that single women are not to go to the men's cavern." She stopped just inside the entrance to yet another cave.

"Here's where we eat. You may make your way here for the meals."

"Wait," I called after her. "What am I supposed to do afterward?"

Mari turned to face me. "Whatever you want, Otherworlder."

"But—"

She waited, motionless, her arms hanging at her sides. When I didn't say anything more, she nodded once and left. I followed her in silence down the corridor to the main cavern, through another corridor on the far side, which ended in another large room.

"Go on," she urged before leaving me.

Inside the cavern, two women washed dishes, the only occupants in the room. The last meal, which I guessed to be lunch, must have come and gone. As I weaved across the extensive cavern, two people washing dishes stopped, watching my approach.

"Otherworlder," the older of the two women greeted, inclining her head.

"Hello, I was told I could get something to eat here?"

"Sit over there, Otherworlder. We'll prepare your meal."

"You don't have to—"

"Yes, we do. Sit."

⁕⁂⁕

The hint of it being evening came when Haniel found me wandering through a small tunnel.

"It's the dinner hour, Otherworlder," he reminded.

"Why that name?"

He turned and walked down another tunnel without another word.

"How did you find me?" I jogged a few steps to catch up to him. "And where is Tristan?"

"My lord is busy with important affairs."

"Will he see me?"

Haniel shrugged. "Perhaps. I am going to the dining cavern now, and it seems you are following me. Lord Tristan may be there."

"Do you have word of my companions?"

"There has been none."

My heart sank. "You don't talk much," I muttered. Maybe I imagined it, but Haniel's lips seemed to quirk for the barest moment.

The chatter filtered down the tunnel. We stepped into the brightly lit cavern, and I tensed.

"More people have arrived, haven't they?"

Haniel nodded, leading the way through the many tables. Some of the faces we passed had yet to wash away the dirt from the road, but there was no sign of Saya or Adnan. *Not that I thought there would be. What if they were captured? Or are dead?* My jaw clenched. It had been two days, yet it already felt like forever. *They have to be alive. How much longer?* My chest tightened, and my fingers curled at my sides.

Haniel led the way to a larger table, which was set away from the others. He gestured for me to take a seat.

"Juliet," Tristan spoke. My eyes darted to where Tristan's voice had come from. He stood and tugged his shirt down, smoothing out the few wrinkles.

"Tristan," I rejoined, returning the greeting. I glanced at Haniel, who took a seat.

Tristan stepped up to my side. "Please sit, Juliet. Have they been treating you well?"

I opened my lips to answer but froze as plates loaded with meat, squashes, and other veggies—some savory, some sweetened with sugar and spices—arrived at the table. The breathy steam carried the smells straight to my nose, and my stomach rumbled. A young woman placed a small bowl of rice in front of me. I dug in, almost inhaling the hot food.

Tristan laughed, loud and hearty. "I believe you are a mite peckish after the many miles you walked today."

"How did *you* know?"

"I do have eyes and ears in this place. Besides, I have ordered my people to guard you, and guard you they do. You may not realize it, but someone is always keeping an eye on you."

"What? Why?"

"To keep you safe."

"Am I not safe enough here?"

Tristan set down his wooden eating utensils. "It is just an extra precaution. So tell me, now that you have explored my domain more fully, what do you think?"

"It's impressive," I said after swallowing. "And a bit overwhelming. It seems to go on and on. Several times I found myself where I'd already been because the tunnels intersect. It's incredible, really. How was it made?"

He leaned back in his chair and laced his arms behind his head. "Many of these caverns are natural, as are some of the tunnels. We just expanded them. There are many such places in this world if you have eyes to see their use."

I pushed my plate away and leaned my elbows on the table surface. "What am I supposed to do here?"

Tristan regarded me for several moments. "Nothing for now. Rest. Strengthen yourself for what is ahead." His shoulders rose as he took in a long breath and relaxed.

"And what is ahead?"

The lines around Tristan's eyes deepened. "I am not sure," he admitted. "But we'll figure that out. For now, the best thing is that you're out of Creulon's hands." His face darkened as he mentioned his cousin's name. "He doesn't know you're here, and we need to keep it that way as long as possible. There are a lot of things in play, but because of the secrecy we have been able to maintain, we have been able to take our time. The Uprising is growing stronger day by day." His gaze grew distant as he stared out over the cavern, his eyes unfocused.

I cradled a cup in my hands, watching him. Nearly imperceptible pain flickered across his face. My eyebrows furrowed. "What are you thinking of?"

Tristan started and poured himself some tea. "Nothing to bother yourself about." He gave a small, tired smile. "Now, why don't you get some rest. There is nothing you need help with here, not yet at least."

"Exploring was fine today," I murmured. "But what about tomorrow, or the day after, or the day after that? I can't just do nothing."

Tristan twirled his cup in his fingers. "I will give them orders to let you do as you wish. I should have known better than to keep you from menial tasks."

I raised an eyebrow. "You're right. You should have. But I don't know that I would use the word menial."

"Oh?"

"If everything your people are doing is necessary to the cause, then isn't everything important, down to the smallest task? No matter whether it's washing the dishes or mending clothes, up to training the men or being a spy?" I leaned forward, emboldened. "They are all important in their own way. Some are more dangerous than others, yes, but without the little people, you would not survive." My stomach churned and I licked my lips, my eyes flickering over Tristan, who said nothing.

He sighed and set his cup down with a soft thud. "You continue to surprise me. Your words reflect your heart and the feelings of my own. Thank you, Juliet."

He does agree. It hadn't seemed like he was agreeing. My eyes narrowed and I glanced away, breaking his intense gaze. I cleared my throat. "Have you had any word?"

"From the Unknown and Saya? No." Tristan laid a hand on my forearm. "My people have just begun trickling in. It could be a few more days before your companions arrive. And there is so much to do in that time." Tristan pushed his empty plate to the side. "Do not worry about Saya, Juliet. I sent several men to guard them and bring them safely back. They will be here before you know it."

I longed for Adnan and Saya, someone to help reassure me, to tell me that what I was doing was right, or at the least, unavoidable. But there was no one, and I couldn't seem to sway the doubts flickering at the corners of my mind and soul.

Tristan and I didn't say anything as the dishes were cleared away and we were handed mugs of spiced wine. Most of the people had cleared out of the room by now, and sharp, clinking noises came from those on kitchen duty as they washed.

I watched Tristan from under lowered lashes as he gazed at the kitchen workers, his brow furrowed.

"You have that look on your face," he noted without looking away from those cleaning up.

I jumped. "What?"

"I can sense it. You have been watching me for the past several minutes."

Warmth began spreading up my neck and into my face. Tristan chuckled and ran his fingers through his short locks. *He saw.* My body grew warmer with embarrassment.

"Juliet, you wear your heart on your sleeve."

"I do not," I fumed.

"Perhaps not always, but you don't realize how much you do. Now what do you want to know?"

"I don't want to pry."

"Don't all females say that when that is what they want most?"

Hearing the lilting way in which he said the words took some of the sting out. "The way you spoke of your..." I hesitated. "Your family dying...you blame yourself, don't you?"

Tristan's eyes widened, and his face paled.

I shouldn't have asked. I searched for something to say, anything, but footsteps alerted us to Haniel approaching. As he bent down to whisper in Tristan's ear, I watched as Tristan straightened, his face brisk. In a second, he had reverted back to Lord Tristan, leader of the rebels, and away from the softer man I had just begun to see. My heart clenched.

Haniel stepped back as Tristan stood. "Juliet, I apologize. I have matters I must attend to. Can you find your way back to your room?"

"Yes."

"Perfect. Sleep well. I shall see you tomorrow." Tristan bowed.

I stood as the smaller, slighter figure of Haniel strode off beside Tristan. *He's different.* I watched as he looked aside at Haniel and tilted his head back in a laugh, which echoed down the corridor. *He's gone through so much, and yet his morals are true. He strives to do what is right.* With slow steps, I made my way down the dark tunnel, the light from my candle flickering on the walls and floor. *The people look up to him. He's earned their trust. He's open about his past—but Adnan...he's different. Why? He won't share about his past, or even much about his life now. And yet I want to trust him. But why?*

Chapter Twenty-Two

There was nothing to do in this godforsaken mountain, although the gods abounded in the prayers of those within the walls. I was the sole person who did not believe in the numerous gods the Ryujin prayed to. There were no books, no entertainment, nor even the barest glint of natural light. A cloud hung over me.

Hours of exploring, hours of walking miles, my feet treading corridor after corridor, burning candles down and replenishing, on and on. Then I slept. Sleeping was a relief from the pain in my ribs and the discontent shadowing my mind. But it was still restless. Three times I woke, unsure of what had pulled me from sleep, and it took me a while to relax again.

Breakfast. Ignoring the stares of the men and women in the caverns. Returning the bows of those I passed with unnatural ones of my own.

It was hard to keep track of time without the rising and falling of the sun. But lunch had come and gone, and I leaned against the wall outside of my little alcove, watching the women bustle around. The ceiling high above loomed over us with rock formations that, if they cracked and dropped, would kill those standing below.

A shout arose, arresting my attention, and I saw Mari standing on the far side of the cavern. I pushed myself off the wall and meandered through, nodding back to the women, both young and old, as I passed. Slipping around three large washing vats, steam rising from the tops, I sidestepped a circle of women winding strips of leather around the hilts of daggers and swords. Then I found Mari.

She turned before I could say a word and raised her eyebrows. "Otherworlder?"

"Juliet, my name's Juliet."

"What do you want?"

I swallowed my annoyance. "I'd like to do something to help."

Mari watched me without blinking an eye or even shifting. "You won't be much help with those ribs of yours."

I shrugged.

"Very well," she acquiesced, raising a hand. She snapped her fingers and the same young girl as the day before darted forward.

"Honoka, the Otherworlder will help with the mending. Please show her what to do and see to her needs."

"Alright, Mari." Honoka smiled at me and beckoned.

I followed her over to a corner of the room where several women sat on the rocky floor, baskets of clean clothing by their feet and needles and thread in their hands.

Silence fell as I sat down next to them. They watched me, their work forgotten in their laps.

"Here." Honoka shoved a shirt into my hands. "Do you know how to sew a button back on?"

"Yes, thankfully that is something I *do* know."

She nodded and gave me a cup full of loose buttons and needles. "Just pick one that matches the best." She sat down next to me and picked up another item from the basket in the middle of our circle. "I'm Honoka, as Mari already said, and this is Yui, Koharu, Rin, Sakura, and Aoi." She pointed to each woman in turn as she said their names.

"Hello—" I bowed with a hesitant smile. "I'm Juliet."

"You're the Otherworlder," Sakura observed, a slight question in her raised eyebrows.

"Shh," another woman hushed, looking at me with frightened eyes.

"Rin, right?" I looked at the speaker, who nodded, eyes furtive. "It's alright. I don't bite."

Honoka grinned back at me. "Can I ask you a question?"

"Sure."

"What's your world like?"

My world? So similar and yet so different.

The woman who had shushed Sakura spoke up again. "Please, Other-worlder. We do not mean to be rude." She turned to Honoka. "That was impertinent."

"I really don't mind," I murmured as I threaded the needle and chose a button.

"Tell us about it," Honoka pressed, unable to contain the excitement shining in her eyes.

I laughed as I looked at her. "It's much like here: beautiful, dangerous, wild, cultured, filled with many different peoples, each with their own unique traditions and ways of living. There are creatures, most of which are probably much like yours." *There are families, just like here, mothers and fathers, just like here, and friends...Cam.* My hands stilled in my lap. *She must be worried out of her mind. Or has she given up on ever finding me?*

Honoka's sewing lay still in her lap. "Like what?"

I blinked, startled. "What?"

"What creatures?"

"Birds, some as small as would fit in the palm of your hand, others large and ferocious, predators of the skies; there are reptiles, amphibians, mammals, and fish. The sun shines as bright and warm as it does here, and the moon at night, just like here. There are forests, trees, lakes, rivers, hills, and mountains."

Sakura, the young woman with small hands and an inquisitive look in her eyes, leaned forward. "And what do you do in your land?"

"I?" The question took me by surprise. *I work. I live with my family. I spend hours talking, laughing, and doing things with Cam. Much like I do things now, with new friends.* I looked around the small circle, the women watching with varying degrees of interest. *I haven't felt free like this in years. The cloud doesn't lie over me like it used to.* I closed my eyes, hiding the sheen of tears. *It's been almost eleven years since Eddie died. What must Mom and Dad be going through, thinking they lost me as well? I can't live my life like this. Was I right to go with Saya?*

A small hand touched me on the arm. I opened my eyes.

Honoka cocked her head and giggled. "Are you all right?"

I opened my mouth—and jumped as a voice spoke from behind me: "There is work to be done."

I glanced over my shoulder. Mari stood there, eyeing the group of women, most of whom had bent their heads back over their work. She met my gaze and nodded once before turning away with a soft swish of her skirt.

"My lady," a deeper voice spoke.

With a sigh, I looked up to see Haniel standing on the other side of the small circle.

"Your presence is requested."

My stomach dropped. "By whom?"

"Lord Tristan."

Lord Tristan. Why? I frowned but let Honoka take the sewing from my lap. *What does he want?* My heart thudded in my chest, and I felt the blood rush from my face. *Adnan. He must have news.* I stood up and brushed the dirt off my tunic and pants. "Fine. Lead the way."

Haniel's eyes widened, and his lips thinned, but he turned away without waiting.

Honoka waved a small hand at me. "See you later?"

I nodded and smiled, but it was forced. "Definitely."

"Come," Haniel urged, almost growling the word. "You should show more respect when Lord Tristan—"

"Me?" I spluttered. "When I seem to be at his beck and call? Or is it just me?"

Haniel's shoulders stiffened, and a tinge of red showed in his cheeks. "He is a very busy man. Besides, this is an important matter. Be glad he called for you."

Adnan. What's happened? I hurried my step, wishing Haniel would walk faster. Sweat formed on my forehead as worry gnawed at me.

Haniel stopped and gestured. "Here we are. Go in."

"Thanks," I murmured, stepping into the small room.

Tristan straightened from where he'd been leaning over a low table. "Juliet," he acknowledged.

Tristan nodded to his advisors. "Give us a moment." He waited until they left through the open doorway behind me. "Please sit."

I sat down in one of the hard-backed chairs.

"Keeping busy?"

I nodded. "Yes, I'll admit I didn't realize how hard it would be with my ribs."

He started forward. "What happened?" His eyes narrowed and his lips thinned.

"I broke a rib or two," I admitted.

Tristan looked into my eyes, and after a few moments, took a deep breath and hunched forward. "I am sorry." He raised his head. "Which of my people was responsible?"

I took a step back. "Tristan, it wasn't one of your people! Why would you think that?"

He strode over and twisted a chair away from the table and sat down, straddling the chair as he faced me. "When?"

"It was days ago, a couple weeks or so."

He leaned forward, his eyes earnest. "I will have the healer sent to your quarters. Why did you not say something sooner?"

"There was no need." I looked down, hesitating. "Saya took care of it for me; her mother was a healer."

"And since then? Have you had no help?"

"The Unknown and Mari—"

Tristan's chair thumped on the floor as he stood.

I watched his back, wondering what was going on. "What did I do wrong?"

"I am sorry, Juliet. I should not have acted the way I did." He turned around. "I let my emotions get the better of me and for that, I apologize. It was nothing about you, just worry for your safety and concern that I may have failed in some way." His eyes crinkled. "You are a strong woman."

"Perhaps, but I don't feel it now. My body hurts and I'm exhausted." I laughed.

"Who did it to you?"

"The king's men...I think." I jumped as his fist landed on the table with a loud thud. "I don't know for sure, but that's what we think."

"You mean Benkei."

I nodded.

Tristan smiled, a grim tilt to his lips. "Then he is right."

"Why would you say so?"

"Because he would know better than anyone. And if he says they work for the king, then they do."

"But why—"

Tristan raised an eyebrow and walked around the edge of the table to face me. "Has he not told you who he is?"

I blinked and felt as though I'd been punched in the gut. "No, I mean, not completely."

"Interesting. I wonder why..."

"What do you know?" I pressed. *Adnan hadn't even seemed to know much about Tristan. Why would he trust Tristan over me with who he is?*

"Sorry, not now, Juliet. There are other things we must talk of." He tapped a finger on the table, his eyes distant, lost in thought.

Anger bubbled up within me, but I swallowed, pushing it back down. *Not now. Find out what he wants.* "Why did you want to see me?"

"It is not enough for me to just want someone to speak to?" Tristan rejoined.

My eyes narrowed. "I—you have your advisors."

"True, but all they speak of is the war. I have word for you. Saya and the seer should be here by the end of the day. Apparently they had to take a detour, as the king's men are searching for everyone who escaped." He stood up and switched chairs, moving into one right next to me. "It presents a big problem. There are many who have not arrived, and the longer it takes them the higher the chance of them not making it."

My breath caught. "And Adnan?"

Tristan's eyes narrowed and an iciness seemed to cast a thin sheen over his features. "Knowing him? He will be just fine. There is no need to worry. But no, I haven't had word of him yet."

What do I not know? I stared at Tristan, who watched me with a searching look. *Will the secrets ever end?*

"Juliet?"

My head jerked, and I looked up at Tristan.

"Will you dine with me?"

I hesitated, and Tristan leaned forward and rested his hand on the table. "Juliet?"

"Yes, yes, I'd like that."

"Good." The lines on his face lessened somewhat. "Haniel?"

The curtain rustled. "My Lord?" Haniel inquired, his hands hanging by his sides.

"Juliet will dine with me tonight. Will you show her the way?"

Haniel nodded and stepped aside, holding the curtain open for me to follow.

"I'll be along shortly," Tristan murmured, nodding to me. "I just have something I must do first."

"This way." Haniel gestured and joined me in a walk. The lantern in his hand enveloped us in a small circle of light.

"Where are we going?"

Haniel shot a sideways glance at me. "My lord thought you might like a private dinner tonight."

"Oh. Just the two of us?"

"Yes, be careful."

I started. "Of what?"

"Of yourself," he paused before adding, "And him."

Tristan knows more about Adnan than I'd realized and keeps so much from me. I'm not here of my own free will, but it's easy to forget that. I watched as Haniel glanced down another tunnel opening as we passed. *Is it Tristan who is a threat? Or is Haniel meaning I am the threat?* Confusion filled me with the warring thoughts. My mouth felt dry and tight. I swallowed. *Tristan is acting strangely. I am kept dangling. He talks when he wants to but isn't available when I want him to be.* I snorted, ignoring the curious look Haniel shot me.

He stopped short in the passageway, and I almost ran into his back. A guard stood outside a door, I realized, and he moved aside to let us in. I glanced over my shoulder as I entered and saw the door close, leaving both men outside.

Be careful. Haniel's words seemed to echo.

A lantern hung from the ceiling, its light supplemented with the soft and romantic glow of several candles propped up in the rocky recesses of the floor. I sat down on a plump cushion before a low table laden with food. My stomach growled at the tantalizing scents.

A footstep alerted me to Tristan entering the small room. He walked over and eased himself onto another cushion.

"You look beautiful."

I blushed. "Don't be ridiculous."

With a smile crossing his lips, the lines of worry and strain faded away. He looked more boyish now, the years sliding away as his humor and lightheartedness grew. "Are you hungry?"

"You have no idea. You?"

"Likewise. I missed lunch today."

"Why do I get the feeling that is a normal occurrence for you?"

Tristan arched his eyebrow and grimaced. "You had better be careful. You are beginning to sound like Haniel."

I chuckled. "Haniel is interesting. He doesn't say much."

"True, but a finer friend and supporter I could not ask for. I do not know what I would do without him."

"It's important to have those. Friends, I mean," I added. "Especially when surrounded by enemies. Sometimes I don't think we value true friendship enough."

"And you, Juliet? Who do you consider your friends in this world?"

"I suppose—Saya and the Unknown. They have been there for me when no one else has. They've protected me with their lives. We have a bond forged by hardship, and I trust them."

"Lucky them. I hope a friendship between you and I might grow." He raised his glass up in a tribute.

"And I as well," I said, raising mine.

⁕⁕⁕⁕⁕ ⁕⁕⁕⁕⁕

Belly full and my worries all but forgotten, I let Tristan heave me to my feet.

"I know it's late, but would you like to go on a walk?"

"A walk?" I repeated.

"There is something I'd like you to see."

"Uhh, sure."

He held out a hand to me.

Haniel warned me. But what if he just doesn't want me around Tristan so much? What if it's not Tristan Haniel thinks is a threat, but me?

Tristan's blue eyes beckoned to me.

I laid my hand in his. The warmth and smoothness of his hand sent a jolt through my body. My face mirrored his own bright smile.

Haniel followed us at a discreet distance as we made our way through dank passageways I hadn't found in my earlier exploration. The breeze grew colder as we continued, caressing my face and causing the candle's flame to throw dancing images on the wall.

"Almost there," Tristan murmured as we rounded a bend. Not five yards from the curve in the path lay an opening in the rock, maybe six feet high and a couple feet wide. Tristan handed the candle to Haniel, and we continued forward without him. The fresh, clean scent of pines suddenly wafted through the air. We walked out and stood on a small ledge cut into the mountainside, the valley below awash in soft moonlight.

"I didn't realize how much I missed this," I whispered.

"I come up here every night I can," Tristan murmured. "It helps me decompress." He sat down and patted the rock next to him. I joined him, my back against the rough wall, and followed his gaze out to the dark landscape.

The coolness from the stone seeped into me. I laid my chin on my drawn-up knees, watching as the soft moonlight gleamed off something in the distance...*a lake?* A darker patch, the forest, lay further off from the mountain, drowned in shadows. No one was about. Nothing disturbed the quiet, slow peacefulness of the dim valley.

"You are right."

I blinked, startled.

Tristan didn't break his stare over the valley. "I do blame myself for the deaths of my family."

"Why?"

He shrugged. "I was so young, too young to do anything, and yet it was because of my birth that Creulon acted. He would have been heir. He would have waited."

"You couldn't decide not to be born—"

"I know." Tristan ran his fingers through his short hair. "I keep telling myself that, and yet the weight is still there. I can't let go of the past. It is what has shaped me and what drives me even now."

"Someone once told me to learn from the past, but also to let it go. Not to be consumed by it."

Tristan turned to look at me. "You think I am consumed by it?" The dark glint in his eyes dissipated. He shrugged his broad shoulders. "Perhaps I am. But that drive fuels me. Sometimes I wish I could let it go."

"Then do it. Try—"

"You do not understand," Tristan bit out.

Yes, yes, I do. My fingernails bit into my palm. "Yes, I do, Tristan. I understand far better than you think I do. My brother *died* because I wasn't paying attention. He drowned because I froze, because I didn't try to help until it was too late. You think I don't know what it's like to have a hard time letting go of the past? I do. I am to blame for my brother's death." My words seemed to echo around the mountainside before silence fell. "I could have done something. I could have saved him. But you were so young. Too young to do anything to save your family. You would have died too, if not for your nurse."

Tristan stared at me, his lips parted, and laid an arm across his drawn-up knees. "Have you forgiven yourself?"

Air felt trapped in my lungs.

"Juliet?"

I started and stared at him. "Sometimes I think I do...but no, no, I haven't. It haunts me every waking day and each night when I fall asleep. He's even in my dreams sometimes."

"I do not fully blame myself for the deaths," Tristan began, his voice low and hesitant. "Not like how I realize you do. And it is less and less with each day. I know I should place all the blame on Creulon. It was his actions, not mine. I had to move on from blaming myself. It was not going to change anything. You're continuing to blame yourself for your brother's death will not bring him back."

"I know," I whispered, hunching forward. "But it's easier."

"So that makes it right? You made a mistake—"

"A mistake?" I sputtered, swiveling my head to look at him.

Tristan raised a hand. "A horrible, life-changing mistake, yes. But still a mistake. You were young?"

I nodded.

"Does your family blame you?"

I shook my head. "No, but they didn't need to. I put it all on myself. I think they knew I felt guilty enough without them also heaping it upon me."

"A lot of time has passed, Juliet. If you ever need to talk, I'm here. But I hope you can begin to heal from your brother's death."

I smiled. "The same goes for you. I want to help if I can."

Silence fell, and as time passed by, I relaxed, leaning back against the rock wall. We sat there long enough that I began nodding off without realizing it.

"Come on. We had better get you to bed."

I blinked, sleepy, and stared up at Tristan's face. He helped me up and guided me back through the tunnels. Haniel walked ahead of us this time with the single candle, pushing the pressing darkness back as we left the fresh breeze behind.

By the time I reached my room, my eyes struggled to stay open. I collapsed on the bed, boots and all, and muttered, "Thanks, Tristan. It was lovely."

I felt a vague tugging on my feet as I dropped into sleep.

⁂

Sweat coated my body, the loose blouse clinging to my skin, damp with perspiration. Sitting up, I looked around the small cave, my breathing heavy. It was pitch black. I didn't know what had awoken me.

Pushing up with my hands, I stood up from the cot and picked at the shirt, peeling it away from my skin. Why could I not remember? There were no memories, just a certainty that I had dreamt, and whatever had happened had been terrifying.

The curtain rustled as a cold breeze blew through, brushing across my skin and causing goosebumps to break out over my skin. But still I felt the clamminess of the sweat coating my body. My hair hung in stringy strands around my face, also damp. I hadn't dreamt, or had I? Another breeze blew through the small chamber, and I shivered.

I brushed the curtain aside and stepped out with a clean change of clothes. The baths would be empty at this time of the night. My ears perked as I noticed the snores ringing through the air, reverberating from the different sleeping places of the women in the cavern. With fumbling fingers, I managed to light the lantern I'd brought with me.

My shadow followed me down the unfamiliar corridor to the bathing chamber. A dull glow filled the room from the lantern, the wavering light revealing steam rising in curlicues above the water, which sprang up from its hole in the ground, filling the pool and cascading down into the second, larger pool.

I wasted no time in peeling my clothes off and flinging them to the ground. Standing under the small fountain of water spurting out of a hole in the rocks above, I felt the grime and sweat wash away and the heat warm my body.

A footstep in the tunnel beyond echoed. My eyes flicked to the fresh clothes lying on the ground, but there wasn't time. Leaping over the rim of the wall, I sank down into the deepest part of the pool, jerking as the hot water hit the stitching of my wound. The heat was almost unbearable, but I stayed put, my head just above the rim of the pool.

A young woman stepped through the opening. She started as she spotted me in the corner. "Oh, pardon me. I hadn't thought anyone would be in here."

"Wait, you're Sakura." I waded closer to the edge of the pool. "You are welcome to stay."

"Thank you, Otherworlder." She nodded and slipped out of her clothes before also showering.

I stared up at the ceiling, waiting for her to join me in the basin. Often I was alone when I used the bathing chamber. *Remember, this isn't weird for them.* I straightened as Sakura slid into the water. *This is normal—a social time...just without clothes.* A small smile curved my lips. Sakura raised an eyebrow.

"Couldn't sleep?" I asked, breaking the silence.

"No, someone's snores were keeping me awake. You?"

"I slept fine until an hour ago. Had to clear my head, so I figured I'd come here."

"It's peaceful at this time," Sakura sighed and relaxed against the wall. "Chases away the night chills as well. Might I ask you something?" I had no chance to respond before she continued, "Why are you helping us?"

"What do you mean?"

"Well, you aren't of this world, and you have no ties to anyone here." Sakura finished washing under the fountain and slipped into the pool. "There's no reason for you to help the rebellion, or to even stay."

"You're right. I'm not from here, but I've made good friends since I've been here. Friends who would sacrifice their lives for me, and who are in this to the end, it seems." I took a deep breath. "I think that though this hasn't turned out the way I expected, I still made the decisions that placed me here now. Or if I didn't, then there was nothing I could do to stop it."

"You make it seem as though fate placed you here."

"Fate?" I sighed and leaned back against the pool wall. "You mean like the seven gods you've mentioned before?"

Sakura shrugged her dainty shoulders. "They aren't the only gods. I do not know who decides fate."

"So do you think you are here because of fate? Because the gods will it?"

"No, well, I don't know."

"But are you happy? Content?"

"I am content. I think I would've gone crazy if I'd left back to my world and didn't know what would happen here. In a way, this is starting to become my Earth, too."

"And you would die for the rebellion?"

I reeled back in surprise and clenched my hands together. "I—I would."

It's just what she wanted to hear.

Guilt gnawed at me.

Sakura nodded. "I'm glad you're with us, Otherworlder."

"My name is Juliet."

"Juliet." Sakura smiled and bowed her head.

"How long have you been here?"

"Part of the rebellion? A year or so."

"Why did you join?"

"It was time." Sakura glanced away, her eyes trailing to my ribs. "Otherworlder," she began. "What happened?"

"Juliet, please." I followed her gaze. "I was injured a couple of weeks ago."

"By whom?"

"I'm not sure."

Sakura raised her eyebrows. "But—"

"It was two men who captured me. My companions and I had rescued people taken by slavers. The two men weren't with the slavers; I know that much."

"Were they the king's men?"

I shrugged. "Possibly." I rose and nodded to her. "It was nice to talk with you a little, Sakura."

"You as well." Sakura inclined her head.

As I squatted to reach the dirty clothing on the floor, Sakura cleared her throat.

"You can leave it there. I'll make certain they're returned to your quarters."

"I can take care of my own clothes."

"I'm not saying you can't." She smiled. "But I am going to wash my own anyways. Let me do this, Otherworlder."

"Very well, thank you."

Once I left the cavern, I realized I'd left the lantern behind but decided to go on without it. Feeling my way across the uneven ground, I squinted as a light appeared ahead of me, coming towards me in a jolting manner.

Haniel came into view, the lantern bobbing in his grip. He grunted. "There you are."

"Is everything alright? Does Tristan have news?"

"He would like to see you, my lady," Haniel responded, gesturing with his arm. He walked just ahead of me and soon pointed at a small tunnel. "Through there," he said.

I walked past him and saw a light at the end of the corridor. It was just enough to show me the way. Pausing in the entryway, a smile lit my face.

"Saya!" I rushed forward and wrapped my arms around her. She relaxed and grinned. Drawing back, I held her forearms. "Are you all right? I've been worried."

"I'm fine," she rejoined with a twinkle in her eye. "You?"

"Thanks to Tristan," I nodded towards him, "I'm safe, as well."

Tristan drew forward at this. "We will leave you two ladies alone to catch up. I have a feeling neither of you will want to sleep. I will have some food and tea sent in."

"Thanks, Tristan."

He nodded, a smile crossing his face for a moment. He gave us a brief salute before turning on his heel.

When we were alone, I asked, "So what happened? How was the trip? Everything went all right? I wasn't sure what to expect. I haven't seen you in days, and then when the attack occurred, all I was told was that you were with the seer and you would join us soon."

Saya laughed. "You never cease, do you? Always full of questions."

I grinned and walked across with her to a couple of cushions on the ground next to a low table.

Saya's eyebrows furrowed. "To be honest, the last couple of days were a blur. We had to take a roundabout way because of the king's men, but I never saw them. We moved at night, slept during the day. The journey would've been boring except for the conversations I had with Drielle." Saya's eyes shone. "She knows so much! There is much I could learn from her. Juliet, there's someone else like me."

"I'm happy for you."

Saya eyed me. "You sound hesitant."

"No, I'm excited, really. It's just everything is happening so quickly."

"That's not just it, is it? Have you heard from Shizukana?"

I shook my head. "No, and it's bothering me. I don't know if he escaped—"

"What do you mean?"

"We left him fighting to cover our flight."

Saya muttered under her breath. "Look, Juliet, I'm sure he's fine. If anyone can make it here safely, it's him."

"I know." I sighed. "That's what Tristan said."

"Right. What is going on between you two?"

I blinked. "Who?"

"You and Tristan."

"What do you mean?"

Saya gave an exasperated huff. "Come on. It's obvious."

"I have no idea what you're talking about," I responded, confused. "There's nothing between us. We're friends."

"Of course, silly me." Saya rolled her eyes. "He is rather good-looking though, isn't he?" she asked. "Juliet?"

"What? Oh, yes, he is good-looking. But we're just friends," I replied, pushing the matter out of my head. "Will the seer take you under her tutelage?"

Saya frowned but let the change of subject pass. "She has offered, yes."

"And?"

"I have accepted. I can learn much from her and possibly help the rebels. Now that I know how the rest of the kingdom has fallen, it won't be long till our coast bears the brunt as well. Things will get worse. That raid was only the first."

"If you believe you can help them better here, then stay. Send word to the innkeeper, though. Relieve his mind that you are safe."

Saya's eyes clouded. "I—I hadn't thought of him."

"You should. He cares for you a lot. I'm sure he's worried to death."

"Juliet," she began, her eyebrows furrowed as she mulled over her words. "Drielle says that with practice, I will be able to purposefully look into the future and see things. Not necessarily exactly what I want to, but I wouldn't have to wait for the visions to come." She looked me in the eyes, waiting for some sort of answer.

Before I could speak, the door opened, and a woman entered with a tray. She kept her eyes averted and set the tray down on the table between us.

"Thank you," I murmured. "This looks wonderful."

The woman nodded and with a small bow and left the room, closing the door behind her. I poured two cups of steaming tea and handed one to Saya.

"Well?" she prompted, staring at me from over the rim of her cup.

"Somehow I'm not surprised."

Saya nodded. "Me neither. I always felt like I should be able to do more. Now I will have that chance, with Drielle's help." Saya quirked an eyebrow. "And you? What will you do now?"

"I don't know. Part of me wants to return home, but I know I can't leave. Especially not now. It's not even possible."

"But do you *want* to stay?"

"Yes," I responded without hesitation. "Yes, I do."

Saya smiled. "I'm glad. I don't want you to leave, either."

Chapter Twenty-Three

Honoka, the young girl with rosy cheeks from the sewing circle, bounded through the curtain into my enclosed room.

I peered at her from under sleepy, half-closed eyes and yawned. "Honoka?"

"Juliet! I thought you might be awake." She looked down at me from the edge of the mat. "Are you tired? I've been up for hours. It's late morning, you know! Breakfast is about done with, but they probably have left you some—"

A laugh escaped my lips and I grinned. "Yes, I'm tired. Why are you so full of energy?"

"Am I?" She skipped a step. "Is it true that your ribs are broken?"

"What?"

"Your ribs? Is it really bad?" She peered up at me, worry mixing with curiosity in her eyes.

"Yes, I do have some broken ribs, but they're healing. How did you hear about that?"

"Oh! Everyone is talking about it. I heard about it hours ago and have been looking for you. Will you be alright?"

I frowned. "Yes."

"And is it true that the king did it to you?"

"What do you mean?"

"Everyone is saying how the king is responsible for hurting you and that he will try to hurt you again if he has the chance." Honoka's eyes were large and innocent as they stared back into mine.

I stood up and set my hands on Honoka's shoulders, leaning down to look her in the eyes, "I'll be fine, Honoka. You don't have to worry about me."

"But—"

"No." I smiled and cupped one of her cheeks in my hands. "Don't think anything more about it. Are you hungry?"

She flashed a grin full of white teeth and bobbed her head.

"Good, me too." I took her hand and set off down the hallway, keeping half an ear open as Honoka kept up her ceaseless chattering.

Where did those rumors come from?

"Here we are." Honoka grinned. "Will you come sit with me?"

I nodded as we entered. Faces swung towards us, emotionless but staring. Honoka almost lost me as she bounded towards a table filled with other young children. Taking a deep breath, I focused in on her receding form and followed her to the table. Before I'd even sat down, Honoka rattled off a list of names. The children stared back at me, their eyes full of curiosity and wonder. Their faces blurred together as I sat, numb. I lifted my eyes and swept my gaze across the cavern. A silence had fallen.

Then the whispers started. They ebbed and flowed like the tide, but one word stood out above all the rest.

Otherworlder.

Honoka stopped talking mid-sentence as I stood up from the table.

"I'm sorry, Honoka, but I have to go speak with Tristan."

She watched me with hurt-filled eyes, but there was no protest as I strode away. As I walked, I could've sworn that those I passed moved aside to form an aisle. My footsteps quickened.

⁂

The guard knocked on the door to Tristan's council chamber, eyeing me as he did so. "The Otherworlder requests to speak with Lord Tristan."

"Let her come in," Tristan called through.

The door opened, and I walked through. Tristan stood at the back of the room, facing me, a table littered with papers and maps in front of him.

"Leave us," Tristan said to his advisors, not taking his eyes off me.

The men left, filing one by one out of the chamber.

Tristan crossed his arms. "What is wrong?"

"Have you heard what everyone is talking about this morning?"

Tristan walked around the table. "About you and the king?"

I tapped my foot.

"Yes, I have heard the rumors. It was not me, if that is what you're wondering."

"You didn't use me?"

"No."

"Well, who did then?"

Tristan turned and poured himself a cup of tea. "Who knew?"

"Just you, Saya, the Unknown, Mari, and...Sakura."

"Sakura?"

"She's one of the women. Last night I was bathing, and she was there. But why would she say anything?"

Tristan shrugged and took a sip of the tea. "Would you like some?"

I shook my head.

"Well, perhaps she admired you for it."

"But I never told her it was the king's men for sure. Just that it was possible." I dropped onto a cushion. "Maybe I will take some tea."

Tristan nodded and walked over to the tray holding cups and a pot.

"What am I supposed to do?"

"Do? Do nothing. There is no harm with their surmising anything. You keep them from thinking of their own troubles. I suppose you might be plagued by a sense of worship in a way—"

"What?" I spluttered.

"Have you not noticed they already view you as some sort of mystical creature?"

"Well, I mean, I've seen their curiosity and how they're afraid to approach me, but then again, everyone here seems to be more closed off until they get to know you, as though they don't easily trust."

"That is partly true." Tristan took a seat next to me. "The people of this country do not easily trust. They are polite and do not open up easily to strangers. They are also superstitious, with many different beliefs about the paranormal and more mystical senses." Tristan handed me a small cup of tea. "When you came to this earth, and they found out about you, you instantly gained superiority, mystery, over them. They don't understand you, don't understand how you came to be here. For all they know, you could be some sort of spirit or sorceress. They fear you just as they are awed by you. But they all share one common enemy, one which you share as well: King Creulon. So they find themselves joined to you even if, in other circumstances, it could go differently."

I took a sip of my tea.

"By them finding out about your injury—and it seems the story plays closer to the truth than I could have expected—they believe you to have escaped the king's clutches. You are quickly embedding yourself here."

"They don't believe I have any powers, do they?" My chuckle was dry and humorless.

"Who knows?" Tristan shrugged. "They might, but they will never be bold enough to ask you."

"I don't like the attention."

"I am sorry, Juliet, but I am afraid it is something you will have to get used to if you continue to stay here, which I hope you will."

I stood up. "I didn't think we had a choice in the matter."

Tristan's eyes narrowed, and he clenched his jaw. "You have to understand why I did what I did. I could not risk all of this. I could not let you, nor Saya, nor Benkei, turn on me and go to Creulon with what you have learned—what you have seen. How could you expect me to do anything differently?"

"I understand, but it's still something I can't forget easily." My footsteps rang through the air as I walked to the door. "But just so you know, I would've done the same thing in your circumstances." I left without waiting for a response and nodded to the advisors standing outside as I strode past.

My feet carried me back to the dining cavern, but it was empty. I turned away with my stomach growling.

"Wait."

I turned to see Mari standing behind me at the entrance to the hall.

"Come and eat."

I didn't move.

"I know you're hungry, even without being able to hear your stomach." She beckoned me forward. "I haven't eaten either. Sit there; I'll be back."

I sat and watched as she prepared two plates of leftover food.

"Here." She set the two plates down and sat on the cushion across from me.

My stomach growled again, and I lifted a bite with the chopsticks to my mouth.

I couldn't help but recoil as the cold eggs hit my tongue. I closed my eyes and focused on chewing and swallowing against the clammy texture oozing its way down my throat.

Mari glanced down at the food. "We didn't always get warm food three meals a day. Took us a while to get to where we are now."

"Where were you before?"

Mari stopped eating and regarded me for a minute. "Always on the run. We were never in the same spot for long. There weren't many of us then, either. But slowly we gathered forces, and Lord Tristan grew as our leader. The more atrocities the king committed, the more flocked to Lord Tristan's banner. In a way, the king is partly responsible for all of this." Mari smiled, but it looked more like her lips cracked, threatening to split at the seams, and there was no warmth in her eyes. "We ate scraps, but Lord Tristan changed all of that." Her eyes narrowed as she looked at me. "He is a good man."

I set my chopsticks down. "Is that a warning?"

Mari took a bite and chewed. After swallowing, she replied, "You can take it how you want. But know this, Otherworlder: the people here would lay down their lives for the Uprising. There's a flame growing in the hearts of every person here. Soon it will become a fire, and then Creulon and everyone who stands with him will fall."

"I don't work for Creulon; I would never serve him."

"Perhaps not."

"Why do you not like me?"

"I do not dislike you."

"Really?" I countered. "So why assume the worst of me?"

"You are embroiling yourself in our affairs, Juliet Barrows. Perhaps faster than you realize. Nothing will be the same as they were before you were thrown into our midst. It might be for the best; then again, it might not. None of us know the path we've been set on, and no one can know how it might have changed. For better or worse, we are in this to the end, whatever that may be and however soon that may be."

I pushed the eggs around on my plate, my appetite lost. "I mean no harm to any of you, Mari. You're right—for better or worse, I *am* part of this now, and you can rest assured I'll do whatever I have to, not only to survive but also to keep my friends safe. Maybe I don't do this for the same reasons as you or anyone else here, but I won't betray you either."

She nodded once and stood. "Otherworlder."

"Mari." I inclined my head in return, watching as she walked away, straight-backed and tall. I didn't finish eating; I had no stomach for the food anymore. Taking the lantern with me, I left the cavern and paused in the inter-section where it branched into three corridors. A figure walked ahead in a faint halo of light.

"Saya! Saya!" I called, hurrying my step.

"Juliet, I'm in a hurry."

I grimaced.

"I'm sorry," Saya sighed, running a hand through her long hair. "I didn't mean it that way. It's just that Drielle is waiting for me, and I'm already late."

"Go ahead then."

"No, it's fine. What did you need?"

"I can't just want to talk with you?" I protested, feeling a stab of jealousy. *Drielle gets all of Saya's time now, and me...hardly anything.*

Saya eyed me and continued on. "Will you walk with me?"

I fell into step next to her. "Any progress with your training?"

"Yes." Saya pulled her hair up and secured it with a thin ribbon and some metal prong-like pins. "Last night we were up late. I was able to see into the future on purpose for the first time."

I gasped. "That's amazing!"

A small smile crossed Saya's face and her shoulders relaxed a little. "Drielle said it's sooner than she'd expected or hoped for."

"What did you see?"

The smile disappeared. "Not a whole lot. And nothing that seems to have much meaning."

"It's still progress," I encouraged, brushing up against her.

Saya brought her shoulders back and lifted the candle she held a little higher. "You're right. I just wish I was making faster progress."

"At least—" I shook my head. *It's not her fault I feel useless sometimes.*

Saya didn't seem to have noticed anything amiss. She stopped where the tunnel branched. "I'm almost there. I need to go."

Drielle takes up so much time. I wish I could go with her.

I perked up. "Saya, can I come and watch?"

Saya bit her lip and glanced down the narrow dark tunnel. "No, sorry. Drielle doesn't allow anyone to watch, not even Tristan."

"Oh, okay."

"I'm sorry."

I shrugged.

She shot me an apologetic look and turned to leave.

"Wait! Have you heard anything from the Unknown? He isn't back yet—"

Saya chuckled, and my eyes grew wide at the sound. "Yes, Drielle told me he's been waylaid and sent on a mission by Tristan, but I don't know what nature it is."

I gasped and my heart leapt inside me. "He's alive?"

"Yes." She smiled. "He is."

Tristan. He must've known. "You said Tristan sent him? He didn't say anything." I crossed my arms.

Saya shrugged. "Maybe you should ask him." A gleam entered her eyes.

I gestured. "There is something you're not telling me."

"What?" She blinked and the gleam disappeared.

"What are you thinking?" I probed, taking a step closer.

"Nothing. Go ask him if you want. He is charming, Juliet. I sat with him during breakfast early this morning. Now I really should go." She lifted a hand in farewell as she turned.

"You'll tell me if you hear anything more, won't you?"

"Yes," she called back over her shoulder.

⁕⁕⁕

The corridor I had traversed a little earlier welcomed me again into its enveloping darkness. The guard in front of the council chamber nodded to me.

"Here again, Otherworlder?"

I nodded and strode through the door. "Tristan, we need to talk."

"Advisors." Tristan nodded towards the door behind me. Once they'd left, he sighed. "I see you're making a habit of this, Juliet. What do you think I did this time?"

I crossed my arms. "You sent the Unknown on a mission."

"Ah, yes, so I did." Tristan beckoned me forward, but when I didn't move, he moved forward and took my hands. "It was needed, Juliet. He's more use to me out there than in here."

Anger flared within me. "When were you going to tell me?"

"I had not realized he was that close to you." Tristan's eyes searched mine, his gaze questioning.

Haven't I been asking for news? My jaw clenched and I wrenched my hands out of his grasp. "He's saved my life before, Tristan. He's a friend."

Tristan tugged at the hem of his tunic and turned away. "He will not be gone long, a few days at the most."

"You know I care!" I blurted. "You know I have been asking every day for news of him. Why didn't you tell me?" My voice cracked.

"It slipped my mind. Honestly. I've had a lot to deal with in the wake of the underground cavern system being discovered." Sincerity shone in his eyes. He held his hands out in front of him, as though pleading for forgiveness. Some of the anger within me dissipated.

Even though the tension relaxed from my shoulders, I kept my arms crossed. "Where did you send him?"

"I cannot tell you that. No, do not press me. It is for his safety."

"You don't trust me?"

"It is not you." Tristan took my hand, but I wrenched it away. "Juliet, let's go get some fresh air."

"No. Not today." Firmness tightened my voice. I spun on my heel to leave.

"Wait, Juliet, I have an idea. There are several farms a few leagues from here—" He paused and I waited, but he didn't say anything.

"What is it?"

"Nothing, never mind."

"It was something," I probed.

Tristan laughed. "You don't give up, do you?"

"Not usually."

"Well, in this case, I think it would be too dangerous."

"Why don't you tell me, and if I think it's too dangerous, I won't go. But you have to realize there is a risk for me in this world no matter what I do."

"Very well." Tristan's shoulders bowed, but I could see a glint in his eyes. "A few loyal to our cause own rice paddies a few leagues from here, and it's time for us to make a supply run. I have a group leaving in an hour. They'll be there all day, helping with the harvest and bringing back the supplies over the next few days. We do the trips in small spurts, under the cover of darkness to avoid detection. If you wanted to get outside for a day or two, this would be the best choice. It's relatively safe if we're careful. There shouldn't be any danger."

"It sounds like you're trying to convince yourself more than me."

"I am," he replied, his lips twitching.

"Would you feel safe enough going yourself?" I asked.

"Yes."

"Considering you're the leader of a rebel movement and *you* feel safe going, then I have no qualms."

"I don't want you out of my sight."

I snorted. "What? Out of your sight? You only see me once a day or so!"

Tristan sighed. "You know what I meant."

"Then I suppose you shouldn't have brought this up. I'll be fine. If you trust your men, then I do as well."

"I'm almost sorry I said anything."

"I'm not. I'm dying to get outside."

Tristan regarded me. "Are you sure your ribs are healed enough for a ride?"

"I think so."

"Very well. Go pack your things. You leave in an hour."

I got up to go.

"Oh, and Juliet? How are you since—since our conversation?"

"I'm fine."

Tristan took a step closer and peered at me.

"I've been thinking about what you said, and you're not the first person to have told me this, but I think you understand, which helps, and"—I gave a nervous laugh—"I'm sorry, I'm rambling. I feel a little better since we talked.

But it's stirred up more questions. And now I look at you and see the constant lines around your eyes, and I wonder if those aren't solely because of the weight you bear with the Uprising but if they are also there because you struggle to let go of the past."

Tristan sighed. "You are smart. Am I so easy to read?" When I didn't answer, he continued, "I think I will always carry the weight of the past with me. I do not think I can ever let it go. Not until justice is served and Creulon is judged for his actions." His voice grew steely. "He has taken *everything* from me. I cannot let that go."

"But will you feel that much better when he does answer for his actions?"

Tristan's jaw clenched, and he turned away. "You should go pack."

I opened the door and walked through.

Tristan's voice filtered through the open doorway. "Stay safe, Juliet."

Chapter Twenty-Four

I knew we'd reached the farms when we topped the shallow hill and looked over vast fields of wet earth filled with plants with their stems blowing in the wind, the green shoots bright in the morning sunlight. Beyond that lay a sprawling farmhouse.

I clicked my tongue, and the packhorse beneath me moved forward.

As we filed into the yard in front of the house, the door opened.

A woman walked out and approached, wiping her hands on a cloth. "Haniel, I saw you from afar. Mari! It has been a long time, but I am happy to see you again."

"Tori, this is Juliet. She'll be helping us out this time."

"Juliet." Tori inclined her head and returned her attention to Haniel. "My husband and the farmhands are already out harvesting. If your men can join them, the work will go even faster."

Haniel nodded, and his men hitched up the packhorses to the two wagons sitting off to the side.

"Mari," Tori began. "Come in for some refreshment. We can bring drinks to the men in a little while."

Mari nodded and followed her inside. I hesitated, wondering if I should go in as well.

"That is the first of four trips," Haniel explained.

I jumped, not realizing he'd crept up on me. "When will we go?"

"With the second or third trip."

"If there are four trips, then why did we bring only four horses?" I looked out toward the wagon growing more distant by the minute. The dust kicked up by the horses' hooves and the wagon wheels created a small cloud about them.

"A few days ago, two men brought the other four horses here. It is easier bringing them down in a couple of trips so that we avoid any unwanted suspicion."

"So, one trip each day?"

"No." Haniel furrowed his brow. "One today, two tomorrow, and one before dawn on the third day. You and I shall head out tomorrow."

"What about Mari?"

"She'll leave on a different route. Two is the perfect number to avoid attention. One is too suspicious, and three is too many. Trust me, Otherworlder. I'm here to make sure you stay safe."

"If this is so dangerous, why did Tristan suggest it?"

"Because of you!" Haniel ground the words out between his teeth.

"Haniel!"

The voice startled us both. Haniel whirled around to face the speaker.

"Don't," Mari stated as she faced us, staring Haniel down.

"Mari—"

"No, it's not her fault."

She's protecting me. She's standing up to him.

Haniel's jaw dropped. "Yes, it is. She's weakening him."

"Come on, Juliet." Mari took my arm and led me away from Haniel. Relief filled me as we strode away from him. He watched us go, his face twisted with frustration.

⟿ ⟻

The work was hard. But the air was fresh, though cold, and the sky stretched above us for miles. I didn't miss being underground or in the mountain.

I sighed and walked away from the wagon to pick up another basket of grain.

It will be difficult going back.

But that would be postponed a little. I'd managed to convince Haniel to let us go with the third wagon instead of the second, so we would not be leaving with this wagon.

The sun continued to rise above our heads as we worked. Morning came in full swing.

"Alright, load up," Haniel ordered, stepping back and wiping his hands on his pants. We stepped back and waved as two men boarded the wagon and started off.

"I have food ready, and there is hot tea here," Tori said, smiling and waving us over to a low table she had set up in front of the house. A small bonfire crackled nearby. "Please come eat."

My stomach growled as I loaded up a plate and sat near the fire. I looked up as I chewed and shaded my eyes from the bright morning sun. Narrowing my eyes, I gazed further into the distance. "Who is that?"

Haniel stood up and peered in the direction I pointed. "A rider." His hands clenched into fists at his sides.

"Scatter!" Tori called, bustling into the house with her arms full of small china cups.

Haniel glanced at me and motioned toward Tori. "Help her."

I nodded and grabbed a couple bowls of food off the table and carried them inside.

Tori almost ran into me as I entered the house. "Oh, thank you. Please hurry!"

Faster than I would've thought possible, all the food was taken inside, the men outside had disappeared, and I watched through a slit in the curtain as Haniel waited in front of the house. Tori stood next to me, her face pale.

We didn't have long to wait.

The rider materialized, approaching fast, thick clouds of dust blooming into the air from under his steed's pounding hooves. The man waved his arm as he approached and pulled his mount to a halt. The horse reared and snorted, a plume of steam rising from its nose.

Haniel and the man exchanged words, their faces serious.

Wait—I know that man. He left with the first wagon last night.

Haniel turned and beckoned to me to join him.

I stepped outside, Tori close behind. "What's going on?"

"King's soldiers," Haniel responded. "They're in between us and the mountain."

My heart dropped. *The king's men. Please, please, not again.*

Tori stepped forward. "What about the wagon that left a little while ago?"

"I was able to intercept it. They're going to take a roundabout way, see if they can get through."

"How many?" Haniel stroked the stubble on his chin.

"I don't know," the rider confessed. "We saw at least two patrols of half a dozen men. More movement than I've ever seen hereabouts."

What if they're here for me? I hoped no one could hear the pounding of my heart.

"We'll have to risk it with the wagons. Take different ways, make sure our cover stories are good. It is harvest season, and the king's men know many will be traveling to the markets with goods." Haniel stroked his jaw. "We need the supplies badly. If we wait, it will be even harder to evade detection, especially if the patrols continue till winter."

We all waited in silence for Haniel to continue. *We could just hide here. It might be safer than traveling back with the possibility of running into the king's men.*

"Plans have changed. The third wagon will leave within the hour, go to the east and circle around to the mountain. The fourth will leave tomorrow morning and go west." Haniel rocked on his heels. "Mari, you'll go this afternoon. You three men, I'll leave it up to you to decide."

Am I to go then? I steeled myself. "What about me?"

"You and I will travel under the cover of darkness. We'll leave tonight and travel alone."

Go it is, then. With Haniel. The men dispersed, but I took a step forward. "Haniel? I'm putting you in more danger, aren't I?"

Haniel regarded me. "I would be lying if I said no. But we cannot live our lives in the fear of what could happen. You, me, Tristan—we all knew the risks of you coming. Don't worry—despite my disposition toward you, I won't let any harm come to you." He beckoned over his shoulder, and I leaned to peer around him. "Tori is going to dye your hair."

"What?" I gasped, my fingers rising towards my head.

Tori stopped next to Haniel and smiled at me. "Your hair is beautiful, but it's *blonde*." She lifted a few strands with her finger and chuckled.

I frowned. "So?"

"It is like gold in a coal yard," Tori explained. "The king's men will know you are not one of us the moment they see you, so I thought we could dye your hair darker. I won't be able to get it to the right hue, but it should help."

My jaw dropped. "I don't want to dye my hair."

"Don't worry. It won't be permanent."

"Go," Haniel grunted. "We don't have much time.

I followed Tori into the house and watched as she grabbed little pots from a cabinet and made a paste.

She noticed my gaze on her. "It's just a mixture of tea and walnut. It won't last long. Your eyelashes are already full and almost black," she murmured, leaning forward to peer into my face. "But for your eyebrows, I will use a hint of the walnut. Your skin I cannot do anything for, but perhaps they will think you have not been out in the sun enough this summer."

I sighed. "Alright, let's get on with it."

"Sit here." Tori gestured to a chair near the kitchen counter. She took the kettle off the fire and poured some of the steaming water into a bowl. "Now sit here and tilt your head back a little."

I closed my eyes as her gentle fingers combed through my hair, ridding it of tangles and knots.

"Try to relax," Tori suggested, her voice soft.

⚘

We left just as the last of the light disappeared, setting off with our bellies full and our packs full of provisions. Trudging off into the darkness felt familiar somehow, yet also strange. Unlike Adnan and Saya had always been, Haniel would not speak to me and was an uncomfortable presence at my side.

Even the flies buzzing by sounded too loud in the quiet. As the hours stretched on, we continued walking. I welcomed the cold air as my body heated up from the miles covered and from the heavy cloaks wrapped around us.

We topped a ridgeline, and I gasped as Haniel yanked me to the ground.

"Look," he murmured.

My gut constricted. Several figures moved about in the light of a fire down in the valley below.

"Must be the king's men. No one else would be so brazen as to set up camp in such an open place. By the gods!" he hissed under his breath and squinted. "We'll have to go around. It'll take longer, but hopefully we can make it all the way around them by the time dawn is here."

"And if we can't?"

"Find a place to hide and wait out the day. I think it best we only travel at night."

I swallowed the lump in my throat. "Good point."

He glanced at me. "You doing all right?"

I nodded and removed my hands from my hips. "Yes, my ribs are just aching a little."

"Here, drink some water. Then we'll go." He handed me a waterskin and waited while I drank.

As we walked forward, Haniel continued to keep an eye on the sky. His face grew darker the longer it took for us to wend our way around the valley with how little cover there was to hide our movement. And the sun only continued to rise.

Pale pink had begun to streak across the sky when Haniel spoke, "Let's stop in that small copse of trees ahead. It's the best cover around."

"Copse? There are three trees there."

"I see that," Haniel gritted. "But do you see any other cover around?"

"No."

"Thought so. Now hurry up."

I sighed and trudged on after him—

Not before hoofbeats pounded the earth.

Haniel's head shot up, and he cursed.

"Here they come. We've been spotted. We can't make a run for it," he muttered. "Just follow my lead. Time to see if Tori's work does the trick."

I resisted the urge to touch my hair as I remembered how it looked when she had finished. In the mirror, I'd gazed into a face almost unfamiliar, framed as it was by hair darkened several shades—blonde no longer, yet not as dark as the almost-black hues of the people around me.

Haniel walked around me. "You still don't look quite like us. But no matter. Here they come."

I shuddered as the sounds of galloping horses drew closer.

"Halt! Halt in the name of the king!" a voice yelled out.

Keeping my head down, I stayed close to Haniel's side as the men surrounded us.

One man spurred his horse forward and dismounted. "What's your business here?"

"We are traveling home from the market, sir," Haniel responded with bowed shoulders.

I blinked. *He usually has perfect posture.*

"Who is she?" The man jabbed a finger at me.

Don't let him see.

"She is my younger sister."

Sister? I licked my lips. *A cover story,* I realized.

"Our parents own a farm to the northeast," Haniel continued, his voice lighter than normal. "We're returning home after selling some wares." He stooped even lower and averted his gaze to the ground.

"No wagon?" The horseman guffawed. "How did you bring your goods in the first place?"

"We sold the horse and wagon. We need the money. It's been a hard year."

The man dismounted and strode forward to stand in front of me. "She's a pretty one." He gripped my chin in his hand, forcing me to look up at him. "Older than she first appeared, too."

Don't let him see, I repeated over and over again. My altered appearance had to be enough—it had to.

Haniel began, "Sir—"

"Taisa!" the man snapped.

"Taisa," Haniel tried again, holding his hands out in a placating gesture. "Please let us be on our way."

The taisa ignored him. "What's your name, girl?"

I bowed, a tendril of dyed hair tickling the side of my neck. "Mari," I responded after a brief hesitation, using the first name that came to my mind. The taisa's eyes bored into mine, and I dropped my gaze to the tips of his boots. Each second ticked by as though hours were passing.

"Such a fair beauty," the taisa muttered, his hand gripping my jaw and drawing my face upward. "Why so fair?"

"Sir, please, she is not normal, you understand—" Haniel stumbled over his words.

A cold hand wrapped its icy fingers around my heart.

"My parents keep her in a lot of the time. She is delicate, you see."

Haniel never stumbles over his words or rambles. He's afraid. His too-soft voice echoed in my mind, and his deep, ongoing bow... My blood curdled. *He's doing this on purpose.*

"Is she now?" A dark gleam glittered within the man's brown eyes. "Should we take her with us, boys?"

A low rumble of laughter came from the throats of the men seated upon their horses.

"We are"—the taisa mulled over his next words—"searching for a young woman traveling, who may not be all she seems."

"Taisa?" Haniel questioned. His cloak swished a little as his hand brushed against something underneath.

What is he hiding? Hope glimmered inside of me.

"A young woman, known to be traveling with at least one companion, possibly two." The taisa strode back and forth in front of me. "Thought younger than you, but then again, even I thought you were younger till I got a good look at your face."

"I don't know who the young woman is—"

The taisa held up a hand, silencing Haniel.

"Sir, please," I began. "My mother—"

He laid a finger over my lips. "I must admit, I quite loathe harming such a pretty face."

"Mayhap we could have some fun with her ourselves!" one of the men called out. "That might make her talk."

"Unless she is indeed innocent," the taisa replied. "Enough. Mari, you'll come with us. If you are as innocent as you say, you should have nothing to fear. You will be released upon confirmation of your identity. You, man, head back to your farm."

Haniel opened his mouth, but the patrol rode their horses forward, driving him away before their dangerous hooves. Around the plunging legs, Haniel shot me a quick look, his expression clear: there was nothing more he could do for me. My breath caught in my throat as I watched them force Haniel farther and farther away. The taisa's grip on my shoulder was firm. It was no use running.

Fear touched the edges of my mind, freezing my limbs. I couldn't have screamed if I'd wanted to; I'd trusted Haniel, and he was gone, his figure small in the distance, too far away to do anything now.

Don't let them see.

When the patrol returned, the taisa barked, "Ribahn, take the woman up on your horse with you."

The other men clamored as they protested, each begging for the duty themselves, but the taisa quieted them with a harsh command.

I was thrown up on the horse without mercy, and I winced as my ribs jarred from the contact. As I began to topple over the other side, I flung my arms around the man before me, clasping him around the middle and closing my eyes against the onslaught of ribald jests and snickers coming from the company.

"My name's Ribahn." The man looked at me over his shoulder, his face unlined by age. A faint shadow of scruff grew in patches on his cheeks and jaw.

"I'm Mari."

"I know—I mean—" His body tensed. "I'm sorry about the others. They don't have good manners when it comes to womenfolk, or anyone really." His voice cracked, and I realized he was younger than I'd realized.

"I'm not her. I don't want to die."

"You're not going to die," Ribahn protested, looking at me again. His brown eyes shone bright under his dark brows as they furrowed.

"How do you know?"

"I—well, I suppose I do not. What does the king want you for anyway? What did you do?"

"Nothing."

Ribahn chuckled.

"No, really. I haven't done anything. I'm not the girl he's looking for."

"Say I believe you."

I sucked in a breath.

"Do you have proof of what you claim?"

"No, and I have no idea how to prove it, whether to you or to the king."

Ribahn laid a hand over my own, which was clasped around his middle. I bit my lip, a sudden queasiness rising in my stomach. He pulled me back against him until I was flush against his back.

"I might be able to make something happen…" He stroked the top of my hand with his index finger. My stomach turned.

"No talking," the taisa ordered, startling both of us. "We'll make camp soon enough."

Ribahn's breath blew against my ear as he whispered, "We can talk more later."

The rest of the horseman drew ahead, and Ribahn spurred the horse to catch up as we fell into the back of the line.

Ribahn did not let another word pass his lips, thanks to the taisa's orders. But when we halted for the night, and the taisa set up the watch, Ribahn lay down a couple feet away from me. I shifted, my bound wrists lying on my stomach, and watched the glowing embers of the fire grow dimmer. Snores filled the air as, one by one, the men dropped off to sleep.

When at last the fire had died down, and even the sentry dozed, I turned onto my side, preparing to rise to my feet.

A hand clasped over my wrist and I bit my lip, stifling a scream. The smell of potent body odor washed over me as a lithe figure lowered next to me.

Ribahn's voice whispered in my ear, causing the hairs on my skin to stand straight up. "So, how about it? I make a deal with you, and after, I'll let you slip away in the night."

"No," I muttered around the hand over my mouth. It tightened.

"You realize this is your only choice." He hardened his voice, the innocence and youth having vanished in his eyes, which loomed over my own. "No one will know. Then you can go back home and continue living your life. Or I could kill you now and the taisa will wake to find your dead body and assume you killed yourself rather than be taken in. I've seen it before. Not a pretty sight." He slackened his grip on my jaw and lips as his other hand began playing with my hair. A shudder ran through my body as his fingers brushed against the tip of my ear.

"I—I—" The words froze on my lips. My hand slid across the ground.

Ribahn's body pressed against mine. "What's this?"

He brought his fingers close to his eyes, peering at something, which he rubbed between his thumb and index finger. He sniffed.

"Tea!" he hissed. "Why would you have tea in your hair—unless to hide something beneath its color."

I held my breath as he ran his fingers through my hair again, leaning closer, his head over my own as he sniffed again.

"You are not who you say you are," he murmured. "We all have secrets, Mari. And what will you do with yours? Will you choose freedom, or will you choose death?"

My hand closed over something hard and firm.

A rock.

"Neither," I breathed.

Then I swung my fist toward his head.

No gasp passed his lips as his body went limp and fell across me, knocking the breath out of me. Seconds of panic passed before I could catch my breath and push his body off my lap.

I leapt to my feet and ran, unsure of the direction in the darkness. I knew that at any moment, stealthy footsteps would approach, fueled by a young man's anger. Then the sound of slick metal and cruel laughter. *I'll be caught,* I thought, panting. *Any second, he'll catch me.*

But the only sound that followed me was the harsh brush of my feet tearing through the grass and the sounds of my own breathing in the otherwise still night.

Searing pain split through my chest, and I stumbled to a slow jog, my hands shaking. Something sharp dug into my palm. I glanced down and found my right hand still gripping the rock. Something wet and sticky covered my palm. I dropped the rock and doubled over. Retching, I wiped my lips. A sour taste filled my mouth.

I could still feel his hands on me.

Chapter Twenty-Five

A gummy dryness coated my throat, and I stumbled on tired feet. I'd tried drinking from the rainwater as it had poured down earlier in the night, but it hadn't quenched my thirst. Not the kind of thirst created from walking through night, day, and now night again.

A sliver of moon high above provided a hint of light, illuminating the never-ceasing plains. The grass, long and thin, brushed against my pants. I buried my hands deep in my damp cloak, shivering from the cold. The air smelled of mildew and dirt, damp from the recent rain.

Dawn came and went as I kept moving west. They would come for me. Even if Ribahn lived, and I hoped to the gods I hadn't killed him, they would come. My escape would prove me guilty, and if Ribahn—if *he* lived, they would know I wasn't Mari, the simple farmgirl.

I twirled the ends of my hair in my hand. The dye had already begun to fade. But it didn't matter anymore. Ribahn knew I'd altered my appearance. He would tell them.

Goosebumps spread over my skin, and I glanced over my shoulder, but no one was there. No one but me, alone and on the run.

Dawn cast her pale-yellow beams over the horizon, pushing back the terrors of the night. A fallen tree lay before me, its trunk large and round. I stepped forward, rubbing my eyes in exhaustion, and saw that the tree was propped up by a couple of large boulders. A little niche, shadowed and hidden, lay under the trunk. I crept into it and curled up. My breathing slowed, my nostrils filling with the musty scents of earth as sleep overcame me.

Pale rose streaked the sky when I awoke, heralding the approach of dawn. With blurry eyes, I examined the angry red line stretching across my palm from where the rock had bit into me. Raw and painful, it burned from the sweat and dirt caking it.

In the east, the first rays of sun streamed across the valley I'd crossed the day before. I blinked and turned my gaze to the west.

There.

At the end of the next valley was the mountain. It loomed before me, large, rocky, cold, and beautiful. I stumbled to my feet, adrenaline banishing my exhaustion to the edge.

As mid-morning came and went, I continued trudging onwards, head aching and vision fuzzy. At the bottom of the trail, I looked up and took a deep breath.

You can do this.

With each turn in the trail, I was disappointed. The entrance did not loom before me, only a continuance of the rocky path. My legs burned, each step a challenge both physically and mentally.

The trail sloped up higher and higher when at last I saw it cut off, seeming to disappear into the craggy face. Tears stung my eyes and slid down my cheeks. I sank down onto my knees in joy and crawled forward on all fours.

I had just passed the illusion when a voice shook the silence.

"Stop!" a voice cried out. "Who goes there?"

I opened my lips, but nothing came out beyond a horrible croaking noise. I tried again, but there was nothing.

Strong hands jerked me further into the blackness, and my face was tilted back as a candle was lit and thrust toward my face.

"It's the Otherworlder," the man exclaimed, letting me go.

"Come on." Another man placed a supportive arm around me and hoisted me to my feet. "I'll be back," he called to the other man as he helped me stumble down the corridor.

My eyes drifted closed in the murky darkness.

"It's her!"

"The Otherworlder has returned!"

"My lady!"

The voices crashed in around me. I blinked in the low lighting, unable to make out anything or anyone with clarity.

"My lord! She has returned! Lord Tristan!" The call was taken up till the caverns echoed with the noise.

"Juliet—" Tristan's voice filtered through the others into my aching head.

I blinked and watched as his form weaved through the small crowd. I swayed, my vision blurring. The guard removed his arm from around me, and I fell toward the ground. Strong arms swept me up before I hit the ground and my head lolled against a shoulder.

"By the gods," Tristan spoke above me. "You are injured. Haniel, fetch a physician. My chambers, now. Mari, please bring food and water and some fresh clothes." He glanced down at me, his brow furrowed, lips clasped in a firm line. The edges of my vision were dark, blurred. His face grew fuzzy as I drifted in and out of consciousness.

Something soft enveloped my body, and I blinked. Mari, Haniel, and another man flitted in and out, murmuring strange words in low voices. My eyes struggled to stay open when I felt myself being stripped.

Mari stood next to the bed. "Don't worry. I sent the men away. It's just you and me now. Here, drink this." She brought a mug to my lips, letting the cool water trickle down my swollen throat.

Then even she faded from view.

❧ ☙

"I'm hungry."

"I'm sure you are," a voice replied.

I opened my eyes. "Did I say that aloud?"

Tristan smiled from where he stood at my bedside. "You did. I will have someone bring some food."

I watched him go and move past a figure who stood at the door.

"Adnan?" I whispered. "You're here." Tears sprang to my eyes.

"Juliet?" His voice hovered above me.

I opened my eyes and smiled up at him. "I'm okay."

"Why do you—" Adnan groaned. He stiffened from where he leaned over me, standing straight and tall again.

I frowned. "Are you okay?"

He cocked an eyebrow. "You have a propensity for getting yourself into trouble. We should have never split up."

"I do not have a propensity for getting myself into trouble."

"Yes, you do. Ever since you've arrived here, one thing after the other has happened." He flung his arms out. "I don't know how you attract it all!"

I glared at him.

"I should have been here."

"What? No, it's not your fault. You said yourself, no one knows the future, and besides, it was my decision to make. I needed to get outside. It was stifling, being in here, and—" I hesitated before reaching over and clasping his hand in mine. "I'll be fine. I am fine, and I can talk again."

His eyes hardened, their green hue darkening to a deep emerald.

The door opened, and Tristan walked into the room. He cleared his throat as he walked over to stand next to him. "Food will be here shortly." His gaze shifted down to my hand.

I slipped my hand out of Adnan's. Heat flushed my cheeks. "Where's Saya?"

"I am not sure," Tristan answered. "But I will send word to her. She is probably eating with everyone else in the dining hall."

I groaned as I tried sitting up. "I can go eat there, too."

Tristan pushed me back against the pillows. "No, that's not necessary."

"But I want to."

"No," Adnan bit out. His eyes softened the tiniest bit as he sat on a cushion next to my mat. "Why are you arguing on this?"

"I don't know," I murmured, closing my eyes and ignoring the warmth spreading through my body. "Will you stay and eat?"

Adnan nodded. Silence fell between the three of us. I looked back and forth between the two men.

"Perhaps it is best you tell us what happened," Tristan began.

Adnan folded his arms and stared Tristan down. "She should eat first."

"It's fine," I reassured. "There isn't much to tell."

"Skip everything up until the patrol." Tristan sat on the edge of the mat by my feet. "Haniel told us what happened up to when he was driven away."

"Well, the patrol didn't know for sure who I was," I began. "One of the men, more of a boy, Ri—" I swallowed down the sour taste in my mouth. "I escaped that night and traveled on foot for about two days before I found my way back here."

Adnan sat back, his eyes expressionless.

Tristan cleared his throat. "That's not all. You began to tell us something about someone. Did he help you escape?"

His face, his hands on me, his voice...flashes of memory washed over me. I swallowed. "In a way."

"What happened?" Tristan pressed.

Goosebumps broke out over my skin, and I looked down at my blanket as I played with the coverlet. "I knew we'd traveled southwest for the most part, so I headed northeast. The third day, I think it was..." I glanced up at the ceiling. "I don't know. It's all a little fuzzy. At some point I found the mountain." My fingers curled as I clenched the quilt.

The mat rustled as Tristan shifted. "Haniel said you were smart enough not to use your real name."

"Mari. Mari was the first name that popped into my head."

A small grunt from the doorway had us all swinging our heads toward it. Mari stood there with a laden tray in her hands, but her dark eyes pierced my own. She shoved the tray into Tristan's hands. He took it with raised eyebrows but didn't say anything as she brushed past Adnan to stand over me.

"You're looking a little better."

I nodded.

"You're none the worse for wear, I see. Your new wounds just blend in with the old."

I nodded again.

"Why are you in bed still? I never thought you to be lazy." She glared down at me.

"No, Mari. I've never thought myself to be lazy, either."

She sniffed. "Then what's wrong with you?"

"Two or three days of no food and leagues of travel will do that to a person," Tristan muttered as he spooned some of the food from the tray onto a plate.

Mari ignored him and stepped back from me. "Eat, and I expect to see you up and on your feet in no time."

"Thank you, Mari."

Mari sniffed again, trying to turn her fiercest glare on me. "You just call if you need anything." She turned on her heels and left with a swishing of skirts. It was enough to send tantalizing smells my way. My stomach growled.

"Leave off, Tristan, and give her some food," Adnan commented.

Tristan turned a freezing look on Adnan but gave up when he saw it wasted. He set the tray on the bed within my arm's reach before digging back into his own food.

"Are you going to eat?" I asked Adnan.

"I will after you."

Seeing the food there, my stomach grumbled again, and my mouth salivated. I helped myself to a bowl of broth and a little meat and rice.

Adnan didn't make a move until I settled myself back into the large feather pillows. Then he leaned across me and heaped some items onto a ready plate.

Tristan watched as he ate, but there was a strange glint in his eyes. "The king would not be happy to hear that one of his patrolmen fell for a pretty face," Tristan stated.

With a shrug, I took a bite of food, but my heartbeat quickened.

"Come on, Juliet." Tristan leaned forward. "There is no way the boy you mentioned would have sympathized with you and your plight."

I shuddered, trying to close out the memories from my mind.

"He fell for a pretty face; he would not be the first to do so," Tristan continued. "And you have an exceptional one."

"Don't!" I blurted out. Cheeks burning, I looked away from the two men, toward the wall. *He's acting just like them.* The knot inside me grew. I closed my eyes. *Those words are so similar to the guards'.* Ribahn's face filled my vision; I could still smell his stale breath, hot and heavy on my skin—

"Excuse me, my lord." A man entered the room and leaned over to whisper something in Tristan's ear, whose face turned stony.

He stood up, a muscle in his neck pulsing, and gave me a short bow. "I must deal with some business that has just arisen. My apologies, Juliet."

I looked down at the food, my appetite gone, and fingered a grape, firm and plump, between my thumb and index finger.

"Juliet—" Tristan began, and I raised my eyes, surprised to see him still standing there. "I am sorry I must go. Will you be all right?"

I nodded and lifted the grape to my lips, trying to show that I was okay. The sweet juice burst across my mouth as I bit down. A wave of nausea swept over me at the taste.

"I will be back later to check in on you. Let me know if you need anything. Benkei." He inclined his head and left the room.

Adnan set his plate to the side. "How are you feeling?"

"A little sick to my stomach," I admitted, handing him my own food to put back on the tray.

"You should eat."

"I'll try again later." I folded my hands in my lap and watched as he leaned back against the wall.

He crossed his legs at the ankles. "Why did you leave here?"

"I felt restless."

"You were safe here," Adnan continued in the same toneless voice.

"Not really. What if a rock fell from the ceiling and dropped on my head?"

"Damn it, Juliet!" Adnan burst out. He took a deep breath, calming himself in an instant.

I watched him, startled. As fast as he'd lost control, he resumed it, his stance nonchalant as he crossed his arms over his chest.

"I'm sorry." He turned his deep, dark green eyes on me. "I can't protect you when I'm not here. And I trusted you to *stay* here, where I knew you were safe and protected. I don't have the luxury of worrying about you. I have to keep my head."

"You don't have to always protect me, Adnan. It's not your responsibility." I sat up and swiveled to face him. Leaning forward, I peered up into his eyes, almost hidden by his shaggy brown hair. "I wanted to see the sun, to feel the warmth of it on my skin. I never saw Saya, never saw you, and—I didn't feel free." I bit my lip, watching as his eyes, inches from mine, lightened a little. "I missed what we had before we came here. With all the uncertainty, maybe I just wanted a bit of that back. I felt antsy, lost in my own thoughts. I felt like I had treaded water, unable to go anywhere. I needed to get out."

"It was foolish," Adnan stated. "He shouldn't have let you go."

"I don't think I gave him much of a choice," I replied, looking back up. "Besides, why is it he who is to control what I do and don't do?"

Adnan raised an eyebrow, a thought flitting across his eyes and disappearing before I could understand it.

"I'm sorry," I continued. "Maybe I shouldn't have left. Maybe you're right. It was too dangerous. But I didn't need to consult you nor Saya to make my decision."

"The boy," Adnan began, his eyes holding my own. "What happened?"

"He offered something to me to let me escape—"

Adnan swore under his breath and stood up, almost knocking me backward.

"Adnan! I didn't! I wouldn't. How could you think that? I hit him in the head with a rock and he fell on top of me. He wasn't moving—I may have killed him—I'm not sure. But he knows who I am, Adnan! He realized my hair was dyed..." I trailed off, my head spinning.

Adnan sat back down and crossed his arms.

"If he isn't already dead, I'll kill him."

"He didn't do anything," I whispered.

"Yes, he did. I've seen that look in your eyes before."

I reeled back. "What?" A wave of exhaustion swept over my body without warning. *He is not listening to me. Why can't he and Tristan just listen?* "Why do you automatically assume he did something? First those other men, and now him?"

"Because I know their kind."

"How?" I grunted, waving a hand in the air. "How do you know them? Are you one of them?"

Pain filled Adnan's green eyes. "No."

"Then how?"

"Because I've lived with their kind. I've dealt with their kind. I *know* their kind." With each word his voice rose. "And I wouldn't put it past either the two men in the woods or the boy you mentioned to take advantage of you. Tristan is right—you are pretty—and even more than that, you are striking in this country with your blonde hair and blue eyes. Those men lack scruples—"

"Unlike you?"

Adnan flinched.

I went too far.

"I may not have as many scruples as some, but I've never taken advantage of a woman who did not welcome my advances. My morals may be blacker than white, but I still have some." The mat rustled as Adnan stood up. "Now get some sleep."

Now he's giving me orders. I gripped the quilt, my skin whitening, mirroring the blood rushing from my face. My lips parted, but Adnan spoke before I could get a word out.

"What's done is done. You're safe now, but we'll have to be more careful. The king will know by now." He picked up the tray and walked to the door but hesitated, turning to look over his shoulder. "I'm always here if you need someone to talk to, Juliet." His voice had lost some of its prior sting.

Are you though? I sat still, frozen. Pain throbbed in my temples. *It's not my fault everything happened the way it did. How was I supposed to see the future?*

But Adnan was gone now. There was no one to speak my thoughts out loud to. And I didn't want to call him back.

I balled my fist and hit the quilt.

"Juliet?"

I opened my eyes. Saya stood in the open doorway, her dark eyes large in contrast to her pale skin.

She moved forward and sat on her heels next to me. "Tristan sent word you were awake. How are you feeling?"

"Weak as a kitten."

She rolled her eyes, and I stifled a chuckle.

"We knew something was wrong," she blurted out. "Before Haniel returned, Drielle saw you had been taken by the king's men. Tristan, he sent out men on horseback, and they found Haniel, but there was no trace of you. When they returned without you, I—I—" Tears welled in her eyes, and she swallowed. "I was so worried. Drielle and I tried without fail to see where you were, but there was nothing. Tristan's had some men out searching for you, but he had to be careful not to let the king's men find us, so he only sent out a few."

I laid a hand on her arm and smiled, though I ached inside. "I'll be all right. I'm here now, aren't I?"

Saya brushed the back of her hand across her cheeks.

"When did the Unknown arrive?"

"Just a couple hours before you. He was all ready to set out in search of you. So was I, but Tristan and Drielle forbade me to go." Saya glanced toward the door and stood. "I have to leave. Drielle told me not to be gone long. I'll see you later."

"See you."

Saya paused at the door. "And Juliet? I'm glad you're back."

Chapter Twenty-Six

Adnan entered the room and sat next to my mattress. "How are you?"

I adverted my eyes. "Tired, but better."

He looked at the floor.

I sat up and sighed. "I'm sorry I accused you the way I did. I didn't mean..." I trailed off, unsure of what to say. *What had I meant?*

"And I'm sorry I lashed out at you. I—" He licked his lips and his eyes rose to meet mine. "I care about what you think. It hurt to think..." He paused. "I'm not upset with you."

Relief filled me. *We can move past this.*

"Do you need to talk more about it?" he asked, each word seeming forced from him.

I shook my head. "No." I picked up the cup of water by my bed and took a sip. My voice sounded distant, stiff. "Thank you for coming."

"How is your ribcage?"

"It hurts a little more after all the walking the last few days." I shrugged.

Tristan slipped into the room and stood just inside the doorway, a shadow over his features.

My hair fell over my shoulder as I leaned forward. *What?* I wanted to ask. *Do you also want to apologize?*

Tristan said nothing, but emotion swirled deep in his eyes, and his shoulders tensed as he stood by the door.

"What is it?" I couldn't keep a note of irritation out of my voice.

The two men glanced at one another—but before either could say a word, a small form darted through the doorway and leapt onto the bed.

"Wait a moment, you little scamp." Tristan scooped Honoka up off the bed and deposited her on her feet. "You do not want to be jumping on beds right now. Juliet does not feel well."

Adnan leaned forward, his hand stretched out to me, but he snatched it back before Tristan noticed.

I gave a thin-lipped smile. "I'm fine."

"Is it her ribs?" Honoka gazed up at Tristan with big, innocent eyes. "Is that why she's been in bed for two days?"

"Yes, and we should let her rest. Perhaps you should run along and find something to do."

"But—" she began, her shoulders drooping.

"Tristan, she's fine. Let her stay awhile," I protested.

He shrugged and crossed his arms.

I beckoned Honoka forward and patted the spot next to me on the bed.

She glanced once at Tristan before sitting down next to me. "Everyone is asking about you." She drew a corner of the blanket over her lap.

"Oh, are they?"

"Yes, and I haven't been able to tell them anything because I didn't know anything."

"Well, now you do know how I'm doing, so if anyone asks you, you can say that you visited me and that I'm doing just fine."

Honoka smiled and tilted her head. "Will you be able to come out of your room soon?"

"I'm sure I will." I glanced at Tristan and Adnan and lowered my voice. "It really depends on those two."

"Why? You're not in trouble, are you?"

I stifled a laugh. "No, I'm not in trouble. But they want to make sure I stay safe and that I don't overexert myself."

"Then you should stay in your room."

"I agree," Mari said from the doorway, the blue of her dress a striking color against the dull gray of the stone wall.

The color was so much brighter than the shades the others wore here. I smiled. *Reminds me of home. Of robins' eggs. And springtime.*

"Honoka," Mari began, "I need your help with something. Come on, now."

Honoka bounded off the bed and walked to the door. "I'll be back to visit you later." She waved and disappeared with Mari.

I frowned as I watched Tristan walk to the doorway.

He hesitated and looked over his shoulder. "I have to go, as well, Juliet. But I will come back later. You look better." The soft smile curving his lips disappeared as he looked at Adnan. "Benkei, I want you part of the next meeting. Will you accompany me?"

Adnan stood up to follow. "Get some sleep, Juliet. I'll check on you later."

"Tristan, you were going to say something before Honoka walked in."

"It can wait," Adnan replied for Tristan. "Now sleep."

"Fine." I crossed my arms and glared at the two men as they turned their backs and left the room. A little of the tension left with them, but my irritation didn't dissipate as I wormed back under the quilts covering me. *What was Tristan going to say? Was it about yesterday?* I forced the thoughts from my mind and closed my eyes.

❧ ☙

Sleep would not come. I tossed and turned, first one way, then the other. A heavy knock sounded on the thick door—a welcome distraction.

"Come in."

The door opened and I started as Haniel entered and closed the door behind him.

"Haniel? What—"

"I want you to stay away from Tristan."

"What?"

"Stay away from him, Juliet Barrows. He's weakened with you about. He can't be concentrating on you; he has other things to think about—to do." Haniel folded his arms. "He doesn't need to concern himself with your safety nor concern me with it, for that matter." He strode closer to the bed, his broad shoulders seeming to form a barrier of a wall over me. His eyes smoldered with a quiet fury as he hissed, "Why don't you just leave? You bring danger to every one of us. But do you even care?"

Anger burned within me, fanning from a slow flame into a brilliant fire. "Did I ask for any of this?" I struggled into a sitting position. "It's not my choice not to leave. Don't you remember? Join or be thrown in prison?"

"Perhaps the latter is better!" Haniel growled, his eyes glittering.

I gripped the sheets beneath my hands as he leaned closer. "Watch yourself, Haniel. You go too far."

"You've not proven yourself, not to me, not to anyone. Why should I trust you?"

"I didn't give you away to the king's men," I snapped. "I went and escaped on my own. You were supposed to protect me, but you did nothing. Did you even try to follow?" A snort escaped me, and I turned my head away. "I doubt it."

Haniel grabbed my wrist and twisted it off the mattress, forcing my gaze back to his. "If you do anything that harms Tristan, I will kill you."

"Does he know you're here?"

"No, and you won't tell him. Who do you think he'll believe?" Haniel sneered. "Me, his long-trusted advisor, friend, and servant? Or you, a woman in a world in which she doesn't belong, far over her head in matters that don't concern her? I think it'll be me, Juliet Barrows. So no, you won't say a word. But mark my words, I swear on the gods that if I ever suspect you of deceit, I will end your life."

"Let go of me," I hissed, glaring at him.

"Haniel!"

We both jumped and Haniel dropped my wrist, springing back from the bed.

Mari approached, her eyes smoldering. "Get. Out."

"Mari—" Haniel frowned.

"Now." She stepped aside to let him pass. "If I ever see you in here again, I will tell Tristan. Don't come near her again."

Haniel disappeared around the corner. I blinked. *Their clothes are the exact same shade of blue.* I opened my lips, but Mari whirled about to face me.

"He didn't hurt you, did he?"

"No." My heart pounded in my chest, and I hid my shaking hands under the blanket.

"Well then, eat your dinner." She set a tray on my lap I hadn't even noticed she'd been holding. I stared down at the food as she bustled around, straightening what few possessions I had. When I looked up, I knit my brows together. Mari's eyes were puffy and red-rimmed.

Concern laced my voice. "Mari? What's wrong?"

She paused for the merest second before continuing her movements.

"Mari?" I whispered.

"Nothing is wrong."

"Is it Haniel?"

Mari blinked. "No."

"Please tell me. Maybe I can help."

A hard mask slipped over her face. She walked to the door. "Leave me alone, Juliet."

"I can tell something is wrong. You've been crying."

She froze. "You won't give up, will you?"

Shaking my head, I smiled. "No, I won't."

The air seemed to still and grow colder with each second that slid by.

Mari sighed and came over to the side of the bed. Her eyes softened. "I have a niece; she lives with her husband in a village not far from me, maybe half a day's ride. She's expecting a baby any day now."

I began, "That's wonderful news—"

"I want to go see the baby."

"Then why don't you?"

Mari frowned, and her arms fell to her sides. "Leave Lord Tristan? Leave all of this? I have sworn myself to the Uprising. What would they do without me?"

"Survive." I took her hands in my own. "They would survive just as they have done so far. Others will pick up your work, Mari. Tristan will understand. Talk to him."

"It's my niece," she whispered. "They think it will be a hard birth. That's why they've asked me to come."

"Then go. Be with her. I'll talk to Tristan for you if you'd like."

"No, no, I can't ask you to do that. She'll be fine." Mari's eyes wandered. "She'll be fine."

"She will with you there," I pressed, my voice soft. "Mari, she needs you. Your family needs you."

"So does Tristan. The rebellion needs me. Get some rest, Otherworlder. I'll send someone for the tray." Her mask was back, and with a soft swish of her skirts, she was gone, and I was left to heave myself to my feet, alone in the small room.

A few hours after she left, I lay in the darkness, staring up at the ceiling. Even without light, I could see the unevenness of the rocks above; the deep crevices in black shadow contrasted against the gray of the lower crags.

Slipping out of bed, I wrapped a blanket around me and opened the door. The hallway was dark and foreboding, and a cool breeze wafted from down the corridor. I shivered and pulled the blanket closer.

"What are you doing?"

I jumped, biting back a shriek as a stern voice cut through the shadows. Taking a shaky breath, I felt a hand touch my shoulder.

"Juliet, it's me." Adnan's pale face loomed in the darkness and into the shaft of candlelight glowing from my room. For a moment, Ribahn's face replaced it. I blinked, startled, and it was gone.

With a nervous chuckle, I gasped, "Way to scare me like that. What are you doing here?"

"I could ask you the same thing."

"I am standing outside my room."

"Fine, I'll reword my original question: *Why* are you outside your room?"

"I don't know."

A sharp grating from a flint and stone cut through the air, and a small glow appeared as Adnan lit a lantern. He quirked an eyebrow at me and waited.

I leaned back against the wall and looked into the darkness surrounding us. "I can't sleep."

"Come on." He took my arm, but I pulled it out of his grasp and took a step back.

"Sorry. I'm just a little jumpy."

He nodded and proceeded the way back through my doorway.

We sat down on the floor cushions, the lantern between us.

"So why can't you sleep?"

"I don't know—I just can't. No matter what I do, it won't come. And I'm so tired that I feel panicky inside. I'm sorry, I didn't mean to ramble on like that. It's just—" I trailed off, unsure of what to say or perhaps how to say it. "Mari is stubborn."

"I've noticed."

I watched the candlelight dance on the wall over his shoulder. "Her niece is having a baby, and she's been sent for, but she swears she can't leave, that the rebellion can't survive without her. For just a moment, I saw a glimpse of her—how she should be, would have been, before all this."

"War, strife, danger...it changes a person. You can't come through on the other side without having been affected in some way." His tone was weary, an unseen weight settling over his voice. Hidden meaning lay over him, so visible and yet so subtle. "She's not the only one. This is all she knows, Juliet. It's all she has known in some time."

"You sound as though you speak with experience."

"I do."

"What happened?" I pulled the blanket a little closer around me to ward off the chill.

"Let's just say that my life has changed me. There were bad decisions I made, and there were other things that were out of my control. It has left wounds not fully healed. Scars." He stretched his legs out in front of him. "What about you? You've been quieter, and I don't think it's just because of your run-in with the king's men."

I shrugged. "There's a lot that's happened. And here—" I looked around at the stone walls enclosing the small room. "I feel like I'm constantly being watched. I stand out here, and I'm not just talking about how I look."

"The Otherworlder. That's what they call you."

I nodded.

"You can't control what they think of you."

"I know," I replied. "But I don't like the attention. I don't like standing out. I feel ostracized..."

"I know how you feel. I've felt that way most of my life, for one reason or another. The Ryujin people are full of superstitions and symbols, and you are now one to them. They are beginning to see you as a beacon of hope." Adnan ran his fingers through his beard, trying to calm stray hairs. "After your second escape, it'll become that way even more so."

"What? No."

"Perhaps not," he admitted. "But I wouldn't be surprised. Just be prepared for that."

"What can I do?" I whispered, watching the shadows dance across his face.

"Do? Nothing." He shrugged. "You can't let them control your actions and what you think or do. You're still your own person, Juliet. You're strong, you're smart, and you can think for yourself. Don't worry about those around you. Just worry about yourself." He got to his feet. "I have to go. I've taken long enough."

"What do you mean? Why did you come?"

"I'm leaving."

"What?" My eyes widened.

"I'm leaving," he repeated.

"Why?" My breath caught in my throat.

He looked at me. "Orders. Tristan has another mission."

"Why you?"

Adnan ran a hand through his hair in frustration, but it fell right back into his eyes. "I'm the best man for the job," he murmured, toneless. "I know the lay of the land, and I'm a good tracker. I can't stay here forever, Juliet. You know he planned on using me."

"Yes, but for what jobs?"

Adnan averted his gaze. "Things others wouldn't want to do. I have to go."

"Like what?"

Adnan growled and ran his hand through his hair again. "Spying. I can't tell you more. It's for the best."

I nodded. *Fine.* "But why can't you stay and do something here?"

"Tristan's orders."

I stood and placed my hands on my hips. "And since when do you respect him? Or want to jump to his every order?"

"Since"—Adnan froze and took a deep breath—"since I have to."

"Why—"

"Juliet, please."

"Fine, but you just got back. I thought maybe…" I hesitated, knowing how petulant I sounded. Steeling my resolve, I forced the words I didn't want to say out. "Whatever it is, I know you're the best man for it. Just come back."

The resolve in his eyes softened a little. "I'll come back. I promise. Besides, Tristan knows my name." He stood up and faced me.

I blinked. "What?"

"Adnan. He knows it."

My mind flashed back over the past few days. "So that's why you feel like you must. But I don't understand. I must have said it. I don't understand; I don't think I did. I swear I've been careful."

"It's no matter." Adnan sighed, weariness crossing his face. "Someone may have overheard us talking."

"Does it really matter so much?"

"Yes, but right now he is the only one who knows it, as far as I know. I think he'd prefer to keep it that way."

I frowned. "Why is it so bad that he knows?"

"Names have power. Names have history."

"But you said you have many names."

"I do." He picked up the lantern.

"But Adnan?"

"It's the one…" He paused. "It's the one my parents gave me."

"When was the last time you were called by that name?"

He straightened, and his voice hardened. "A long time ago."

"Wait, when are you leaving?"

"Now."

I stiffened and hesitated, my hand outstretched. I let it drop back to my side. "Stay safe, please," I whispered. "Come back."

He took a step back toward the door. "Maybe I should ask Tristan if I can stay longer, at least until you have your strength back."

"No, I'll be fine. But, Adnan, do you trust him?"

"As much as I can trust anyone."

I blinked, surprised at the bitter tone.

"I think we're safe, at least for now. Promise me you'll stay here, though. Don't leave again. I shouldn't be gone long, I don't think. Just please promise me you won't go gallivanting off again."

"Where are you going?"

"Please don't ask. I can't tell you that," he replied, his tone soft. "Will you promise?"

"I can't make those promises. What if I break it? You'd never forgive me." I smiled. "Don't worry about me."

He walked to the door and paused a moment. "I have to go. I'm late as it is."

"Wait," I called out. "Does Saya know?"

"Yes, I stopped by her room on the way here. And Juliet, remember what I said: don't play into what they think of you. Be you. Try not to let the stares, the questions, the comments—whatever they send at you—try not to let them get to you. Don't let them shape you."

And he was gone, his words reverberating through my head like hushed echoes.

CHAPTER TWENTY-SEVEN

"It's been two days since the Unknown left"—I sighed—"and I haven't seen any sign of Saya."

Tristan glanced at me as we walked. "She's been busy."

I took a deep breath of the cold night air as we reached the ledge cut into the mountainside. "Where have *you* been?" Goosebumps carved a path across my skin. *Mari...I need to talk to him about Mari.*

"I have been busy too. Here—" Tristan raised the lantern a little higher. "Sorry we haven't had a chance to speak. I missed talking with you. It has been difficult here."

I raised an eyebrow. "Can't have missed our conversations that much. I'm pretty sure the last few we've had have either been because I've been irritated at you or I've been too exhausted to really talk much."

And now Mari. I bit my lip.

Tristan eyed me. "True, but I missed you—your company," he stumbled. "Now I'm getting the impression something has come up." His eyes probed as he waited for an answer.

Finally. I sat down and turned to face him. "Mari."

He set the lantern down. "What about her?"

"You should let her go visit her niece." I waved my hands in the air. "She's had news that her niece isn't doing well and is expecting a baby any day now and—"

Tristan raised his hands. "She's already gone."

I reeled back. "She is? She spoke to you?"

"She did."

"And you let her go?" My shoulders relaxed, and I smiled.

Tristan blinked. "Of course I did. She can be spared a few days." He shifted and glanced out at the valley below. "I'm glad you're here—back—and you're safe. I hated feeling like I couldn't protect you."

I groaned.

Again? Everyone tries to protect me, but what about teaching me to protect myself? I don't want to be at the mercy of those around me all the time.

"What is it?" Tristan frowned.

I sat down next to him. "Nothing. Tristan, I think you've done what you could. Don't blame yourself."

He chuckled. "No, I haven't. You could have died, or worse. I couldn't protect you."

"Tristan, it wasn't your fault. We couldn't have known. I don't want to live my life in fear every day of the unknown. Besides, it's not up to you to protect me."

Tristan's shoulder brushed against mine for a moment. "I do not want that for you, either. You are here, safe and sound. But I do not know that I can easily let you out of my sight again. I wanted to thank you for encouraging me to try and let the past go, to not let it consume me. While I struggle to agree with you, I wanted you to know I am trying."

I smiled. "Good."

"It is hard, though. And I still want justice more than ever."

"You should." I took a deep breath of the fresh night air. "None of that should change." I looked up. The stars twinkled in all their white brilliance above our heads. A shooting star streamed across the sky, leaving a glittering trail of streaking light which disappeared in the blink of an eye.

"I have had a rough time," Tristan whispered, his voice soft.

I looked at him as he stared up at the sky.

"There are more reports of raiders, of ransacks..." He inhaled. "I keep thinking of Creulon and everything he's done—not just to me and my—our family—but to this country." He placed a hand over his eyes.

He's hurting. We're all hurting. I leaned back against the wall of rock. "You're doing what you can, Tristan. You're not responsible for his actions."

"I keep trying to tell myself that," Tristan bit out. "But every time, I think of that night when I was forced to flee my rightful place on the throne, leaving my family to die."

I leaned forward, my voice soft. "Look at what you've built here. You can't keep hiding in the past."

"Hiding?" Tristan lowered his hand. "I am not hiding."

"Sorry." I held up a hand. "That wasn't the right word. Dwelling, I guess. Use your energy for the now, not for what happened then. As you said, think of everything he is doing to this country. It doesn't mean you can't have justice for what happened in the past, but you have to try not to let that cloud every decision you make."

Tristan sighed and sat back against the wall, as well.

I looked down at the valley, listening to the wind whistling in the treetops. I shivered. The temperatures were dropping.

Something warm and firm pressed against my skin. Startled, I sat up straight, staring as Tristan lowered my hand from his lips. My heartbeat quickened. His fingers were gentle and strong as they rubbed the back of my hand in slow circles. Keeping his eyes locked with mine, he leaned closer.

Another shape leaned toward me, younger, darker hair, more sinister... *Ribahn*. With a jerk, I ripped my hand out of his grasp and turned away. My heart beat in my chest, erratic and out of control. *It's not Ribahn. It's not him.*

Tristan stood up after a moment, his posture weary, his face lined. "Come on. I'll walk you back to your quarters."

As we neared my room, a small light bobbed toward us. Tristan stiffened but relaxed as Haniel's face loomed in the near darkness.

"Haniel," he greeted.

"My lord, you're wanted." Haniel shifted his gaze to me, his dark eyes expressionless.

A pit grew in the bottom of my stomach.

Tristan brushed past me as he took a step forward. "I'll be there soon."

"My lord—"

"Haniel, I will escort Juliet back to her rooms. I will be there momentarily."

Haniel nodded and cast one last lingering look at me before leaving, the thud of his footsteps echoing. They hadn't echoed before. I knew he was angry. He'd approached in silence but left with spite. My brows furrowed.

"Don't mind him." Tristan smiled. "He can be a little grouchy sometimes, but he means well."

"Are you sure?" I asked before I could bite the words back.

Tristan hesitated, a questioning look in his eyes. "What do you mean?"

"Nothing." I kept walking, forcing him to follow. *Could Haniel know Tristan just tried to kiss me?* I shook the thought away. *He wasn't watching.*

"Juliet, I do not know what could make you distrust Haniel, but he has been one of my most loyal supporters. There is a reason he is my right hand. You can trust him."

I nodded, watching the light send shadows flickering over the rock walls. It became cooler the further we descended, and I shivered.

"You are cold," Tristan murmured. "We are almost there. I will speak to Haniel."

My eyes widened. "What? No!"

Tristan stopped and turned to face me. "I do not want you mistrusting him so. Has he said something to you?"

"He—" I licked my lips. "He..."

"Juliet, you can trust me. What happened?"

"He said to stay away from you!" I blurted out in a low tone.

Tristan ran a hand through his hair—an action he seemed to do when thinking hard about something. "That is not for him to decide."

"But he came across..." I struggled to find the right word. "Strongly."

"That is his character. He does not want me distracted and thinks you are a distraction for me." A rueful smile crossed his face. "Perhaps he is right. But that is not going to stop me from continuing to enjoy your company. You help give me clarity, and I have had more energy to do the work I need to do because of the time I get to spend with you." Tristan glanced up past my shoulders. "There is your room. Get some rest. And don't worry about Haniel." He lit my candle and handed it to me. "Good night."

"Good night," I responded, watching as he headed down a tunnel a short ways off. The echoes of his boots faded. Taking a deep breath, I turned to head back inside when I caught a glimpse of someone coming. Haniel appeared and I stiffened, my heartbeat loud in my ears.

"I thought you were meeting Tristan," I said when he neared.

He stopped a few feet away. "I am. But I wanted to speak with you. I know you talked to Tristan on Mari's behalf, and while he had already allowed her to go, I wanted to acknowledge what you did for her." His eyes would not meet mine. He turned and left. I watched, my mouth open as his blue tunic rustled with each step.

Wait. I took a step forward. *Blue tunic. Mari. That's right—the color is the same.* I'd noticed when Mari had confronted Haniel but hadn't thought to ask. Now...I frowned. "Wait, Haniel." I raised the candle higher, which stretched the small halo of light a little farther.

He paused and turned to face me. "Yes, my lady?"

I ignored the derision in his voice. "I'd like to ask you a question about Mari."

"What is it?"

I eyed the blue material again. "Have you known her a long time?"

He nodded, his eyes flickering toward Tristan's receding footfalls. "Longer than most can claim."

"She's not naturally cold and distant," I murmured. "I've seen the warmth in her. She cares more than she wants to admit."

Haniel regarded me for several long moments. "Not many have had the privilege of seeing past her mask."

"Why does she put it on? What happened to cause it?"

"That's a question for her."

"But she's not here," I pressed. "Haniel, I truly do want to know."

"Fine, but don't blame me if she finds out."

I nodded and waited, my arms folded.

Haniel leaned against the doorframe, his eyes searching the cracks in the floor. "We both came from the same village," he began, "the village where Mari has gone now. My parents live there still. Before Mari and I joined the movement, I was busy helping with the farming, taking care of my family, and living a normal life. Mari was married—"

"She was?" I blurted out.

"Yes, they'd been married a year or two when it happened. Her husband had gone to the big city with a couple of friends from our village. Night came, and they didn't return. The next day I set out to find them. It was a day's journey, and by the time I got there, it was too late." Haniel bowed his head. "I found them, but not alive. The king had made an example of them. I don't know why, and I wasn't able to find out. So I brought back their bodies. Mari was devastated, and from that moment on, she wasn't the same. She used to be bubbly and full of life and laughter." He closed his eyes. "But those days have gone."

I couldn't speak past the thick lump constricting my throat.

"We both joined Tristan and have been here for a few years now, long enough for Mari's heart to have hardened but not long enough to ease the pain of the past." Haniel turned his face away from me and took a step down the corridor.

"Why would you go after her husband?" I asked, reaching out to him. "How do you know so much about her?"

"It was a small village."

"That's all?" I whispered.

"Don't pity us—either of us. We both chose our paths long ago." Haniel turned to face me, his face hard. "As did you, Juliet Barrows—*Otherworlder*."

"Wait, and the color? The robins' egg blue? You both wear it."

"It's the traditional color of our village. Generations back, we discovered the dye combination." He shrugged. "It is cultural for us." He closed the door and I stared at it, the light from the candle I held flickering in my trembling fingers.

⁕⁕⁕⁕ ⁕⁕⁕⁕

Clean clothes, delivered by one of the women, glared at me, urging me to get up and move. I stood and picked them up, along with my thin candle. The curtain hung across the way. I squared my shoulders and took a deep breath before walking through, taking the long way around the edge of the cavern to avoid the majority of stares and whispers from the women within. *Adnan told me not to let them shape me.* I blinked. *He said not to become an outsider.* I bit my lip and continued on. I refused to take the endless, questioning looks.

I made it to the bathing chamber without having to speak to a single person. Perhaps they could sense my moodiness. I grinned. It was empty. I lit the lantern by the pool before blowing out my candle. The soft light flickered over the water cascading down the rocks.

A familiar voice echoed down the corridor into the chamber.

Saya.

I relit my candle and snuffed out the lantern before leaving the chamber. At the end of the corridor, where it branched into two more tunnels, Saya stood speaking to a young man.

"It's fine!" she exclaimed, crossing her arms over her chest.

"Good. I'll pass on the message." The young man grinned and strode away.

"Saya!" I called, jogging forward.

"What?"

"What are you doing here?"

"Looking for you, actually." Saya glanced at the candle she held. "I've been looking all over for you."

I blinked and raised my candle a little higher. "Oh, really? You couldn't *see* where I was?"

Saya frowned. "What's wrong?"

"Nothing."

"It's something. What's going on?"

"You're asking me? Aren't you the one who just said you were looking for me, not the other way around?"

"Yes."

I sighed. "Sorry, it's me, not you. I'm frustrated because I've barely seen you. Do you know how many times I asked after you and was rebuffed every single time? I've been wanting to talk to you for ages, but all you seem to do is spend time with Drielle." I stopped and hung my head. "I don't know what's wrong with me. I'm sorry."

"No." Saya's voice sounded tiny and vulnerable. "You're right. If I'd known how you felt, I—I just didn't think you'd miss me."

"What? What do you mean?"

"You make friends so easily. Everyone likes you. You have two handsome men at your beck and call, and I just didn't think you'd miss my company."

"Saya, you're my friend. I'd hoped you thought so, too. And what do you mean about two men at my beck and call?"

"I did—do." She shook her head. "I've just been excited about learning there are other seers and spending time with Drielle." Saya turned shining eyes upon me. "It's amazing. She can do so much. Every minute I feel like I learn something new, like I belong, like someone actually cares about me and my ability and wants me to hone it, not hide it away like some rabid animal. For the first time, I'm actually doing something, not just for myself, but for others. It's elating, Juliet." Saya took my hand in hers and squeezed it. "I would let you come join us, but Drielle won't even let Tristan or anyone else in."

"Are you getting better at seeing the future at will?"

"Yes. Drielle said the practice is good for her too. Teaching me is honing her own ability."

I smiled at her enthusiasm, my annoyance and jealousy fading away. "I don't know why you think I'm that popular," I said in a teasing way. "You're the one with the abilities, after all."

"Yes, but you're the one with the following."

"The following?" I repeated, my smile fading.

"Yes." Saya rolled her eyes. "You're all everyone can talk about—even Drielle talks about you, but it never makes much sense, and she refuses to explain herself to me. She always says the time will come. The Otherworlder, Juliet."

I laughed, cutting her off. "Saya—"

"Have you not noticed how everyone clamors to meet you? To ask you questions? How, when you enter a room, all eyes turn toward you?"

"Yes, but—"

"So you have noticed?"

"Yes, but—"

"Juliet, you have a title, and names hold power—titles hold power. Don't think you go unnoticed here. It'd be a far cry from the truth."

I rolled my eyes.

"Times are changing, Juliet, and we must change with them."

"You're completely in, aren't you?" I realized.

"In what?"

"The Uprising."

Saya's voice was quiet when she answered. "Yes, and what about you?"

"If you'd asked me a few days ago, I would've said no, but now? Now I've been maneuvered into it all, and there is no escape until it is all over. There's no use spending time and energy figuring out the answer to your question when I do not have a choice in the matter."

Saya grasped my hand. "For better or for worse."

"For better or for worse," I echoed. "I don't think I'm as important as you make me out to be. I'm just different, and everyone knows it. They're curious; that's all."

"I wish it was just that," Saya replied. "But I don't think so, and neither does Drielle. You're meant for something."

I chuckled. "Something embarrassing probably."

Saya shook her head and frowned. "I don't think so. You should start taking everything more seriously."

"So that I don't miss my moment?"

"Juliet, I'm serious. You need to take this more seriously, as well. Something is coming—and you're going to be instrumental in it."

I blinked. "Wait, you've seen something, haven't you?"

Saya averted her gaze.

"Saya?"

"I'm not supposed to say anything. Drielle said I can't share this—"

"Saya."

Her shoulders sagged a little. "Fine. But you can't tell anyone. And don't say that I told you."

I nodded.

"Do you promise?" she pressed.

"Yes."

Saya hesitated and glanced up and down the corridor as though to make sure we were alone. "I saw you in a dress—"

My jaw dropped. "A dress?"

"Please, don't interrupt. Yes, a dress, a nice one, as though you were at a fancy party or something. The material was above that of which our people normally wear. And you were changed somehow—" She shook her head. "I can't explain it."

I watched her. She wouldn't meet my eyes. *Can't or won't?*

"There were a lot of people around you, but I couldn't see their faces. And a voice, deep, frivolous almost, as though knowing he would get his way in anything."

I stepped forward. "Anything else?"

"Not much," she admitted. "But you weren't here. And you were smiling, but it didn't reach your eyes. You—" she hesitated again. "You seemed like a snake, coiled as though to strike but afraid of what was around you."

"You don't know what it means?"

Saya shook her head. "No, and nor does Drielle. Are you alright?"

I gave a dry chuckle. "I don't know. It doesn't make sense."

"It's clear enough you play a role in what's to come, Juliet. Just be careful, alright?" Saya started. "I should go. I'll talk to you later, okay? Just don't forget, you can't tell anyone I told you this."

I nodded but couldn't speak. Saya turned to leave, casting one last concerned look over her shoulder at me. I managed to force a smile onto my face and waved at her. *What does it all mean? What am I supposed to do?* I watched as she walked away. *A snake coiled as though to strike but afraid...* I shivered. *And I forgot to tell her of what passed between Tristan and me.* With a sigh, I turned back to the bathing chamber, my heart heavier than before seeing her.

Chapter Twenty-Eight

"Juliet!" Honoka called out as she rushed through the curtain into my small room.

I straightened and grinned at her. "Hey, what are you in a hurry about?"

"Nothing! What are you doing?"

"Stretching."

"How are your ribs?"

"Sore but healing." I eyed her. "Why do you ask?"

Honoka drew a circle on the rocky flooring with the toe of her small boot. "I didn't have anything to do, so I thought I'd come find you."

"Uh-huh. Nothing to do?"

Honoka nodded.

"Why do I have the feeling you're just avoiding the duties you've been given?"

Honoka averted her gaze, her round apple cheeks reddening. "I just thought it would be more fun if I did something with you."

"True. I can't argue with you there. Is it a little easier with Mari gone?"

"I—no—"

"I'm teasing you." I laughed. "Want to explore with me?"

Honoka grinned, and her dimples appeared. She nodded, brown eyes shining.

"Alright, let's go."

She peeked around the curtain and glanced back over her shoulder at me. "It's safe," she whispered. "Come on."

"Okay," I whispered back. "Where are we going?"

She shrugged and beckoned before slipping into the cavern. I followed as she hugged her way around the rim, her eyes darting here and there as though trying to hide from someone. We made it to the entrance to the tunnel without any interference. Honoka's shoulder relaxed and she flashed a smile.

"Honoka!" a sharp voice snapped.

Honoka froze and turned around with a sigh.

Sakura stood behind us, her thick eyebrows drawn together in a downwards 'V'. "Honoka, what are you doing?"

"She's just spending some time with me," I said, jumping in. Honoka bobbed her head and looked between us.

"That may be, but she has chores unfinished."

Honoka pouted. "But—"

"No buts. You may play after you finish, not before."

"Go ahead." I nudged Honoka with my hand. "You can come find me later." I watched as they turned to reenter the cavern. *What will I do now?* I bit my lip. Sakura's cloak rippled as she strode. The memory of the hooded stranger flashed before my eyes. I'd been powerless to save myself then, or when the king's men had taken me, but now that I was here... I furrowed my brows. *I need training.* Energy surged through my body. "Sakura! Wait!"

"Yes, Other—Juliet?"

"Is there a training hall or something like here?"

She blinked. "Yes, there is. Just follow this corridor to the dining cavern and take the second right at the fork, and then the middle at the next fork, and then right at the next, and you will find it. You can ask for help if you get lost."

"Right, middle, and right. Got it. Thank you."

She nodded.

"Sakura, wait—"

She swiveled around to face me again.

"Were you responsible for telling everyone about my ribs?"

Her cheeks reddened, and she hesitated. "Yes. I'm sorry, Juliet. Was I not supposed to say anything? I didn't think you would mind. I didn't know others would not know of it."

I waved a hand. "Never mind. It's fine. I was just curious."

"Come on, Honoka," Sakura murmured. "Otherworlder." She nodded to me, and Honoka waved as she was ushered away.

She treats me like I'm above her. I sighed and followed the directions Sakura had given me. The light from my candle flickered on the walls, and my shadows stretched out before me, long and thin on the floor as I walked.

Right.

I repeated to myself as I took the second right fork.

The rest was easy.

Long, narrow, and rocky like all the others, the corridor ended in a wide, squarish room lit by many lanterns hanging from the ceiling. I hesitated in the doorway, watching as about a dozen men trained with swords against one another. In another corner of the room, a few jabbed with spears at targets set up against the wall. A small doorway stood in the far side of the room, and through it echoed filtered hisses as that of the rush of air. *Archery?* I wondered, tilting my head to try and see through the open door.

"Can I help you?" a gruff voice asked, breaking through all the others. A man walked up to me and crossed his arms over his broad chest.

"I was hoping I could train here."

He raised an eyebrow and flicked his long hair over his shoulder. "Really? And why would you think that?"

I motioned with my head towards the men fighting. "Because it's a training room."

His frown melted into a hearty laugh. "Good point. What would you want to learn? How to kill someone with your bare hands? How to be an effective killing machine?"

I blinked. "No, I just want to learn how to defend myself. The Unknown began to teach me, but we didn't make it very far."

"Who is that?"

"He's also known by Shizukana?"

The man shook his head. "I don't know of him. Why don't you show me what he taught you?"

I blew out my candle and set it down on the floor next to several others.

"Go ahead," the man urged, taking a step back.

I took a quick step forward as I raised my arms up, my elbows out in front of my face as I lowered my upper body and used my hips to ram into an invisible enemy. Dropping my hands on the imaginary shoulder, I brought my knee up into the groin and tucked my right ankle around where the other's ankle should be and pushed as I swept the leg out.

The man clapped. "Very good. Basic defense. Not bad. What else?"

"That's it," I admitted. "I have knocked someone out with a staff before—"

I grimaced. *And a rock...*

"Alright, I'll train you. Come on."

I jogged forward to catch up to him. "I'm Juliet."

"Ah yes, the Otherworlder, as you seem to be known."

"I prefer Juliet."

"Good, because that's all you'll go by here. No special privileges."

"I'm not looking for any."

"Good," he grunted.

"What can I call you?"

"Sensei. Now, let's build off a little of what you already know."

"Am I going to learn how to use a sword?"

He frowned. "No, not yet. What do you do if someone has you in a choke-hold?"

I shrugged. "Struggle?"

"Come put me in a chokehold." He beckoned to me.

"I don't think I can reach you. You're taller than me."

"Jab me in the stomach or chest area as you demonstrated before." He stepped a little closer. "Okay, now lower your hand to grab my shoulder." He adjusted my stance. "Good. Your right fist will swing down to hit me in the groin, but don't actually!"

I took a deep breath, sweat already beading on my forehead.

"Now, slip behind and around me and use your foot to drive into my shin." He paused and tapped my other leg. "Make sure you're keeping yourself light on your feet but in a solid stance at the same time. Better. Now run your arm under my chin as I buckle back a little. Good. Good." He smiled. "Grab your bicep with your hand and grab the back of your neck with your other hand. Perfect. See how your left hand is now tucked in and reinforced by your right arm?"

"Yes." I panted, wishing I had a free hand to wipe away the droplets of sweat already beading on my forehead.

"I'll tap you but squeeze as hard as you can while driving me back and down a little."

I flexed and squeezed as hard as I could.

Two seconds later he tapped my shoulder. I released him and let him stand up straight.

He rubbed his neck a little. "How did that feel?"

"Awkward."

He shrugged. "It's always going to be when you're facing someone bigger and taller than you. Not that it isn't always awkward, but it'll get easier and more natural. Now, let me show you how to get out of a chokehold."

⁂

Sweat dripped down my face, and my shirt clung to my skin.

"Here, drink some water," Sensei ordered, handing me a full waterskin.

"Thanks." The water rushed down my cheeks.

"That's enough for today."

I nodded, breathing deep to recover my breath.

"Why did you keep favoring your ribs?"

"I broke a couple a few weeks ago."

He nodded. "Make sure to not overdo it. It's good to get some movement but stop if anything causes you severe pain or discomfort." He took the waterskin back. "I'll see you tomorrow."

"Tomorrow?"

Sensei leaned over to light my candle and handed it to me. "Yes. Don't you want to continue your training?"

"Yes, I do."

"Good. Then I will see you here."

"Thank you, Sensei," I remarked with a bow. As I left the cavern behind, the grunts and yells of the men within faded. My stomach growled, but I headed back to my chamber first, hoping my clothes from the day before had been cleaned already.

Sure enough, they sat waiting for me on the table. I grabbed them and headed to the bathing chamber to wash off the grime.

As I approached, a woman leaving the chamber held up a hand. "Otherworlder?"

I peered at her. She was one of the women from the sewing circle, but I couldn't remember her name.

"It's Rin," she reminded me. "I was sent to find you. Haniel told me to tell you that you're invited for dinner with Lord Tristan this evening."

"This evening?" My eyes widened. *But what about the almost kiss...?*

"Yes. Haniel will come find you when it's time. He just asks that you stay close to, or around the women's cavern, so that he does not have to look for you." Rin said the words in a halting way, not meeting my eyes.

"Oh, does he?" My jaw clenched.

"I'm sorry—"

"Don't be," I interrupted. "I'm sorry. It's not your fault. Thank you for telling me."

Rin nodded and left me alone at the entrance to the bathing chamber.

I walked inside and left my dirty clothes in a pile on the floor while I washed myself. The running water coming out of the rock face washed away the sweat and grime. I redressed without getting in the bathing pool and picked up the pile of clothes.

"Juliet!" Saya strode forward, a soft smile on her face. "I didn't realize you'd be here."

"I was just leaving."

"Stay and chat a while?"

I hesitated. *There are only a couple hours left before dinner...* I sighed and raised my eyes to Saya's face. The smile hovering there faded. *She'll leave. She'll realize she has other things to do and will leave.*

Saya's eyes narrowed in concern. "Please?"

Haniel can find me. I don't need to be exactly where they tell me. I took in a deep breath. "Sure."

While Saya bathed, I slipped back out of my clothes and lowered myself into the steaming basin.

Saya slid in with a sigh and grinned. "This feels amazing."

"I can't stay long." I leaned back, feeling the smooth rock press into my back.

Saya frowned, droplets of water falling from her hand as she gestured. "Do you need to leave, then?"

"No, not yet." Steam rose in curlicues around us, and the air was heavy with moisture.

"How are you doing?" She slid a little farther under the water. "With what I told you, I mean."

The vision. An icy dread trailed through my veins. "I haven't given it much thought," I admitted. "I've been busy."

Saya nodded to my side. "Looks like that is healing well, but those stitches will have to come out soon. Who did it?"

"A—the Unknown. He said stitches were needed to help it heal."

"You've done that a couple of times now," Saya mused. "Start to call him something starting with an 'A', but you always catch yourself. Is there a different name he's given you?"

"Yes."

"What is it?"

"I—I can't tell you."

Saya blinked. "What? Why?"

"Because I don't have his permission. I'm sorry, but you'll have to ask him if you want to know."

"But we're friends," Saya protested, leaning forward. "I don't understand."

"It's not for me to tell."

"You should be careful with him. He's not to be trusted."

"You still don't trust him? Saya, hasn't he proven himself?"

"No, especially not after hearing the other name he is known by." Her face darkened.

"Benkei?"

Saya nodded, her face paling. "Don't say that name, not here."

"Why? What do you know?"

"I'd rather not speak of it. Just be careful."

"You'll have to give me more than that. What is it about that name?"

Saya clenched her jaw. "Do you remember the other name Tristan mentioned that day? A name Shizukana did not deny?"

"Vaguely. What was it?"

Saya peered around as though to be sure no one was listening. She leaned forward and whispered, "Oniwaka."

"And?" I asked when she did not continue.

"Those names are for the same person. They're myths, legends, really. They're passed down through the generations, but to have a living person go by those names...it's not good, Juliet. Darkness must surround that person."

"What do the myths say?"

"Some say that he is the offspring of a man who was the head of a temple shrine, a man who raped the daughter of a blacksmith. Another says that perhaps he is the offspring of a temple god, granting him his strength and feats of power. It's said he's killed hundreds of men—"

"Seriously, Saya? You've already said it's a myth, nothing more."

"I didn't say it was anything more," Saya protested. "But all myths and legends have some semblance of truth."

"And what, do you think the Unknown is hundreds of years old?"

She blinked. "No, I didn't say that. But if he's been named after the legend, then some of it must be true. I knew all along he couldn't be trusted." The water splashed into the air as her hand came down on it in a fist. "He's good with weapons, just like the legends say, and he carries many."

"So? What's wrong with having more than one weapon?"

"Nothing!" Saya replied with a hint of exasperation. "But the legends say seven, and he seems to have quite a few on his person."

I rolled my eyes. "Saya—"

"What, you don't believe me?"

I know he has seven. I saw them. A small sigh escaped my lips. "He does have seven."

Saya's eyes shone. "See?"

"But you said it's just a legend. And what about what you said about the man who took you being so similar to Shizukana? That seems like an odd coincidence, doesn't it?"

Tristan knows something but won't tell me about Adnan's true identity. A hint of doubt wormed its way inside of me. *He keeps it a secret from me.*

I shook my head and took a deep breath. "You already know that's impossible. He was with you the whole time, so it wasn't him."

Saya frowned. "We don't know what powers he may have."

I stood up and got out of the pool. "I'm done with this conversation, Saya. I think you're grasping at straws, and it's ridiculous."

"Fine. Maybe I am, maybe I'm not. Maybe you should ask Tristan what *he* knows."

"Maybe I will!" I bit out as I dressed, my hands shaking. The cold air in the corridor beyond was a refreshing blast against my heated body. As I walked, my temper cooled, and I stopped.

Perhaps I should go back.

"Juliet Barrows," a voice ground out behind me. "Lord Tristan is ready for you."

"Haniel." I nodded to him. "It's a little early, isn't it?"

"He has a meeting this evening, so yes, the dinner is a little early."

"Alright," I sighed. "Lead the way."

He glanced at the clothes in my arms and blinked. "Come this way."

I followed him down a tunnel. Down the corridor shone a faint ball of light bobbing our way. It grew as we approached it, and an older woman with a lantern came into view.

"Please take those and have them cleaned," Haniel ordered, stopping her. The woman extended her arms, and I gave the clothes to her without a word.

"Come on."

I turned to see Haniel had already continued on down the corridor without waiting for me. Running to catch up, I commented, "You're still mad at me."

Haniel grunted.

"I didn't ask for dinner tonight."

"But you didn't say no."

"Did I have a choice?"

"I suppose not."

A wry grin crossed my face.

The fabric across Haniel's shoulders tightened as if he tensed. "Here we are. Go on in. I'll wait out here."

I entered through the open archway and saw Tristan lighting another candle. The table was spread with two steaming plates of meats and veggies.

Tristan smiled. "Juliet, please sit."

Cross-legged, I watched as he also knelt, his weight on his heels.

He regarded me, his hands clasped together in his lap. "You trained today."

My jaw dropped. "How did you know that?"

"I was told."

"So you were spying on me?"

"No!" Tristan exclaimed, running his hand through his short hair. "But I have told you I always have men keeping an eye on you."

"Yeah, and I'm pretty sure I—"

Tristan's eyes narrowed, and his lips thinned. "You never told me not to."

"Fine." I crossed my arms and flipped my hair over my shoulder. "Maybe I didn't."

"I would prefer if you do not train anymore."

"What?" I blinked, lowering my arms to my sides. "Why?"

Tristan took a deep breath, his hands whitening as he clenched them. "Because I don't think you need to. We can protect you—"

"So you don't want me to be able to defend myself?"

Tristan's blue eyes darkened, and he took a deep breath. "Juliet—"

"Don't *Juliet* me, Tristan. I can't believe this. First you..." I paused.

"First I what? Tried to kiss you because you looked breathtaking in the moonlight and because you are strong, brave—" He took a deep breath. "And now I don't want you training because I don't want you to hurt yourself? I don't think you're weak, Juliet. Far from it. But I do know that you're still healing and you need to be careful." His smooth voice filled the room, a soothing cadence. Without thinking, I felt my heartbeat slowing as a sort of calm settled over me. "I apologize if I came across as overbearing." He sighed and ran a hand through his blond hair. "It has been a long day. Do you forgive me?"

I shook my head. *Everyone either has something that comes up, or they're mad at me.*

Tristan's jaw clenched and he took a step back, his boots a soft thud against the floor. "I apologize. I should not have disrespected you the way I did." The fire in his eyes dulled. "Juliet?"

I stared at him. *He's trying to do the right thing. We're all under a lot of pressure.* I tucked a few strands of hair behind my ear, uncertain. My mouth opened. "Yes, I forgive you."

"Thank you. Are you hungry?"

I nodded, eyeing the bowl of rice in front of me and the wooden sticks lying next to it.

"Good." His white teeth flashed in his smile. "Let's eat then."

"My lord," Haniel interrupted, striding into the room. "It's urgent."

I exhaled. *I knew it. Something always comes up.*

Tristan's jaw clenched. "Juliet, I'm sorry. I should go; please eat your fill. I'll see you later." He clasped my shoulder briefly before following Haniel out of the room.

I didn't flinch away. I blinked and stared down at the food, my appetite vanishing. The spot where he touched my shoulder seemed to tingle. *Rib-ahn is the past.* I gritted my teeth. *Everyone leaves me.* First Saya, then Ad-nan—Benkei—now Tristan. The pit of emptiness within me grew.

Chapter Twenty-Nine

The sweet scent of roses filled the air as I walked through the curtain into my little alcove. A small, white note lay next to the bouquet.

Juliet,

I am sorry for how defensive I got of you yesterday. I hope you do not hold anger against me. I just want to keep you safe. I do not think I have hidden that I care for you. If I can, I will slip away to have dinner with you in the dining hall.

~ Tristan

The curtain rustled behind me. "Juliet?"

I set the note down and turned. "Saya."

She lowered herself onto my mattress and crossed her legs.

"Shouldn't you be training with Drielle?"

She frowned. "Yes, but I needed to talk with you. Will you sit?"

"Alright."

Saya waited until I'd sat down across from her before she began, "I'm sorry I got so mad at you yesterday. I know Shizukana is hiding something, but I didn't distrust him so much until I heard Tristan call him those other names. And when he didn't deny them—well, I haven't been able to forget it. But I don't want us to be mad at one another. And you're right. I should give Shizukana the benefit of the doubt until we know more. I'll try to keep my feelings in check."

"Thanks. And I'm sorry, too," I replied. "I shouldn't have gotten so mad at you. I think I trust him. Most of the time I do, anyway."

Saya smiled. "So are we all right?"

"Yes."

"Good." She made to get up but caught a glimpse of the roses over my shoulder. "Where did you get those?"

"Tristan."

Her eyes widened. "Really? And you accepted them?"

"Yes, why wouldn't I?"

"So you like him, then."

"What is that supposed to mean?"

Saya shrugged. "When a man gives flowers to a woman, it's a sign of his pursuing her."

My breath caught as I reeled backward. "What?"

"You didn't know?"

"I mean, yes, I suppose, but can't it just be an innocent gesture?"

Saya shook her head, her dark strands of hair flying through the air. "No, not with flowers."

I stared at the floor, thoughts flying through my mind like a whirlwind. *Flowers.* I glanced up at Saya, my eyes wide. *They meant more to him.* I knew she was right. My heart beat faster. *He's been hinting this whole time.* I placed my fingers against my temples. *The almost kiss, the comments that were more than encouraging...he likes to compliment me. He enjoys spending time with me. Dinners with just the two of us—*

"Juliet?"

"Yes?"

"Are you going to keep them?"

"I—I don't know. What should I do?'

Saya held up her hands and leaned back against the wall. "Don't ask me. I thought you said you might like him."

"I don't know! This is a lot. This isn't even my world! And he's keeping us here without a choice—"

"But I thought we'd all decided to help."

"Eventually, yes, but it wasn't much of a choice in the beginning," I reminded her.

She waited with her lips pressed together.

"What?"

"Juliet..." Saya sighed. "Anyone who has eyes to see knows that Tristan cares for you deeply. He's head over heels, to use the expression. The people all love you, though I'm not in the least sure why." Saya looked me up and down, a twinkle deep in her eyes. "But everyone here has formed an attachment to you, and you don't even realize it. And they respect and care for their leader. The rebels are anxious to see if you return Tristan's feelings."

"Well, they will be disappointed," I huffed. "And I think you're mistaken anyway. "There's no way I'm seen that way."

"It's more complicated than you think." Saya hesitated. "I've heard and seen a lot during my time here. The movement is larger than you realize, and word spreads among them as fast as a wildfire. You are a symbol of the Uprising now. Your escape from the king's men—twice—is no small feat. Most think you have powers you have brought over from your world."

"But I don't," I protested.

"But they think you do, and that makes you powerful, one to be feared and respected."

"So you think Tristan knows about what you're saying?"

"Yes, he does." Saya nodded.

"Then why doesn't he refute the rumors?"

"Because he needs someone like you. His people look up to him, but not as much as they look up to you. He would be a fool to ignore this. I wouldn't be surprised if he has put fire to the rumors, growing them into flame."

I groaned. "Is that the reason he—"

"No," Saya interrupted. "He does care for you. From what I've seen at any rate. You are in a hard position, Juliet. Reject Tristan, and you do harm to the rebel cause." She paused. "You could be what they have needed this whole time. You could be key to overthrowing the king."

I swallowed, my throat dry. "Saya, I don't think—"

"War calls for sacrifices, Juliet. You will have hard decisions ahead of you. Think on this but make your decision. And remember what I told you: *I* know you're meant for something big in all of this. I just don't know what yet. And I don't doubt that Tristan will have an open conversation with you soon, much along the same lines I have just said."

"You're suggesting I sacrifice myself and my future for the sake of this country?"

"No, I am not. The decision is yours. I just want to make sure you know exactly what you're doing. This is my country, and I care about it."

"It seems silly, though. That I should begin dating someone, that it should matter so much to everyone else?" I bit my lip in frustration.

"You realize no matter what path you may take, you may never return home. The idea of a portal is new. No one has heard of this being possible. What if you can't return home?"

"What does that have to do with this?"

"Plain and simple: this may become your Earth, your country. Do you care what happens to it? What will the world you raise your children in be like? Do you fight for something you believe in—or do nothing?" Saya waited, watching from where she leaned against the wall. "They want a love story," she continued. "Do you care at all for him?"

"Yes, I do. He's handsome and charming, but—"

The silence stretched on and thoughts whirled around my mind like tornadoes going round and round.

Saya rested a hand on my shoulder. "You need to make a good decision for yourself too, Juliet. I think Tristan is a good man, and I think he would be good for you. I trust him. You should just see where this takes you, no matter what the people think. You've already admitted you're attracted to him."

"I think I might keep the flowers—"

Saya nodded.

"—and just see what happens—"

She nodded again.

"—because it's not like I'm promising to marry him or anything like that..."

She continued to nod encouragingly.

"So there's no harm in accepting some beautiful flowers," I finished.

"I don't think so," Saya agreed. "There will be a lot of jealous women, you know. He's quite the catch."

My cheeks flushed. "Stop it."

"I should go now. Drielle will be waiting for me."

"What are you working on today?"

"Drielle wants me to try and see more about you."

I dropped the hair I'd been twirling about in my fingers. "What?"

"That vision I had about you. She wants me to try and see more. So that's what I'm going to be working on today."

"Will you tell me if you are able to?"

She nodded. "Yes. I will. But this is my second time trying, so I don't know." She stood up. "Oh, before I go, do you know where Shizukana is?"

"No."

"It's been what, two days, three, since he left?"

"Four."

"Have you asked Tristan?"

"No."

"If he trusts him, then I probably should, as well." She sighed. "Shouldn't you go to the dining hall?"

I started. "How did you—"

"The note. I read it before I sat down." She shrugged and pulled me to my feet.

"Why don't you come with me?"

"No, but I'm sure you'll have more fun without me anyway."

"What is that supposed to mean?"

Saya pushed me out of the door. "Hopefully it doesn't take you forever to figure it out." She closed the door behind us.

"Wait, Saya, you haven't said what you mean about the Unknown."

"And I'm not going to. You'll be late, and I have something I need to do. I'll see you later." She turned and walked off, her lantern bobbing along with her.

I barely noticed my surroundings as I strode in the direction of the dining cavern, my footsteps echoing down the dark corridor.

When I arrived at the entrance, I hesitated, my eyes roving around the room. The cavern was full. Each table brimmed with people, most young and middle-aged, but the table of children had grown. Honoka sat there, beaming as she shoveled food into her mouth. Tristan's blond hair stuck out in the crowd as he wove his way toward me.

"There you are," he said with a smooth, low voice. He held out his arm, and I took it. He escorted me around the tables towards the small dais where he always sat when he ate in the hall.

"Everyone is staring," I murmured.

"That's nothing new." He grinned and sat down beside me.

"But it's more than normal."

Tristan averted his eyes and drank some water.

"Tristan?"

He cleared his throat. "It's probably because word has gotten out that I gave you flowers."

I blinked. "So?"

"So now we are an—an item of attention, you could say. You accepted my gift, so you are open to my pursuing you, and the people don't have much else other than the rebellion to occupy their thoughts and time, so it's easy for them to focus on us."

"So the only thing I'm good for is comic relief." Bitterness laced my words, and I pushed my bowl of rice back.

Tristan's face blanched. "That's not true. You train, you mend torn clothing, you help with other tasks, which I remember you saying were not so menial."

"I'm sorry," I murmured. "That wasn't fair."

Tristan shrugged his broad shoulders. "Juliet, Saya and Benkei are of us, there's no doubt about that. We need them. But as it stands, we can't let you fall into the king's hands. You're what he seeks, what he wants more than anything else."

"Then maybe I should leave, try going back home again. You should just let me go."

Tristan's eyes darkened. "No!" he blurted out. "Please. You don't realize, do you?"

"Realize what?"

"We need you. *I* need you." He leaned forward as he spoke, his hand resting on the table.

"We?"

"I think you give the people hope. You've escaped the king's clutches twice now, and they like you. You're becoming a symbol to them."

"What?" My jaw dropped. "Why?"

"It's just happened. The rumors about you have grown, and most here haven't ever had more than a brief conversation with you, if that. My followers are growing, and you've seen how those who were already here respect you and tiptoe around you as though, well, as though you're otherworldly."

"But—" I shook my head. "I haven't asked for any of this. I've noticed how most don't seem to be comfortable around me, and I know Sakura spread those rumors about me and the king, which I wasn't happy about, but I've not made myself out to be any sort of symbol or hero. I'm not. I don't even belong here."

Tristan laid his hand on mine and squeezed it.

I stared down at his hand. *Saya said he has feelings for me. This isn't the action of just a friend.* My throat constricted, and the room felt warmer. I moved my hand, and Tristan let go.

"The people believe you've come to help us vanquish my cousin. Thankfully, I haven't lost being the face of the uprising." He chuckled. "But you are the fuel. You are instrumental in keeping them going."

"I still don't understand. I haven't done anything—"

"You didn't have to." Tristan smiled. "You're from another world, you've escaped twice, and you've rescued villagers from raiders, all for a world that is not your own."

"How do you know all of this?"

"Have you not heard the murmurs, the whispers, the gazes that turn away as soon as you look upon them when you enter a room? The hushed voices all around you?"

I nodded, silent.

"Then you have your answer. It also helps that I have Haniel and others who report to me." Tristan shrugged. "And do not forget, I want you here. You know how I feel about you, and I need people I can trust, people I can lean on. In a war like this, friends can become enemies, but I trust you implicitly. Every rebellion needs a symbol, Juliet," Tristan murmured. "You *are* one now, whether you like it or not."

"I don't want to be that."

"Please, Juliet, I want you to stay. You are helping me—more than I think you realize." Tristan rolled the sleeves of his tunic up a little and poured himself a cup of hot tea. "I am here to help you also. But I would like you by my side."

I tossed and turned. Tristan's words slammed against the walls inside my brain, keeping me from sleep. The minutes ticked by, and so did the hours, until I rose and headed for the training quarters.

A noise emanated from the cavern as I drew near. I turned the corner and stopped dead in my tracks. The last person I expected to see stood there.

Tristan.

His shirt lay on the floor a few feet away, and sweat glistened on his lean, muscled torso. He stiffened and glanced over his shoulder. He relaxed at the sight of me and lowered his sword. "What are you doing here?"

I raised my eyes back up to his face. "I could ask you the same question."

"I couldn't sleep."

"Me neither."

He gestured for me to come forward. "Come on, then. We can spar."

"I've never seen you down here before."

"I prefer to come when it is quiet. It gives me space to think. Besides, I am not the best when it comes to fighting." He grimaced.

I quirked an eyebrow, trying to keep my gaze on his.

Tristan ran a hand through his hair. "Are you all right?"

"What? Yes, I'm fine." I waved a hand through the air and gulped.

"M-*hm*," he responded, flashing another grin.

Was that a wink?

I ran straight at him and gave a right hook, which he blocked. My hands slid onto his shoulders, and I grunted as my knee came up—and was blocked by his hands.

I backed away, defending against a quick series of punches and feinting to the side. In one fluid movement, he moved to my side and slipped behind, his arm slithering under my chin until he had me in a chokehold. I tapped him on the arm, and he lessened his grip just the slightest, his soft panting brushing against my ears.

With a deep breath, I kicked him in the chin and thrust backward into his torso and twisted out of his chokehold.

"Impressive." Tristan grinned, his chest still heaving with effort. "Could be a lot better if you were not favoring your ribs so much."

I bent over, gasping for air. "You were toying with me."

He smirked. "Teaches you to always be on your guard. Even when you think you are winning, it may be the opposite."

"Fine." I glared at him, my side burning. Sweat dripped off my face, and my hair felt sticky and wet.

"Come on, try again." He beckoned with his fingers.

Steeling myself, I rushed him, but the tip of my boot caught in a small divet in the rocky floor and I crashed to the ground, knocking the wind out of me.

"Juliet!" Tristan knelt next to me. "Are you all right?"

"No."

His hands brushed over my arms. "Where are you hurt?"

"My pride."

He laughed and stood up. "Well, if that is all."

"If that's all," I grumbled. "It's everything. Sometimes pride hurts the most."

A muscle in Tristan's cheek pulsed. "Yes, it does," he whispered. "Come, let us call it good for the night." He offered me a hand up.

"I'm okay." I lunged to my feet but tripped over a drop in the floor. My hand shot out for balance, but I stumbled into him. He wrapped his free hand around my back to keep me from falling. His heart beat in a smooth rhythm beneath my left hand, and my breath caught deep in my throat.

The stench of sweat entered my nostrils.

He stayed stock still, his mouth an inch from mine, his eyes staring into mine. I trembled and blinked. *We're friends...nothing more.* Stepping back out of his grip, I chuckled and slid my fingers through my hair. *Or are we?*

Tristan shrugged. "Not the most romantic of moments, I know."

"I'm sorry." I blinked, my cheeks flushing. "It's hot in here, isn't it?"

"Not really," Tristan murmured, his white teeth flashing in a quick smile. "Should we call it a night?"

I nodded, relief washing over me as he moved on from the awkwardness. "I should probably try to get some sleep."

"So should I. Good night, Juliet." He leaned down and grabbed his shirt off the floor.

Frozen, I watched as he pulled his shirt on. It clung to his damp skin, doing nothing to hide the muscles beneath.

"Here you go." He handed me my candle.

"Thank you." I followed him out of the room. His lantern lit the way through the enveloping darkness. *What am I doing?* My damp clothing clung to me with sweat. *He has so much he is dealing with. Maybe Haniel was right…what if I am a distraction?* I bit my lip.

Tristan glanced over his shoulder, his eyes soft.

Or maybe he does need me. Maybe we need each other.

CHAPTER THIRTY

A hand shook my shoulder, jolting me to awareness.

"Juliet, you must hurry. Come with me." Haniel waited, holding out my boots. He tapped his foot as I pulled them on.

"What's going on?"

"You'll find out." He led the way out of the room.

I hurried to catch up and pulled my cloak closer around me as I yawned. "What time is it?"

"Close to dawn."

"Do *you* know what's going on?"

"No."

"Nothing?" I pressed.

"A messenger arrived in the middle of the night. Tristan wants us all there, and I was sent to get you. That's all I know. Here we are."

The two guards at the door nodded at us and stepped aside to let us through.

"You're here!" Saya murmured, coming alongside me. Tristan nodded to me, and I nodded back.

"Do you know what's going on?" I asked without looking at her. Drielle stood next to Tristan, her gaze inscrutable; beside her, Tristan's advisors.

"No," Saya whispered.

Tristan sighed, his shoulders bowed under an invisible weight. Lines of weariness crossed his face. "Thank you all for coming," he began. "Some of you are new to this circle, but you're here because I trust you. A disturbing message came in not long ago. There is a village several leagues to the south, where Haniel and Mari both came from. It's small, not even marked on a map." Tristan gestured to the drawing on the table in-between us. "A few days ago,

Mari left to visit her niece, who would soon give birth. There is a band of raiders from the north whose progress we have been semi-tracking. Their movements suggest they are returning home. They've kept to a relatively straight path, one which—if they continue upon—will go right through the village."

Haniel stiffened, and my heart skipped a beat.

Had he not known?

"With their current progress, they should reach the village within two days. I'm sending someone to warn them." Tristan spared a single glance for Haniel before turning his eyes to me.

Haniel took a step forward. "My lord—"

"Haniel, my friend, no." Tristan gazed at Haniel with sadness in his eyes. "I can't let you go."

Haniel raised a hand, his bright blue tunic rustling. "But—"

"I'll go," I spoke, the words coming out before I'd thought them through. "Tristan, let me go with Haniel. They are his people, his family. If the band is two days away, as you say, we can be there and back within a day."

"No," Tristan bit out, his fist coming down on the table.

"But Tristan—"

"No, Juliet. I will not let you go." His tone softened. "This is too dangerous. You cannot put your life in jeopardy again."

"But Haniel and I know Mari the best. Let us go. It's his village, his family." I strode around the table to face Tristan. "Let me do this. Mari is my friend too."

Tristan's face was white with anger. "No."

"I'll go." Saya stepped forward, her chin tilted up in resolution. "I'll go with them."

Tristan started. "No—"

"Please, Tristan. I—and Haniel, we wouldn't be able to stand staying here, knowing we could be out there."

Tristan's shoulders slumped a little.

One of his advisors stroked his long, thin beard. "Lord Tristan, it is not the worst idea. Perhaps you should let them go. Haniel does have a right. It is his village." He glanced at his companions and licked his lips before continuing. "And the Otherworlder, it might do good if the people see her going forth to try and save the villagers. I do not think it a bad idea that she goes."

Tristan turned his weary gaze from the advisor to me.

"I know," I whispered, staring at him. "Believe me, I am not doing this out of a sense of rebellion. I *have* to do this. I'm the one who pushed Mari to go. I need to help her."

He sighed, whispering words meant for my ears only. "You, Juliet, are—"

"I know." I grinned.

Tristan turned to the rest of the group. "Haniel and Juliet will go."

"I as well." Saya took a step forward, voice firm. "I'll keep an eye on Juliet." I rolled my eyes.

"Very well," Tristan replied. "Haniel, take them with you. I expect you back within twenty-four hours." He waved a hand in dismissal, but before I could leave, he whispered, his breath blowing against my ear. "Be careful. Come back."

"I'll see you soon," I responded and turned to follow Haniel and Saya.

⁘⁘⁘⁘ ⁘⁘⁘⁘

After the intensity of the last hour, the cold air caressed my face. We picked our way down the mountainside on horseback, a precarious journey to be done in the dark.

Small rocks, jostled by the horse's hooves, rolled off the path, the noise leaving clanking echoes behind them.

I followed behind Haniel, with Saya taking up the rear.

"We'll warn them in time," I assured, trying to convince myself as well as Haniel. Not a word came from his lips, and I could not see his face in the darkness. Light had begun to streak in from the west, denoting the rising of the sun, but it was a pale sort of morning, dull and colorless.

Saya followed behind me. "Juliet?" she called. "Look, dawn is approaching."

"I noticed," I replied over my shoulder. "Saya, did you see any more—"

Saya shook her head, shooting me a glare, and glanced down the trail at Haniel to see if he'd noticed. "Not here. Later."

"We don't have much time," Haniel growled. "Save your focus for getting down this mountainside."

I glanced behind at Saya, but it was too dark to see more than her silhouette.

The sun continued to rise, and soon the murky pale morning made way for a brighter sky filled with a rosy glow.

But it did nothing to dampen the dread in the pit of my stomach.

❧❧❧ ❧❧❧

"There." Haniel pointed ahead.

Straight ahead, lit by the warm afternoon sun, lay a small village, no more than a dozen rooftops visible. Smoke curled up into the air from invisible chimneys. There was no sign of movement.

Dust burst around us as hooves drummed the earth, disturbing the quiet peace. I held the sleeve of my jacket over my nose and mouth, trying to keep the endless dirt from coating my airways.

The village loomed closer with every stride, and the smoke grew thicker as it drifted towards us with the breeze.

Something was wrong. It was a slight feeling, disturbing, but unable to place. The others must have felt it, too; Haniel straightened, peering under his hand against the glare of the sun, and Saya's horse shifted beneath her, sensing her uneasiness. The smoke curled further.

Too much smoke.

We careened around the corner of the first house and into the center of the village. My breath caught as though my chest was being squeezed by an invisible hand. Through a haze, I saw Haniel and Saya rein in.

I slipped off my horse, releasing the reins. Small clouds of dust rose into the air as my boots hit the ground.

The small boy at my feet stared up with glassy, sightless eyes. His mouth was rigid in death, a frozen expression of fear upon his little face.

A sheen of tears welled in my eyes, blocking my vision. I gasped, struggling to take in air.

Then a cry of fear, longing, sadness, of lost hope and of heartache, ripped through the air.

Again, it came.

I dragged myself away, following the sound of the voice.

Another cry split the air and chickens squawked as if unnerved by the chilling sound.

I peered in the open doorway of the nearest house. Haniel knelt inside, the late morning sun sending his shadow further into the house. In his arms lay a woman, her brown hair hiding her face from view.

Another wail ripped from his lips.

He looked up at me in anguish, tears rolling down his cheeks, his mouth open as if to speak. I'd seen that look before. My heart clenched in my chest. My parents had looked at me the same way. Eleven years ago. I gasped for breath.

Beyond Haniel I saw the still form of an older man, a pool of scarlet beneath him.

And then I knew. *His parents. They're dead.* The smell hit me, clogging every part of my airways with the sharp, metallic scent of blood. My legs trembled, but I couldn't break my stare from their still bodies.

Eddie. He had been so still when we pulled him out of the water. So pale. I gasped for air. Haniel's mother's face, tilted toward me, eyes blank and staring, was replaced by my own. *Is that how my parents think of me now? Am I dead to them?* Sound disappeared. I could hear nothing through the buzz in my ears. *Will that be me before I have the chance to go home?* I backed out of the room, stumbling over the doorsill.

I clasped a hand to my nose, trying to block out the overwhelming stench of death and decay permeating the air. *Mari. Where is she?* I looked around, my movements jerky, as though I were a puppet. "Mari!" I called, the name sounding strange to my ears. "Mari!"

Nothing. Nothing but the sounds of Haniel rocking in the house behind me. I looked up to see Saya still standing where I'd left her, holding the reins in her limp grasp. No tears wet her eyes, but she stared unseeing. I took a step toward her—

A hand clapped over my shoulder, and I screamed.

Haniel's eyes stared out at me from a tear-streaked face. "Mari's niece lives there." He pointed at the house beyond, and I put one foot in front of the other. I couldn't hear Haniel behind me and knew he hadn't followed.

"She's fine. She's fine," I whispered over and over. The words were not convincing, but they pulled me closer to the house.

The house stood at the end, on the outskirts of the small village. With each step, it grew harder to keep moving forward. As I neared the open door, I glimpsed a hint of blue—there, in the field beyond, a hint of blue against the stark yellow of grain.

A knife pierced my heart with each step as I rounded the corner of the house, leaving the village—and Haniel and Saya—behind. The noisy blurs of color around me deadened until that hint of blue was all that remained.

Three bodies.

Three lay in the dirt, left to rot. Beings who, hours before, had been alive and breathing, working, playing, talking, laughing—now the last glint of life had seeped from them. I sunk to my knees, recognizing that robins' egg blue in an instant.

Mari.

She loved that color, the color of the sky after a storm, the deep gray-blue...

Her brown hair clung to her scalp, curled and dried by reddish-brown blood. I reached a hand out and closed her sightless eyes. Her skin felt warm and dry to the touch from the sun. Even for the mere second my hand had touched her, I expected her to jump at me.

Beyond her lay a young woman, facing away from me. I crawled to her side and pushed her over. I gasped and fell backward, my hands and wrists breaking my fall. My throat constricted, aching as it tightened.

A newborn babe lay in a bundle of bloody blankets upon the ground from where the mother had fallen. A beautiful little baby, its features ravaged by death.

Time passed as I sat there, staring at Mari and her loved ones. *This is my fault. This is my fault. This is my fault.* I rocked back and forth. *I told her to go.* The baby lay in the dirt, helpless, wisps of his downy hair flying in the slight breeze.

Breathe. In for four, hold for eight, out for three. I raised my eyes to the darkening sky above. The gray clouds had begun to billow in, hinting of rain.

I couldn't leave the baby there. On hands and knees, I inched forward, saliva pooling in my mouth from the taste of dust and smoke. Unable to swallow because of the tightness in my throat, I spit onto the ground.

The newborn was light and small. His limbs had stiffened, his body cold yet warmed by the sun all the same. I held him close to my chest, not minding the dampness of the blood seeping into my shirt.

My jaw ached, and my eyes stung. I breathed, and the fresh, clean smell filled my nostrils from the newborn.

A cry tore from my throat unbidden and I sobbed, dropping to my knees. Rocking back and forth, salty tears slid down onto my lips and past my chin until they bathed the infant's head.

The sobs wracked my body until I had no more.

Then I cried without them. It hurt to live, to breathe—to see what lay before me if I opened my eyes.

The baby, his parents, and his great-aunt were the sole witnesses to my grief.

And I knew what I would have to do.

A bout of rain began in a drizzle, taking the place of tears upon my cheeks. Then came the downpour. Within a minute I was soaked to the skin. The cold shocked me out of my stupor, and I gasped, opening my eyes to see blood running in rivulets upon the ground from the bodies.

I stood and turned away, walking toward the village square with the baby in my arms.

Saya glanced up from where she dragged bodies, laying them in rows. The mud lay slick, marking the paths she'd taken. She watched me with dry eyes. "Mari?"

"Dead." I gestured back over my shoulder. "Along with her niece, the baby, and the father. They tried to flee." I heard my own words as if another had spoken them.

Saya didn't say anything. She couldn't. There were no words.

Haniel appeared, carrying his mother. He laid her down, pushing the wet hair out of her face, his hand lingering over the smooth curve of her cheek. "Mari?"

"She's dead."

Haniel bowed over his mother, his body stiff and unforgiving.

"We can't leave them here like this," I stated when the silence became unbearable. I sniffed before I could take it back, not wanting to smell the blood, the death that lay at our feet, but there was nothing, nothing at all. I couldn't even smell the rain.

Haniel's lips moved, though he didn't look at us. "We won't. But we can't take them with us, either. There's no way to transport them." He closed his mother's eyelids, leaving his hand resting there.

The motion, small as it was, pierced me. I took a deep, shaky breath. It hurt to breathe. "Will we bury them?"

"No," Saya blurted out before Haniel could say a word.

"What?" Haniel growled as he stood and clenched his fists.

"We can't," Saya repeated, gentler this time.

"We have to. It is our custom." He took a step toward Saya as his tone grew more furious. "They will not be honored if we do not lay them to rest. We must bury them."

Instinctively I took a step forward, putting myself between the two of them. I laid my hand on Haniel's chest and exerted enough pressure to draw his attention to me.

"Haniel," Saya continued, walking up behind me. "We don't have the time or the resources to dig graves for so many." She laid a hand on his forearm. "I'm sorry, but you know we can't. They'll understand."

Haniel's eyes brimmed with tears. I followed his gaze down to the bundle I still clutched in one arm.

With numb hands, I laid the baby down next to Haniel's mother, tucking him to her side. "Just until we bring Mari from the field," I explained, my voice shaky. Haniel nodded. "What will we do?"

"We're burying them. One massive grave," Haniel bit out, his eyes glaring at each of us in turn, daring us to defy him. "It's what they deserve."

⚜ ⚜

Somehow, drenched from the rain and exhausted from the hours of digging, we made it back before our twenty-four hours had passed. We hadn't slept or eaten. Those hours were ones I never wanted to remember...but couldn't get out of my head.

Once we entered the mountain hideout and dismounted, Haniel took the lead down the familiar tunnels and passageways to Tristan's council chamber.

The guards stepped aside, their eyes traveling up and down our wet bodies.

I glanced behind me and started. "Where's Saya?"

"Don't know and don't care," Haniel growled, walking through the doorway.

Inside, Tristan looked up from where he pored over papers. "You're back." His eyes roved over us, seeing everything from the wet clothes which clung to our bodies to the dark circles underneath our eyes. He stepped around the table. "What happened?"

"They're dead," Haniel growled. "We were too late."

"Haniel, I—"

Haniel held up a hand. "Not now. Please." He left the room, leaving the door open behind him.

Tristan approached me, his bootless feet soundless against the ground. "Juliet?"

I opened my mouth, but the words wouldn't come out. *What could I say?*

"They're all dead," I uttered. "Every last one, the woman and children too."

"And Mari?"

"I found her with her niece, nephew, and the baby. They even killed the baby, Tristan." I closed my eyes at the gruesome sight conjured in my mind.

Strong arms enclosed around me, holding me tight in an embrace. I hunched as I buried my face in his warm shoulder.

"I don't feel anything, Tristan. I feel empty."

Tristan ran a hand over my damp hair. "I'm sorry, Juliet," he whispered. "I'm sorry you saw that. It's all my cousin's fault. With him on the throne, raiders run wild, whether from the northern kingdom or others. His own men are guilty of acts just as cruel and evil. You see why we have to fight, why I and those who follow me live to remove the king from his throne. I will kill him myself if that's what it takes."

The words sent shivers down my spine, and I backed away. Tristan released me, but his gaze held my own.

"The faces will fade, Juliet. It will take time, but the memories will dull."

I shook my head, tears welling up in my eyes. "No, they won't!" Using the back of my hand, I brushed away the tears.

Tristan took my hands in his. "They will. Believe me. I should know."

I stared at him through blurred eyes. *Like Eddie. The memories are no longer as sharp.* I gasped. *Who else? I keep losing people.* It started as a small flame before blazing into a roaring fire within me. *The raiders could have done the same in Umi no Machi.* Dead faces swam before me as I leaned back and looked into Tristan's eyes. *It could happen again. It will all keep getting worse.* Anger flared deep inside me, and I gritted my teeth. A pit grew in my stomach. *This is all Creulon's fault.* I cleared my throat.

"We can't let him get away with this." My voice grew stronger. "I'll help. I'll do whatever I need to. Tristan, I can't get their faces out of my mind!"

"Juliet, you need food and rest. We can talk about this later when you've had some time to think—"

"No, I'm not going to change my mind. I'm in. I'll help however I can. I want to do more than sew. I want to be there when you take the king down."

Tristan leaned forward and planted a light kiss on my forehead. "I want you by my side, Juliet Barrows. Together, we will take down Creulon and end his reign. The gods help us."

I looked into his eyes, my own vision blurring as I fought to keep back the emotion building up. *At home, my past haunted my every move. I could never escape the guilt over Eddie's death.* I swallowed, my eyes dry. Here, we were also bonded by the all-too-recent past. The gods only knew what the future would be. But I knew who I was doing this for; it was as much for them as myself.

For all of them.

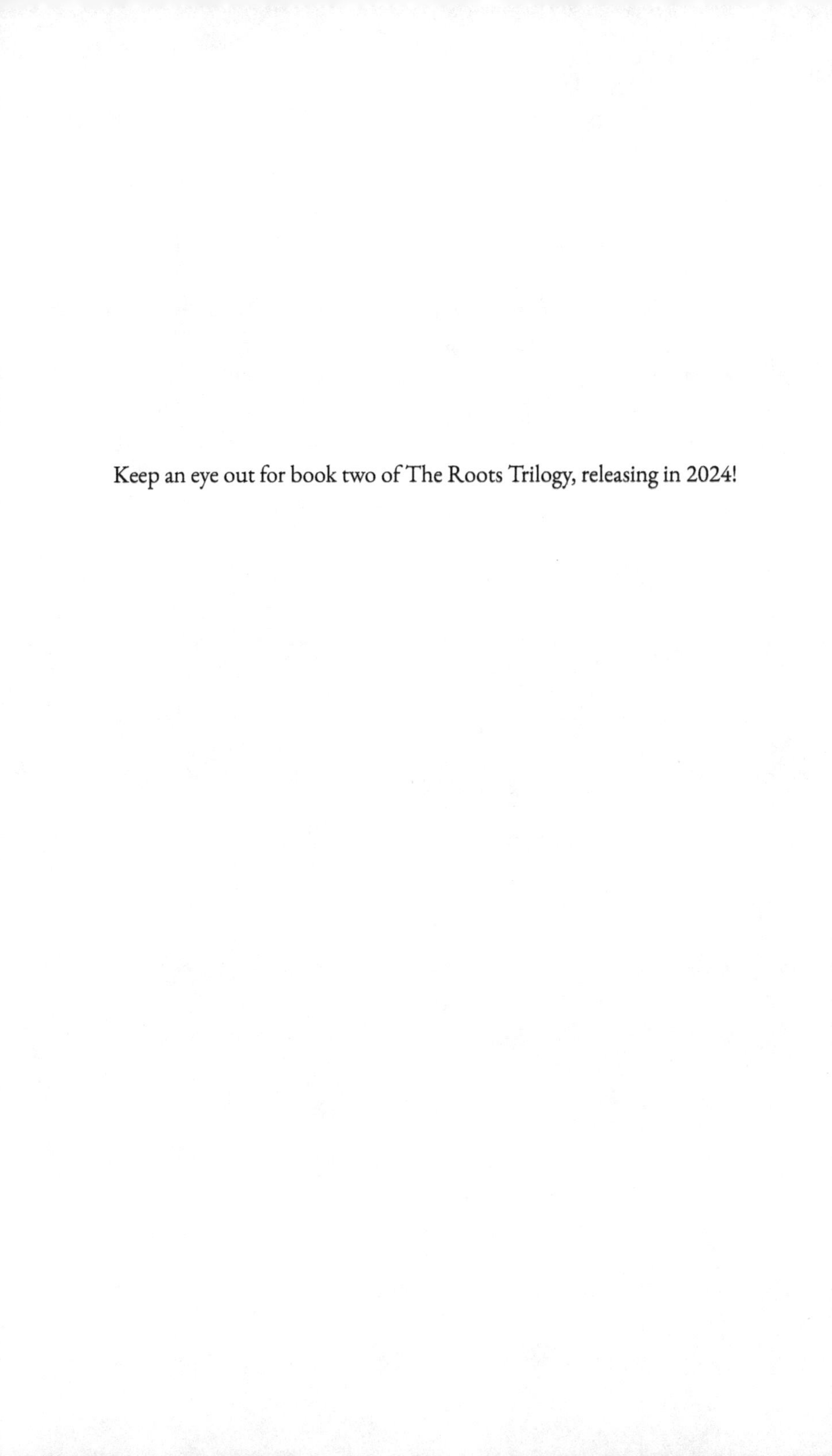

Keep an eye out for book two of The Roots Trilogy, releasing in 2024!